BEYOND THE PORTAL

BEYOND THE PORTAL

and
other
strange
tales

by

Keith J. Hoskins

A Blue Stone Media Publication

ISBN 9781697621693

BLUE STONE
MEDIA

Published by Blue Stone Media

Story art by Frankie Green
Cover by Alan Amrhine

For Donna, who loved, supported and encouraged me, and let me slip into my various universes.

And for Bail, who was honest in his readings, and imaginative with his suggestions.

ACKNOWLEDGEMENTS

Thanks to everyone who read my stories and encouraged me to write more.

Thanks to the Bel Air Creative Writers Society. Specifically: Lisa, Alan, Dave, Mark, Jodie, Amy, Tim, Diane, Peggy, and Jim. You wonderful people scoured every word of every page and gave me your honest and earnest opinions and guidance. I would not be where I am without the lot of you.

Thanks to Lerxst, Pratt, and Dirk for your inspiration.

And a special thanks to Robert Broomall for his teachings and leadership. It all started with you, Bob. Thanks for guiding me to the finish line.

TABLE OF CONTENTS

WHEN YOU STRIKE AT A KING

"Don't mistake my kindness for weakness. I am kind to everyone, but when someone is unkind to me, weak is not what you are going to remember about me."
– **Al Capone**

Sitting in an easy chair, the woman lit her cigarette, crossed her legs, and glanced around the dimly lit hotel room. This wasn't the typical hotel her affluent lifestyle had her accustomed to, but it was certainly no dump either. It might not have been as elegant as the Plaza or the Carlyle, but she needed a place to perform a certain task, and this establishment served that purpose quite well without costing her too many amenities.

Coming to the city was not very brow raising, nor was her selection of hotel. However, her bodyguard, Clint, insisted on two rooms with a connecting door. When it came to her protection, he was the one who called the shots. So, any travel and hotel plans had to be run by him. She didn't begrudge him that. It was his job, after all. And he, like most men in his position, was gruff and stoic, though he could also be very kind and understanding at times. Rarely did he question her judgement or actions unless it was a matter of her safety, and she could usually trust him with almost anything of concern to her. Almost anything. For this particular matter, she needed him to be in the dark. And at this late hour, he was hopefully sound asleep, oblivious to the conspiracy happening a room away.

Picking up her wine glass and taking a sip, she glanced at the coffee table in front of her, where sheets of paper, nestled together by tri-fold creases, taunted her. They sat on an envelope, which had been steamed open to covertly retrieve the pages that had been its dirty secret. Her anger boiled with the thought of what those pages said, what they represented. Though not the sole reason for her being here today, they were the final straw that made her realize that the current situation wasn't going to get better, but worse.

The only other person in the room was a well-dressed man who stood vigilantly at the window, observing the cars entering the hotel's parking lot. After yet another car proved not to be the one they were waiting for, he turned and addressed the woman.

"He's late," he said, his English accent not hiding his nervousness.

"He'll show," she calmly replied, looking at the Cartier on her wrist.

"And if he doesn't?"

"Then we'll find someone else."

"There *is* no one else." He stepped away from the window, letting the curtain fall back into place, and approached her. "It was a miracle I found *this* chap. There won't be time to find anyone else. Not if you want to do this where and when you have planned." He put a hand on her shoulder; she lifted her head and met his eyes. "You know, it's not too late to back out of this, Jaybird."

Jaybird. That was his nickname for her. He'd first jokingly called her that when she was a sophomore at Vassar, and he a junior at Yale. Now, it was a term of endearment that she couldn't imagine him not using. Though they were from different backgrounds—she a New York socialite, and he the son of English journalists—they immediately connected and had been inseparable ever since. He was her dearest, closest friend. And if he hadn't preferred the company of men in the bedroom, she might have married *him* ten years ago instead of that womanizing egomaniac she was introduced to at some random party. Her life would have been completely different; that was for certain. And she undoubtedly wouldn't be in her current situation.

"Back out?" She shook her head and pursed her lips. "No, Ian, we've come too far and I'm not stopping until it's finished. I told myself 'no more.' I cannot bear this any longer. It has to end. You know it does."

"I know," Ian conceded with a sigh. "But most women simply get a divorce. They don't have their husbands murdered."

"Yeah, well, most women aren't married to *him*. If I were to divorce 'mister perfect,' I'd be ostracized like a leper. And he'd probably get full custody of the kids. And his family—God, they would make sure my life was a living hell. Or worse. No, it has to be this way. As the distraught widow, I will have everyone's sympathy and no one's suspicion."

Ian nodded and took a seat.

"Besides," she continued, "he has it coming. I gave him ten great years—I got him where he is right now, you can't deny that—and what does he do? He fucks every girl that bats her eyelashes at him. And the worst thing is that everyone knows it. I must be quite the laughing stock"

"No, Jaybird," Ian consoled. "Everyone adores you. I'm just so sorry that the man you married is such a pig. You deserve better."

"Damn straight I do." She took a sip of wine, then watched the Bordeaux hypnotically swirl around in her glass.

"Jaybird, would all of this have anything to do with your little trip to Greece a couple weeks ago?"

She shot him a look. At first, she was angry with him for daring to suggest something like that, but their relationship was one where they could be frank with each other and not worry about hurting the other's feelings. There were no lies between them, and she really appreciated that about their friendship. And Ian did have the uncanny ability to see through bullshit. Trying to deceive him would be an act of futility, and, moreover, she had too much respect for him to do that. "I'd be lying if I said it didn't, but this has been coming for a long time. No ... this is all on him. My trip to Greece, if anything, helped me to open my eyes about what needed to be done." She took another sip.

Ian nodded. He was completely on her side, a fact she considered an axiom. She cherished Ian; he was one of the very few male friends her husband allowed her hang out with, knowing that the relationship would never blossom into anything more than the platonic friendship it had always been. Being as it was, their friendship remained strong, and Ian became privy to everything in her life. Especially her marriage.

"And it's not just the sex," she said after swallowing the wine, "I would be fine if he fucked every girl from here to Kalamazoo. But now he's trying to replace me. Me! And I won't have it."

"Replace you? What do you mean? Why on Earth would he replace you? He's not that stupid. His affairs are more like conquests. Trophies, if you will. They are never about replacing you."

"See for yourself." She pushed the papers on the coffee table toward her dear friend.

He picked up the pages laden with large handwritten script. As he gave each page a look, he said, "Is this the surprise you told me about?"

She gave a curt nod.

He creased his brow in a frown and began to read.

"Read it out loud, please," she said. Not that she wanted to torture herself, but hearing the words fueled the rage inside her. That rage gave her strength and focus that made her feel righteous in her actions. Ian obliged her and began reading in a somber tone.

"Dearest Mary. Why don't you leave suburbia for once, come and see me, either here, or at the Cape next week, or maybe in Boston on the 19th. I know it's unwise, irrational, and that you may hate it—on the other hand you may love it—and I will love it. You say that it is good for me not to get what I want. After all of these years, you should give me a more loving answer than that. Why don't you just say yes?"

"My God, Jaybird. I can't believe this."

She sniffled and took a deep breath. No, she wasn't going to cry. Not today. She let her anger swallow her sadness like a snake devouring its prey. She wasn't going to feel sorry for herself. Not anymore. Today was about taking action. "That bitch," she said through clenched teeth, "has been after him ever since I can remember. And he decides *now* that he wants her in his life? After everything I've done for him? After everything I've been through?"

"Unbelievable." Ian folded the papers and placed them in the envelope. He tossed the envelope onto the coffee table in front of her. "Where did you get this?" he asked.

"His secretary."

"Bollocks! Evelyn? You're pulling my leg."

She gave him a wry smile. "He asked her to mail it for him. On a hunch, she opened it and couldn't believe what she saw."

"That makes two of us," Ian said shaking his head in disbelief. "Then she just gave it to you?"

She nodded and extinguished the remainder of her cigarette in a glass ashtray that rested on a brass pedestal stand.

"When was this?" he asked.

"A couple days ago."

"How much does Clint know?" Ian jerked his thumb towards the adjoining room's door.

"About the other women? About Mary? Probably everything. Everyone else does, I'm sure. I'm the one who's been living in denial for the past ten years."

"Does Clint know about … this?" Ian pointed down, referring to what they were currently doing in the hotel.

"Of course not. And we need to keep it that way. He's loyal to a fault, but more to the job than to me."

"Why does he think you're here?"

"He thinks I'm here shopping to help cope with my depression."

"In a way," Ian said, "that's not too far from the truth."

A knock at the door startled them both.

Ian leapt from the sofa, dashed to the ingress, and peered through the peephole.

"It's our guy, he finally showed," he said, looking back at her. He placed his hand on the door knob and gave her a nod.

She nodded back. *This is it. There's no turning back.*

Ian turned the handle and opened the door, revealing an unassuming man dressed in a plaid button-down shirt. He had a slight build and was a couple inches shorter than Ian; not what she was expecting of a former Marine.

"Are you Ian?" the man asked with a slight southern twang.

"Yes," said the Englishman. "Please, come in."

Ian directed their visitor to the sitting area and gestured to the couch. The man sat and folded his hands in his lap.

"Good evening, Marine," she said. Looking down at his lap, she noticed the Marine Corps ring he wore on his right hand. Good. That meant he was proud of his service.

"Ma'am?"

"I said, 'good evening'." She reached for her cigarette case on the side table.

"I—I heard that, ma'am," he said nervously. "But did you call me 'Marine'?"

"You were in the Marine Corps. Am I correct?" She lit a cigarette with a small gold lighter, then placed the case and the lighter back on the table.

"Y-yes, ma'am," he said. "But the key word there is *were*. I been discharged goin' on four years now."

"I'm aware of that," she said matter of factly. "But I need a soldier, former or otherwise. Someone who can take orders and follow them to the letter. Someone who is trained to kill. Someone who won't hesitate when it comes time to pull the trigger. Is that you? Or do we have the wrong person?" She blew out a pillar of smoke and let it dissipate above their heads.

"Yes, ma'am—I mean, no, ma'am." He grimaced and shook his head. "I mean ... I have the training and can be the man you need me to be. In fact, I had the highest marksman score in my battalion. And this isn't my first hoedown. I've done this sort of thing before."

"So I've heard," she said as she lifted her glass for Ian to pour her some more wine. He did so, then took the chair adjacent to her. "May I offer you some wine? It's a fine vintage. Or so they tell me."

"No ma'am," the former Marine said. "Thank you, though." He wrung his hands and avoided prolonged eye contact.

She took a sip and gave him a discerning look. "So, if not Marine, then what shall I call you?"

"My name's Alek. Alek Hidell, ma'am."

She and Ian exchanged glances. That wasn't the man's real name. It was the name he'd given Ian over the phone, but after doing some digging, Ian had found out that Alek Hidell was an alias the man created to separate himself from his more nefarious deeds. Not a big deal. The man was being careful. She could appreciate that.

"Okay, Mr. Hidell, what did Ian tell you?"

"Well ... he told me that you need someone ... taken care of."

"Murdered, Mr. Hidell. It's okay. You can say it. We're all adults here."

"Yes, ma'am." He nodded and gave her a half-smile.

"What else did Ian tell you?" She sat back in the chair with her legs crossed, letting her confidence control the conversation.

"Just that you need me to kill someone."

"Not just anyone," she corrected. "My husband."

"I see," he said with a swallow. He sat up straight as if this sudden revelation demanded more attention. Or maybe it was the Marine in him coming out now that he knew the severity of his mission. Either way, she was glad he didn't balk or look like he was going to run out the door. Of course, he might have just been frozen in his seat.

"Is that a problem?" she said.

"No, ma'am. No problem."

"Good."

"Just one question, ma'am—why me?"

"We needed someone with a particular skill set, notably an expert marksman. We wanted him to be from this area so that no unusual travel was needed. My associate, Ian, has contacts all over the country, and one of them came up with a list of individuals. You were at the top of that list."

This was mostly true. Ian did have numerous contacts across the U.S. His job sometimes had him meeting with persons of questionable vocations and backgrounds. Which sometimes meant for uncomfortable meetings in shady establishments. But the network he had developed over the past decade had proven to be an invaluable business tool and asset. Especially in this case.

The list of potential candidates, however, was mainly composed of known criminals with ties to various crime organizations across the country and beyond. And if there was one thing she didn't want was for this to look like a mob hit. At first it would seem ideal and plausible, but it would draw investigators from all over, and her chances of remaining innocent in all this would be slim.

But Hidell was another story. He had no ties to the mob. He was an independent with his own agenda, and he could never be traced back to Ian or anyone else she knew. And certainly not her.

Hidell smiled; he seemed to like the idea that he was 'at the top of the list.' Ian had said that from his conversations with Hidell on the phone that he was a man who wanted to be larger than he really was. He wanted to be someone of importance. And after this job, he certainly would be. She almost didn't have to pay him the fifty grand they offered him. And if things went how she thought they would, they might not have to. Not completely, anyway.

Three knocks sounded and everyone jumped.

"*Ma'am?*" came a voice. But it wasn't from the main door; it was Clint from the adjoining room.

"Shit!" whispered Ian as everyone stood. "What do we do?"

"Get him in the bathroom," she whispered. "Quietly!"

Three more knocks. "*Ma'am?*"

"Coming, Clint," she yelled toward the wallpapered door.

Ian grabbed the confused hitman and ushered him into the bathroom while she tiptoed toward Clint's room. Once Ian had Hidell in the bathroom and the door latch clicked, Ian gave her a nod, and she opened the door to reveal her impatient and curious bodyguard.

He was dressed in boxers and a t-shirt which were hastily covered with a complimentary hotel robe that remained uncinched, the straps hanging loose by his sides. In his hand, down by his waist, he held his black snub-nosed revolver. Behind him, on the bed, his shoulder holster lay on the corner as if he had just retrieved his weapon.

"Clint," she said with a touch of surprise, "what are you doing up?"

"I heard voices," he said and took a step into the room. "When I saw that it was one in the morning, I became concerned." He looked around, examining every visible inch. If he had just woken up, he didn't appear so. He was alert and seemed ready for trouble. That's what made him good at his job.

"Oh," she said, changing to a more contrite expression, "I didn't realize it was that late. Did we wake you? I'm so sorry."

"Yes," Ian said as he walked toward them. "Sorry about that, my good man. We were trying to keep it down. It appears we failed miserably."

Clint continued to look around the room. “Was there anyone else in here? I thought I heard three voices.”

“No,” they said in unison and looked at each other, frowning and shaking their heads.

“It’s just us here,” Ian said, spreading his arms.

“Oh,” she said, getting an idea. “You may have heard Ian doing an impression of one of his old college professors. He was from Georgia and had a funny way of speaking.” Then she turned toward her friend. “Go on, Ian. Show him.”

Ian shot her a glance that could have frozen lava, but he recovered quickly and changed it to an amused smile as he continued her ruse. “Yes,” he said. “He was a funny chap. Talked a bit like this—'Today, we’re going to have a test.’ ” Ian did his best to sound like the man they had hidden in the bathroom. ‘I’m going to swear I told you about the test two weeks ago, and it’s going to be about material we haven’t even covered yet.’ ”

They both laughed at each other and looked at Clint, who did not seem amused nor fully convinced of their reason for this mysterious third voice. When he took another step into the room, Ian approached him.

“Say, Clint,” Ian said in a slightly more sibilant voice. “Jaybird and I were just about to play some cards.” He reached into his jacket pocket and pulled out the souvenir pack of cards he had purchased from the hotel gift shop. Ian loved card games, and he usually had a deck on him. He often said ‘if you have a deck of cards, you are never bored.’ “Gin rummy, in fact,” he continued. “Care to join us?” He placed his hand on Clint’s upper arm. “It certainly would be more fun with you in the game.”

Not everyone knew Ian preferred men, but Clint was one of the few who was privileged to that information. And, ever since finding out, he had been very uncomfortable whenever in close proximity to the Englishman, which was apparent at that very moment.

“No, thanks,” Clint said with a polite smile. “I need to get back to bed. And you should too, ma’am, if we’re to hit those stores before lunch tomorrow.” He turned to walk back to his room, but not before giving another quick scrutinizing look around.

"I will, Clint," she said, trying to hide her relief. "We won't be up much longer. I promise."

"Very good, ma'am. Good night." He went back to his room, closing the door behind him and making sure not to make eye contact with Ian.

"That was close," Ian said in a hushed voice. He started walking toward the bathroom until she grabbed his elbow.

"Wait," she whispered. She tiptoed to the door Clint had just exited through, put her ear up against it, and listened. After a few seconds of silence, she finally heard the faint squeaks of bedsprings as her bodyguard apparently did as he said he was going to do, and went back to bed. She carefully twisted the lock on the door handle to make sure there were no surprise walk-ins later.

"Come on, Jaybird. Let's start that game," Ian said in a normal speaking voice. He had sat on the couch and opened the deck and began shuffling, causing the cards to make the very distinctive ruffling sound on the coffee table.

She nodded approvingly. It was smart to keep up the pretense just in case Clint was keeping an open ear for anything unusual including that phantom third voice. "Just a sec," she said, matching his own volume and proceeded to walk over and reclaim her former seat. "I just need to get some more wine." When she reached her card shuffling friend, she leaned over and whispered, "Get him out of the bathroom, then get the bag."

He nodded, stood, placed his cards in his pocket, and made his way to the bathroom. He returned with their potential hitman in tow. Hidell again sat on the sofa while Ian went to the sleeping area.

"Who was that?" asked Hidell.

She held her finger to her lips to silence him, then made a slow push-down motion with her hand to tell him to speak quietly. He nodded that he understood.

"Who was that?" he repeated in a whisper.

"We're in enemy territory," she said. "We need to keep our heads down."

He nodded, understanding the metaphor.

Ian returned with a leather carrying bag that he gently placed on the coffee table. Hidell looked at the bag, then at his two hosts.

"Mr. Hidell," she said, "in this bag is my husband's itinerary for our trip when we return here in two weeks. Memorize it, then destroy it."

He nodded.

"Use this information to pick the best place and time for you to take your shot." She held up a hand, cutting him off before he had a chance to reply. "Don't tell me about it—I don't want to know. I want it to be a complete surprise. It will help with the acting, you see."

A look of understanding came over him, and he grinned at her cleverness.

"Also in the bag is ten thousand dollars—"

"Ten thousand?" Hidell said. "The English guy told me the job would pay fifty."

"Perhaps he did, but if I'm eating dinner at LaGrenouille, I don't pay for a thing until I have received my escargot prepared perfectly, and the wait staff service has been exemplary. You'll get the remainder of the money when the job is finished. Is that understood?"

He gave a quick nod, and his eyes flicked away in embarrassment. "Yes, ma'am."

"Now," she continued, "take the bag and prepare for your mission, Marine. We will contact you when the deed is done."

Hidell nodded, then stood. Ian escorted him to the door as the player they had just put into motion quietly exited the room.

Ian returned and took the seat next to her. "I don't know, Jaybird. There's something about that chap that's got me worried. What if he gets pinched? What if they interrogate him and he implicates you?"

"I'm planning on it."

"Planning on it?" he said in a raised tone. She gestured for him to lower his voice. "What do you mean, 'planning on it?' You *want* him to get caught?"

"No, of course not. I'm just saying that in the likelihood that he does get captured by the police, we need to have a fail-safe plan in place to ensure his silence."

"And how do you plan on doing that?"

"That's where our next guest comes into play."

"Our next guest? Who in blazes is that?"

"The owner of the club we visited last night for drinks."

"That sleazy Al Capone-looking chap? You told *him* about our little scheme?"

"No. Not yet. I need to feel him out, but I have a feeling he will be quite accommodating."

What makes you sure we can trust *him*?"

"I had a nice little conversation with him at the club last night. He has financial problems that have made him quite desperate."

"You mean he owes money to the mob." Ian continued shuffling the cards— part out of habit, part out of keeping up the ruse.

"Yes. And his debtors want his balance paid—in full—by the end of the month, or they collect his dead body instead. And then, perhaps, go after his family."

"How much does he owe?" Ian asked as he sat on the edge of the sofa.

"A quarter of a million dollars."

Ian whistled. "How the hell did he do that?"

"Gambling problems or something of that sort. But I will offer to pay off the mobsters, saving his life and that of his family. When I dangle that carrot in front of him, he'll be more than willing to do my small favor."

"And where are you going to get that kind of money?" Ian smiled. "Oh wait. Let me guess. Greece."

Her only response was to take a sip of her wine.

"Where was I when you two were having this little talk?" Ian asked.

"You were at the bar ogling that French bartender."

"I was not 'ogling' him. We were just having a nice talk. He was telling me about his family home in Dijon. And I said 'Your family's home is in mustard?' He laughed so hard at that and then we—"

A soft knock came at the door. Ian jumped from his seat and both of them looked toward the adjoining room, hoping Clint was fast asleep and hadn't heard it as well. After a few unresponsive seconds passed Ian made for the entrance before their visitor could knock again. He looked through the peephole then back at her. "Speak of the devil."

"Okay. Let him in."

Ian opened the door and a stocky man wearing a black overcoat and gray Fedora stepped inside. Ian took the man's coat and hat, then led him to the seating area.

"Please, have a seat, Mr. Ruby."

The club owner sat on the sofa across from her, his hands shaking, and a bead of sweat trickled down his temple. "Thank you, Mrs. Kennedy. And may I say that it is an honor to again be in your company."

She lit another cigarette and crossed her legs. "Please," she said, letting smoke escape through her nose, "call me Jackie."

CLEAN SLATE

"Blessed are the forgetful, for they get the better even of their blunders."
– Friedrich Nietzsche

"Good afternoon, Mr. Peterson. Can you hear me?"

The man in the hospital bed slowly, painfully, opened his eyes. Squinting against the light, he blinked and looked around.

"Mr. Peterson." The man that addressed him smiled and waited for an answer. He was thin, dressed in a long white jacket; an ID badge with his picture hung from the breast pocket.

A doctor, perhaps.

Also, in the room were several other presumable doctors, nurses, and, behind them all, a man in a black suit stood in the shadows, trying to look unassuming. But all eyes in the room were fixed on the man who lay before them.

"Mr. Peterson," the doctor repeated. "Do you know where you are?"

The man in the bed looked around at each of the faces, their eyes focused, waiting for his reply. He looked around the room and the distinctive bed he lay upon.

"I'm guessing ... I'm in ... a hospital?" The words slurred from his mouth. His tongue seemed not want to cooperate, as if it were still waking from a deep slumber.

"That's correct," said the doctor.

The man tried raising his hand to touch a tube that protruded from his nose, but the arm could barely move. His wrist was limp, and he seemed to have little, if any, control. A nurse reached over and gently pushed his hand down and told him, "Don't touch that. It's okay."

"And do you know why you are here, Mr. Peterson?" the doctor continued.

"Why ...?" The man's brow wrinkled in confusion.

"Yes?" the doctor prodded.

"Why ... do you call me ... Mr. Peterson?"

That evoked a response from the entire room. The doctors and nurses exchanged glances with each other. The black-suit man's face became concerned as he glared at the lead doctor.

"That is your name, is it not?" said the doctor.

The man's gaze dropped, his eyes flicked side to side. "I ... I don't know. I'm not sure." Dropping his jaw, he stared wide eyed at the doctor. "I don't know what my name is."

Another response from the room. This time whispers were exchanged.

"Your name is David Peterson," said the doctor.

"David ... Peterson?"

"Yes. You don't remember your name? Do you remember me? I'm Dr. Hawkins. I'm the one who operated on you."

David—that's what they said his name was—slowly shook his head and gave the doctor a blank stare.

"What's the last thing you do remember?" asked the doctor.

"I remember ... I remember ...." He shook his head again. "Nothing. I can't remember anything." David suddenly looked scared, almost panicky.

"It's okay, Mr. Peterson. That's to be expected."

"Expected?"

"You were in a car accident. Do you remember that?"

"No."

"You suffered severe head trauma. You've been in a coma for three months."

"Three months? What happened? How bad was I hurt?"

"You broke both ulna and radius bones in your arms, as well both tibias and your left fibula in your legs, and you had seven broken ribs—all of which have completely healed. There was some facial damage from the glass, but we had our top plastic surgeons working on you, and we are quite pleased with the results."

Several of the doctors nodded in acknowledgement. The man-in-the-suit looked on with impatience, anticipation maybe.

"What about my head? You said I had trauma? Do you mean brain damage?"

"In a manner of speaking, yes. There was damage to your paleomammalian cortex. That's the part of the brain responsible for long-term memory as well as other functions. We were able to control the bleeding and repair what we could. However, your brain went into a coma to heal itself, and all we could do was hope you healed enough to come out of it."

David tried to raise his hand to feel his head, but his muscles did not want to cooperate. Exhausted from the effort, he let his arm fall into his lap. "And am I all right? What about my memory? Will that come back?"

"Physically, your injuries have completely healed. Your brain, on the other hand, could only do what it could. To be honest with you, we're not sure if your memory will ever return. We want to run a battery of tests on you to see how much your brain was able to heal before we can talk about sending you home."

"Home? I don't know where that is. Do I even *have* a home? A job?"

"We'll get that all sorted out. Meanwhile, we're just glad you're awake and responsive. The nurses will set you up with your diet and schedule your physical therapy sessions, and we'll begin those tests on your brain in a few days."

"Why do I need physical therapy?"

"You haven't moved or eaten properly in three months, so there is some muscle atrophy. Don't worry, Mr. Peterson, with proper diet and therapy, we'll get you back up to snuff."

The other doctors filed out of the room, each one giving Hawkins a congratulatory nod and smile as they passed him. The man-in-the-suit turned to leave, but not before addressing Hawkins. "Keep me posted on his progress. I want to know the results of those tests." With a final glance at the patient, he exited the room.

"Who was that?" David asked Hawkins.

"That's my boss. He's always worried about cases such as yours."

"Cases like mine?"

"Cases where death was a possibility. There's always insurance and public relation issues to deal with."

"I see."

"Anyway, I'll leave you in the hands of our highly capable nurses. They'll take good care of you."

"One thing ..."

"Yes?" the doctor stopped mid-exit and turned around.

Can I see a ... thing ... to see my face ...?" David struggled as he tried to remember what that reflective object was called.

"You mean a mirror?" he said.

"Yes."

One of the nurses gave the doctor a concerned look, but he nodded, and she retrieved a mirror from the drawer of a nearby table and held it up in front of David's face.

David gazed at the face that gazed back at him. After a long, quiet minute, Doctor Hawkins stepped a bit closer.

"How does it look?"

"Doc," David said, "I have no idea who that guy in the mirror is." Then he turned his head away, not wanting to see any more.

Doctor Hawkins nodded to the nurse, and she pulled the mirror back and placed it back in the drawer. "Like I said," Hawkins reiterated, "the nurses will take good care of you. I'll be by later to see how things are going."

"Thanks, Doc."

The rest of the afternoon and the evening had the nurses doting over David Peterson. They removed his catheter and feeding tube. They assisted him in limited movement and gave him a dinner consisting of bread, mixed fruit, and a bowl filled with noodles and a yellow liquid.

"What's this?" he asked.

"Chicken noodle soup," the nurse replied with a sympathetic smile.

In a hollow tone he repeated, "Chicken noodle soup."

* * *

The next morning, David Peterson was awakened by more nurses. They checked his vitals, and forced him to eat a breakfast of eggs, cereal, milk, strawberries, and wheat toast. Though his stomach, which was not accustomed to eating solid foods, told him that he was full just a third through his meal, the nurse insisted that he eat every morsel lest she stick the feeding tube back through his nose. David complied, and almost felt sick when finished.

Shortly after breakfast, a tall man wearing matching navy-blue shirt and pants entered David's room pushing a wheelchair. His movements were slow and precise, his face was stoic, and his dark, bald head reflected the fluorescent lights in the ceiling. "Mr. Peterson," he said in a baritone voice. "My name is Mike, the orderly assigned to you. I'll be taking you to your appointments while you are recovering."

"Hi, Mike. Pleased to meet you." David struggled to sit up, and offered Mike a shaky hand.

Mike hesitated, looked at David's extended hand, then finally gave it a firm, but brief, shake.

"That's quite a grip you got there, Mike. You work out?"

Ignoring the question, Mike positioned the wheelchair next to David's bed. "Your first appointment is physical therapy. We need to be there in fifteen minutes."

"Fifteen minutes, huh? I guess we better get going."

After Mike helped—pretty much lifted—David into the wheelchair, the two headed down to physical therapy, on the first floor. There, Mike guided David towards the rear of the gym where a beautiful woman with red hair pulled back into a ponytail looked over papers on a clipboard.

Hearing David's wheelchair pull up next to her, she said, "You must be my nine o'clock." When she raised her head to look at David, he could have sworn she seemed a bit startled.

David nodded. "Yes, ma'am."

"I'm Pam, your physical therapist for the next few weeks or so."

He offered her his hand, trying hard to control the trembling. "Very nice of me to meet you," David blurted out. "I mean ... very ... nice ... to meet you." Frustrated and embarrassed, he closed his eyes. "Sorry," he said looking back up at her. "My mind is a bit jumbled."

"No worries," said Pam. "I know all about your accident, and I received an updated sheet on your memory loss. I'm sure your speech will improve every day. My job is to improve your body."

"I'll leave you in her care, Mr. Peterson," said Mike. "I'll return in an hour."

David had almost forgotten about Mike, who was halfway across the gym before David looked in his direction.

Pam grabbed David's wheelchair and pushed him towards some equipment, where she introduced him to her instruments of torture. That's not what she called them, of course. She told him they were devices that would strengthen his arms and legs and get him walking on his own within a couple weeks, but in reality, they seemed to mock his efforts, and his only reward was pain and frustration.

After an hour, David was back in his wheelchair, with Pam handing him a banana and a protein drink.

"Here, eat this."

David took the food, his tired hands barely able to grip the fruit and box drink. "I'm not really hungry. Do I have to?"

"Only if you ever want to ever get out of this hospital one day. Your muscles need to be fed. Especially after a workout like that."

"Oh, is that what you call that? I thought you were working on your Gestapo merit badge." David flashed her a smile, but Pam's face remained indifferent. David's demeanor turned grim. "How do I know that? How can I remember what the Gestapo and a merit badge are, but I can't even remember my own name?"

Pam shrugged. "I don't know, David, but this afternoon, you have your first appointment with Dr. Watley, your psychologist. Maybe she can help you figure all that out."

"I hope so. Right now, my mind feels more useless than my legs. What are you staring at?"

"Just noticing your birthmark, right there, behind your ear. Almost looks like a star. Interesting."

"Funny, I was just thinking your eyes look like stars. One could get lost in them."

A smile almost broke her granite-like composure, but she quickly reeled it back.

"I'm sorry," he said. "I shouldn't have said that. That was ... that was ..."

"Inappropriate?"

"Yes. I'm sorry."

"Don't be sorry. It's fine."

"It doesn't seem like you're fine with it."

"I am." She forced a fake smile. "We're good."

"Good. I hope so, I don't want to get off on the wrong—"

David's leg began to shake. Pam firmly put her hands around his knee, steadying the leg, until the tremor stopped.

"What was that?" David said, gawking at his leg.

"Just a muscle tremor. Perfectly normal, nothing to worry about. They might happen now and again, but their frequency will subside over time."

"I'll take your word for it. Strange. Doesn't even feel like this is my body."

"That'll pass. When you're done your therapy, you'll be as good as new." She paused her movements and a faraway look came over her.

"You okay, Pam?"

"Fine," she said, snapping out of her fog, her professional tone and demeanor returning in full force. "And it appears Mike is right on time to pick you up."

Mike folded his arms in front of him. "All finished, Mr. Peterson?"

"Yeah, Mike." David said, puzzled by Pam's quick change of moods. But before the orderly wheeled him away, he said, "See you tomorrow, Pam?"

"Of course. Same time."

David flashed her a smile, and then Mike wheeled him out the door.

Back in his room, David sat in an easy chair and skimmed through some magazines, watched a little television, and fiddled with a tablet the nurses had given him. After lunch, Mike came to fetch him once again.

"Okay, Mr. Peterson," said the orderly. "Time for your next appointment. And bring your tablet."

"Hey, Mike. Okay, got it. Let's go."

Mike helped him into his wheelchair and maneuvered him to the elevator. Once inside, he pressed the button for the eighteenth floor, the top floor.

"You're a quiet guy, Mike. You don't talk much."

Ironically, silence was the only answer David received.

"You don't smile much either, Mike. Why's that?"

"I smile. When I have something to smile about."

"What makes you smile?"

"Thinking about family. My parents. My siblings."

"I don't even know if I have a family," David said. "I guess I don't. No one's been here to see me. Nurses told me I didn't have any visitors while I was ... unconscious."

More silence ensued, and just when David was about to try another icebreaker with Mike, the elevator doors opened, and Mike pushed the wheelchair down the hall. They came to an office door with *Charlotte Watley, Doctor of Psychology* printed on the opaque glass. Mike opened the door and pushed David inside.

Dr. Watley sat behind a desk and stood as soon as David and Mike entered. "Mr. Peterson. Nice to see you."

She motioned for Mike to push David's chair to a spot that seemed purposefully vacated to make room for the wheelchair-bound man. "Thank you," she said to Mike. "I'll take him from here."

Mike gave the two a final glance before closing the door behind him.

"So," said Watley, "how are you doing, Mr. Peterson?"

"Fine, Doc. I guess. Fine for someone who's been in a horrible car accident and in a coma for three months."

She chuckled. "I see. Are you comfortable? Would you like a pillow, or your legs propped up, perhaps?"

"I guess I wouldn't mind a pillow. This chair isn't as comfortable as it looks."

She smiled and grabbed a cushion off of the adjacent couch and placed it behind him, giving his upper back and neck some support. "How's that?"

"Nice. Thank you. Sorry to be a nuisance. I guess it's going to be a while before I can do things like a normal person."

"No problem." She took a seat across from him. "I've dealt with coma patients before. You'll be dancing your way out of this hospital in no time." Flipping over a couple sheets on her legal pad, she began writing on a fresh page. "So, they tell me you can't remember anything."

"No. Nothing. Except certain general things. I mean ... how can I remember what a wheelchair is, or an elevator, but I can't remember my name, my home town, my favorite baseball team—if I even like baseball? But I do know what baseball is. How is that possible? And how can I speak English with no effort and then can't come up with a simple word like 'mirror.' "

"Certain things you will remember, certain things you won't. It's all relative to the damaged area in your brain. Which, to be honest, is still a mystery to modern medicine." After a thoughtful pause she said, "Do you smell my perfume?"

"Uh ... yeah. Smells nice."

"Do you recognize the scent?"

"No." David sniffed and concentrated. "I mean it kinda smells familiar, but I can't tell you what it is."

"It's vanilla. A very distinct and common aroma. You remember smelling the scent before, but you have no association for it. You'll have to relearn many things all over again. As far as English, I'll wager that thirty percent of your vocabulary is gone. You may be speaking and then stumble on a word that you feel you should know. Again, you'll have to re-learn them. Sometimes you'll remember the most arbitrary thing without even trying. Other times, you'll wrack your brain trying to think of the name of an object sitting on a grocery store shelf."

"Okay. Sounds scary, but okay."

"Good. Now, let's do some exercises to see just how much you do remember. Maybe we can jumpstart that mind of yours."

Watley stood and retrieved a box from the corner of her desk. She placed it on the table next to David, opened it, and removed several straps and cables, revealing a machine underneath.

"What's this? You going to torture me? I had enough of that at physical therapy."

"Torture?"

"Never mind. Just a joke," he said as he focused on the machine.

"Ah," she said as she sorted out the different wires. "No, this is to monitor you as we go over the exercises." She connected two of the wires to David's fingers, then two straps around his chest and midsection, then finally a blood pressure cuff on his arm.

"Wow," David said as he watched Watley hook him up to the machine. "This seems pretty serious."

"Just dotting our I's and crossing our T's. We need to make certain of the present state of your mind, especially your memory. Ready?"

"I suppose."

"Don't worry. It's quite painless. Promise." She gave him a wink then took a seat in the chair on the other side of the table and next to the machine.

The next few hours were long and tedious for David. Not to mention frustrating. Watley asked him question after question, often repeating herself, or asking a question in a different manner. They did word association, flash cards, and an audio recognition game that she created herself. All the while she made notes on her legal pad. Some were short and quick; others were more detailed. When they were finished, she disconnected him from the machine, placed everything back in the box, and then placed the box back on her desk.

"Well?" David prodded.

"Everything checks out," she said.

"Checks out?"

"I mean your mind is about where we thought it would be, but I think your memory may not be as recoverable as we had hoped. We'll conduct more tests and get you started in some education classes. You can probably start them in a couple days. Is there anything on your mind? Anything you want to talk about?"

"Actually, there is." David leaned closer to her. "Can you tell me about my accident?"

Watley's eyes widened in mild surprise. "Has anyone spoken to you about it yet?"

"No."

"Okay. Well, I only know what I've read in your file. Are you sure you're ready to hear this?"

"Yes, please. Maybe it'll help me remember some things."

Watley sat back, paused a few seconds before continuing. "You were driving down the road when a deer ran out in front of you, forcing you to swerve into the other lane and into oncoming traffic. You hit another car head on."

"My God. Was anyone hurt? Besides me, that is."

Watley took a breath, looked hard into his eyes. "There was a family of four in the car you hit, David. None survived."

David's jaw dropped; his eyes glazed over. It was almost a full minute before he said, "Anyone else?" When Watley didn't answer, his eyes bored into hers. "Doc? Was there anyone else hurt?"

"There was, David. Your ... your wife and son were in the car with you. Neither of them made it."

David slumped in his chair. His head turned, and he stared out the window.

"David?" said Watley. When she got no response, she said, "David, I know this is a lot to take in. What are you feeling right now? Is this triggering any memories?"

"What were their names?" he mumbled almost incoherently.

"I'm sorry?"

"Their names. My wife and son. What were their names?"

"Margaret and Steven."

"Margaret and Steven," he echoed.

"Do you remember them?" Anything?"

"No," David said flatly. An ironic grin crossed his face as a tear streaked down his cheek. "It's like you're talking to me about someone else's life, something terrible that happened to a stranger. Maybe it's good I can't remember."

"I know it's upsetting, but if memories do come back to you, I'll be here to help you sort it all out. Okay?"

David gave her a nod, and a natural smile almost diminished his somber expression. Almost.

Watley gave David a couple of puzzle books to take back to his room to work with, and instructed him on applications on his tablet that would benefit his memory and maybe fill in some gaps with language and math. When the session was over, Mike showed up promptly to retrieve his charge.

During the trip back to the room, Mike was his usual reserved self, but this time, David matched Mike's distant demeanor. As Mike helped him into the bed he said, "Looks like you are the quiet one this time."

"Yeah, Mike. Sorry. That session with Watley was kinda tough."

"How so?"

"She told me about my car accident. She said I killed a family as well as my own wife and son."

"Interesting."

"Interesting? It's not interesting, it's horrible!"

Mike showed no reaction. He only stared at David with an unreadable face.

"But you know what's really horrible?" David said. "The fact that I can't remember any of it. Not just the accident, but my family. I remember nothing, so I feel nothing. Nothing except sorry for myself. I feel bad for killing that family—and mine too, of course—but no remorse. Not really. Like it was someone else behind the wheel that day. Like it was someone else's wife and kid that were killed."

"Some might call that a blessing," Mike said matter of factly.

"A blessing?"

"That you can't remember." Mike turned from David and began to leave the room.

"Do you?" David said. "Do you think it's a blessing?"

Mike stopped but didn't turn around. "No." And then he was gone.

* * *

The next two weeks became routine for David—breakfast, therapy with Pam, then lunch. He saw Dr. Watley Tuesdays and Fridays. And he spent afternoons and evenings working with his tablet and the puzzle books Watley had given him as well as attending re-education classes.

His favorite part of it all was seeing Pam. Of all his puzzles, she was the hardest to crack. Her beauty was captivating, and her cold professional demeanor only made her more attractive. David's desire to get to know her better was maybe greater than his wanting to walk again. He was relentless, as he prodded her for friendly conversation and personal information. And she spurned his attempts every time.

He began eating most of his meals in the cafeteria, and he would often ask Pam to join him, but her answer was always the same. "It would be inappropriate for you and I to see each other outside of our sessions."

But one day, Pam surprised David by giving in to his request, and she met him in the cafeteria for lunch.

"I gotta say, David, I'm a little disappointed in you"

David looked up from his spaghetti and meatballs. "You are? Why?"

"I thought you would be further along in your rehab. You're making me look bad."

"Sorry. Maybe I just don't want our sessions to end." He tried to smile while chewing.

She gave him a look that either said 'don't push your luck' or 'you better be joking.'

"But honestly, I do enjoy your company, and I'm hoping we can become friends. Even after my rehab is done. And maybe I'm not in such a hurry to be done here. I mean, I have nothing to go home to. No real life to speak of."

"Don't you want to get out of that chair?" She nodded to the corner of the cafeteria where David's orderly sat alone, eating his lunch. "And not have to rely on *him* to get you around? What's his deal anyway?"

"Who, Mike? What do you mean?"

"He's so quiet. Very stern. Kinda gives me the creeps."

"Mike's not so bad. He grows on you. But I don't know why he's still attached to me. I can get around in this thing pretty good on my own."

"It's hospital policy," she said. "But don't use him as an excuse."

"I'm not. But seriously, I do want to get better. I'm sure that I'll be walking into your gym one day soon. No chair, no crutches, or anything. And I'll take you to lunch somewhere outside of this hospital. Just you wait."

David watched Pam for a reaction as she ate, her eyes occasionally glanced at him though she never smiled. That was something she and Mike had in common, so David found it a bit ironic for her to call Mike creepy. But as he watched her eyes darting randomly over her plate, David could tell she was thinking about something. He hoped she was considering his offer for a more casual meal somewhere, sometime in the future.

"Hey!" Pam's eyes lit up with an idea. "Do you want to get some fresh air?"

"Yeah. Sure." He hoped he didn't sound as surprised and hopeful as he felt. "Mike sometimes takes me to the courtyard. Want to go there?"

"No, I've got a better idea." She looked over to where Mike sat, focused on his meal and reading a magazine. "Let's go, before your babysitter comes and steals you away."

She stood, grabbed the handles of David's chair, and pushed him toward the exit, far away from Mike's table. Once in the hallway, she doubled her speed and made a beeline for the elevator. Inside she pressed the button for the eighteenth floor.

"Where you taking me?" David asked. "Not to see Watley, are you?"

"No, you'll see. I think you'll love it."

On floor eighteen, the doors opened and Pam pushed the chair down the hallway, the opposite direction from Watley's office. They reached the end of the hallway and another elevator, a much larger one. Pam pushed the call button and the doors opened immediately.

"What's this?" asked David.

"Service elevator," Pam said and pushed him inside. "Window washers use it." She pressed a button at the top of the panel marked with the letter R. The doors closed and the elevator slowly took them up. When the doors opened, bright sunshine and a summer breeze welcomed them

"Wow," said David. "The roof. Amazing—I do love it."

"Told you," Pam said and pushed him out to the perimeter wall. "Hopefully, you can see enough over the wall to really appreciate the view."

David placed his hands on the warm concrete, craned his neck and looked about the city and the people going about their busy day. He looked up toward the sun, closed his eyes, and let the rays cascade over him like a long overdue shower. "This is truly wonderful, Pam. Much better than the courtyard."

A clattering noise made David twist his neck to look behind him. He saw Pam placing a long piece of wood in the elevator, preventing the doors from closing.

"What are you doing?'" he said, still grinning.

"Just assuring a little privacy." Pam walked over to an air conditioner unit and reached behind one of the ducts. When she pulled her hand back, it held a shiny object that reflected the sunlight.

It was a handgun.

Pam sauntered over to David; her face full of hateful determination.

"Pam?" David said. "What are you doing with that gun?"

"Oh, this?" she said, appraising the large weapon in her hand. "Just another instrument of mine, David. This one, however, is an instrument of revenge."

"Revenge? What do you mean? What are you talking about?"

"Oh, David—which isn't your real name, of course—I plan on taking your life, just like you took the lives of my family."

"What?"

"I had planned on doing this much later, setting you up, savoring your death. I spent all this time healing your body so I could relish in the irony of breaking it. But then I heard that you were being moved to another facility out of state, so I had to act a little sooner than I originally wanted. It took me too long to get this position, and I knew there wouldn't be another chance."

"Pam," David pleaded. "I don't know what you're talking about. I didn't kill anyone. I was in a coma for three months. I just woke up—" he paused as his gazed turned inward. "My God." He looked at her bloodlust eyes. "Was that your family in the other car? Were they the ones killed in the accident?"

"Accident? There was no accident, you imbecile." She stepped closer, raised her leg, and pushed David's wheelchair over on its side. David landed with a thump and a surge of pain cascaded though him.

Pam raised the pistol to point at David's face. "You murdered them. In our house. After you tortured and raped my mother, and my sister, and my grandmother." Tears ran down her face, the hand holding the gun began to quiver. I've been dreaming of this moment a long time. I just wish I could have done it the way I envisioned. But I guess this will have to do."

She pulled the hammer back; her hand began shaking even harder.

"Pam," David pleaded. "Please. You got the wrong guy. I'm David. I had a car accident. That's what happened."

"No," she said, trying to steady her nerves. "I was there at the trial. They found you guilty and sentenced you to rehabilitation. They may have changed your face, but I'll never forget that stupid birthmark behind your ear. They forgot to remove that, didn't they?"

"Rehabilitation?" David said, stumbling on the word.

"Yes, rehabilitation, asshole. Since the amendment outlawing capital punishment, and with the overpopulated jail system, the courts decided to take all assholes like you and wipe their memories and make them productive members of society. They call it the "Clean Slate Initiative."

"Clean Slate Initiative?"

"Stop repeating everything I fucking say!"

"Okay, okay. Just lower the gun, Pam. Please. I think you've got the wrong guy."

"Oh, no, I don't. I spent every penny I had, and then some, to find out where they had taken you. Then I applied here as a physical therapist. It was pure luck that you landed in my lap as one of my patients. Maybe it was God delivering you to me."

"No—no ... they've been trying to make me better—the doctors, the nurses, Watley. They all've been—"

"They're all in on it. Yeah, that's right. And all that testing you went through, that wasn't to help you get your memories back. It was to make sure your memories were really wiped so they could get you started on your new life. But I can't let that happen. No, uh-uh. Why should you get to go on living like nothing ever happened? You deserve nothing less than what you did to them, what you did to me. It cost me a lot to be here, but here we are. I had so badly wanted to torture you the way you did my family." She began to cry. "How could you have done that? My sister was twelve. Twelve!" She wiped away her tears with her free hand, then placed it back on the gun to help steady the revolver. "You're a monster, and no amount of rehabilitation will ever change that. You need to die."

A door behind them burst open, and Mike ran out, holding a pistol in his hand. Seeing Pam's gun trained on David, he raised his own and pointed it at her.

"Drop the gun, Pam!" Mike yelled. He kept his firearm leveled on her. "I'm a U.S. Marshal. Just drop the gun and back away."

Pam's arm didn't waver. Her gun was still aimed at David as she snapped her head to look at Mike behind her. "Marshal? Then you know who he really is. What he's done."

"Pam," Mike said. "If you pull that trigger, life as you know it is over."

"My life was over when he tortured and killed my family. Why does he get a clean slate? He should be rotting away in a hole somewhere."

"Hey, Pam," David said in a calming voice just above a whisper. "I need to tell you something."

"Don't waste your breath, David. There's nothing you can say that would make me change my mind. Nothing."

"No," David said, continuing his hushed tone. "But what I was going to say was I know how you must feel."

"David," yelled Mike. Still a good thirty feet away, he tilted his head as if trying to hear over the din of the city background noise. "What are you saying to her? Don't aggravate her. Let me take care of this."

"You don't know shit," Pam said to David. She glanced behind her to make sure Mike hadn't gotten any closer.

"Your eyes, Pam—"

"Yeah, yeah, my eyes. Blah blah blah. That shit isn't going to work with me. You make me sick, you piece of shit."

"No," David continued in his soft voice, "it's just your eyes ... your sister had the same look on her face when I was raping your grandmother."

Pam's face hardened, her nose flared. "What?" Her anger now mixed with disbelief. "How?" Her voice trailed off and her gun lowered.

"Good. Now drop the gun, Pam." Mike said.

"That's right." David's lips stretched into a sardonic smile. "I remember. I remember it all. Good ol' Doc Hawkins must have screwed up, because I remember everything. Every little detail. And I savor every moment I was with them. Your parents—"

"Shut up," she spat.

"Your grandmother—"

"I said, shut up!"

"And your little sister. Oh, she was the sweetest of them all. I don't know what I enjoyed more. Raping her or killing her. Or maybe it was the looks on your parent's faces as they watched me do both."

Pam, her face now twisted in an angry grimace, and tears streaming down her cheeks, raised the gun once more and pointed it at David's head. "I'm gonna enjoy killing you more, you bastard."

There was a loud *bang* and David flinched, but it wasn't Pam's gun that discharged. It was Mike's.

Pam's lifeless body crashed down next to David. Their faces mere inches apart, her unseeing eyes still seemingly focused on him.

David smiled inwardly. "Just like your sister's."

THE BRIEFCASE

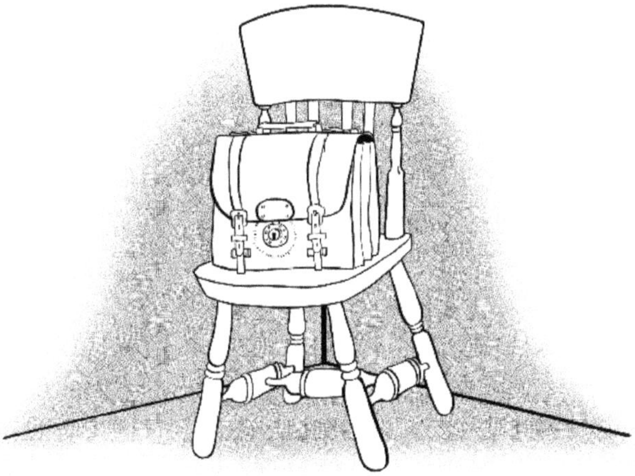

"The only thing necessary for the triumph of evil is for good men to do nothing."
– **Edmund Burke**

Frankfurt, Germany, Sachsenhausen District – 1937

Hans Dietrich looked at his pocket watch for the sixth time since entering the Donderbrauen Kneipe, a quaint tavern in a small town on the outskirts of Frankfurt. His contact wasn't late, but time was crucial; Dietrich was a wanted man, and quite possibly his country's last hope for a peaceful future.

From his small table in a quiet corner of the tavern, he looked around at the patrons and staff, making sure no one paid him any more attention than he deserved. He was just an old man, after all, drinking his schnapps and minding his own business. As far as they knew, he was there to enjoy a drink or two after a hard day's work. He lifted his glass and had a sip. Apples. *Was everything in this town made from apples?*

He looked around the bar and scrutinized all the people again. Everyone seemed all right; minding their food and drink, and sharing the latest gossip or news. The barkeep kept busy preparing for the evening rush, and the kellnerin who had waited on him, occasionally glanced at his drink to see if it needed tending. Nothing more.

No, everyone was fine; no one seemed suspicious or looked out of place. Dietrich postulated that the only one who fit that description here was himself. He hoped he wasn't that obvious. He was normally better at this sort of thing; he had done it a hundred times. But this was different; he wasn't meeting a fellow member or informant, the man he waited for was a stranger. He wasn't even German. And by the end of their conversation he would have to trust this man with, not only his life, but the lives of every citizen of Germany. Dietrich glanced around again; he had to be careful. The others were all dead, but he couldn't afford to die. Not just yet.

Dietrich looked to the chair to his right and at the large, brown leather briefcase that stood upright on the seat. It was a quality case; it had two strong straps that kept it securely closed, and a large brass latch in the center that locked with a key. It had cost him sixty marks at the luggage store in Berlin. A bit expensive, but the price that had been paid for its contents was immeasurable.

Dietrich checked his watch: two minutes past four. Damn! Now he was late. *Where is he?* But the man he was meeting was a doctor, and doctors were notorious for being late.

He'll be here. He'll show. Dietrich nodded to himself reassuringly. *He has to.*

The tavern door opened and the cool, early May air seeped into bar. Although the calendar said spring, winter refused to let go. A tall handsome man wearing a tan overcoat and matching hat walked in. He was about thirty-five years old, but he had a bit of old-soul look in his eyes. He wore brass trimmed glasses, and a billiard style pipe hung from his mouth.

This could be the doctor; the description matched. He was alone, and he casually glanced around as if looking for someone. He stopped a kellnerin carrying a tray full of drinks and asked her a question. She pointed in Dietrich's general direction, and the man in the overcoat walked over. Dietrich picked up a newspaper he had abandoned to the tabletop twenty minutes earlier and pretended to read the editor's column. The man placed his coat and hat on the rack off to the side, then took a seat at a small table adjacent to Dietrich's. He unfolded a newspaper of his own, and with the pipe still balanced in his mouth, he began to read.

Both men read their respective papers and now Dietrich had to make the next move.

"It's a beautiful day to go fishing," said Dietrich, not taking his nose out from his open pages.

"It is," said the man, "but I prefer to do my fishing on the lake."

Both newspapers dropped. "Dr. Adler?" said Dietrich.

"Yes," replied the other. He stood and approached a chair opposite Dietrich. "May I?"

"*Bitte.*"

Adler sat down, placed his pipe in his suit pocket, and then folded his hands on the table. "One of my patients said you wanted to meet with me?" He smiled. Dietrich did not return the smile. This wasn't the time for pleasantries, but he knew he had to ease Adler into this. Too much too fast would certainly scare him off. "Something very important, she said," Adler added.

Adler's smile wasn't a nervous smile, but an appeasing one. One he had probably used many times to woo a woman, or calm a patient, or get a better price on a new watch. It was more of a politician's smile, and it was one he'd likely learned honestly.

"That would be an understatement, my good doctor. This will be the most important meeting of our lives. And I have had many important meetings."

"Really?" said Adler, his face now showing a seemingly well-rehearsed look of concern. "Well, you have my full attention, my good sir."

A kellnerin came over and placed her hand on Adler's shoulder. "And what can I get for you, *mein herr*?" asked the waitress. She wore a red and white dirndl that flaunted her more prominent features. Her honey-colored tresses framed a beautiful face, and cascaded off her shoulders. Her smile was warm, her eyes alluring.

"What do you recommend?" said Adler.

"Well, we are famous for our apfelwein. It is the best in Sachsenhausen."

"Then that's what I'll have," said Adler, his politician's smile shining brightly.

The waitress blushed, then turned to Dietrich. "And you, sir. Would you like another schnapps?"

Dietrich picked up the drink he had been nursing for the past hour, downed the remainder, and placed the empty glass on the table. "*Bitte*," he said to the waitress in a raspy voice as the alcohol drained down his throat. She grabbed his glass and headed back to the bar, but not before giving Adler a glancing grin.

As Adler gazed at the departing view of the waitress, Dietrich cleared his throat to get the doctor's attention back where he needed it. "If you are done flirting, Dr. Adler, we have urgent business that needs your complete attention."

"Right," said Adler, "the all-too important conversation." He furrowed his brow, feigning that he knew the gravity of the situation.

Dietrich frowned and shook his head. "I know men like you, Doctor. Just observing the world around them, but not willing to be a real participant when true action is required."

"With all due respect ... I'm sorry, I don't even know your name."

Dietrich hesitated. He normally wouldn't give up his name to a man he just met, but it didn't matter anymore. After tonight, his name might be all that would be left of him. Dietrich exhaled and answered. "Dietrich. Hans Dietrich."

"With all due respect Herr Dietrich, you don't know me."

"I know more about you than you think," said Dietrich. "For one, you're a spy working for the American government."

"I assumed you knew that much since my patient who set up this meeting is one of my informants."

"I also know that you are an American citizen, and that you send monthly reports to the United States government on regular actions involving key Nazi personnel, up to and including Adolf Hitler."

"You've done your homework, Hans, but that doesn't—"

"Your reports go directly to Senator Henry Thomas, who just happens to be ... your father."

Adler's jaw dropped a bit, stunned by Dietrich's revelation.

"Which brings me to your real name: Steven Thomas. You were born in West Chester, Pennsylvania, to the daughter of German immigrants. Her name was Hilda Adler, which is where you took your pseudo name after you agreed to spy on my country at your father's behest. Growing up in a house with a German mother and grandparents, you learned the language and speak it almost flawlessly. You are a real doctor, and you received your degree from Harvard Medical School. Currently, you have a wife and two sons living in Chevy Chase, Maryland. How is that, Doctor? Do I now know you sufficiently?"

"How the hell—" Adler cut himself off as the kellnerin returned with their drinks.

"Here you are, *mein herren.*" She placed the glasses on the table. "Is there anything else I can get for you?" Although she spoke to both men, her eyes flicked to Adler who was too rattled by Dietrich's disclosures of him to pursue any more flirtatious activity and barely gave the waitress a look in return.

"That will be all for now, fraulein," said Dietrich. "*Danke.*"

"*Bitte, mein herr.*" She turned and headed for another table of patrons.

Adler waited until the kellnerin was out of earshot before he said: "Who the hell are you, Hans?"

Now that Dietrich had the American's attention, it was his turn to smile. "Dr. Adler, have you ever heard of the Widerstand?"

"Yes. It's a small underground organization that is attempting to undermine the current government in Germany."

"There is nothing small about it. There are dozens of cells all around Germany, all operating independently. I should know; I was the organizer of one of those cells. And now, I am its last surviving member."

"The rest of your cell is dead?"

"Murdered," said Dietrich with venom in his voice. "We were about to complete our task of stopping the Nazi regimen once and for all when we were hunted down by the Gestapo and executed by their SS monsters."

"Stop the Nazi regime? Stop them from what?"

"From plunging Germany into another great war, Herr Doctor."

"Another great war?" Adler asked in surprise and took a sip of his apple wine. "Isn't Germany still licking its wounds from the last one? Besides, the Treaty of Versailles—"

"The Treaty of Versailles is a slap in the face to the people of Germany. Our country's citizens have been suffering for *years* because of the harsh penalties laid upon us after the war. And Adolph Hitler and his followers plan to make everyone responsible pay for it all." Dietrich's voice had started to rise along with his anger. He took a deep breath and stared at his schnapps as he tried to reel in his rage. When he was once again in control of his emotions, he raised his gaze back to Adler and spoke in a much calmer tone. "We Germans do not want another war, Doctor. We don't want to see our beloved country go to the brink of annihilation and thousands of her countrymen killed for the ideology of a few madmen. But that is what Hitler has planned for us. And if he gets his way, Hitler's war will make the last one look like a petty skirmish."

"I don't think you have anything to worry about, Herr Dietrich. The rest of Europe—the rest of the world won't let that happen again."

"But it *is* happening, Doctor Adler. In all the reports you've sent to your father, you have to have seen the signs that Hitler is building his army and the retaking of former German lands."

"We know about the conscription of the people for the army, and we were surprised, but not too concerned, about the reoccupation of the Rhineland. Many of our statesmen believe that is France's fault."

"You mean France's problem," Dietrich corrected. Adler gave him a half smile. "Believe me, Doctor, those things you mentioned are just the beginning." Dietrich motioned to the chair next to him. "You see that briefcase? In it is a two-year collection of information showing that the Nazi party has plans to have Germany 'claim that which is rightfully hers.' To use the words of Hitler himself."

Adler glanced at the briefcase. "So, you have a few notes on the Nazis complaining about how unfair the treaty was. Everyone knows how they feel, and everyone knows Hitler isn't bold enough to start an all-out war with Europe. My informants and contacts have shown me no evidence that anything serious is stirring in Berlin."

"With all due respect, Doctor, but I believe you and your colleagues are being naive. As well, I'm sure, you have been intentionally fed disinformation by your so-called informants. Inside the briefcase are documents, photographs, recordings, and letters from and to Hitler himself. All of it showing plans for the expansion of Germany and the purification of its people."

"Purification?"

"Yes, Doctor. Every Jew, homosexual, and communist will be targeted. Essentially, anyone who is not of pure German descent, and who is not a true representative of its people."

"I assume you're speaking of the Nuremburg Laws stripping the Jews of all their rights. But you make it sound like Hitler wants to eradicate these people. What's he going to do, have them lined up and shot in the streets?"

"It may be just that simple." Dietrich took a drink of his schnapps. "The details are in the briefcase."

"And what of this 'expansion of Germany'? I assume that means he wants to take back more of the land Germany lost in the treaty."

"That and more. By this time next year, Austria could very well be an annexed state of the Third Reich."

"Austria?"

"Yes. And then Czechoslovakia, and then possibly Poland. In fact, Hitler is meeting with Stalin next month to discuss a possible invasion of Poland. A photograph of a letter to him from Hitler is in the briefcase. In fact, a copy of Hitler's itinerary for the entire months of May and June are in there as well."

"Do you realize what you're saying?" Adler said. "If Germany puts one soldier into any of those countries the treaty would be broken and would cause ..." Adler paused as the realization hit him.

"It would cause war, my good Doctor." Dietrich nodded, knowing Adler had finally caught on. "It would thrust Germany into another massive war with Europe."

It was Adler's turn to take a drink from his glass, and he managed to down its entire contents in one gulp.

The door to the tavern swung open with seemingly angry force. A man in long gray overcoat walked in followed by two men in black uniforms. The man in the gray overcoat casually ambled through the bar while the uniformed men stood guard by the door.

The man in gray had the swagger of one who had no fear. Why would he? When you are above the law and have the power of judge, jury, and executioner, you bestow fear, you are its embodiment. Such was the existence of agents of the secret police.

"Gestapo," Dietrich whispered to Adler who was himself carefully watching the men.

"And SS," said Adler.

Dietrich noticed the distinctive insignias on the collars of the black uniformed men. Adler was right. Of course he was; wherever the Gestapo goes, their SS dogs are not far behind.

"Why are they here?" Adler asked.

"They are looking for me," Dietrich said matter-of-factly.

Adler shot him a look. "They followed you here?" A bit of panic was in his voice.

"Most likely doing random searches, but they may know I'm in Frankfurt. They shouldn't have a picture of me, and I'm almost certain that my fellow members wouldn't have divulged my identity to them."

"Almost?"

Dietrich shrugged. "That depends on how persuasive the Gestapo was in their questioning."

The Gestapo agent worked his way around the establishment, questioning patrons and employees. Dietrich could see fear in the people's wide eyes. Although they knew nothing about the resistance cells, they all feared the Gestapo and their free-reign, ruthless rule they had over the populace.

"What do we do?" asked Adler. He was a bit more nervous, but otherwise kept his composure.

"We do nothing, Doctor Adler. We are simply two men having a drink on a Monday afternoon."

It took no time for the Gestapo agent to make his way to Dietrich's and Adler's table. He made a casual, but purposeful beeline straight for them.

"*Guten tag, mein herren*. May I ask what you gentlemen are doing here in Sachsenhausen this fine afternoon?" The agent was young, maybe a few years younger than Adler. He had straight, blond hair, and he was brimming with confidence. He was probably one of Hitler's fine examples of the perfect German citizen.

"We are merely having a few drinks at the end of a hard day," replied Dietrich.

"I see. May I see your papers please?"

Dietrich and Adler both reached for the inside pockets of their jackets and handed their identification papers to the Gestapo agent. He opened Adler's first.

"It says you are a doctor, Herr Adler."

"Yes," replied Adler and signaled the waitress for another drink.

"And your practice and residence are both in Berlin," continued the agent. "Why are you so far from home, Doctor?"

Dietrich couldn't let Adler ruin this whole operation, so he interjected. "He came to see me—"

"I was addressing the doctor," said the agent with a scowl and condescending tone. "When I want answers from you, I will address you."

Dietrich nodded and grabbed his glass.

"I am waiting for an answer, Herr Doctor."

Adler swallowed, inhaled, and answered. "My main practice is in Berlin; however, I have a second office in Frankfurt to accommodate my patients that live in the south."

"I see," said the agent. "And what is the address of that Frankfurt office?"

"24659 Schillerstraub."

"And you, Herr Dietrich, it says here that you are a cabinet maker in Dusseldorf. What are you doing in Frankfurt?"

"To see Doctor Adler. I'm a patient of his."

"Do they not have doctors in Dusseldorf?" the agent asked as he continued inspecting the identification papers.

"Yes, but Doctor Adler came highly recommended. You see I have—"

"Recommended by whom?"

"A friend. He said Doctor Adler was—"

"Name?"

The barrage of questions was an attempt to get Dietrich to slip up in a lie. An old but effective trick. Fortunately, Dietrich was too good for that; he had perfected the befuddled old man routine years ago. "My name? I thought you knew my name. Isn't it on my papers?"

"Not your name, your friend's name."

"I have many friends. Which—"

"The friend that recommended Doctor Adler."

"Oh, that would be Fritz Zimmer. He's a longtime customer of mine."

"And if you are seeing Doctor Adler as a patient, why are you here in this tavern with him?"

"You don't like this tavern?" Dietrich asked innocently.

"At the moment, Herr Dietrich, I don't like you. Now, tell me, why are the two of you here?"

"To have a drink, of course," Dietrich said as he raised his glass and gave a very toothy grin. The Gestapo agent looked from Dietrich to Adler. He was obviously frustrated from talking with the old man and on the verge of venting some of that frustration.

"He insisted on treating me to a drink," Adler said in response to the agent's glare.

"For being such a great doctor!" Dietrich said. He took his schnapps, threw it down his throat, and placed the empty glass back on the table just a little too hard so that it clumsily fell over.

"Do you normally have drinks with your patients, Doctor?"

"No, but Herr Dietrich wouldn't take no for an answer." Adler gave Dietrich a concerned look. He probably thought they were pushing their luck with the Gestapo agent, but Dietrich knew that lying to the Gestapo was a unique skill that had to be done convincingly.

The Gestapo agent looked at Dietrich, suspicion lingered in his eyes. Dietrich did his best not to make eye contact with him. A well-trained agent could read a man by deciphering his eyes.

"I think your *patient* has had one too many drinks, Herr Doctor. Make sure he finds his way home."

"I will," Adler replied.

The agent closed their identification booklets, placed them on the table, and walked back towards the door where the other agent waited. The kellnerin brought Adler his drink; she must have been waiting for the agent to leave before she approached the men's table. Dietrich was ready to breathe a sigh of relief until the agent turned around in mid-stride.

"So, whose idea was it to come here?"

"Pardon?" said Adler who was started at the agent's return.

"This tavern," said the agent as he waved his arm to gesture the entirety of the place. "Whose idea was it to come to this particular establishment?"

"It was mine," replied Adler.

"And why did you pick this place?"

"For the apfelwein, of course," he said, raising his glass. "It is the best in Sachsenhausen."

"Yes," said the agent, forcing a smile. "So I've heard." He was about to turn around again when he noticed the briefcase sitting on the chair. "That is a nice briefcase, Herr Dietrich."

"Actually," said Adler, "it's mine. It's a bit too big for my use. It cost me fifty marks in Berlin. It's yours for forty." The agent gave Adler a stone-faced look. "Thirty-five, then?"

The gestapo agent looked to Dietrich, to Adler, and then back to the briefcase. His eyes focused on it for what seemed an eternity. If he insisted on opening the case, not only would the entire mission be killed, but so would Dietrich and Doctor Adler. And maybe half of Europe.

"*Guten tag, mein herren.*" The Gestapo agent turned, and along with the SS officers, he left the Donderbrauen Kneipe.

"That was too close," said Dietrich. He motioned to the waitress for another schnapps. Adler grabbed his apple wine and drank it slowly until his hands stopped shaking. He placed the glass down and gave Dietrich a stern look.

"What are you trying to get me into, Hans?" Adler was visibly angry, and Dietrich couldn't blame him.

"I'm sorry, Doctor Adler, but—"

"Sorry?" Adler said at a slightly elevated volume. He looked around to see if he caught anyone's attention and then continued in a voice of more discretion. "You bring me here all the way from

Berlin, tell me a tale of exaggerated fears about unfathomable deeds that most likely won't happen, and then the damn Gestapo and SS come in and interrogate us here in our seats." Adler grabbed his wine again and drank the remainder in the glass.

"Believe me, Doctor, that was hardly an interrogation. If they had suspected that either of us was with the Widerstand, we would be in the back of their car heading off to meet our end, but not before they did everything they could to get as much information out of us as possible."

"What do you want from me, Hans?" said Adler with a bit of exasperation. "I may be a spy, but I am very low level. I'm not much more than a glorified messenger."

"Right now, that's exactly what I want. I need—Germany needs— you to take this briefcase to your father in America. He needs to see the truth behind all our 'exaggerated fears' as you call them. And then he must share that knowledge with his fellow senators."

"I can send it to him via my standard—"

"No," Dietrich interrupted. "*You* must take it to him. It must be hand delivered by someone he and I both trust, someone who can vouch for its contents."

"I can't vouch for anything that's in there," said Adler. "I don't know where any of it came from. And, how do I know *you* aren't trying to give me and the United States disinformation?"

Dietrich sighed and took off his glasses. He rubbed the ridge of his nose, cleaned the lenses with a handkerchief, and put the glasses back on. "I know this is a lot to take in, Doctor Adler, but I need you to have faith in me. Dozens of people have died getting the information in that briefcase. Good people; friends and good honest citizens. We love our country, Doctor, but we don't like where our Fuhrer is taking us. We need to show the world what is happening, so they can help us before it becomes too late."

"Why me?" asked Adler. "Why the United States? Why not France or England?"

"If Hitler begins his conquest of Europe, France and England will not be prepared for him. And the United States will, once again, ignore what is happening over here, and hope that it goes away. We need them to intervene before Hitler becomes too powerful. We need the Allied forces that banded together twenty years ago to do so again; this time not to fight a war, but to prevent one. We calculate that the United States is the best choice to spearhead that endeavor." Dietrich grasped one of Adler's hands. "The beast must be killed before it becomes an unfathomable monster."

"And you have real proof that war is inevitable?" Adler asked.

"In here," Dietrich said as he placed his hand on the briefcase. "Everything is in here. The proof is irrefutable. And as far as the authenticity of it goes, I'm sure your nation's government has highly competent individuals who can verify that the items in here are very real and quite damning."

Adler sat there digesting all that Dietrich had told him. After a minute of silence, he said, "Why me?"

"As I said, we need someone of notoriety and trust to hand deliver this information."

"No, it seems that you are coming to me rather hastily on this; things seem rushed and desperate."

"Very true, Doctor. Two nights ago the man we had arranged to take this briefcase to the United States was killed. He was the unfortunate victim of an automobile accident."

"I take it that you don't believe it was an accident."

"Not for a minute. After his 'accident' our group members were hunted down one by one until only I remained. There is no question that we had been revealed by a traitor in our midst. Fortunately, I was the one in charge of meeting our courier and giving him this briefcase. Also, fortunately, I was aware of you and who you truly are. You seemed like the most logical choice to replace our fallen man."

"How was this courier going to get this package to America? Who was he?"

"Are you familiar with Jonathan Bishop?"

"The ambassador's aide?" Adler's eyes went wide with realization. "Jon Bishop, the aide to the American ambassador to Germany, was your delivery man?"

"Yes. And now that task must fall onto you."

"And if I refuse?" asked Adler.

"Then we have no hope of stopping Adolph Hitler." Dietrich raised his empty glass to signal the kellnerin that he needed a fresh schnapps, then he gave Adler a rueful stare. "Besides, Doctor, it may be too late for you to say no."

"What do you mean?"

"I will most likely be caught and killed just like my fellow members, and when they do catch me, they will find all the people I have had contact with over the past couple days. That means they will find out that I have been to this tavern and that I was talking with you."

"No one could know th—" Adler paused as the afternoon's events came crashing upon him in a shower of reality. "The Gestapo agent."

"Exactly," said Dietrich.

The kellnerin came with two bottles in her hands. One was the schnapps for Dietrich, the other was a carafe of what appeared to be apple wine for Adler. "More schnapps?" Dietrich nodded and the waitress poured. "And you, *mein herr*?" Adler nodded slightly as he stared blankly at the table. She filled his wine glass and left the two men alone.

Dietrich sipped his schnapps and stared at Adler. This was a lot for the doctor to accept in one night, but he seemed like a decent man and would make the right decision. At least, Dietrich hoped so. But Adler was an American, and Americans cared for nothing save their own selfish lives. Most of them anyway. Living so far away, the problems of Europe were nothing more than stories. And if Adolph Hitler became the monster that Dietrich feared, America would see him as just another one of Europe's problems. Adler needed to be different; he needed to be the man he hoped—

"I'll do it," said Adler, still looking at the table. He slowly raised his gaze and looked into Dietrich's eyes. "I'll deliver the briefcase to my father."

Dietrich smiled; a smile of happiness, a smile of relief. "Thank you, Herr Doctor. You will be our savior." He reached across the table and took Adler's folded hands in his. "You have my and my country's eternal gratitude."

Adler forced a smile. Dietrich could tell that he was still a bit unsure and probably a bit scared. Good. That would keep him on his toes and possibly alive.

"I assume you have a plan for getting me home," said Adler. "To America, that is."

Dietrich reached into his inside pocket once more and removed an envelope and placed it on the table. "In here is the key to the briefcase as well as a ticket for a ship that will go directly to the United States." Dietrich paused and stared at the envelope. "This was supposed to be Bishop's ticket."

"I understand," Adler nodded. "When does the ship leave?"

"Tonight at seven o'clock."

"Tonight? Seven?" Panic was in Adler's voice. "I need to go home and pack. I have patients to see tomorrow. I need to call—"

"There is no time for that, Doctor. You must leave here and go straight to the ship."

Adler looked at his watch. "But I'll never make the docks in two hours."

Dietrich gave Adler a reassuring smile. "It's not that kind of ship, Doctor." Adler frowned and gave Dietrich a puzzled look. Dietrich pushed the envelope toward Adler. "Welcome to the resistance." He raised his glass and toasted his new recruit. "Prost!"

"Prost!" Adler returned the salute with his own glass, then the two men drank.

"It really is good apfelwein," Adler admitted.

"The best in Sachsenhausen," Dietrich added.

They both smiled.

Adler put down his glass and looked at the briefcase. It sat there like a punished child, waiting for one of its parents to rescue it from its place of abandonment. Was Adler ready for this responsibility? Dietrich prayed he was; he was their only hope. Dietrich needed to have faith in Adler just as Dietrich needed Adler to have faith in him.

"You will have three days before you reach America; take that time to look through the briefcase and really look at what we have accomplished. Look at all the information, and then you will truly believe all that I have said here this afternoon."

"I will," said Adler. "I promise." He picked up the envelope that sat so ominously in front of him, opened it, and removed the small brass key. He placed the key in his breast pocket and gave it a pat. He then removed the ticket, read it, and smiled.

"Something amusing, Herr Doctor?" asked Dietrich.

"There is one good thing about this mission."

"And what is that?"

"I've always wanted to ride on the *Hindenberg*."

HELD CAPTIVE

"Jealousy, that dragon which slays love under the pretense of keeping it alive."
– **H. Havelock Ellis**

Jill Temple stepped onto the curb and walked toward her assistant Brian to get an assessment of the situation. Scanning the area, Jill noticed her team's van parked in the driveway with most of her people preparing for the daunting night ahead of them. Neighbors from the surrounding houses watched with eager curiosity from the safety of their porches or lawns. And across the street, a group had gathered to witness and gossip about the evening's terrifying events.

Jill shook her head. *Every night this week. Will I ever get a break from this job?* This was supposed to be her night off. She had planned on a diet Dr. Pepper and a pepperoni pizza from Pepe's for dinner. For dessert, the latest Stephen King book to get lost in for the rest of the evening. *I guess it just wasn't meant to be.*

Brian was standing in front of a large tree stump that he was using as an impromptu table for his laptop and various folders. He smiled with relief when he lifted his head and saw his boss approaching.

"What do we have?" said Jill.

"The Porter family was chased out of their house. The invader's name is Alan Campbell, but everyone calls him Buck."

"Okay, so what's Buck's problem?"

Brian handed her a manila folder filled with papers, which she proceeded to skim through until she came to the page she was looking for. Her brow wrinkled in a frown, and she shook her head. "Where and when did this happen?"

"Check out the address," Brian said using a pen to point to a section of the police report. "And there's the time."

"Interesting."

"Makes sense, right?" Brian tapped the stump with his pen.

"Yeah, but what was the trigger?" Jill said, still focused on the papers. After a few seconds, she started scanning through the pictures that were paper-clipped to the folder. She let out a sigh as the photos brought to life the gruesome details from the report.

"And that's not the worst of it," Brian said.

"Oh?" she mumbled.

"He has hostages."

Jill shot him a look. "Hostages?"

"Yeah. His wife and daughter—Carol and Heather respectfully."

"Dear Lord," Jill said. "That's gonna make this more difficult."

"Without a doubt."

"Tell me about the wife and daughter," Jill said, then closed the folder and tossed it onto the stump.

Brian, holding a clipboard, flipped through a few pages. "Let's see. Carol, the wife ... an accountant for a firm that specializes in payroll. Heather, the daughter ... an honor student at Gilmore High. Seems like a very typical American family."

"Yeah, well, horrible things can happen to typical American families. We know that all too well. Just ask the Porters."

"Speaking of," Brian pointed to the group of people across the street. "The Porters are over there with some neighbors. Do you want to talk to them?"

Jill glanced over at the freshly evicted family, who were still visibly shaken by the experience. She had almost forgotten about them. Normally she would have talked to the family and reassured them that everything was going to be okay. But tonight, she just didn't feel like putting on the mask of concern. "No, just have Michele talk to them. She knows the drill." Jill gave the house a long cold stare. "Let's have a team meeting. Call everyone together so we can go over a few things. Then I'll get ready to head inside."

"By yourself?" Brian asked, surprised.

"Yeah. This may not end well, and I don't want to put any of you in danger." Seeing the concern on his face, she continued. "I'll be fine. This is what I do. Remember?" She gave the house a final glance. "Let's hurry up and have our meeting and get me hooked up. I don't want to waste any time."

Brian acknowledged her with a nod, then got on his walkie-talkie to call everyone together.

* * *

The house smelled of oregano, garlic, and roasted tomatoes. The Porters must have been having spaghetti for dinner when the incident had occurred. Jill Temple stood in the foyer of the large colonial and let the fragrance of the spices and herbs calm her shaky nerves. The loud ticking of a nearby clock unnerved her more than the Italianesque aroma could calm her. It was a battle of her senses that she had to quickly dismiss.

Breathing a heavy sigh, she was hesitant to proceed any further. Fear and trepidation kept her planted firm in the entranceway of the Porter's house, but duty kept her from turning around and going back to her team outside. And that duty meant risking her safety for the sake of others.

Jill forced her legs to move. From the foyer, she had three options: ahead of her were the stairs leading to the second floor; to her right was the large family room; and to the left was the living room. She decided to head left.

"*Do you see anything*?" came Brian's voice through her discreet earpiece.

"Not yet," Jill said in a soft, almost inaudible voice. She knew Brian could hear her reply, she just hoped no one else could. "Just left the foyer, heading to the living room."

"*Be careful. He could be anywhere.*"

"Yes, Dad," she said mockingly. Though ten years her junior, he tended to dote over her like a worried parent.

Jill knew she was fortunate to have a well trained and experienced team. In the whole scope of the situation, she wasn't alone. But when it came down to actually entering the scene, she felt very alone and almost naked. *Just another day at the office.*

"Hello?" Jill said, letting her voice carry throughout the house. "Anybody here?"

She listened.

Nothing, save for that infernal ticking.

"Mr. Campbell? Buck?"

Still nothing.

The lavishly decorated living room appeared to be more for decoration than actual use. It was filled with beautiful, ornate furniture including an antique secretary, a grandfather clock, which was the source of the loud ticking, and an angled-back Devan that was similar to the one Jill's grandmother had in her old farmhouse. The ticking of the clock gave an unnerving heartbeat to an otherwise empty dwelling. Jill had never cared for the timepieces; they reminded her of old Alfred Hitchcock movies she had watched as a kid and had nightmares about for a week afterwards. She would give anything if those were the worst nightmares she had these days.

While taking in the room, Jill mentally recalled all the information Brian had given her about Alan—call me Buck—Campbell. She imagined that's what he would say when he was introduced to someone. She had made sure to memorize every little detail about Campbell. She didn't want to walk in there carrying a memo-pad full of notes, as if reading from a script. She had to appear to care about what Buck was going through. Fortunately, she had Brian in her ear to fill in any gaps.

The police report itself had plenty of gaps. The report was inconclusive; some of the facts didn't add up. Jill hoped Brian and the rest of her team would be able to dig up more information that would shed some light on this situation, especially on Campbell himself. Buck was possibly guilty of manslaughter—maybe even murder—but she wasn't there to make that call. Someone way above her pay grade would decide his guilt. Jill was just there to get him out and rescue the hostages. Hopefully, saving all three in the process.

As she glanced around the family room, nothing seemed out of the ordinary, so she proceeded to the dining room.

The dining room table was set for five people; Mr. and Mrs. Porter had a teenager, a six-year-old, and a baby. A highchair was nestled at one of the table's corners. Its tray had been hastily removed and its former contents lay strewn on the floor. The plates on the table were laden with half-eaten food, the forks and knives appeared to have been dropped in mid-use, still piercing the homemade Italian food. The dinner, hours old and no longer piping hot, still looked delicious to Jill. And she had been wrong;

the Porters hadn't been eating spaghetti, it was lasagna. The four chairs had been pushed far from the table, some knocked over, in an apparent rush to leave. Other than the evidence of a hasty family departure, the dining room seemed normal. Jill turned toward the kitchen.

The kitchen was a mess. Not from the family's departure or any other disturbance, but from Mrs. Porter's hard work to make her family a nice meal. A glass Pyrex tray still hosted half of the lasagna. Dirty mixing bowls littered the counters as did containers of various ingredients, as well as a large recipe book opened to a page of highlighted text. In the center of the kitchen table, looking freshly made and delicious, was a chocolate cake. On top of the cake were two number-candles making a wax '14' amid the sprinkles and frosting. It was the oldest child's birthday. Karen, she believed, was her name.

"Happy birthday, Karen," Jill murmured to herself as she read the piped frosting letters below the two candles. What a crappy birthday this turned out to be. One thing was for certain: she would definitely remember this one for the rest of her life.

"What's that?" Brian's voice came over the earpiece.

"Nothing. I think they were celebrating the teen's birthday." Jill's stomach growled. Teased by the smell, she was half-tempted to steal a piece of the lasagna. No. Not a good idea.

"Oh. Yeah, you're right. Says here her birthday is today. That's strange."

"What's strange?" Jill asked.

"Buck's daughter Heather. It's her birthday too."

"How old?"

"Fourteen."

"Interesting. That could explain something."

"I was just thinking the same thing."

"Hopefully we can salvage what's left of *this* birthday."

"Who are you talking to?" came a orotund voice from her right.

Jill spun around to see a large man standing in the entrance to the family room. From the picture in her briefing folder, she knew the man standing ten feet in front of her was Alan Campbell.

"Mr. Campbell," Jill said. "There you are."

"Oh shit! You see him? Is he there?"

Jill responded to Brian with a barely audible "Uh-huh."

"Okay. Going radio silent. Cutting chatter."

"I asked who you were talking to," Campbell demanded. The man's anger was chilling. The scowl on his face and the fire in his eyes only reaffirmed that he was dangerous.

"N-no one," Jill stammered. "I was just mumbling to myself."

"Who are you? What do you want?"

"My name's Jill Temple. And I'm just here to talk to you. I'm with the San Francisco—"

"I don't know you. Get out!"

"I'm afraid I can't do that, Mr. Campbell. This isn't your house."

"It is now. I'm claiming it. Finders keepers." He chuckled to himself. "And there ain't nothing you can do about it." He glared at her menacingly. Jill took a reactive step backward though Campbell remained just inside the family room side of the doorway. Campbell sneered at her, seeming to simultaneously loath and enjoy her fear of him. "Now, do as I said and get out!"

Jill fumbled for the chair at the table beside her, not taking her eyes off of the terrifying man. She pulled it out and slowly sank into the seat. "I can't leave, Mr. Campbell. Not until we resolve this."

"There's nothing to resolve. I'm not going anywhere. And nobody; not you or those damn Porters can make me."

Seeing that she wasn't getting anywhere with this line of conversation, Jill decided to address the other issue. "Are Carol and Heather with you?"

He seemed taken aback by her question, but he gave her a quick and harsh response. "Maybe. What of it?"

"Could I talk to them? Would you allow me to see them?"

"No. They're fine and they're stayin' put."

"I just want to talk to them. Make sure they're okay."

"You want to take them from me. Don't you?"

"No. I just want to make sure—"

"I said no!" he screamed. "Don't make me do something you'll regret."

"Listen, Mr. Campbell. You're in charge here. No one's trying to take that away from you. But you gotta let me see your wife and daughter."

Campbell glared at her, baring his teeth like a dog guarding a precious bone.

"This is your show," Jill said reassuringly. "I'm just here to make sure everyone's okay." She paused to let that sink in. "Please, Mr. Campbell."

Campbell hesitated as he seemed to ponder this. Finally, he said, "Fine. But you stay in that chair. And no funny business. If you try anything, they're the ones that'll pay."

"I understand completely. No funny business. You're the boss." Jill set her jaw firm and breathed in, letting her body language show Campbell that she was serious about obeying his rules, but that she was also not going to back down from what she wanted.

Campbell walked backward, moving to the right and out of the frame and out of Jill's view. Seconds later, two women walked into the doorway.

Their movements were slow and hesitant, and they kept glancing in the direction to where Buck must have stood waiting, watching for them to slip up or try something. The older woman wore a gray and black business suit that reflected the professional woman that she was. Her daughter, Heather, was wearing denim overalls that barely covered a Backstreet Boys t-shirt. Both of their heads hung low as if they were emotionally beaten into submission. Their eyes showed fear and defeat.

"Carol?" Jill said softly. "Heather?"

The two women looked at her, seeming to notice her for the first time. Jill gave them a reassuring smile. They did not smile back.

"Hello, ladies," said Jill in a friendly, soothing voice.

"Hello," was Carol Campbell's nervous and subdued response.

"Hello," said Heather, echoing her mother's somber tone.

"My name's Jill, Jill Temple. It's very nice to meet the two of you."

The only reply from the Campbell women was a curt nod from Carol while Heather clung to her mother's arm.

"Are you women all right?"

"Does it look like we're all right?" Heather snapped. Her mother, startled by her daughter's outburst, cast worried eyes toward the direction of her husband. Then she grabbed her daughter's head and pressed it into her chest in a protective fashion. Both women's eyes were wide with fear that a rebuttal would soon be coming.

"I'm sorry," Jill said. "I'm going to do everything I can to resolve this ... situation."

"How?" said the mother pleadingly. "He's got us trapped here. There's nothing you can do."

"What happened, Carol? Why did he do this?"

"It's my fault," Carol replied. "I made him mad. I guess I deserve it."

"You guess you deserve it? No one deserves what you've been through. And what about your daughter? Does she deserve any of this?"

"Alan Campbell left work early." Brian's voice was fast but steady as he relayed Jill new information. *"He told his boss he had to go home and see his wife and kid. We're still making calls now to get more info."*

"Why did Buck leave work early?" Jill asked Carol. "Was he sick? Was one of you sick?"

"No," Carol said. "He came home to take us out to dinner."

"For Heather's birthday?" Jill asked.

Carol nodded. Heather raised her head at the mention of her name.

With none of the pieces coming together yet, Jill needed more information from the women. "Were you two fighting? Were you having marital problems?"

"Every couple has marital problems. Right?" Carol's eyes flicked nervously side to side.

Jill could always tell when someone was lying; avoiding eye contact was a dead giveaway. And though she had only just met Carol, she knew the woman was not telling her everything.

"What aren't you telling me, Carol? What happened that set Buck off like that?"

"That's enough!" came Buck's voice as he bullied his way into the doorway. The women, terrified, rushed out of sight in the direction from which they had come.

"Mr. Campbell, I was just trying—"

"I know what you were trying to do. You're trying to take them away from me. Why does everyone want to take them from me? Well, I won't let you! I won't let anyone! They're mine! You hear me? Mine!"

And with that, Alan Campbell rushed off towards his wife and daughter, his maddening scream echoing throughout the house. Jill stood and started to go after him until Brian's voice crackled to life in her ear.

"Jill, Buck hired a P.I. for a couple weeks to follow his wife."

"And ...?"

"She was cheating on him. She was having an affair with a guy from her work. We managed to track down the guy, and he says that Carol had planned on leaving Buck, and that he and Carol had plans to get married."

"Christ. That's it. That's when he snapped."

"Yeah. Apparently the P.I. had lunch with Buck and gave him the news."

"Okay. Good work, Brian." Turning her attention to the family room, Jill called after Campbell. "Buck? Where are you?" The family room was empty save for children's toys and a baby walker that Jill almost tripped over. She cautiously walked through the large room to where it met the foyer and wondered where they could have gone. She turned her gaze up the stairs and realized that was the most likely place.

She climbed the stairs slowly, keeping a wary eye out for Campbell. When she reached the top, she observed that there were too many rooms for them to have possibly entered. There were three doors to the left, one ahead, and a set of open double-doors to the right.

Jill stepped forward and opened the door in front of her. It was a bathroom. No sign of the Campbells. *One down, four to go.*

She was headed toward the group of three doors when a vase hurtled past her head and shattered against the wall next to her. Unable to shield her face in time, Jill was struck by a piece of the broken glass that had ricocheted off the wall and across her cheek.

Jill spun around to see Alan Campbell standing in front of the doorway of, she presumed, the master bedroom. His face full of anger and loathing.

"See what you did?" he said through clenched teeth. "You tried to trick me. You tried to get them away from me." His posture was that of a tiger ready to pounce on its prey. But who exactly was that prey? Herself? Carol? Heather? She wiped the blood that trickled down her cheek with her sleeve and took a calming deep breath.

Some people would have tried to calm Buck down, tried to reason with him. But Jill knew that would be like throwing a log onto the fire. Many people riding a wave of anger don't respond well to placating or patronizing. But how was she going to approach this?

The radio in her ear crackled to life. *"We checked on Buck's criminal history. He has none."* Brian's voice came hurriedly on the radio as if a doomsday clock ticked away in front of him. *"There were never any domestic violence issues, not even a visit from the police. And his neighbors said he was always a great dad and husband. At least, from what they observed."*

Okay. She knew what she had to do. Empathy was going to be her ally tonight.

"I know what happened, Buck," she said with her hands raised instinctively in front of her. "I know about the private eye, and the affair."

Buck's face changed. It softened a bit as his brow creased in puzzlement.

"She was going to leave you, wasn't she?"

"Yes," he spit out. His expression softening more.

"And she was going to take your daughter with her. Am I right?"

"Yes."

"That doesn't seem fair," Jill said. Her tone reflecting understanding and confusion. "I mean, you were a good father. Right? A good husband. Why would she do that?"

Jill wasn't merely acting; she truly didn't know Carol's reasoning for the affair. It could have been that she was simply bored with Buck. Or, perhaps, this boyfriend of hers was filthy rich. Who knew?

"I don't know," Buck said, his anger replaced by grief and sadness. "I tried to be a good husband and father. I worked hard—"

"I'll tell you why." Carol emerged from the bedroom, her daughter Heather in tow. "Because that's all you did was work!"

Buck turned to face her, tears forming in his eyes.

"Twelve—thirteen—hour days, six—seven—days a week. You were never home, Buck. You loved your job more than your family." It was Carol's turn to be angry. Jill knew this could be good, but she realized it could be dangerous as well. She just hoped Buck was the man she thought he was.

"That's not true, Carol," Buck reasoned. "I liked my job, but I didn't like working all those hours. I did it for you. Both of you." Bucked nodded to Heather.

"Did it for us? How was not being home to be a father and husband for us?"

"I didn't make a lot of money as a mechanic," he said, explaining himself to Jill as well as his wife and daughter. "It's hard work and not very rewarding. And I didn't want that kind of life for our daughter. I wanted her to go to college—something I never did—and get an education, get a real job. So, one day I made a bank account, a college fund for her, and have been putting money into it ever since."

Heather's eyes widened. She seemed like a bright kid and her good grades in school showed she had an aptitude for higher education. Just from her expression, Jill could tell the teenage girl was surprised and delighted at the news her father just shared. Then her expression was replaced with sorrowful despair as she seemed to remember their current situation.

"And you, dear," Buck said to his wife. "I started saving for you, too."

"Me?" Carol said incredulously.

"I was saving to take you to New York in the fall. Stay at a fancy hotel. Go to a couple Broadway shows. Even check out those twin towers."

The corner of Carol's mouth raised in a thoughtful smile. "Really?"

"Yes." Buck returned her smile and nodded. "And a couple years later, for our twenty-fifth wedding anniversary, I was going to take you to Hawaii. For two weeks. Cruise the islands, luaus, surfing—the whole bit."

Carol's face lit up, and she turned to Jill. "Those are the two places I always wanted to go." Then she looked at Buck. "I told him that on our very first date." She smiled up at her husband and gazed at him with eyes that seemed to remember a time when her love for him was pure and real. He responded with a loving, caring grin.

"Well, we're not going to do any of that stuff now. Are we?" Heather's statement snapped everyone back to reality. The smiles disappeared, replaced by gloomy and defeated expressions.

"Heather's right," Jill said. "I'm sorry that everything turned out the way it did, but you need to face reality." She paused to let that sink in. "Buck?"

Buck turned his head toward Jill as if she had just awakened him from a trance. He nodded slowly. “I know.” Then, addressing his wife and daughter he said, “Can you forgive me? I’m so sorry for what I’ve done. I’m so sorry for not being there for either of you.”

Carol and Heather exchanged glances then turned to Buck. “Only if you can forgive me,” Carol said. “I should’ve talked to you. I should have told you how I was feeling.”

“Of course I forgive you,” Buck said. “I think after all this time, we just forgot what was really important to each other, and we let ideas and dreams steer us off course.”

“Buck?” Jill said. “Are you ready to let them go?”

Buck looked at his family, tears swelling in his eyes. “What if—what if I don’t see them again?” Hopeless despair resonated in his voice.

“I think you will, Buck.” Jill said. “But it’s been twenty-four years. It’s time to let them go.”

Buck’s eyes glanced from Jill to his family then back to Jill. He nodded; unable to speak.

“Okay ladies,” Jill said to the Campbell women in a comforting voice. “It’s time.”

A bright light—almost too painful to look into—suddenly emanated from the bedroom. It glowed with a brilliance that could rival the sun, almost causing Jill to avert her eyes. As difficult it was to look at, it was just as hard not to. The light was blinding, but inviting, like a hot bath. It was as if the light itself went beyond a mere optical existence and was somehow ... alive. A calming peace came over Jill, and she wasn’t sure, but she could have sworn she smelled the sweet aroma of honeysuckle. *Funny*, she thought, *the smell changes every time.*

The two women turned toward the light, then Carol twisted her head back toward Jill. “Thank you, Miss Temple.” And then to her husband. “See you soon, honey.”

Heather stepped through the light first and disappeared in an enveloping glow that seemed to eagerly suck her in.

Carol was next, but before she stepped into the light, Buck grabbed her ethereal arm.

"Wait, Carol," he said, his eyes darting from side to side in uncertainty. "I ... I'm scared."

"Why, Honey?" Carol asked. "What's wrong?"

Buck looked at Jill, trepidation in his eyes. "I don't think I can do this. I'm afraid." Turning back at Carol he said, "What if I never see you again?"

"What do you mean, Honey?" Carol said, a little confused.

But Jill understood what Buck was saying. "I know how you feel, Buck," Jill said, "but this is what you're supposed to do. You can't stay here forever." Jill needed Buck to let his wife cross over. That was the only way this situation was going to get resolved. She only hoped she could convince him. *He's so close now ....*

"But I've been bad, Miss Temple," Buck lamented. "I've done something terrible. What if—what if I end up somewhere else?"

"What you did was an accident, Buck. I saw the police report. You were driving too fast. You lost control. It's not like you hit that tree on purp—" Jill hesitated as she tried to read the husband and wife who were exchanging worried looks. "Is it?"

"That's where you're wrong," Buck said. "I didn't lose control. I meant to hit that tree dead on." Buck lowered his head in shame. Carol looked away as if not wanting to hear what her husband had to say.

Jill gaped at Buck, unprepared for what he had just confessed. She had thought it could have been a possibility, but after all that had been said, she would have bet anything that it had been an accident.

"I left work early," Buck began to explain, staring down at the floor. "After hearing what the P.I. found out, I had to get home and see my family. I picked up Carol and Heather, it was Heather's birthday. I was going to take them to dinner. Pepe's, Heather's favorite place."

"Yeah," Jill sighed. "Good pizza."

"Right," he said, looking back up at her. "But before we even got there, we got in an argument, and I brought up the P.I. and what he found out, and then she told me everything. How she met someone else, was going to divorce me and marry him. Then, I just lost it. I couldn't take no more. I said that I'd be damned if I let anyone take my two girls from me. So, I saw that big tree, and I stepped on the gas."

She closed her eyes as she realized the police report had been correct all along. She had thought the estimated speed and the lack of skid marks in the report had been a mistake. But after hearing Buck's confession, maybe it had been spot on. Murder-suicide. This definitely throws a wrench into the works. Jill remembered the large tree stump outside. Another innocent victim of the crime? Or a hapless participant?

Jill shook her head, angry at herself for not seeing this coming. She just assumed this would be another happy ending. She was on a roll after all. Four in a row. Four.

Buck put his face in his hands and began to cry. "What did I do?" he sobbed. "I destroyed the only things that mattered to me."

Carol put her arms around her husband to console the sobbing man.

"Maybe I was right," Buck said to Jill with a grimace.

"Right about what?" Jill asked.

"Maybe I *am* damned." His crying turned to laughter as he realized the irony. He gazed at his wife and a semblance of clarity came over him. "But you are right, Miss Temple. I need to let them go. If I love them—and I most certainly do—then it's the right thing to do." Placing a hand on Carol's shoulder, and with a gentle push, Buck coaxed his wife toward the light. "Go on, Honey. Go be with our daughter. I'll be right behind you."

Carol gave her husband a sympathizing, yet loving smile. Her own tears streaked down her face. "See you soon, Dear." Then she turned and started for the light. Stopping short, she turned to Jill. "For what it's worth, Miss Temple, I appreciate everything you've done." With a final glance at her husband, Carol stepped into the light.

But instead of being enveloped in the brightness like Heather had been, the light faded as quickly as it had appeared, leaving the hallway in darkness save for the chandelier hanging above the foyer.

Confused, Carol turned around, her gaze going from Jill to Buck, then back to Jill. "I don't understand."

Suddenly, a small rumbling noise began to echo through the house. On the floor, between Jill and the spectral couple, a small black circle appeared out of nowhere. It was the size of a dinner plate, but it swirled and grew until it encompassed most of the hallway's floor, separating Jill from the Campbells. Jill wrinkled her nose; a pungent smell had cut into the air, replacing the aroma of honeysuckle with what Jill could only compare to rotten eggs.

The rumbling sound had increased to a roar, sounding like a freight train running through the house. The Porter's home shook as if a continuous earthquake rocked the neighborhood. Jill grabbed hold of the newel post to keep her balance. Several pictures fell as cracks appeared on the walls and ceiling.

As black as pitch, the churning mass on the floor appeared hollow and solid at the same time. As if it existed and didn't exist; it fought to remain in this realm. It violently twisted around and Jill got a feeling like she was floating in the sky during a horrible storm as she looked down into a frightening tornado. The swirling pit filled her with terror, just as the light had filled her with peace.

Carol and Buck held each other tight as their eyes became fixated on the event in front of them.

Eddying in the blackness were things that Jill couldn't quite make out. Moving independently of the storm, they slowly reached the top of the maelstrom where Jill could finally comprehend what they were.

Creatures. Manlike creatures that spun naturally in the storm as if the swirling mass of terror was their home as well as their prison. Their faces were contorted in anguish and hatred. Horrible shrieks emanated from their gaping mouths. Their skin was blotchy gray, and their eyes were piercing red spheres.

"Demons," Jill muttered to herself.

She took a step back; no matter how many times she had seen them, the demons still gripped her with an almost overwhelming fear. Wide-eyed and shaking, she gripped the railing tight until the grooved wood bit into the flesh of her hand.

Several of the demons' arms stretched out of the maelstrom, their long bony fingers reaching out and grabbing hold of Buck's and Carol's legs. Buck kicked and Carol screamed, but it was no use. The demons' hold on them was too strong, and they fell into the pit of blackness, joining the evil tempest and the creatures that had dragged them in. Carol screamed for help, and they both cried in agony, but the storm of blackness swallowed the couple like writhing bugs being washed down a drain.

Hovering near the top of the black storm, one of the demons set his gaze upon Jill. An evil, satisfied smile rested on its face as its glowing red eyes seem to drill into Jill's soul. It raised a gnarled hand and tossed something shiny at her feet, hitting the floor with a resonating *ding*. The evil creature gave her a nod, then joined its fellow demons in the storm of the damned.

And then, like waking from a bad dream, the hole was gone, and the hallway was empty and calm once more. The only sound was that of the grandfather clock downstairs. Its loud thumping ticks mocking her racing heart. Ironically, she was glad to hear it.

Jill Temple crossed herself and kissed the silver cross that hung on a chain around her neck. She said a prayer for Heather and continued to stare at the area where the hole of darkness had been. "I'm sorry, Heather. I didn't know you would be going on alone."

Jill hesitantly walked over to the shiny object that the demon had tossed, and she carefully picked it up. As she had expected, it was a gold coin. Ice-cold to her touch, it was almost painful to hold. Ancient writing adorned the coin and, like the others, was most likely priceless.

And, like the others, she hated it. She despised what it represented. But she wouldn't accept the coin, not for herself. That would make her complicit in the dark actions that transpired this evening. No, she would give it to someone who needed it. Someone who was affected by the situation. Someone who wouldn't know what this soul-costing blood money represented. This coin she would leave for the Porters to find. She placed it on a small table where the glass vase had once rested.

Jill breathed a sigh of relief that all of this was finally over, though the images of all she had seen will join the collection of horrors that would haunt her for the rest of her life.

But that was her job. That was how she helped people. Like it or not, it was her life. Some might say having a gift like hers was a curse, but Jill saw it as an obligation. A cloak of responsibility that she wore with both pride and dread. Did that make her a good person? A saint, possibly? Or just someone with no choice but to heed her calling? Right now, she was simply tired.

No longer hungry, she just wanted to go home and crash in her bed and sleep. Sleep until her cat woke her to be fed. Sleep until the pangs of hunger made her get up and eat something herself. Sleep until the next unnerving call that would ask her to resolve yet another ghastly situation.

But it wasn't that simple. The dreams—the nightmares would not let her rest so easily. They never do.

"Jill? Is everything okay?"

"Everything's fine, Brian." She turned towards the stairs, but not before giving the hallway floor one final look. "You can tell the Porters they can have their house back."

"It's over?"

"Yeah. It's over."

"Thank God!"

“Yeah,” Jill said as she descended the stairs. “But tonight, He wasn’t working alone.”

DOG YEARS

"A dog is the only thing on earth that loves you more than he loves himself."
– **Josh Billings**

I know what you're thinking. What's an old man like me doing in a dog kennel? Well, this is actually an animal rescue shelter, and I'm not that old. I'm a very spry seventy-two. I walk three miles every day and do all my own cooking and cleaning. I live in the same house I've had for over forty years, and I take care of it just like I always have since the day I bought it. No one's keeping this former Marine down, not even Father Time.

So, why am I here? Well, I'm thinkin' of getting a dog. But you probably guessed that. Maybe you mean, why am *I* getting a dog? Why not? I love dogs; always have. But getting one now, at my age .... This was actually my son's idea. He lives in Beeville, Texas with his wife and my three grandkids. Not for too long, though. They're moving back to Maryland next year. I was talking to him last week and, well, I guess he was worried about me.

"Hello?"

"Hey, son. It's me"

"Hey, Dad. Everything okay?"

"Sure, fine, fine. How are the kids?

"They're good."

"Is Lisa still picking on little Alan and David?"

"Ha. Yeah. She is, but they hold their own. I keep telling her that her little brothers won't be little for very long. Soon they'll be bigger than her."

"And Donna? She having any more problems at work?"

"Nah. She's good. Everyone's doing okay."

"Great."

Silence

"You sure everything's okay, Dad?"

"Sure. Why wouldn't it be?"

"Because this is the third time you called this week, and it's only Wednesday."

"Is it so bad that a man misses his son and grandkids?"

"No, but it tells me that you're feeling lonely."

"Me? No. I'm fine, son. Really. I enjoy my solitude. I go out and do things all the time. I go to the movies, the diner, the park—"

"How is Winston Park? I haven't been there in years."

"It's good. They finally replaced that one bench I've been bitching about for damn near a decade. I sat on it while I ate my lunch last Monday. Or was it Tuesday? Great sandwich. Cuban from Maria's."

"Speaking of the park, dad, have you ever thought of getting another dog?"

"A dog? At my age?"

"Yeah, why not? You've always had a dog. I think having one now would do you some good."

He was right. Ever since I can remember, I've had a dog in my life. You could say my life has revolved around dogs. Funny, they say on average, every year a dog lives, is like seven years to a human. And in my lifetime, I've had seven dogs. The math seems to work, doesn't it? Even though I've had all these dogs, I remember each and every one of them with great detail and fondness. In fact, my earliest memory I have is of my first dog. His name was Lucas.

* * *

Lucas was an Alaskan Malamute, and his coat was as white as virgin snow. He was a beautiful dog—big and strong. I would tell my friends that he was half wolf, and they believed me. He certainly did look the part, and after a while, I think I started to believe it myself. My parents got him when I was two years old, and because I was an only child, he was my constant companion. But he was more than that; he was like a brother, and I loved him no less than I did my parents.

What a great dog. And strong—did I mention that? During the winter, after a nice snowfall, my father would strap a harness to Lucas, and he would pull me around in my sled like it was nothing. And he loved doing it, too. When he saw my father bring the harness and sled out of the garage, he got all excited. His tail would wag like a windshield wiper on a cheap car.

We did everything together. Any game or activity I did, involved him. Whether I was a dinosaur hunter, or a cowboy, or a spaceship captain, he was there for the ride right alongside me. We were inseparable, and were best pals to the end. That end, however, came just a little too soon for me. It was something I was completely unprepared for.

Lucas died when I was fourteen. He had developed some serious medical problems—I'm not sure exactly what—and went downhill quickly. At least he didn't suffer long. I should have been grateful for that, but the pain I felt inside clouded any sort of rational thought. It was the first time I had lost someone really close to me. He had been my big strong pal, and I thought we would be together forever. When you're a kid, you live in the moment, you don't think about the future, and that someday things will change or come to an end. But they do. There are some things in life you have to learn the hard way. I'll never forget my last day with Lucas. My mom took him to the vet to be put down. She asked if I wanted to go with her, but I couldn't. I just couldn't bear to go and take him to his death. So, I said goodbye to my best friend, my brother, in our driveway as he sat in my mom's station wagon. Teary eyed, I watched as they backed out and rode down the street until they were out of sight. My mom returned later with his collar and tags. I cried for a week straight. It seemed like a year.

* * *

Summer vacation began just a few weeks later, but I couldn't be as joyful about it as I usually was. What was the point? After a few months of moping around the house, my parents, in an attempt to cheer me up, got another dog. He was a Jack Russell Terrier. They named him Willy. And he was the nastiest, most malicious dog I had ever known. And I mean that to this day.

We should have known something wasn't quite right with Willy the first time my mom turned on the vacuum cleaner. Now, normally, when a vacuum is turned on, a dog will run for the hills. They'll dive under a dining room table or jump on the sofa. They'll do something, anything, to get away from the infernal contraption making all that noise. Lucas always sought the solace of my mom's walk-in closet when the Electrolux monster roared through the house.

But Willy was different. He attacked the machine like it owed him money. And I mean *attacked.* As my mom pushed the vacuum from room to room, he would bite and snap and chomp at the nozzle with intent on killing the mechanical creature. It was quite a spectacle to behold. He actually broke two vacuum cleaners, and when the destruction was done, he would walk away, staunch pride in his gait.

I lost track of the number of dead animals he brought into the house. If he were human, one might say he was a serial killer in the making. And we're pretty sure Willy was the cause of the constant rotation of postal workers in the neighborhood, as well as my mom's tulips and perennials being ripped out and strewn across the lawn. We never caught him in the act, so a canine court would never have convicted him, but my father constantly threatened to send the mangy mutt, as he called him, to join Alice Kramden on the moon. My mother, however, always intervened and saved Willy from any impromptu interplanetary travel.

Now, there wasn't a dog in the world that could have replaced Lucas. It would take years for me to come to terms with his death. So, in a way, I was glad Willy was the mean little monster that he was. That way, I couldn't feel bad about not loving him the way I had Lucas. But between all the destruction and mayhem, Willy was a dog and did a lot of good dog things. I just can't think of any right now, but I'm pretty sure he did.

* * *

When I turned eighteen, I was drafted into the Marines for the war in Vietnam. I said goodbye to my parents and Willy, and I was shipped off to Paris Island. After boot camp, I saw a posting for the Marine's War Dog unit. I applied and was fortunate enough to be accepted. I spent almost a year training with a one-year-old German Shepherd named Oscar. He was big, very big, and such a friendly dog. And, by George, he was smart; he absorbed everything he was taught like a sponge. He was an easy dog to like, if not love. Our instructors, however, told us not to get too attached to our dogs; they were just a piece of equipment like our rifle or gas mask. But it was hard for me to see Oscar as just a piece of equipment. The more we trained together, the closer we became. And after the day's training, we ate together and slept together. We were more than just dog and handler, we were best-mates. And though Lucas still had a huge part of my heart, I was making room for Oscar in there as well.

When our training was done, Oscar and I, along with a couple hundred other teams, were shipped to South Vietnam for various deployments. We were assigned to First Marine Division, first battalion, fourth regiment, bravo company, second platoon. We were designated scouts and lookouts. And all training from then on out, was on-the-job.

At first, I wasn't quite sure what to expect. We were trained well, but reality usually has its own thing in store for you. We would go out ahead of patrols to look for traps and snipers. It was pretty hairy at first, but once Oscar got a real-life taste of what was expected of him, he became a pro. A combination of training and instinct made him an invaluable part of our platoon. I guess I should say, made *us* an invaluable part of the platoon, but in all honesty, Oscar was the star of our duo. If he was King Kong, I guess that would make me Fay Wray.

On hot dark nights, when we had to camp away from base, Oscar and I would take up watch while most of the other Marines slept. Our job was simple; don't let the enemy sneak up on us and kill everyone in their sleep. But hell, it was so dark, I couldn't see my hand in front of my face, but Oscar—that dog could hear or smell a Vietcong soldier a hundred feet away, no matter how stealthy they tried to be. And once he got a whiff of one, he would let me know with a low growl and a stare in the direction of the intrusion. I would then signal the other's on watch, the clamors would go off, and the enemy learned a powerful lesson as their comrades were ripped to pieces by shrapnel.

The Vietcong learned to hate the war dogs very quickly. They even placed bounties on the lives of the dogs and their handlers. I was both proud and terrified when I learned of that.

Some Marines kept track of how many Vietcong they killed; my and Oscar's success was measured in Marine lives saved. Every other day, we would foil an ambush or discover a trap well before it could be triggered. Corporal Steve Roscoe, a skinny guy from Oakland, even kept a tally of men Oscar saved. Eventually, he lost count.

On those life-saving days, the men would show their gratitude by sharing a bit of their evening meal with Oscar. I got the occasional clap on the shoulder, but it was Oscar that got most of the accolades, and I didn't mind that one little bit, he certainly deserved it. Everyone in our platoon said Oscar was our ace-in-the-hole when it came to dealing with the VC.

But not every encounter with the enemy was perfect.

While humping to a firebase out in the middle of nowhere, it rained like nothing I'd ever seen before. The raindrops were heavy and hit hard like bullets from heaven. We had to shout above the deafening sound, and the humidity was so high, it felt like we were breathing water.

We hurried to take cover in a nearby village, and that's when we came upon an enemy encampment that was just as surprised to see us as we were them. With it raining as hard as it was, Oscar couldn't hear or smell anything to give us a warning. After initial shots were fired, the situation turned into a close-quarter melee, and my dog was more than up for the challenge.

With Oscar being so lean, powerful, and fast, they had no idea how to deal with him. With lightning speed, he took down several Vietcong by hitting each one like a linebacker and tearing at the arm that held their weapon. Once the VC was down, a Marine would finish him off, and Oscar would move onto the next one.

After the skirmish, I saw Corporal Roscoe writing in his book on the page he designated for Oscar. Instead of checks, he marked four X's. I asked him what were the X's for, and he said they were four the enemy soldiers Oscar helped take out.

I had mixed emotions about that. It was one thing for us to save lives, but I wasn't too keen on Oscar taking them. Later, I expressed my feelings to the company chaplain, and he told me that this was war, and a lot of times killing was necessary to save lives. I knew that he was right, but that didn't mean I had to like it.

After a year, I was due to rotate out and could have left the country to serve a year in Okinawa or, if I was lucky, Hawaii. But I opted to stay in country and be with Oscar so we could continue serving together like we had for the past year. I did, however, apply for a new assignment. I'd had enough of scouting; we saw more than our fair share of carnage. Things I have forced myself to try to forget and will continue to try 'til the day I die.

No, it was time for something different, so we were assigned sentry duty at a nearby base. It was a little boring at times, but no less dangerous than scouting. Along with other dog teams, we would patrol around our base to prevent any enemy incursion. A tactic used by the VC was to covertly send sappers, in the dead of night, into a military base, and do as much damage, and kill as many people, as they possibly could. They accomplished that by wrapping themselves in explosives and blowing themselves up once inside a building or tent.

Imagine sitting with your buddies, enjoying your evening meal after a long day on patrol. When suddenly, a Vietnamese man runs in the mess tent, screaming at the top of his lungs, and when he reaches the middle of the group, he detonates all the explosives strapped to his body. As you can imagine, the results were quite horrifying.

Oscar and I did our job well, and no enemy ever breached our perimeter. In fact, I heard no enemy incursion ever occurred at any base during the war where there were dog teams on sentry. The Vietnamese hated and feared our war dogs, so they always steered clear of them whenever they could. They estimated war dog teams saved the lives of over 10,000 American servicemen. Not too shabby for a couple hundred canine-marines.

Sometime during my second tour, while NASA was sending regular excursions to the moon, my parents wrote me telling me that Willy had died. They said that he had gotten hit by a car while he'd been chasing the gas meter reader across the street. I was sad when I heard about that. He may have been a mean dog, but we did have some good times, and he had a special place in my heart. Of course, I'm sure, there were many mailmen and meter readers that celebrated the day of his death as an annual holiday for many years afterward.

I ended up serving just two tours in Vietnam before being forced to rotate back to the States, where I would then have the option of re-upping or being discharged. In doing so, I had to leave Oscar in the hands of another handler who was an FNG fresh from training, and whose name I can't even remember.

I worried for Oscar; he had several years of experience, and this new handler had none. I knew this guy was trained well, but I just hoped he didn't go and get my dog killed. It was a tearful goodbye when the jeep came to take me to the airstrip. As I knelt there saying goodbye to Oscar, I felt so bad for him because he didn't understand what was happening. And he probably didn't understand until days later when I never came back. On the plane home, I wondered if he would miss me like I would miss him. Would he forget about me and make a new best pal in this new handler? One thing was for certain, my heart broke that day. Not just for the fact that I would never see Oscar again, but because he would never see me again and not understand why. Why did the man who took such good care of him and show him so much love, leave him in that dangerous land? That plane ride home was the most heart-wrenching flight of my life.

* * *

When I came home from Vietnam, I was given an honorable discharge and entered civilian life. I moved back in with my parents, and I knew the best way to get over Oscar and put the horrors of war behind me was to get a job. Something I could focus my mind and time on. I found such a job at the local bakery. Rick Fauston, a friend of my father, and a former Marine himself, owned a bakery and wanted an apprentice, someone for him to teach the business and cultivate into a great baker. He was tired of the summer and holiday help that was there for only three or four months at a time. With no kids of his own, Rick needed someone he could pass the business down to one day. It sounded like a good opportunity, and I applied within days of being back. I got the job almost immediately; we Marines ... we look out for each other.

I lived with my parents for about eight months until I had enough money to put down as a deposit for an apartment. But during those eight months, I reflected on my time in Vietnam. Did it change me? Sure. It was war. I saw things, horrible things. Things which people just shouldn't be a part of. It was unnatural and evil. My parents could tell right away that I wasn't the same naïve boy who left home just three years prior. I couldn't put my finger on it at first, but I realized that they didn't smile. Not like they used to, anyway. Oh, they tried to put on a facade of happiness; welcoming me home, making my favorite foods, but they treated me more like a stranger than their son. I couldn't blame them really, they had no idea what I had gone through, and they didn't really know what to say to me, so they usually said nothing. My father was drafted into the Army just as World War II was ending, so he didn't see any action, just the end result.

War is hell, that's for sure. And I don't think I would have come back halfway sane if it hadn't been for Oscar. I sure did miss him. I missed the company of a dog. I missed the presence of a dog in the house. Even having Willy around would have been somewhat comforting. And his vacuum cleaner attacks were always entertaining. But Willy's antics were just a memory that echoed in a depressingly quiet house.

I felt like all that sadness was my fault. I wanted to apologize to my parents; tell them I was sorry their little boy was gone. Sorry this man they barely recognized came home instead of that boy who made forts out of couch cushions. Sorry that the happiness in the house was extinguished like the flame on an old candle.

One day, while helping my father out in the garage, I saw my old sled and Lucas' harness. I was filled with warm memories as I rubbed the cracked leather between my fingers. A few strands of hair were caught in the brass buckle. White hairs. My mind raced back in time to when I was ten and being the happiest I had ever been. Those were great times, not just for me, but for the whole family. As I stood there holding that harness, I knew it was time for a new dog to take up residence in the house.

I brought the idea of a new dog up with my parents, and they weren't exactly receptive to it. You see, they were still recovering psychologically from Willy, and they had no interest in getting another dog while the images of broken vacuums and civil servants running for their lives were still fresh in their heads. But I told them if I got a dog, I would take it with me when I got my own place. They agreed, and that's when I got Kasie.

* * *

It was actually by happenstance that I got her. I mentioned to someone at the bakery that I was thinking about getting a dog, and he said that his parents' neighbor had a dog that had pups about a month before, and they were looking to find good homes for them. I jumped at the opportunity and went to check out the litter. I picked the first one that ran up to me and took her home.

Kasie was a red golden retriever and a full-grade sweetheart. She loved everyone, and everyone loved her. She was the complete opposite of Willy and won the hearts of anyone she came in contact with. She learned tricks, never barked unnecessarily, and most of all, she helped bring happiness back into the house. There's nothing like a puppy to melt the hearts of the people around her. My parents smiled. I smiled. And we talked. We talked about everything, and even though that boy that used to live there was gone forever, the man that replaced him found love in his parents that he had almost forgot existed. But they reminded him, and he never forgot again.

When I finally found an affordable apartment that allowed dogs, I packed up my stuff, and Kasie and I left my parent's house and headed for a quaint apartment on Quaker Street, about a half-hour away. My mother did everything but beg me to not take Kasie with me. But I told her that I needed Kasie in this new chapter of my life, and my mother couldn't agree more. Two months after I moved out though, my parents got another dog, a female cocker spaniel. They named her Valentine, after my mother's sister who passed away when she was just eight years old. She was a pretty good dog. Over the years, Kasie and Valentine would make many trips to visit each other and became great friends.

It was early spring when Kasie and I moved into the apartment. The last of winter's ice had melted allowing us to take plenty of walks. She quickly made friends with all the dogs in the neighborhood, as well as those that frequented the park a couple blocks away. We became regulars there, at Winston Park. Little did I know the impact that place would have on my life. The apartment didn't have a lot of room for Kasie to run around in, so visiting the park was part of our daily routine. Between working at the bakery and playing with Kasie, my days were pretty full, but also pretty great.

* * *

Two years had come and gone and our lives had changed very little. Mr. Fauston opened another bakery and made me manager. I had increased income, but also increased responsibility. My time in the park with Kasie was reduced a bit as I started working twelve-hour days. At least I worked close enough to home that I could visit her during my lunch break. My social life was almost nonexistent. I dated a little here and there, but there was always something that didn't work out, so my relationships with women were short lived.

In early May of '75, I heard that the war in Vietnam had come to an end with a disappointing, anticlimactic whimper. I immediately thought of Oscar and made some phone calls. What little information I discovered wasn't encouraging. The mass exodus of our troops was done so hastily that a lot of equipment was left behind. And that included most of the dogs that served in the war dog programs of the various branches of the armed services. In the end, only 200 out of the 5000 war dogs returned home. The remaining dogs were either euthanized or just plain left behind. And I'm sure the Vietnamese people didn't take care of those poor creatures the way they deserved to be treated. To us—the handlers, and the soldiers, and the Marines they protected—those dogs were war heroes. To the Vietnamese ... well, let's just leave it at that. I shuddered to think what might have happened to them and I hoped and prayed Oscar wasn't one of them. My mind went to dark places, and my heart broke again. With soul wrenching empathy, Kasie could sense my sorrow, and laid her head in my lap. If she were human, I swear she would have cried. I sure did.

* * *

A few months later I was in the park with Kasie. It was a warm Saturday, and we were playing fetch with her favorite ball. The park was busy with people having picnics, walking their pets, or doing other leisure activities. As Kasie and I played, I noticed a blind woman with a seeing-eye dog—now days, I believe they call them service dogs. Anyway, I was amazed at the ease with which she navigated the sea of people and their pets. As she got closer, I noticed her beauty was as graceful as her stroll through the weekend crowd. And I'm sure it was, in no small part, due to her guide dog, a yellow Labrador Retriever. It was a beautiful dog for an even more beautiful woman. She had red hair that uncannily matched her outfit, and dark sunglasses with stylish frames that hid her eyes in a mysterious rather than pitiful way. You really wouldn't have known she was blind, if not for the special brace-like leash she had for her dog.

As I watched her, a Frisbee sailed over the lab. Its intended recipient backpedaled between the woman and her guide, causing all three to collapse in a painful-looking pile. I ran over to the heap of arms, legs, and paws and helped the woman to her feet. The lab got up immediately and gave the assailant the stink eye. The Frisbee player got up, apologized a dozen times, and gave the lab a wide berth as he headed back to his partner in crime.

I handed the woman her dog's harness handle and introduced myself. She thanked me and told me her name was Annie. I introduced her to Kasie, and she introduced me to her lab Sam, which was short for Samantha. We talked all afternoon as we walked with our dogs around the park. We had ice cream cones that we bought from an elderly Italian man with a little white cart, and then we talked some more. And then some more. Before we knew it, the sun was setting. We parted before it got dark, but not before exchanging phone numbers. We ended up having dinner later that week.

As the months went on, Annie and I became closer and closer, and so did Kasie and Sam. They became as close as if they were sisters from the same litter. Soon, all my free time was spent with Annie, Kasie's as well, for she needed to have her time with Sam. My mother would joke that the four of us made an interesting, but happy couple. We did, actually. And we were blissfully happy. And sixteen months after that fateful day in the park, almost to the day, Annie and I were married. And where was the ceremony held? In Winston Park, of course. It seemed only fitting, after all. And because it was our dogs that brought us together, Kasie and Sam were there, too.

Shortly after the wedding, Annie and Sam moved into my place. I would have preferred that we would have moved into her's; my place was smaller but was the only one that allowed two dogs. So, we merged all her stuff with mine, and what wouldn't fit, we stuffed in the second bedroom. And after only a few months, Annie told me she was pregnant. After a huge yard sale, that second bedroom was empty, and we turned it into a nursery. The following March, our son Robert was born. We called him Bobby from day one, but once he started college, he preferred to go by Robert. It probably made him feel more adult-like, but we still called him Bobby.

Happily, we lived in that cramped little apartment with two dogs that seemed to dominate every inch of living space, and a little boy who had the dogs, and his parents, wrapped around his finger. We knew we should have found a bigger place, but the apartment was close to both our works and a ten-minute walk to the park. We weren't in a hurry to leave, but we kept our eyes open for a place that would be great for Bobby as well as the dogs.

One Sunday afternoon, two weeks after Bobby's first birthday, the five of us were in the park, eating, playing, doing our normal routine, when Annie started to get one of her headaches. She said that she needed to lie down and wanted to go back home. I said okay and started packing everything up, but she said she wanted me to stay and let Bobby and Kasie play some more. Again, I said okay, and she and Sam headed back to the apartment.

It was about twenty minutes later when I heard the sirens. Hearing them almost every day as background noise to a busy community, you didn't really think much about them. Until they get closer. The closer they got, the more interested you became. When the firetruck stopped just a block up from the park, I craned my neck for a better view. When people started running out of the park and towards the firetruck, that's when I grabbed Bobby and sprinted toward the gathering crowd, Kasie on my heels. I was beaten by an ambulance that filtered through the parting people. I was there in record time though it seemed like an eternity. With my son in my arms, I muscled my way through the onlookers. And there they were.

A drunk driver had run a red light. Annie and Sam lay on the asphalt, bloody and still. Paramedics worked on Annie. Sam lay next to her, not moving, blank eyes staring at nothing. I kept frantically asking the EMTs questions, but they continued working and would occasionally say things like, "I don't know, sir", or "please let us work, sir". Then they put her on a stretcher, in the ambulance, and screamed away. I would have ridden with her, but I had Bobby and Kasie. And then there was Sam. She was gone. Red/brown stains on her once beautiful yellow coat told some of the story. She took the brunt of the impact and hopefully died instantly. Days later, I would learn from a neighbor, who witnessed the accident, that Sam tried to pull Annie from the car's path, but the car's erratic movement had made it impossible.

I stood there on the street surrounded by my neighbors, a crying baby in my arms, not sure of what to do. Kasie plodded up to Sam, lay next to her, and whimpered. I think I was in shock; I was frozen, unsure of anything. My world had been shattered. I felt hopeless and helpless at the same time. Then, Mrs. Miller from 1B said she would look after Robert and Kasie so I could go to the hospital. Mr. Garand from 3A said he would take care of Sam. I thanked them both, got in my car, and raced to the hospital.

Annie wasn't too badly hurt; lots of scrapes and scratches and a few bad cuts that required some bandages and some thirty-odd stitches. She had a concussion that had her throwing up for a day or so, and a couple cracked ribs that hurt every time she took a breath. Considering what she had been through, that wasn't too bad at all. After a week in the hospital, I took her home. After a few more weeks, the doctor said she could go back to work. But Annie wouldn't, she couldn't. She couldn't even leave the apartment unless it was to go to the doctors. She told me she felt naked and afraid going outside without Sam. She was beyond depressed, as was Kasie. And, once again, I found myself in a home devoid of happiness. Not that I could blame anyone, certainly not Annie. She loved Sam so much. They had been together for eight years, and she had depended on her, not just to help her get around, but Sam always made her feel ... normal. With Sam gone, she felt more handicapped than ever.

On top of all that, she felt guilty for what happened to Sam; she felt responsible. And I understood that. That's when I told her about Oscar. Oscar didn't ask to be in a war, but he was more in danger of getting killed than anyone. And I would have blamed myself entirely if anything would have happened to him. Annie appreciated my empathy and knew it was genuine. When the center called and told her that they had a new guide dog for her, she was reluctant, but I was finally able to convince her to go and get the dog, to go and get her life back.

A couple days later, I took a day off from the bakery and drove Annie to the center to get her new guide dog. It had been three months since the accident, but it felt like three years. After an hour of paperwork and waiting, we were taken to the "meet and greet" room where Annie would be introduced to her new dog. Annie was shaking quite visibly; I had never seen her that nervous before or since. The trainer came out with the dog and stood at the far side of the room for a few seconds. This was to allow the dog time to slowly get to know its new master. But the dog made a bee line straight for us, ripping the lead from the trainer's hands. And before I knew it, the large German Shepherd had jumped up, put his paws on my shoulders, and proceeded to euphorically lick my face. And then I knew. I couldn't believe it, but I knew.

It was Oscar. My god, it was Oscar.

* * *

How in the world could it be? At first, I thought my eyes were playing tricks on me, or my mind was making me see what I wanted to see. But I held my head back and gave him a good look, and it was him. It was really him! I hugged him and petted him and cried tears of joy.

As you can imagine, Annie was more than a little confused. As was the trainer. I told Annie it was Oscar. She was just as stunned as I was. I explained to the trainer the history I had with Oscar, how we fought the enemy together in Vietnam, how we slept in foxholes together, and how thousands of soldiers, Marines, and Airmen would call him a war hero. The trainer just stood there with his mouth hanging open, slowly shaking his head in disbelief. I asked him how Oscar could be here, and he explained that many of the dogs that had come back from Vietnam were donated to various organizations including the Federation of the Blind. They were then trained for new tasks and given to needy recipients.

I was beside myself. What were the odds? How was it possible? Heck, if an actor could become governor of California, then I suppose anything was possible.

Annie's anxiousness was replaced with excitement. Her guilt over Sam's death was now replaced with the joy at causing the reunion of two friends. Annie trained with Oscar for about a week before she was able to take him to his new home. He was a perfect fit, like he had lived there his entire life. He and Kasie got along famously, and Kasie was as happy as I had seen her in a long while. It was quite amazing; from the ashes of despair rose a new phoenix of joy.

After the euphoria wore off, I told Annie that I felt guilty for being so happy to have Oscar in my life again. It took the tragedy of losing Sam to make Oscar's being there possible. She told me not to feel guilty, for she was happy that something good came out of that tragedy. She was truly a remarkable woman.

The next year, settlement money from the lawsuit against that drunk driver helped to put a hefty down payment on a nice split-level home. The best thing about it, was that it was only half a mile down from where we were living, still on Quaker Street. And closer to the park, if you can imagine that. It had a nice little back yard where Bobby would play with the dogs and plenty of space inside for us to live comfortably. It was a great home, and still is to this day.

* * *

Five years later, at the ripe old age of fourteen, Oscar left us. Oscar was old but dutifully performed his job as Annie's guide to the end. Just like a good Marine. And knowing Oscar didn't die over in a country far away, surrounded by people that he didn't know, made all the difference in the world to me. He was where he belonged, with people that loved him. And that's where he was to the very end: in my arms until his eyes would open no more. And two months later, Kasie joined him. Some might say Kasie had died of a broken heart. Maybe she did—I don't know—but I do know I was blessed with the time I had with them both. Of course, we cried when they both died, but we smiled and laughed as we remembered them in our lives. Bobby cried the hardest. It was the first time he had really experienced death. But Annie and I showed him how to mourn them and appreciate them, and to be thankful to have had them in our lives. He did, and he joined us in remembering the great times we had with each of them. Sadness did not triumph in our house on that day.

Eventually we had to talk about getting a new dog. No one really wanted to; it just didn't seem right—it was too soon. You know what I mean? But Annie did need a new guide. So, we said we would just do that; we would get a new guide dog for Annie and that's it. So, once again, we went to the center and filled out all the paperwork. In two weeks, they called us saying that they had something for us. And that's how we got Jesse.

Jesse was a black lab. He was a great guide and a great pet. Especially to Bobby. As I watched Bobby and Jesse play, my mind was transported to the past and I saw myself with Lucas. It was an uncanny feeling, but a good one.

For medical reasons, Annie wasn't able to have more kids, so that meant Bobby was an only child, just like I was. And Jesse was his faithful companion just like a good dog should be. So many of Bobby's games and activities included Jesse. Sound familiar? Bobby's happy childhood had emulated mine and I was so grateful for that.

Another thing I was grateful for was that my son went to college instead of going to war. Instead of a few years in another country watching his friends get blown to bits, he was studying computer programming and living near home. He came home often to visit. He would take Jesse to the park and play fetch with an old tennis ball that once belonged to Kasie.

* * *

By the time Bobby had graduated from college, Jesse was finishing his twilight years. Old and arthritic, it was time for Jesse to leave us. And Bobby did what I couldn't those many years ago. He took his best friend to the vet and had him put into that endless slumber. When Bobby returned, he wasn't crying, but I could tell that he had been. He asked me if he could keep the collar and tags, and I said that he could. Then, I watched my son ride up the street, tears in my eyes. Not just tears of sadness, but of pride as well.

Annie and I were in our fifties and usually the last thing we would think about would be getting another dog, but we needed one. Not only because of Annie's blindness, but because she had been diagnosed with multiple sclerosis. So, we went down to the center, and we picked up a yellow lab named Jodie.

She was a smart one. Not only was she trained as a Seeing Eye dog, but as a special needs dog as well. As Annie's MS got worse, she relied more and more on Jodie to pick things up for her or push and pull stuff around the house that would have been too much for Annie to do. And when she wasn't helping Annie, she was my TV buddy. We watched everything together: movies, ball games—you name it. Of course, we went to the park. Just not as often as I would have liked. I retired early from the bakery so

I could spend more time with Annie and Jodie. Those were tough years for Annie, but I made sure they weren't as tough as they could have been. I'm sure glad I had that extra time with her.

Nine years later, MS got the best of Annie, and we lost her on a warm September day. Not too unlike the day that we first met. Jodie was devastated by Annie's passing. The director of the funeral home let me bring her in to see Annie laid out in her casket. Jodie hesitantly walked up to the coffin, sniffed all around, whimpering occasionally. She then lay on the floor next to her for a couple hours, until it was time to go. Jodie wasn't quite the same after that, but we became closer than ever. Between the park and watching TV, we mourned Annie and enjoyed our time together.

That time was another three years. Jodie died quietly one night in her sleep. She looked so peaceful. And although she couldn't feel it, I petted her head and told her that's how I wanted to go, quietly in my sleep, hopefully dreaming of something pleasant.

My son had moved to Texas a couple years after his mom passed. He had gotten a job with a great company that he couldn't pass up. So, with Annie gone, Bobby halfway across the country, and then Jodie ... well, for the first time in my life, I was all alone. Now, don't go feelin' sorry for me. Like I said, I'm doing quite fine. I do enjoy my solitude.

But ... I have to admit ... I do get lonely at times. When I am sitting alone in the house or at the park, that's when I think about Annie and Bobby, and how I miss them so. And the dogs, of course. Oh, I miss them all. So much.

* * *

No. I'm good. Bobby will be coming back home next year and everything will be as right as rain.

So, why am I in this animal shelter? Do I really need a dog? Is this silly? Maybe I should just turn around and go home. I could grab a sandwich at Maria's and take it to the park and eat it on that new bench under the shade tree. But, maybe having a dog to take to that park wouldn't be so bad. It would be nice to feel that unconditional love once again. One last companion for a man who has known dogs all his life. It's actually kind of fitting. Wouldn't you say? Oh, what the hell. Why not?

Here comes a girl that looks like she works here. Let's see if she can help me.

"Hello, sir. How are you today?"

"I'm fine. Thank you."

"And what brings you in today?"

"Well, I'm thinking of adopting a dog."

"Great. We have many to choose from. Our adoption fee covers the animal's initial shots as well as spaying or neutering."

"That's fine. So, what do you have?"

"Did you have any preferences, sir? Boy? Girl?"

"No, not really. Maybe a boy. I don't know. It doesn't really matter."

"Okay. How about size? Big? Small? Medium?

"Not too small and not too big. Medium, I suppose."

"How about age?"

"At least a couple years old. No puppies. Don't have the patience for that anymore."

"Gotcha. Not a problem. Let's just see what we have here ...."

"Oh, there is just one more thing."

"Yes, sir. What's that?"

"He must be afraid of vacuum cleaners."

IT'S A SMALL WORLD AFTER ALL

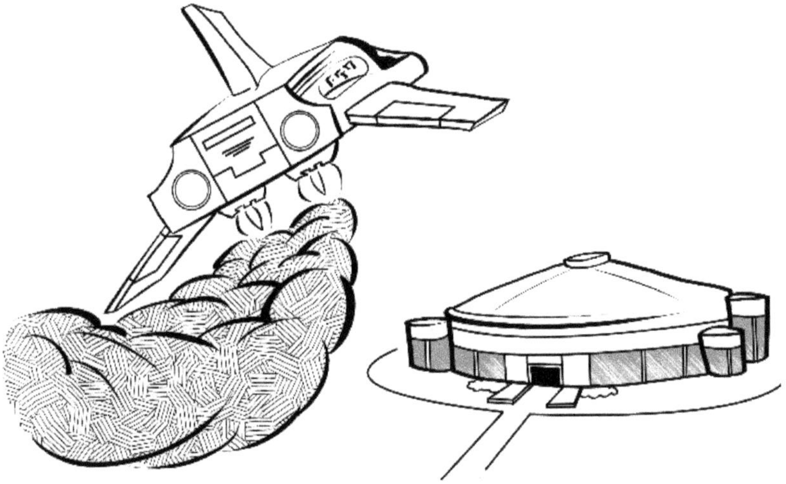

"Man begets, but land does not beget."
– **Cecil Rhodes**

"Daddy, I'm scared."

With all the commotion going on in the house, Steve Rogan hadn't noticed that his five-year-old daughter, Allison, had come up behind him. "Why, Munchkin?" he asked as he picked his youngest child up and placed her on his hip. "What's wrong?"

The house was a blur of motion; more than a dozen government workers had converged on his family's home to assist, or more like commandeer, their move to their new home at the colony. The workers wore grey uniforms with Terran Reclamation Project printed bold across the back and Roosevelt City Team on their bright blue baseball-style caps. One of the workers, or blue-caps, as Steve liked to call them, squeezed by with a box, apologizing for the intrusion of personal space.

"Billy says we might die," Allison buried her face in her father's shoulder. The sweetness of her scent that only a parent could appreciate permeated Steve's own sweaty stench.

Steve gave an exasperated sigh. This move was stressful enough, he didn't need his son scaring his baby sister right before they left for the Roosevelt City colony. "We're not going to die, Munchkin," he said in a consoling voice.

"But Billy said—"

"Your brother is just trying to be a trouble maker. Are you finished packing your immediates?

"Almost," she said. "But I'm still scared, Daddy. What if something happens?"

"There's nothing to be scared about, Munchkin. Nothing's going to happen. It's going to be a smooth ride, and you are going to love our new place. We're going to be perfectly fine. Just you see."

"Promise?"

"Promise. Now. Go finish packing. We leave in about an hour."

"Okay."

Steve placed Allison on the floor where she turned and ran through the obstacle of movers and packed boxes, reminding Steve of Br'er Rabbit and what he must have looked like running through the briar patch.

"What's that about?" Linda, Steve's wife, had come up behind him, in her signature hands on hips pose. Like her husband, Linda was a bit sweaty, and patches of filth dotted her hands and face. Regardless, she looked as beautiful to Steve, at that moment, as she had the day he asked her to marry him nineteen years ago.

Linda had been outside directing the movers as to which boxes were which, determining what went in the shuttle headed for storage, and what was called "immediates" and going to accompany them on the voyage. Linda excelled at organization and directing people, which was why she tended to be the leader of the family.

"It's Billy," Steve said. "He told Allison that we could die on our way to the colony."

Linda sighed and rolled her eyes. "Not this again. I thought we told him not to say anything like that in front of her."

"I know, I know. I'll talk to him again. You may want to talk to Ally, though. Make sure she's okay for the trip. If the doctors sense she is having any sign of anxiety, they could delay our passage for God knows how long, or possibly bump us off the list completely."

"I'll talk to her. But you better have a serious talk with your son. He hasn't been cooperative with us ever since our briefing with Talbot."

Steve nodded and his wife went deeper into the house. The house he grew up in, the house he raised his family in, and the house that would soon be torn down to make way for reforestation, or hydroponics farms, or whatever the government was going to do with this neighborhood. The Terran Reclamation Project was in full swing now, and Steve was proud that he and his family were a part of it. Now, he had to find his son and have one final talk about the sacrifice he and his family were making for the good of their planet.

Steve headed up the stairs and made a left towards his son's bedroom when he was intercepted by his oldest.

"Dad," said Michelle. She was seventeen and a beautiful carbon copy of her mother. "They won't let me take the poinsettia Grandma gave me."

In her hands, she held the potted plant Linda's mother had given her last year for Christmas. Their grandmother loved flowers and gave one of the red season-blooming plants to each of her grandchildren during her holiday visit. Since her passing in May, all the plants had died; all but Michele's. She had taken that as a sign. She had always felt closest to her grandmother, and she had taken her death very hard. This move was supposed be good for her. She didn't like her school, and several of her friends had already made the trip to the colony. She needed this drastic change in her life.

"Sir," a blue-cap holding a clipboard said from behind his daughter. "No biologicals can make the trip. This should have been explained to you during your briefing."

"It was," said Steve and turned to his daughter. "Michele, we've been over this. No biologicals can go."

"What about us?" she demanded. We're 'biologicals.' How can we go, and not a plant? This was ... this was ..." she tried fighting off the tears, but they came like an unexpected rainstorm.

"I know, honey. But that's different. You know that. We can't take everything. We're all leaving something behind."

"But before Grandma died, she asked me how the Poinsettia was doing. When I told her it looked great, she smiled at me and said I had her green thumb."

"Sir," said the blue-hat, his nose buried in the papers on his board. "Do you have a pet? A dog? Cat?"

"No," Steve said as he put a consoling hand on Michele's shoulder.

"We brought along a small stasis unit for a pet. Must have been a mix up with the equipment designation team."

Mike gave the blue-hat a puzzled look. Glancing at the man's name badge he saw it said Fischer. A circular team-lead patch stood out on his shoulder, and a sympathetic look comprised his face.

"We could place the plant in the spare unit and ship it with the rest of your immediates." Fischer gave Michele a reassuring nod. "It should be fine for the trip."

"Really?" Michele beamed, wiping tears from her cheek. "Oh, that would be great. Thank you. Thank you!" She gave the man a one-armed hug while carefully securing the last gift she had received from her grandmother in the other.

Steve mouthed 'Thank you' to Fischer, who turned to lead his daughter away so they could secure the plant. He was thankful that everyone from the TRP was supportive and friendly. It was a much-needed positive.

Steve entered the last bedroom on the right and found his thirteen-year-old son lying on the blue-carpeted floor tossing a tennis ball towards the ceiling, seeing how close he could get it without the ball touching. It was a game he sometimes played when he was bored or worried. Steve guessed that Billy was experiencing the latter. Glancing around the room, Steve saw that it was completely empty save for his son. It seemed much bigger than it normally did; an outer space themed mural encompassed two of the walls, giving the illusion that the room expanded way beyond its twelve by ten dimensions.

"How you doing, buddy?" Steve sat on the floor next to Billy who didn't stop tossing the ball.

"Okay," said Billy flatly.

"Ally says you told her we were going to die. Did you tell her that?"

Billy caught the ball and held it. He turned his head towards his father and said, "I guess."

"You guess? You don't remember telling your baby sister that we're going to die on our way to Roosevelt City?"

"I remember. But I said we *might* die."

"Well, you scared her pretty good. You're her big brother, you're supposed to watch out for her, not frighten her like that."

Billy swung his legs around and sat crisscross style, facing his father. "I'm sorry, Dad. I didn't mean to scare her. It's just that ..." Billy dropped his head and focused on the tennis ball.

"What?"

"It's just that I'm worried."

Steve breathed in and nodded. "I see. What brought this on? I thought you were fine with everything. You were the most excited when your mother and I broke the news to you kids."

"I was. But when Colonel Talbot explained all the details and made you and Mom sign papers saying you understand that something could go wrong and we could all die ..."

"We're not going to die, bud. That was just government paperwork covering their butts just in case the one in a million chance that something does go wrong, they won't be held liable. It's perfectly safe. Thousands of people have already made the trip."

"And what about that one boy who died?"

Steve closed his eyes. The only casualty in this program was a boy from Dallas. He was just a year younger than Billy. He wished his son had never found out about that, but it was hard when it was all over the internet.

"That boy had an extremely rare condition that caused him to have an aneurism during the trip." Steve didn't want to explain what an aneurism was; he was pretty sure Billy knew, but in the off chance that he didn't, Steve didn't want to scare him any more than he was with details about blood vessels in the brain bursting. "Since then, they test everyone who's going for that same condition, including us, and none of us have it."

"But what if there's something else? What if our bodies don't work right when we get there? I heard the gravity's different."

"Some say that the weird gravity shift takes a while to get used to, but it's nothing that can hurt us. In fact, I saw an interview with some colonists, and they said they love it. They feel lighter and have more energy."

Billy dropped his head and stared at the old tennis ball in his hands. Nothing Steve said seemed to comfort his son.

"Is there something else bothering you? You know you can tell me anything. We're buds. Remember?"

Billy nodded and gave his dad a placating grin. "I know. It's just that ..."

"What?"

"It's just that I'm going to miss my life here. I'm leaving my friends and my school. When Colonel Talbot said this was a one-way trip, I guess I didn't think that I would be leaving everything for good. I thought maybe I could come back once in a while and visit. I can't believe we'll never go to another Dodgers game again or fish at the lake. I know it sounds dumb to be sad about all that, but I am. I'm sorry."

"Hey, kiddo. There's nothing to be sorry about. It's not dumb. We're all going to miss some things. Michele has dozens of friends she's leaving behind. Your mom has her brother in Buffalo, your uncle Phil." Steve spread his arms in a grandiose gesture and looked around. "Your great great-grandfather built this house. Four generations have lived here. There's a lot of memories that I really don't want to give up."

"Then why are you?"

"Times change. Things change. This isn't the same world my father and his father and his father lived in. The planet's overpopulated, there are hardly any jobs, there's a food shortage as well as an energy shortage. We've cut down so many trees that our atmosphere is changing, and countless animal species have gone extinct in the last hundred years. It breaks my heart that you will never get to see a real rhinoceros or see the almost human like intelligence in the eyes of a mountain gorilla. We need to make changes if we are to save the rest of what we have. And that means we all need to make sacrifices. I gave the government this house and the land it sits on in exchange for a place in Roosevelt City. Don't you think that's a pretty big sacrifice?"

Billy looked up at his dad and slowly nodded.

"And just think, bud," Steve said. "We'll be pioneers of a sort. Like the ones who set out to conquer this land hundreds of years ago. They left their homeland and everything and everyone they knew behind. All so they could make a fresh start in a strange and far off place. And there was no going back for them either. But they did it anyway. And why? Because it was the right thing to do, and they were brave enough to do it. We need to follow their example. We need to be brave and take this huge step to help save the human race. So, how 'bout it? Are you as brave as those pioneers?"

A smile grew on Billy's face. "Yeah. I think I am. If you can make sacrifices, and Mom, and Michele. I can do it too."

"That's my boy." Steve stood and helped his son to his feet. "Now, go help your sisters finish getting ready."

Billy started for the door then turned around. "Yeah, Dad, I guess what the government is asking us to do is no *small* task."

Steve laughed. "Go on. Go help your sisters."

Billy ran from his old bedroom with an exuberance that inspired Steve and helped give him a renewed assurance that they were doing the right thing. They were doing this for the children. And their children.

It had been a hectic six months preparing for the trip. But now that the big day was here, Steve could appreciate his son's fears, for he had them also. Not fears for himself, not really, but for his family. Would they be okay? Would they adjust to the strange new place and way of life? Billy was right about it being a one-way trip and never getting to see things again. Sure they would be living in a city designed with all the latest comforts and amenities, but they would be trapped there, unable to leave, unable to come back home. They would live there, work there, and die there. It would be like a prison of paradise. What the government was asking of its people was indeed no small task. Steve shook his head and smiled.

* * *

The shuttle's engine began its slow building hum and whine that could not only be heard, but felt throughout the vehicle. Once the Rogan family was secured in their seats, as well as the handful of blue-caps that would be accompanying them, the doors closed, and the shuttle lifted off the ground with all the grace of a flying elephant.

Each family member looked out the closest viewport to their seat, the ones not sitting next to a window craned their necks to get one last glimpse of their former home. And once the shuttle had reached its desired altitude, it accelerated into the clouds, leaving the house behind but carrying hearts full of memories and ready for adventure.

Once above the clouds, the shuttle's flight path smoothed out and everyone relaxed.

"*Good afternoon, Rogan family*," came a voice from speakers overhead. "*This is Captain Wilkes, and I'm piloting the shuttle today. We'll reach the TRP facility in about thirty minutes where your journey will begin. So, just sit back, relax, and enjoy the ride*."

The Rogans exchanged smiles after the pilot's comforting welcome-speech. Steve was sure it helped alleviate a lot of the tension and apprehension the family had been feeling.

From the front of the shuttle, near the cockpit, a group of the agents gave a cheer and patted each other on the back. Their faces beamed with happiness as if a great event had just taken place.

"What's going on?" Steve said to the closest blue-cap who had just finished giving another a solid high-five.

"Mrs. Anderson had the baby," he answered and proceeded to high-five Steve as well. "It's a girl and she's perfectly fine. They're calling her Baby Eleanor."

"Wow, that's great," Steve said and copied the agents smile.

"Who's Mrs. Anderson?" said Ally.

"She's the first woman to get pregnant in Roosevelt City," said Billy.

"And now, she's the first woman to give birth," said Linda.

"Wow," said Michele. "Baby Eleanor. That's pretty cool."

"Do you think I'll get to meet Baby Eleanor, Daddy?" Ally asked.

"I don't know, Munchkin. She's gonna be pretty popular, but we'll make sure we try to visit her."

"Guess what, Ally," Billy said enthusiastically. "Now you won't be the youngest one there. You won't be the baby of the colony."

Ally seemed to ponder this and a smile grew on her face. "Yay. That's right. Awesome! I didn't want to be the baby at Roosevelt City. I'm a big girl. Right, Daddy?"

Steve smiled and ruffled the hair on top of Alley's head. Then he did the same to Billy; he was proud of his son for saying something positive like that to his sister. It helped make up for her earlier scare.

* * *

The trip was over before they knew it, and the shuttle started its descent in the same manner it had taken off; slow and precise. And like before, everyone looked out the nearest viewport to glimpse their destination.

Steve recognized the building, though it had been severely modified since the government procured it for the TRP. The building used to be a football stadium back before American football was basically made illegal and the pro football league closed its doors. Dozens of stadiums were either demolished or repurposed. This particular one was snatched up by the government and transformed into a unique structure to serve a very unique purpose.

The sightseeing was cut short, however, for the shuttle immediately entered a hangar attached to the main building.

With the natural sunlight now blocked by the shuttle hangar, it suddenly became quite dark inside the passenger cabin until the interior lights flickered on, encompassing everyone in a pale illumination. The rear door opened and outside were more blue-caps who assisted the Rogan family out of the shuttle and into the hanger where they were greeted by a short, stocky man in a military uniform. Steve smiled and extended his hand to Colonel Talbot.

"Greetings, Rogans," Talbot said with a broad smile. He shook Steve's hand as well as Linda's. "How did this morning go? Any problems?"

"No, everything went fine," said Steve. "Your men have been great."

"Excellent," Talbot said. "Glad to hear it. I'm going to escort you from here." Talbot then addressed the lead blue-cap, the same man who had helped Michele with her plant. "Captain, what is the status of their immediates?"

"The ETA for that shuttle is two minutes. When it arrives, we will begin the transfer of their property to the delivery platform. Shuttle three is headed for Storage Facility Thirteen-Bravo."

"Very good," said Talbot, giving a satisfied nod. Turning back to the Rogan family, he said, "Shall we?" He motioned to a short corridor that led to an open elevator.

Steve and his family followed the Colonel inside the elevator and rode it up in nervous silence until they reached their floor. When the elevator doors opened, they were immediately greeted by a team of doctors, nurses, and medical assistants.

"This is where the fun begins, everyone," Talbot said. "These people are going to take good care of you as they prepare you for your journey."

Several of the medical staff each took a family member into an individual prep room. The only exception was that Allison accompanied her mother, holding her hand all the way.

After a final physical exam and an oral questionnaire by a psychologist to assure psychological stability, each family member was given a one-piece, skin-tight suit that would not only help with the medical monitors for the trip, but would also be accommodating upon arrival at the colony.

Once everyone was done in the examination rooms, they were led to an adjacent room where a row of tube-like pods stretched along the back wall. Talbot explained these pods in his briefing; they were the stasis units for the trip. Each one, custom programmed for its guest, would carry a member of the family to the colony.

Opposite the row of pods was a wall of glass, possibly leftover from the old stadium, for it allowed one to look out onto what was once the football playing field. The family immediately gravitated to the window-like wall and stared out in wonder and amazement.

Steve couldn't help but be impressed; though he had seen many videos on the Internet and the packet from Colonel Talbot, seeing this in person was a whole other experience. At first it didn't seem real, it was certainly something you don't see every day.

Before them, in all its glory, was the miniature colony known as Roosevelt City.

The city and its outlying communities took up the entirety of the stadium bowl. It reminded Steve of the train garden his father used to take him to when he was a kid. But this was no toy; every building, every vehicle, every tree, was real. He imagined that he could almost see the ant-sized people that inhabited the micro-city going about their business. But he couldn't; they were too small and he was too far away.

The stadium roof was open, letting the sun highlight every detail as well as provide endless energy to the city. Thanks to the virtual tour they received in their welcoming packet, Steve could identify most of the buildings and was happy to spot their new neighborhood.

Welcome to Roosevelt City," Talbot said. "Since I won't be going with you, this is your official welcome from me."

"It's amazing," said Linda.

"So cool," Billy agreed.

"Good afternoon, Rogans," said a voice from behind them. Everyone turned around to find a tall woman in a white jacket standing with her hands clasped behind her back. "I'm Doctor Abatantuono, but you can call me Dr. Aba. I will be overseeing your journey today. The pods behind me will be your vehicle to the city. Once inside your pod, we will shrink you to about two millimeters in height. Some of you a bit smaller." She gave Ally a wink. "My techs and doctors tell me that you are all ready. So, that just leaves one question: who's first?"

"We've decided that it will be ladies first," said Steve.

"Very good," said Dr. Aba. "Let's begin."

Linda, Michele, and Ally were each taken to a pod and helped inside by a few nurses. As the techs worked on the control panels for each unit, Steve and Billy each said their goodbyes to the three most important women in their lives. Steve, however, spent a few extra minutes with his wife.

"Goodbye, my love," he told her and took her hand in between both of his.

"Bye, honey," she said and a tear ran down one cheek.

"Hey," Steve said. "I'm gonna be right behind you. Don't worry." And he kissed her hand.

Linda nodded, gave a quick sniffle, and wiped away the tear. "You better." She cracked a smile. "This was your idea."

"Yeah," he laughed. "I'll be right there. Just don't go decorating the new house without me."

"No promises."

Steve finally let go of her hand and stood back by the window with Billy and watched as the doors to the pods closed. A countdown began and the room started to hum. Through the oval windows of the pods, each of the girl's faces were visible. Steve and Billy gave them a wave, they smiled in return. When the countdown reached zero, the pods were gone.

Vanished. As if they were never there to begin with. Steve knew that they were miniaturized and sent through a tube system to the city, but the process had been so quick, it had given the illusion of disappearing as if from a magician's trick.

"Gentlemen next," said Dr. Aba.

Steve watched as the techs helped his son into his pod and brought the medical monitors to life. Steve was then helped into his own pod and given the same meticulous attention as the rest of his family.

"Hey, Dad."

Steve turned his head to see Billy in the pod next to him, a huge smile on his face.

"I'll see you in a 'little bit'," his son said.

"Hey," Steve smiled back at him. "Don't get short with me."

Billy laughed which made Steve laugh.

The techs, once satisfied with their work, and the medical readings, closed the pod doors and initiated the main system and the countdown began. A tech's face appeared in front of the oval window, mouthed something unintelligible, then gave Steve a thumbs up sign. Steve returned the sign and relaxed.

The tech looked from side to side as if to make sure no one was watching, then he reached into his breast pocket, and removed a piece of paper. After glancing around again, he unfolded the paper and placed it flat against the pod's window.

Steve squinted as he tried to read the handwritten note.

Be careful down there. All is not what it seems. Whatever you do, don't go near the—

But the tech then quickly removed the paper and disappeared out of sight.

"Don't go near what?" Steve said. "Don't go near what?" He yelled louder this time, though he knew his muted voice would just be lost in the hum of the surrounding machinery. "My God," Steve said to himself, fear and dread starting to take hold. "What have I done?"

TIME ON THE ROAD

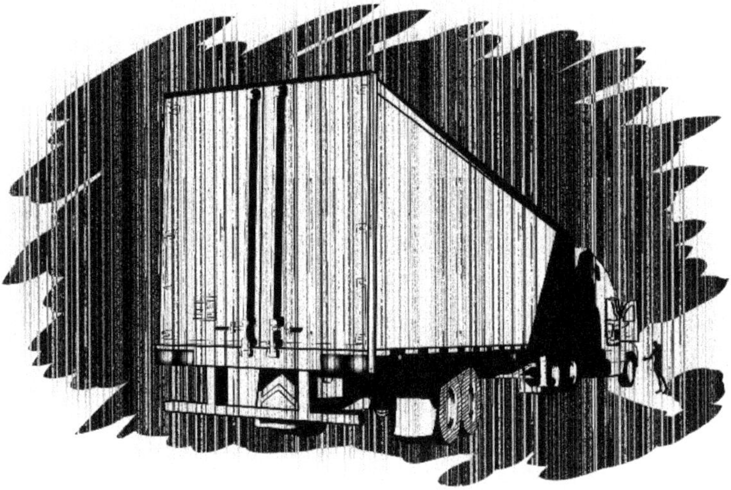

"We are each our own devil, and we make this world our hell."
– **Oscar Wilde**

A car horn blared as it went by. Harry Bukowski snapped his head up and straightened the steering wheel as he fought off the siren song of sleep. He blinked his eyes wide and slapped his face. The mountain road came back into focus as he watched the headlights of his rig roll hypnotically over the yellow-dashed asphalt.

"Damn it, Harry," he said to himself. After a month of shuttling freight all over the Midwest, he was finally going home. Just in time for Thanksgiving. He just had to make it there. "Wake up. Just another hour, and you'll be home with your wife and kid and in your nice warm house." He nodded at the thought. "And in your nice warm bed," he added. But he had to stay awake. He'd been driving for thirteen straight hours and hadn't slept for more than five hours at a time in over a week. "Just a little bit longer."

His eyelids felt like manhole covers. Harry realized that fighting off sleep was a losing battle. *Stay awake, stay awake, I need to stay awake.* He reached for the coffee he bought back at the 7-11 in Broadmont, but it was empty. He crushed the cup in frustration and threw it on the seat next to him. *What else? What else?* An idea came to him, and he unholstered the CB mike from its cradle.

"Break one-nine, break one-nine. Anyone got their ears on?" Harry released his mike button and waited.

Silence.

"Break one-nine," he repeated. "This is the Snow Dog in the Bulldog Brawler. Wonderin' if there're any Kojacs with a Kodak on forty-three in Dawson County. Come back." After a few quiet seconds Harry was about to hang up his mike until the CB speaker crackled to life.

Snow Dog, this is the Chrome Rabbit. What's your twenty on forty-three?

Harry smiled; someone was actually driving as late as he was up here. "I just passed mile marker sixty-three, Rabbit."

"Copy that, Snow Dog. You're all clear all the way up to the state line. I'm at my home twenty and need to log some Z's. So, keep the whites on your noise and the reds on your tail. Clear after you."

That's it? Harry was hoping for a little more conversation than that. He looked at the clock on his dashboard and saw that it flashed 12:00. Lifting his wristwatch, he noticed the second hand wasn't moving. He gave it a shake, then pushed the button on the mike again. "Thank you kindly, Rabbit. . . uh. . . my daggone time piece has stopped dead. Can I get a ten thirty-six?"

"My Timex says quarter after twelve. Heck, that means it's Thursday and officially Thanksgiving. Happy Turkey Day,

Snow Dog. Threes and eights to you and your family. Clear after you."

"Copy that. Thanks again, Rabbit. Threes and eights to you and yours. Snow Dog out."

Harry hung up the mike and fought hard to suppress a yawn. "So much for exciting conversation keeping me awake. I know. How 'bout some fresh air?" He rolled down the window and breathed in the cool November air. "Aaahh," said Harry as his lungs filled with that mountain chill. "That's the ticket." The air did feel good, and it seemed to breathe new life into him.

The pleasant aroma of burning wood made him take a deep breath; someone had a fire going. Maybe it was a fireplace keeping a house warm, or perhaps it was a group of people sitting around a campfire, telling stories and roasting marshmallows. Harry smiled; soon he'd be doing that with his wife and daughter. Two summers past he made a fire pit in their back yard, and since then he'd had some memorable evenings with his family and friends sitting around the fire and having a great time. His daughter Emily loved it and constantly asked her father to make a fire so they could make s'mores or burn a few dogs.

Harry pulled a Polaroid from his visor. It was one of many that populated the cab of his truck. He kept the one in his hand within easy reach; it was his favorite. It showed Emily, her sandy-colored hair in pigtails, with her Cocker Spaniel Millie. On the white space below the picture he had written the caption "Em and M".

"I'll be home soon, Em. We'll get that fire going."

A water droplet touched his forearm. And then another landed on his cheek. Within seconds it was raining and fairly hard. Harry rolled up his window and switched on his wipers. "So much for fresh air. Damn."

Harry squinted through the water streaked windshield. He hated driving in the rain; he needed new wipers, and the moonless night made seeing that much more difficult. Since it was late at night, and no one else on the road, he decided to turn on his high beams. He switched on the additional lights that angled straight ahead, and that's when he saw her.

A long-haired woman in a denim jacket stood on the shoulder of the road. She had her thumb out to hitch a ride and was dangerously close to the traffic lane.

Harry hit the brakes and swerved his rig to make sure he missed her. Trying to control his truck as well as the empty trailer, he crossed over the yellow line and he prayed no one was coming the other way. When he came to a stop, he noticed he was mere feet from hitting the guardrail that protected vehicles from falling down the mountainside. Harry let out a sigh of relief and gave his head a shake; he knew those guardrails were as about as effective as tin foil stopping a charging bull. He knew that if he had been pulling a fully loaded trailer, he would have done an Evel Knievel right off the mountain.

Harry squinted into his raindrop laden side mirror to see if the woman was okay. She appeared fine except for the fact that she was getting soaked by the sudden downpour. He grabbed the gearshift and threw the truck into reverse. Then he hastily, yet carefully, righted his rig so that it was in the proper lane. He looked in the mirror once again. The woman hesitantly moved towards him and he debated whether to let her in or not. He normally didn't pick up hitchhikers, but it was cold and wet out. And he had almost killed her. And it was Thanksgiving.

He undid his seatbelt, leaned over, and opened the passenger door. He listened as the woman's splashing footfalls got closer.

She reached the trucks in seconds flat, climbed into the cab and plopped herself onto the seat that was usually reserved for maps, five-dollar sunglasses, and half-eaten meatball subs. In fact, there were enough marinara stains on the seat that it could have been mistaken for a horrific crime scene. Today, however, the only occupants were yesterday's newspaper, an old baseball cap, and a crumpled paper coffee cup. Harry gathered up all three and threw them into his sleeper.

The woman closed the door and took off her drenched jacket. Harry reached behind her seat and removed an old beach towel he kept for emergencies. He traded her the towel for the jacket and then placed her denim water-soaked coat on a hook behind her head.

"Thanks," she said as she rubbed the towel on her face and then through her hair.

"You're welcome," Harry replied, not sure if she were thanking him for the towel or opening the door or both. He turned on the interior light and got a better look at the woman. She looked several years older than he was. She was thin; had brown, grey-streaked hair; brown eyes; and an almost gaunt face. But what really caught Harry's attention were the marks on her forearm that were revealed when she moved her sleeve while drying. *Great. I picked up an addict.* But one of the many things his mother had taught him was to never judge a book by its cover. He would get to know this woman before passing judgement. He waited for her to finish drying off, as much as the old towel would accomplish anyway, before he addressed her again. "My name's Harry." He waited for her to give her name, which she seemed to stall in doing.

"M-Marie," she finally said. "I'm Marie."

"Pleased to meet you, Marie. That's a great name. My grandmother was named Marie."

Harry was trying to break the ice, but Marie only gave him a small smile and a nod which seemed a bit awkward to him. Was she was acting a little suspicious? Maybe she was just wary of the strange man that was giving her a lift. *Was she in trouble with the law? Should I be worried? I hope this isn't a mistake.* He blew off the thought. She looked harmless enough and couldn't have weighed more than a buck and a quarter soaking wet, which she just happened to be. Maybe another ice breaker was needed.

"Here's a question for you: What gets wetter the more it dries?"

That elicited a chuckle out of her. "A towel," she replied as she gave him back his. That seemed to work a little, she was able to look him in the eye, though she still seemed a bit distant. "Thank you, again."

"You're welcome, again." He then took the towel and hung it on the same hook as her jacket. "Heard that one before, have you?"

"A couple times," she said.

"Where you headed?" Harry put the truck in gear and got moving up the road once again.

"Middleton."

"What a coincidence, so am I. Heading home for the holiday?"

"Uh-huh."

"Got family there?"

"Yeah."

"So why were you on route 43, out in the middle of nowhere? Did you come from Broadmont?"

"Yes."

"That's gotta be fifteen miles back. And Middleton is another twenty. You were gonna walk all that way?" He paused to give her time to answer. It seemed odd to Harry for someone to walk a mountain road over that distance. But he wasn't grilling her, just trying to start up a conversation. He had to be careful though, he knew that sometimes he went on little talking sprees. Being on the road alone for long periods of time can do that to a person.

"When you don't have a car, you do what you gotta do." She rubbed her hands together between her knees. Harry realized she had to be freezing, so he turned up the heat a couple notches and pointed the vents in her direction.

"Couldn't someone from your family have picked you up?"

"They don't know I'm coming."

"Oh. A surprise. That's great. Not worth risking your life though. Lucky for you I was driving by."

"Yeah. Lucky me."

Marie's short responses were starting to worry Harry. Something was definitely up with this woman.

"Is everything okay with you? You running from something?"

"No."

"I'm not gonna hurt you or anything, if that's what you're worried about. I got a wife and kid waiting for me at home."

"No. I'm fine. I'm just cold, that's all."

Harry understood; she didn't want to talk, and he could appreciate that. Not everyone was as gregarious as he was, and perhaps shame kept her from being more open. His wife, Loretta, wasn't a big talker either. Maybe it was because he always dominated a conversation. She always seemed to prefer listening to talking, and he would rather talk than listen. That's probably why they got along so well all the years past. She was the perfect yin to his yang. Emily, on the other hand, had a bit of both of her parents in her. She could hold a conversation with the best of them, but could really listen to someone when they needed an ear to bend. He imagined her becoming a psychologist or counselor when she grew up. She would need a good college for that. And good colleges cost good money. And he certainly—

"What are you doing? Wake up!" Marie grabbed the steering wheel attempting to right it the best she could from her position. Harry gripped the wheel in a panic and waved her off.

"I got it. I got it. I'm good."

"You're not good. You're falling asleep at the wheel. You're gonna get us killed!"

"I'm fine. I'm fine. I'm sorry. It's been a long week."

"Well, you better wake up and pay attention to your driving if you ever want to see that wife and kid of yours again."

"Jeez. What got into you? That's the most you've said to me since you got into my truck."

"I tend to be more vocal when my life is in danger."

Harry was about to tell her that he liked her better when she wasn't talking, but he did almost kill her. Twice now. *Not really a good track record here, Harry. Let's try again.*

"Want to see them?" he asked her.

"What?" she said as if he pulled her out of some deep thought.

"My family." Harry reached up and grabbed a handful of pictures that were stuffed in the passenger visor and handed them to Marie. “Here. This is my wife, Loretta, and our nine-year-old, Emily.”

Marie took the photos and began looking through them. But she didn’t just flip through them like someone might do to be polite. No, she carefully examined each one as if every detail meant something to her; as if she could feel the emotions within each picture. She placed her fingers on each face as if she were touching that person for real and with true, deep feeling.

Perhaps they reminded her of her own family. She had said they didn’t know she was coming. Had she been gone for a long time? Had she been banished for her misdeeds? Was she on her last rope and needed help from her loved ones, if they were indeed still loved ones?

Harry felt for her, and his sinuses cleared as he fought off a tear.

“I didn’t know you had all these,” she said in a soft voice.

“Excuse me?” said Harry.

“I mean ... the pictures. I wouldn’t have guessed you had so many of your family.”

“Oh, that’s nothing.” He turned on the interior cab lights again and pointed to the ceiling where dozens of pictures stared back at them from overhead. Marie’s mouth hung open. “And back there,” said Harry as he jerked his thumb towards the sleeper.

Marie turned around to see the compartment filled with even more pictures. That’s was Harry’s treasure; all those photos of Loretta and Emily, as well as the dog Millie. The pictures covered every major holiday, as well as birthdays, and Emily’s school events. With all these pictures around him, Harry never felt alone on the road. Not truly anyway.

“My god. So many.” Marie said as she seemed lost in the collage of images.

“Does that surprise you?”

She turned back around, a dumbfounded look on her face. “I just never knew.”

“Why would you know? We just met a half hour ago.”

Marie looked at the pictures still in her hand and a tear ran down her cheek.

"Are you all right?" Harry asked.

Marie looked at him, and he could see a tear running down her other cheek. "Harry, I have to tell you something."

"Okay."

"I told myself I wasn't going to say anything, but I just can't sit her any longer, right next to you, and not say anything."

Harry was not sure where this was going, but he played along. "Okay. What's up?"

"Harry," she began and paused as if not sure how to start. "I'm ... I'm Emily."

"I thought you said your name was Marie."

"No. I said that so I wouldn't confuse you."

"Ma'am, I *am* confused. What are you trying to say?"

"Harry. I'm Emily. *Your* Emily."

"Marie—or whatever your name is—this isn't funny. I've given you a ride out of the kindness of my heart, but I don't need no funny business from you. I'm sorry if I scared you when I dozed off there, but there's no need for this."

"No, Harry. I *am* Emily. I'm Em. I'm your Em. I'm from—Christ, this is going to sound stupid—I'm from the future. I'm trying to fix a wrong that has plagued me all my life."

Future? Is this broad crazy or did I fall asleep again? The pothole one of his tires just clipped felt very real. He was awake. With one eye on the road and one on Marie, he decided to play along. "Oh yeah. And what is that? This wrong that's plagued you."

"You. Thirty-two years ago, you died coming home for Thanksgiving. They said you fell asleep at the wheel and went through the guardrail and off the mountainside at mile marker seventy-eight." Her eyes were wide, practically pleading, as she spoke.

Almost out of habit, Harry looked off to the shoulder as his headlights illuminated the small green interstate mile marker. It read fifty-nine.

"I've traveled back through time to save your life and fix what became—will become of our family."

"And how did you do that?" Harry asked sarcastically. "You know, the whole traveling back through time thing." She was either crazy or high. He wasn't sure which, but he was interested in hearing more of her tale. He thought it might prove entertaining. As long as she didn't cross any lines.

"A man," she said, looking down. "He gave me a gift."

"A gift? Want kind of gift?"

"He offered me anything I wanted. He asked if there was anything in the world, in my life, that I could have, what would it be."

"And you told him you wanted to save me."

"Yes," she said looking Harry in the eyes once again. "I told him that I wish I could go back and save you from going off that mountain road."

"And he just happened to have the power to do such a miraculous thing?"

"Yes."

"How? Was he an angel?"

"No," Marie said. She looked down again, her face became flush and full of guilt.

"The devil then," Harry devised.

She nodded.

"So, you made a deal with the devil, for your soul, I assume, so you could travel back to this very place and time, to save my life."

She nodded again.

"Why?"

She looked up with a furrowed brow. "Huh?"

"Why," Harry repeated. "Why would you sell your soul to the devil to save me? You'd give up one life to save another? And not only that, but the devil gets a soul in the end. Doesn't sound very smart to me." Harry enjoyed brain teasers and 'what if' scenarios. He played them all the time with Em and Loretta. This crazy druggy was no match for him.

"Why?" Marie asked, a tinge of anger and surprise in her voice. "You ask me why? Wouldn't you trade your life for that of your daughter's or wife's?"

"Yes, but—"

"But nothing. You always taught me to be generous and self-sacrificing. You said that's what people do in a society. And it goes way beyond that. Do you know what my life was like after you died? Mom became depressed and detached from me. She wanted nothing to do with me because I reminded her of you. For years I hated her for that. I hated *you* for that. She could barely hold a job, and there was never anything to eat, so I left home when I was seventeen. I worked bad jobs and turned tricks to get by. I sold crack and became a user myself. I got pregnant from who-knows-what-guy and lost the baby because of all the shit in my system."

The tears were flowing hard now, giving the rain outside a run for its money. Her crying became sobs, and her nose accompanied her leaking eyes.

Harry removed a handkerchief from his jacket pocket and handed it to her. She blew her nose and wiped her eyes and tried to continue.

"So, if I could fix all that by bringing you back, by having you come home instead of leaving us, it is every bit worth my soul. Every bit."

Harry was stunned and for the first time in a long time, he was speechless. This poor woman had been through a lot and seeing all the pictures in his truck must have triggered something inside her. He didn't know what to say so he just gave her shoulder a comforting rub.

"So, you see," she began again, "if I can keep you alive 'til we get to Middleton, then my life won't become so shitty. We'll just continue to be the happy family we were before that all happened."

"Marie—"

"Emily," she corrected.

"I can't imagine the life you have lived so far, and I'm sorry for all the grief you've had to endure, but you can't bring your father back. All you can do is make the best of everything from this moment forward. It might seem overwhelming and impossible at times, but it can be done. You just need some help and guidance. A friend of mine had a son of his get into some trouble, and he found some great support groups for him. And now he—"

"Stop." Marie was shaking her head. "Just stop. I'm not having some kind of episode here in your truck. I'm telling you the truth. You're my dad. I'm your Em."

"And you're from the future."

"Yes."

"Okay. If that's true then who is the president where you're from? Or I should say 'when' you're from?"

Marie's face crinkled as she thought. "I ... I can't remember. A guy ... a famous guy. An astronaut I think."

"You think? You mean you don't know who the president is?"

"He said going back in time would mess up my memories. I would forget things. Get things confused."

"He? You mean the devil."

"Yes. I know it sounds crazy, but I'm telling you the truth. You've got to believe me."

"Okay ..." Harry reached for his favorite photo once again from his visor. "Then tell me who's in this picture."

"That's me and my dog."

"And what's the dog's name? Here's your clue." Harry pointed to the caption.

Marie stared hard at the worn picture. "Man—no...Mol... Molly? Molly."

"Millie. So close."

"Millie. Yes. I know that. I do. It's just my memories—"

"Yes, your memories are all mixed up."

"I'm telling you the truth." Her eyes darted back and forth as she desperately tried to convince Harry. "Your name. Your name is Harry Bukowski. Your CB handle is Snow Dog. You've had this truck for years, you call it the Bulldog Brawler because it's a Mack truck and their symbol is a bulldog which is the ornament on the hood, but yours broke off last year when ... when ... you did something ..."

"Good try, honey, but all that info is on the door of my truck which you could have easily seen when I picked you up. And anyone can see my ornament has broken off."

"Mom—your wife Loretta, she likes to crochet. She made you blankets and ugly sweaters. She made my baby clothes."

"Yup," Harry said. "You have a pretty good memory after looking at all my pictures."

Marie slumped hard in her seat, looking frustrated and on the verge of tears.

After a minute of silence, Harry spoke up. "What if you fail?"

"Huh?"

"What if you fail to save me? What then?"

"He said that if my mission fails, and I don't prevent you from driving off that cliff, then I'm sent back to where I came from as if nothing ever happened."

"Well," said Harry with a half-smile and stifled laugh, "at least you got a guarantee."

Marie shook her head and let out an exasperated sigh. She stared out her door window, Harry could only imagine what she was thinking. But one thing was for certain: this has gone on long enough. As he rounded a curve, neon lights up ahead gave him an idea.

Harry pulled the truck into a gas station called Gary's. The spot had been blasted out of the side of the mountain decades ago for all the work trucks when they were making the roads. When the roads were finished, the state kept the excavated lot for salt storage and whatever else they wanted to cram in there. About ten years ago they put it up for sale for a halfway decent price. That's when Gary Stenson bought it and built a gas station, mini mart, and sub shop. He called it Gary's Gas and Gulp. The logo was three huge neon "G"s that loomed proudly at the top of the center of the building. It was great little place in a perfect spot between Broadmont and Middleton and Gary's had been doing good business ever since it opened.

"What are we doing?" Marie asked.

"*We* are pulling into this truck stop. *You* are getting out and calling a cab."

"A cab? Wait. No. You can't leave me here. I need to see you to Middleton. I gotta make sure you get there. You need to live!"

"Honey, I—"

"Wait," she said as she desperately removed a chain from around her neck. The chain hosted a silver round medallion the size of a half-dollar, which she presented to Harry, hanging from a shaky fist. "Here. This was recovered from the crash. They said you were holding it in your hand when they found your body."

"What is it?"

"It's your Saint Christopher medal." She shook the medal, begging him to take it.

Harry took the silver medal and its chain from Marie and examined it. In the center was a man with a staff and a baby on his shoulder. The coin-like object was worn with age and handling, but Harry could still read the words "Saint Christopher" engraved along the top edge and "Protect Us" on the bottom. After a few seconds, he gently took her wrist, and with eyes soft yet filled with pity, he placed the necklace back in her hand.

"I'm sorry. But I've never owned a Saint Christopher medal or anything like this. I'm not very religious, and I don't like jewelry. I only wear this watch because it's practical."

Marie looked at the medal then at Harry, clearly confused and looking hopeless. "I ... I don't understand," was all she could say.

"I'm sorry, Honey. Here." Harry pulled his wallet from the liner pocket of his jacket, opened it, and pulled out two twenties. "Take this and get yourself something to eat and a cab to wherever you want to go. Just talk to Gary or whoever's in there, and they'll help you out."

Marie looked at the money like she didn't know what it was, then her eyes met Harry's and tears started forming again.

"Go on," Harry said. "Take it."

Marie slowly grabbed the cash and pulled the handle to open the door. Before she took a step out of the truck she turned to Harry.

"Please," she said. "Please be careful going home. Promise you won't fall asleep."

The corner of Harry's mouth rose. "Honey, I'm am so wired right now, I'm not sure when I'll be able to fall asleep. Not for a long while. That's for sure."

Marie nodded at that and continued her slow exit from the truck. Once out on the ground, she turned around to address Harry one last time.

"Thank you again, Harry."

"You are most certainly welcome."

Then she closed the door and walked toward the entrance of the mini mart.

Convinced he did the right thing, Harry put his truck in gear and got back onto the road, determined more than ever to see his family and make sure they'd have the best Thanksgiving ever.

If Harry was right about anything, it was the fact that he was wide awake. The way he was feeling at that very moment, he was certain that he would be awake all night. Marie's story certainly made him evaluate his life with new founded appreciation. Not that he hadn't appreciated his life; his family meant the world to him, and he knew he could have it much worse. But now, after hearing Marie's story, he knew more than ever how lucky he was. And how precious every second was that he had with his wife and daughter. From now on, he was going to live each day to its fullest. As if it were his last.

Looking at the seat to his right, where the hapless Marie had sat just minutes ago, Harry hoped she would be fine. He hoped that whatever demons she was wrestling with could be silenced, and that she would find peace at last. Behind the seat, he noticed the towel still hanging on the hook and a bit of the denim jacket was visible underneath. "Crap. She forgot her jacket." Although it was still drenched, Harry knew she would need it once it dried out. He couldn't turn around and go back; the road was too narrow for him to do so. Maybe he would give Gary a call when he got home and ask him to give her more money for a new jacket, and he would pay him back. Yeah, that should be okay. Gary would do that, no problem.

Another thing caught his eye while he pondered the jacket dilemma. Something shiny was caught in the passenger seat on the far side right between the seat itself and the back of the chair. Harry stretched for it with his right hand while keeping his left on the wheel. Just inches short of reaching it, he realized the object was Marie's Saint Christopher medal.

The medal!

Harry sat up quickly and saw he was at a sharp turn in the road and was heading straight for the mountain edge. He slammed on the brakes; the truck slid on the wet asphalt only to come to a halt just before the precipice that would have been the doorway to his death.

Harry's heart pounded in his chest, he sat there trying to calm down and catch his breath. After a minute, he unfastened his seat belt and reached over to retrieve the medal. He stared at it in disbelief. *If I had spent another second longer trying to get that damn thing* ... He then looked out at the mile maker on the side of the road. It read seventy-eight. Harry's eyes darted from side to side as his mind processed everything.

"This would have been it," he said aloud. "I could have died right here. Or actually, down there." Harry gazed past the guardrail and the mountain's edge. "One more second ... and I would have surely reacted too late and would have plummeted down the mountain"

"This was recovered from the crash," Marie had said. *"They said you were holding it in your hand when they found your body."*

"Holy cow, Marie. You were right. You were right ..." He blinked a few times and, with realization and clarity, he said, "Em?"

Though still finding it hard to swallow, Harry had to accept that the woman that was in his truck had been telling the truth. *And was she really Em? Did she really make that deal with the devil?* A plethora of possibilities and scenarios ran through his head. In the end, Harry knew what he had to do.

"I'm coming home, Em. I'll be dammed if I'll let you become like her." Harry squeezed the medal tight in his hand before placing it in his jacket pocket.

The rest of the ride seemed to take forever. Harry kept thinking about the horrible things that had happened to Marie—Em—whoever she was. But that was her life; that was Marie's. Whether she was actually from the future or not, his Em wasn't going to grow up to be like her. He just couldn't let any of that happen to his Em. He would live his life dedicated to making sure of that.

Harry pulled into his driveway and drove his truck to the backyard and parked it in its usual spot next to the shed. He hastily exited his cab, not bothering to locked it up. He then raced for the back porch and the wooden screen door. Normally he would have been quiet this time of night, not wanting to awaken anyone in the house, but tonight was different. Harry had to hug his family; he had hold them like he had never held them before, even if that meant waking them from their peaceful slumber.

"Loretta!" Harry yelled as the screen door slammed closed behind him. "Em!" They were in bed, of course, so Harry climbed the stairs, yelling their names as he ascended to the second floor. "Loretta! Em!"

"Harry. What's going on?" Loretta had emerged from their bedroom, putting on her robe and tying it closed. Squinting as her eyes adjusted to the hallway light, she gave her husband a puzzled look.

Harry smiled upon seeing her and wrapped his arms around her and gave her a hug that conveyed every emotion he was feeling. "I missed you," he whispered in her ear.

"I missed you too," she replied as she returned his embrace.

Pulling away enough to look into her eyes, he said, "I love you, and I appreciate everything that you are."

Loretta smiled. "Are you feeling alright?"

"Yes. I am feeling great. Now that I'm home." He pulled away completely and started to go toward the opposite end of the hall. "Now, I just need to see Em."

"Who?" asked Loretta.

"Emily," said Harry and turned to his wife. "Is she in her room?"

"That isn't funny, Harry."

"What isn't funny?" he said as he reached his daughter's bedroom door. He gave the handle a twist and swung the door open. Turning on the light, he couldn't comprehend what he saw. Instead of her bed and dresser and the plethora of stuffed animals, he saw that only cardboard boxes filled the room. Some were marked 'summer clothes' or 'Xmas decorations.' Perplexed, he faced his wife. "I don't understand. What did you do to Em's room? Where's Emily?"

"How can you say that?" she asked, her brow contorted into a deep frown. "You know how that miscarriage upset me. Why would you joke about that?"

"Miscarriage?" Harry said. His eyes lost focus as he tried to understand what his wife had said. "What do you mean?"

But he knew what she meant. He knew what had happened. And he knew where Em was.

He had her. The son of a bitch took her as he had promised. Emily was successful in saving Harry's life so the devil had taken her soul. And he had managed to take it before she was even born.

Memories started to flood Harry Bukowski's mind. Memories he did not have before, but were now as real to him as the ones they tried to replace and force out of his head. He grimaced as fought to retained those precious moments of his life that revolved around a sandy-haired girl. A girl so full of love and joy. She had loved her parents more than anything. And she especially loved that dog named ... named .... But Harry couldn't remember the dog's name. Or the breed. Or the color. In fact, he couldn't remember the girl's name either. It began with an "N". Or was it an "M"?

"You bastard!" Tears streaked down his face. He fell to his knees and pounded the floor with his fist, his forehead pressed against the carpet. "Damn you," he sobbed. "Damn you, damn you, damn you."

THE EAGLE'S TALON

"Cage an eagle and it will bite at the wires, be they of iron or of gold."
– Henrik Ibsen, The Vikings of Helgeland

Road Trip

"You were screaming again last night."

Jackson Gyle diverted his eyes from the road long enough to look at his wife, Ellen. He turned down the radio so that David Bowie's "Suffragette City" was barely audible through the 4runner's abused overpowered speakers. "I was?" he said, then looked back to the road, attempting to keep at least half his attention on his driving. “Sorry.”

Ellen caressed his hair. “Another nightmare?” His wife was a worrier. Whether it was about him, or the kids, or the dogs; she was always preoccupied with someone. She cared deeply about her family and just about everyone she knew. It was who she was. Her nurturing nature not only helped make her a great wife, but it also made her the perfect mother for their three children. She also had great empathy and patience, but she could be quite persistent when something got stuck in that brain of hers. Jackson had a feeling this conversation wasn’t going away anytime soon.

He gently took her hand, brought it to his lips, and kissed her soft skin. “Don’t worry. I’m fine. It was just a dream. I barely remember what it was about.”

“But you do remember some of it. Was it about your father again?”

“Yeah,” he conceded. “But I’m fine. Really. Everyone has nightmares.”

“True, but you have them more often than anyone else I know.” She hesitated, but Jackson knew what was coming next. “I want you to see Dr. Bernstein.”

“Please,” he pleaded, “not this again. I’m not seeing some quack. We’ve been over this.”

“He’s not ‘some quack.’ He’s a good man, Jack. Becky and Rob have been seeing him for a while now and they swear by him.” She placed her other hand on top of his and gave a little squeeze. He winced and pulled away as a small sting reminded him of the injury that lingered underneath the bandage on the back of his hand.

“I’m sorry,” Ellen said. “I forgot. How’s it feel today?”

“Not too bad. It doesn’t hurt like it did.”

“Good. We should change your bandage tonight. I’m glad Steve was there at the gym with you when it happened.”

“Me too,” said Jackson. “Doctor friends come in handy.” He looked at his covered wound. “Can’t believe I was so clumsy.”

Ellen said nothing more. She didn't have to; the mix of emotions on her face said it all: guilt, concern, dismay. Then her features softened and, in a cheerful voice, she said, "It's nice to get out for the weekend. Away from work and the kids and dogs. Just the two of us."

He smiled and grabbed her hand again. "Us and about a hundred party guests. But I know what you mean. It is nice."

"And I'll finally get to meet Steve."

"Yeah," said Jackson in a flat tone. "You'll finally get to meet Steve."

"You okay?"

"Yeah. Why?"

"The way you just said that. Everything okay between you two?"

"Sure. Fine." Jackson gave his shoulders a quick shrug. "Just tired from driving I guess."

"Want me to take over for a while?"

"No. I'm good. It shouldn't be much longer."

Ellen gave her husband a comforting smile and laid her head on his shoulder before changing the subject. "Who is the birthday boy anyway? And to have such a big party."

"Not sure. Steve only referred to him as Mr. Kralle. And it's his ninety-fifth birthday."

"Ninety-five? Wow."

"I really don't know much else. He just said that we'll fit right in at the party."

"I guess after ninety-five years in this world you make a lot of friends and deserve a big party."

Jackson nodded. "I guess so. Steve says this guy Kralle has a really nice place."

"And he's sure there's a guest room we can use? I don't want to be imposing on some man that we haven't even met yet."

"Steve assured me that Mr. Kralle insisted we stay the night since we had to drive all the way out here."

Ellen sat back up and gazed outside at the passing trees and endless fields. "And where exactly is 'out here'? We've been driving since early this morning, and I haven't seen a living soul in over an hour. Are we still in Maryland?"

Jackson glanced down at his GPS and shook his head. "West Virginia now. And according to Steve's directions, we should be there in another hour."

Normally Jackson would have keyed the address into his GPS unit and followed the computerized directions, but Steve had told him this place had no address. It was just a house out in the middle of nowhere. A set of hand-written directions was all Jackson had to work with. That really didn't surprise him; when he was a teenager and worked for his father, shipping generator parts all over the country, some of the places didn't have addresses, just bizarre directions. One such delivery might have said something like: four miles up Route 101, then make a left at the fire station, then the green house next to the old mill. Jackson smiled and shook his head as he remembered that. But his smile soon disappeared at the thought of being out on the middle of nowhere and not knowing exactly what this was all about. *It's all right, Jackson. No need to worry. Go in, do what you have to do, then leave.*

Ellen raised her eyebrows and sighed. "Well, I'm going to call and check on the kids." She pulled her phone out of her purse and pushed a few buttons to call the house. After a few seconds, one of the kids must have answered.

"Hi. Manda? ... How are things? ... The boys being good? ...

There was a pause as their oldest, Amanda, undoubtedly was giving Ellen the low-down as to the irritation her younger brothers were causing her. She was a good kid and a quite responsible sixteen-year-old. Though her little brothers seemed to live to make her life difficult, she loved those boys to death and enjoyed being a second mother to them. She seemed to relish the times when her parents asked her to look after them. There was a lot of her mother in her; Jackson was grateful for that. Still, he thought he and Ellen should get her something nice for looking after the boys on such short notice. *We'll stop somewhere on the way back*, he thought.

Ellen rolled up her window to better hear her daughter. This caused a slight swirl of wind to whip through the car until Jackson used the controls on his door to raise the remaining windows. His tie had managed to get flopped over his shoulder, and as he fixed it, he touched his newly acquired tie clip. His thoughts transported him back to Wednesday, when he had gotten the fancy accessory, and the encounter that made him question everything.

* * *

After a couple games of racquetball at the gym, Jackson had stopped at the local grocery store. Ellen wanted dinner rolls. The kids wanted ice cream. There were a few other odds and ends they needed, and because the store was on the way home, he didn't mind stopping, even against the protest of his very audibly pleading stomach.

Somewhere between the deli and seafood counters, a man in a black suit approached him. He was African-American, tall, and Jackson wagered that he hid a plethora of muscles beneath his custom fit clothes.

"Mr. Gyle?"

"Yes," Jackson replied, totally baffled as to who this person was and how he knew his name. Let alone, what he wanted with him.

"I need you to follow me out to the parking lot." The man in the suit then opened his jacket, pulled out a leather bi-fold, and opened it to reveal a gold badge on one side and an ID card on the other. Both said FBI.

Finding it all hard to believe, Jackson said, "Is this some kind of joke?"

The tall, brawny man peered into Jackson's eyes and said, "Does it look like I'm joking?"

Jackson swallowed "I suppose not." He then left his little red grocery basket by the lobster tank and led the assertive gentleman out of the store.

Once outside, they headed to the back of the lot and entered a black Chevy van through its side doors. Inside the van, a man, another agent Jackson presumed, waited for them. He dressed in a nearly identical suit as the first man, but this guy was white with short brown hair. Other than that, the two agents were like bookends.

"I'm special agent Hart. You've already met S.A. Mumford. Please sit."

His head swimming with questions and concerns, Jackson sat on the narrow bench that ran along the inside wall of the van. He tried his best to control his shaking, but his heart pounded so hard that he was certain the agents could hear it. The door slid shut with a *slam* causing Jackson to start.

For the first minute or so, the agents just sat there staring at him. Probably sizing him up, gauging his fear. Who knows, really? Jackson certainly have a clue as to what was going on. Maybe this *was* a joke, some kind of prank. Afterall, he had nothing to fear. He hadn't done anything wrong. Jackson only wished that they would say something.

"Christ, guys, can one of you please tell me what this is about?" Jackson regretted those words as soon as they left his mouth. But at the same time, he almost felt a surge of pride at his small show of bravery.

"Mr. Gyle," said Hart. "Do you know this man?"

Hart held up a 5x7 picture of a white man in his mid-thirties. It was a head-on shot of the man giving a forced smile and wearing an Izod polo. Jackson figured that it must have been a driver license photo. And yes, he did recognize the man.

Jackson nodded. "That's Steve—Dr. Strasser. I play racquetball with him every Monday and Wednesday at the gym. In fact, I just saw him about an hour ago."

"And how about this man?" Hart held up another 5x7. This one was of a man in his late forties or early fifties. The gray five-o'clock shadow he was sporting in the photo might have made him look older than he really was. A curved scar on his chin made Jackson think he might have gotten the injury in a bar fight. He certainly looked the type.

"No. Never seen him before." Jackson looked from one agent to the other. "Can you tell me what this is about? Is Steve in some sort of trouble?"

"Let's just say he's a person of interest in an ongoing investigation." Hart put the pictures in a folder, then set the folder off to the side.

"Have you ever been to Steve's house," said Mumford, "or any other place with him? Other than the gym?"

"No," said Steve shaking his head.

"Has he *asked* you to go anyplace with him?" Hart asked. "A meeting place of some sort? Dinner, perhaps?"

Jackson thought for a moment, then replied, "He did ask me to go to one of his friend's house for a birthday party this weekend."

Hart and Mumford looked at each other. "This could be it," said Hart. The other nodded.

"*What* could be it?" asked Jackson. "What's going on here? What kind of trouble is Steve in?"

Hart looked to Mumford then back to Jackson. "Mr. Gyle. We believe your friend Steve is involved in an organization whose sole purpose is the undermining and dismantling of our country's government."

"Undermining?" Jackson said; half not believing, half not understanding. "What?"

"And we believe that he has targeted you for possible ... recruitment."

Jackson shook his head trying to make sense of what he was hearing.

"The FBI has been trying to infiltrate this group for several years," Hart continued, "but have failed at every turn. They are highly organized and highly secretive. Any agent that we've tried to get in there has either hit a dead end or ..." Hart trailed off as if he caught himself before saying too much.

"Or what?" asked Steve.

"The party this weekend," Mumford said, diverting Jackson's attention, "could be the opportunity they'll use to recruit you. And we want you to play along."

"Play along? What, you want me to be a spy for you?"

"Mr. Gyle, that's exactly what we want."

"Whoa, whoa, whoa," Jackson said as he held up his hands. "I'm not a spy, or a fed, or anything closely resembling those things. I'm just a high school history teacher. I'm not cut out for anything like this."

"Believe me Mr. Gyle," said Hart. "We wouldn't be here right now if there was another way."

"And we don't mind telling you," said Mumford, "that the fate of our government could rely on the information you obtain for us."

Hart pointed to Jackson's bandaged right hand. "You hurt yourself, sir?"

"Cut it at the gym last week. Clumsy. Luckily I'm left-handed."

Hart nodded, accepting his answer.

Did he think that someone had hurt me? Did he know how I hurt myself and was just testing me?

"Do you love your country, Mr. Gyle?"

"Of course I do."

"Then will you help us?" said Hart. "Can we count on you to be a patriot and do the right thing?"

"I do love my country, and I am a patriot, but I'm not comfortable with what you are asking me to do. And not to sound selfish or anything, but what's in it for me? Why should I risk my safety to play Jack Bauer for you guys?"

Mumford leaned forward. "We're prepared to compensate you for your assistance. We're aware of that professorship you've been seeking at the state college. If you help us, I'm sure we can make that happen for you."

"And we're pretty sure your life will be in no danger," Hart added. "They wouldn't try to recruit you if they thought you were working for us, or if there was the slightest chance that you would reveal their organization."

"They, no doubt, have already run a background check on you and probably know more about you than *you* do," said Mumford.

"But what if they find out I'm working for you? What then?"

"They won't."

"How can you be sure?"

Hart hesitated, then said, "Because they've had you under surveillance for the past few weeks. Multiple vehicles, various personnel. They are just as thorough as we are, maybe more so. But there is no one on you at this particular hour. The Bureau was able to get the trajectory of a satellite changed for this evening. We have eyes on us as we speak." He pointed up with his index finger. "But our time is limited. In fact, that window closes in ..." He checked his wrist watch. "Ten minutes."

"We need an answer from you now, Mr. Gyle." Mumford said.

Jackson sat there dumbfounded. It was like something out of a movie, but it was happening to him, right here. If he did it, were there dangers? Sure there were. But they were probably very minor. And if he didn't do it, he would regret not helping his country when it needed him. He always regretted not going into the military; maybe not to make a career out of it, but at least to give his country four years of service. Maybe now was the opportunity to make up for that.

The agents looked at him with anticipation; they expected an answer. No time to think about it, talk to his wife, or anything. He had to decide right here and now.

"Okay," Jackson squeaked out. "I'll do it."

Hart and Mumford looked at each other with relief. Hart smiled at Jackson and said, "Great. This is what we need you to do."

Mumford produced a small white box, sort of like a cheap box you might get when you buy a piece of jewelry from Target. He opened it to revel a gold, diamond studded tie clip.

Jackson looked at him and said, “You shouldn’t have. I didn’t get you anything.”

Hart took the box from his partner and removed the accessory. “This is more than a tie clip. On the back is a micro recorder. Under the diamonds on the front is a microphone as well as an HD video camera. Push this diamond to turn the unit on. Again, to turn it off. You should have about twelve hours of recording time.” He handed the clip and box to Jackson who took them and examined the clip, holding it gently as if it were made of glass instead of gold and diamonds.

“Wow, this is some real James Bond stuff here,” he said in complete awe.

“One other thing,” said Hart. “You can’t tell anyone about this. Not even your wife. Is that understood?”

Jackson nodded.

“Mumford looked at his watch, then to Hart. “We gotta go.”

“We’ll be in touch next week when we have another opportunity,” said Hart. “‘til then, keep the recorder safe. And good luck.”

“And be careful,” added Mumford.

The agent who had brought Jackson to the van opened the door and let him out. Without another word, the side door closed and the now all-too-obvious FBI vehicle sped away toward Cedar Street, leaving Jackson standing in the middle of the parking lot. Before heading back inside the store, he looked at the small white cardboard box that held the high-tech Q-like device inside and said, “What have I gotten myself into?”

* * *

“It’s okay,” Ellen said into her phone. “Tommy can go over Vance’s as long as his mother is okay with it.” Another pause. “He can spend the night, but he can't go anywhere else. Just Vance's. Hello? Manda?"

Ellen pulled her phone away from her ear and looked at the screen. Jackson glanced over at it long enough to read 'Call Lost' across the middle of her iPhone and 'no service' at the top.

"Damn," said Ellen. "There's no signal."

"Steve said that would happen. There aren't any more cell towers from here on out. I'm surprised your call even went through."

Ellen stuffed her phone back into her purse, a look of concern resided on her face.

"Don't worry, you can call the kids again on a landline once we reach this guy's house. They'll be fine. Amanda's a great kid. She'll take care of the boys."

"You're right," she said with a sigh. "I'll call them later. Right after we eat. I hope they have decent food. I'm starving."

Jackson rolled the windows down once again and Ellen turned the volume to the satellite radio back up. The couple started singing along to Tom Petty's "Runnin' Down a Dream" and laughed as one would catch the other singing the wrong lyrics. The rest of the way to their destination, they continued to enjoy their favorite classic rock bands while letting the crisp mountain air roll through the car.

* * *

They had traveled along a surprisingly well paved road past miles of beautiful scenery, but nothing that led Jackson to think he was on the right track. He was about to stop and read Steve's directions for the umpteenth time to see if he missed a turn somewhere, when they finally came across a chunk of civilization. *Here at last.*

The hilly, vegetation strewn terrain, gave way to a huge manicured property overlooking a picturesque valley. Meticulously trimmed trees and hedges guarded multiple flower gardens and marble statues and fountains. Behind it all sat a house; the home of the birthday boy and their host.

"My god, Jack," Ellen said, wide-eyed and mouth agape. "I haven't seen a house this big since we took the kids to D.C. a couple years ago. And that house was white."

No, Jackson thought. *The word 'house' didn't do this justice. It was a mansion. A castle.* It was three stories tall, four in some places, complete with balconies, a parapet, and a few conical towers. The structure resembled something right out of Victorian Europe, but with a mid-twentieth century flair. And there was nothing intimidating about the structure at all; on the contrary, it was actually quite inviting. There was something comforting just being in its presence. A truly remarkable building. And here it was in Nowheresville, West Virginia.

"Amazing," Jackson said. He whistled a soft tone and shook his head.

They followed the road to a circular driveway which encompassed a multi-spout fountain that would have made Vegas envious. Jackson stopped the car at the Mansion's portico where several men in white tuxedoes waited for them. Jackson put the car in park as one of the tuxedoed men approached his door and opened it with a white-gloved hand.

"Welcome, sir," the valet said with a modest smile and gestured for Jackson to exit the vehicle. Another valet opened Ellen's door and offered his hand to help her out of her side. She accepted and waited for her husband to join her.

Their Toyota zipped away leaving the bewildered couple to gaze up the wide steps that led to an enormous set of wooden doors. There, a sobersided man in a black tux stood at a podium, looking down on them. *Probably in more ways than one,* Jackson thought as he adjusted the knot of his eighteen-dollar tie.

Jackson and Ellen climbed the steps and approached the podium and its austere attendant. Behind him, two more valets stood, framing the ornate embossed oak doors. Or were they mahogany? Jackson really couldn't tell.

"Your names please," said the man behind the podium. His attitude was a tad snooty, which matched his demeanor, but wasn't too condescending.

"Jackson and Ellen Gyle," Jackson replied. "We had overnight bags in the back of our car—"

Ignoring Jackson's comment about their bags, the man opened a leather-bound book and began to flip through the pages. As he ran his fingers through the innumerable names printed on the sheets, the purr of a throaty engine increased behind them. Jackson and Ellen both turned their heads to see a Rolls Royce Phantom pull up to the spot previously occupied by their 4runner. A pair of valets rushed to the doors and assisted a well-dressed couple from their seats in the back of the luxury vehicle.

"Yes," the serious man said. "Mr. and Mrs. Gyle." He made a mark next to their names in the book then closed it gracefully. "Welcome. I'll see to it that your bags are taken to your room. Please enjoy yourselves." He gestured behind him to the double-doored entrance. The two doormen each grabbed a handle and pulled the massive doors open with surprisingly apparent ease.

Facing the open doors, Jackson offered his arm to his wife. She switched her small purse to her other hand, dropping it in the process. One of the doormen quickly stooped over to retrieve it for her. As he bent over, his jacket opened above the buttons just enough for Jackson to see a handgun resting in a shoulder holster under the man's left arm. Jackson did his best not to appear alarmed and gave the doorman a smile of gratitude as Ellen said, "Thank you."

Taking her husband's arm, Ellen gave him a nervous smile. She didn't appear to have noticed the gun, but Jackson could tell she was just as excited and apprehensive as he was about entering the impressive house which, no doubt, hosted an equally impressive party. He, of course, had more to worry about than she did. With his free hand he reached for his tie clip and pressed the diamond button that turned on the micro recording device the agents had given him.

Jackson returned her smile, and the couple walked into the house, not really knowing what to expect.

The Party

Jackson and Ellen stood in the mansion's foyer, which was as big as their living room back in Maryland. They let their eyes adjust to the sudden absence of bright sunlight and gave each other's hands a squeeze.

The doors closed behind them as if it were a signal to proceed into the rest of the house. They walked ahead slowly and were immediately greeted by a man carrying a tray of drinks.

"Dom Perignon, sir? Madam?"

They both took a flute from the tray, said thank you to the waiter, then sipped. With a small nod, the waiter scooted off in search of more thirsty guests.

"Wow," said Ellen, looking to make sure the waiter was out of earshot. "I've never had real Dom Perignon before. Isn't it wonderful?"

"Yeah. Incredible," Jackson agreed as he sipped more of the champagne and took in his surroundings.

The outside of the house was more than impressive, and the inside did not disappoint. Paintings and tapestries hung from the walls. A spectacular chandelier dangled on a gold chain from a ceiling forty feet high. Twin staircases snaked upward to the second floor where dark wood railings guarded some party guests as they looked down into the atrium. The hardwood floor was polished to a mirror finish and covered sporadically with fringed rugs.

The couple walked through several rooms, nodding politely to the few guests they encountered. Some of whom gave Jackson a strange, maybe judgmental, look but never said a word to him. Jackson frowned and looked down at his clothes: his Farrah slacks and Van Heusen shirt practically screamed middle-class.

He glanced at his wife's lavender dress she had recently purchased from Penny's, specifically for this occasion. Pretty, but far from extravagant.

"Do you think they're judging us by our attire," he said to his wife. "I didn't know it was black-tie." Not seeming to care, Ellen pulled him into the next room.

The room was the size of an elementary school gymnasium, but had the appearance and feel of a museum. And the theme was music; instruments of all kinds decorated the walls and floor. In the center was a grand piano adorned with rhinestones and featured a glass—or maybe acrylic—top so that all the strings and hammers were completely visible. Above the keys, a mirrored faceplate bore the name "Baldwin" in its center, and something written by hand on one side. Jackson bent down to read the writing.

"*Too much of a good thing is wonderful.*"

He strained to read the rest, but shook his head. "Can't make out the signature."

They walked to a corner where another piano sat. Unlike its Baldwin cousin, this one was more traditional looking and seemed much older, yet in excellent condition. It was thin with a two-tiered keyboard and the underneath of its open top revealed a painted picture of a town by a harbor.

Jackson and Ellen stepped closer to better examine the curious looking instrument.

"What kind of piano do you think this is?" Ellen asked.

"Actually, it's a harpsicord," came an answer from behind them. The couple turned around to find a handsome man in a white and black tuxedo wearing a broad grin.

"Steve," Jackson said and put on a Pam Am smile. *Don't act like you know anything. Act natural.* Jackson thought of his wife and kids and the fake smile became more genuine.

"Jacks," said Steve extending a hand. "Great to see you. Glad you made it. I hope the ride wasn't too bad. How's the hand? Giving you any trouble?"

Jackson shook Steve's hand. "Wouldn't have missed it for the world. And the hand's much better. Thanks."

Steve softened his smile and offered his hand to Ellen who let him take hers. "You didn't tell me that you were bringing your daughter." He raised the back of her hand to his lips and gently kissed. Ellen blushed.

"Steve, this is my wife Ellen. Ellen, this is Steve."

"It's a pleasure to finally meet you, Steve." Ellen allowed her hand to be held a few seconds longer than Jackson would have liked. "I've heard so much about you."

"The pleasure is all mine," said Steve. "Jacks didn't tell me his wife was so young and beautiful."

Ellen blushed again, and her huge grin told Jackson that she was eating up the compliments.

Recovering his wife's hand into his own, Jackson put his arm around her and said, "Okay, Dr. Smoothie."

"This house is incredible," said Ellen, looking around with wide eyes. "Especially this room."

"Glad you think so," said Steve. "Mr. Kralle spent eleven years building this house and another fifty filling it with various treasures from history and around the world. Every little thing you see has a story behind it. That piano, for instance." Steve pointed to the Baldwin in the center of the room. "That was a gift from Liberace himself. The keys are pre-ban ivory and black alabaster from Italy. That guitar over there on the wall is an original C.F. Martin owned by Roy Rogers. That clarinet belonged to Benny Goodman. And the trumpet right next to it was Dizzy Gillespie's."

"How about this—what did you call it—harpsichord?" asked Ellen.

"This is a Couchet," Steve began. "Made in Antwerp, Belgium, in the mid-seventeenth century. Later it was expanded by a man named Paskal Taskin in Paris around the late eighteenth century. It's rumored that Adolph Hitler himself played with it during Germany's occupation of France during the war. This is one of Mr. Kralle's earliest acquisitions."

Jackson's and Ellen's eyebrows raised in fascination.

"How much is it worth?" asked Jackson.

Steve thought for a second. "Oh, about six-hundred thousand dollars."

"My God," said Ellen. "You're kidding."

"Oh, that's nothing," said Steve. "See this cello?" He led them across the room to where a large stringed instrument sat on an ornate wooden stand. "It's an original Stradivari. It's called the Duport Stradivari, named after the famous cellist Jean-Pierre Duport. Great story for this one. See that scratch near the bottom? According to legend, this scratch was caused by the spurs of Napoleon Bonaparte while he was trying to play it. And over the centuries it has been owned by some of the world's greatest cellists until Mr. Kralle acquired it a few decades ago. Yo-Yo Ma performed with it at a function held here a few years back. It was recently appraised at a little over twenty million dollars."

Jackson and Ellen stood looking at the instrument in stunned silence.

Steve frowned at the glasses in their hands. "What are you drinking?" he asked, reaching for their flutes. "Here, let me have those." The couple surrendered their glasses and Steve placed them on a small side table. "Let's go out back. That's where the good stuff is."

Out back was also where the real party was. After Steve took them though the house and out a set of double glass doors, they stood before acres of land that served as the house's back yard. From a marble surfaced patio that stood twenty feet above the land, they could see tennis courts, horse stables, and several swimming pools. Next to the tennis courts sat a large concrete slab that might have once been the foundation of a structure that had been long gone.

Immediately before them, approximately four hundred well-dressed party guests were enjoying live music from a thirty-piece orchestra and food and drink from trays carried by waiters who weaved through the crowd like bees in a field of flowers.

"I thought you said it was only a hundred people coming," said Jackson.

Steve shrugged.

"And you didn't tell me that there was a dress code," Jackson added.

Steve clapped him on the shoulder. "You look fine. You both do. I want you to meet my wife. Let me go find her. Be right back." He then walked down the salmon-colored stone stairs and into the sea of mingling people.

"Oh my god," said Ellen.

Jackson looked at his wife who was gazing out onto the guest-strewn lawn. "What? What is it?"

"I think that's Olivia Hamilton."

"Who?"

"Olivia Hamilton." She looked at Jackson. "The actress." Seeing the befuddled look on her husband's face, she said, "She was in that movie *Star Frontier* with Tom Cruise."

Jackson shook his head; he didn't watch sci-fi movies and he wasn't a huge Tom Cruise fan.

Ellen sighed. "She was in *Love Always Wins* with Matthew McConaughey."

"Oh," said Jackson. "Okay. Where?"

"Over there." Ellen pointed. "Next to the man with the cowboy hat.

"Yeah. That might be her. She—" He cut himself off. "Do you see who she's talking to? That's the governor of Texas."

"You sure?" Ellen asked looking more closely at the pair.

Ellen might have known more about Hollywood starlets and actors than Jackson did, but he knew way more about politics. He must have seen the governor's picture a hundred times on the news and internet. He was a good man. Some said he might run for president someday. There was no mistaking that the tall man in the Stetson was him. "Positive."

Jackson's curiosity had him scanning the crowd to see who else he could find. "Look. Over there. That's Bret Billings, third baseman for the Dodgers. And over there is Rick Sachs, the

Mayor of New York. And he's talking to Peter Williamson, the majority leader of the Senate."

"And that's Eddie Krantz, the talk show host," Ellen chimed in.

"Where?"

"By the orchestra. With the platinum hair."

"Cool. And there's Iggy Mann from Blade Strike."

"Really? I love that group." Ellen was enraptured with the party; Jackson could tell she was star struck.

As was he; all these celebrities and politicians in one place. It was amazing. And bizarre. *What the hell is going on here?* "Who is this old guy?" he said aloud. "And how does he know all these people?"

"I don't know," said Ellen. "But I'm liking him."

Steve emerged from the crowd with a beautiful woman in tow. They climbed the stairs and Steve signaled for a waiter's attention.

"Jacks. Ellen. This is my wife Claire."

Claire had, what some people call, classic beauty; she emanated sophistication and grace. She was tall, had long blonde hair, and a figure that said she watched what she ate, as well as spent time in the gym. She certainly belonged here among the celebrities that peppered the estate.

She extended her hand to Jackson, who took it and gave it a gentle half shake.

"Pleased to meet you," he said.

Turning to Ellen, Claire took both of her hands in hers and said, "You're right, Steve. She's absolutely beautiful." Claire gave Ellen a tender embrace. "I'm so glad to meet you. I know we're going to be great friends."

A waiter appeared with a tray full of glasses; champagne flutes like the ones inside. The only difference: the sparkling wine in these glasses had a slight pink hue. Steve took two full glasses and handed them to Jackson and Ellen, and then took two more for himself and Claire. "Let's toast," Steve said raising his glass.

"What shall we toast to?" asked Ellen.

Steve placed a hand on Jackson's shoulder and gave it a firm squeeze. "To friends," he said.

"*To friends*," the others repeated. They all drank.

"This is really good," said Ellen. "I mean *really* good."

"It should be," said Steve. "It's Armand de Brignac."

"And what's that mean?" asked Jackson.

"It means," said Claire, "that it's about ten-thousand dollars a bottle."

Jackson almost choked as he sipped. "Did you say ten thousand?

"Yeah," said Steve. "The Dom Perignon Rose goes for about twelve, but Mr. Kralle prefers the Armand."

The *thwop thwop thwop* of a helicopter rose above the din of the party crowd, forcing everyone to peer skyward. The sleek, tapered aircraft circled wide around the house before landing on the concrete slab by the tennis courts. That's when Jackson realized that the old foundation was actually a helipad.

Everyone watched in silence as a door lowered from the copter's rear, serving as a ramp for its passengers. The only people to emerge: a man pushing a wheelchair in which a slight figure nestled under a blanket. They proceeded down the ramp and along a cement walkway that led from the pad to the house, and the patio itself. As they got closer, Jackson could see an old—no, an ancient-man in the wheelchair. "This must be the birthday boy," he said whispered to Ellen. "The mysterious Mr. Kralle."

The aide pushed the wheelchair to the rear of the patio and into a small glass room the size of a closet. Only when the "room" rose to bring its occupants to the patio's level did Jackson recognize it as an elevator.

"Pardon me, folks," said Steve as he placed his glass on the railing. "That's my cue." Steve walked across the length of the patio to greet the men in the elevator once it finished its ascent and opened.

Jackson noticed the entire party crowd had been transfixed on Mr. Kralle ever since the helicopter had landed. Their collective silent gaze was almost unnerving.

Steve escorted the man in the wheelchair, and the aide pushing him, to a podium by the patio's railing where a microphone sat waiting on a stand. Steve pulled the mic loose and gave it a tap to ensure that it was on before beginning to speak.

"Ladies and gentlemen. Thank you all so much for coming today. I know some of you have come from great distances, and that only goes to show the influence our host, Mr. Kralle, has had on all of us." The crowd murmured in agreement. "And why are we here? We are here because today is Mr. Kralle's ninety-fifth birthday."

The crowd erupted in enthusiastic applause and cheers. Mr. Kralle smiled, at least Jackson thought he was smiling, and gave a shaky wave to his guests. The crowd continued to clap, some acknowledging Mr. Kralle with fervent waves of their own.

"Now," Steve began as he waited for the crowd to quiet down again. "Now, Mr. Kralle. Do you have anything you would like to say to everyone?" Steve stooped down and held the microphone to the old man who leaned forward to speak into the mike.

"Thank you," he said in a strained voice.

Everyone gave a small laugh; Steve even let out a chuckle.

"Anything else?" Steve said encouragingly.

"Eat. Drink. And enjoy!" Mr. Kralle's voice was a bit stronger this time and that elicited a cheer from the guests. Jackson wasn't sure, but he thought he detected a bit of an accent in the old man's speech.

Steve stood back up as the aide turned Mr. Kralle around and toward the house, all the while, the orchestra played a jazzed-up version of "For He's a Jolly Good Fellow." Before going inside, the old man met Jackson's gaze and gave him a look of ... recognition? Satisfaction? Jackson didn't know what to make of it, but the stare had him mesmerized. In contrast to the old man's frailty, his brilliant blue eyes were almost hypnotic and energetic. It was if the old man's eyes were that of a much younger person who had only lent them to Mr. Kralle so he could gaze upon his guests for the day. After a curious few seconds, the mysterious Mr. Kralle disappeared into his lavish home.

Steve walked back to Jackson and the two wives and retrieved his champagne glass.

"Ellen," said Claire abruptly, as if she had a brilliant idea. "Would you like to meet Olivia Hamilton?"

"Would I?" Ellen answered. "You bet."

"Great. C'mon." Claire took Ellen's arm and led her down the stairs and into the crowd.

"There's some people I'd like you to meet as well, Jacks." Steve jerked his head to the direction the wives headed. "Let's go."

For the next couple hours, Steve introduced Jackson to more famous people than he had ever imagined he would meet, especially in one place. Politicians; actors; athletes; and the occasional musician and artist as well. What surprised Jackson, although pretty much this entire day had been one big surprise, was the number of high-ranking officers from all branches of the armed forces. There were admirals and rear admirals; generals, two stars and up; and there were men and woman who represented the Department of Defense, all very enigmatic about their jobs. Almost everyone he met that afternoon was someone of acclaim. It was the most humbling experience in Jackson's life.

And the main topic of the day: politics. Usually politics and religion were taboo conversations in mixed groups, but everyone seemed to be on the same page, and Jackson found that to be quite refreshing.

Steve was well received amongst the guests. Some called him Dr. Steve, or Dr. Strasser, but most seemed close and comfortable enough to just call him Steve. Everyone shook his hand and thanked him for the invitation to the party. Steve usually replied with something like, "It wouldn't be the same without you," or "Mr. Kralle personally asked for you to attend."

The guests' reactions to Jackson were a bit more mixed. Some treated him like a long lost relative, while others regarded him with trepidation and what almost seemed like suspicion. But

Jackson wasn't about to let it all overwhelm or intimidate him. He held conversations with the best of them, and he was both gracious and formidable when discussing politics or other topics, for that matter. Being president of the debate team back in school had come in handy. Steve seemed impressed.

"I knew you would fit right in," Steve told him. "You're a natural. You had them eating out of your hand."

"Speaking of eating," Jackson said with a mouth full of food, "this spread is incredible."

Steve called it a stand-up lunch; that's where waiters just keep circulating various trays of hors d'oeuvre sized food. The variety was insane; everything from little crab cakes to Escargots a la Bourguignonne. Jackson never saw the same tray twice, and he took something from almost every one. There were these mushroom polenta things that were delicious, and Jackson couldn't get enough of the grilled sea scallops wrapped in prosciutto. Amazing.

Occasionally they would run into their wives. Ellen would beam at Jackson, and he couldn't help but return her smile. She seemed to be having the time of her life as Claire introduced her to some of Hollywood's elite.

Everything was so wonderful, so incredible. So much so that Jackson had almost forgotten he was on a mission for the FBI. *How could Steve be mixed up into anything nefarious? Everything here is so perfect. And harmless.* Jackson shook his head, not wanting to believe anything the agents had told him. *They have to be mistaken.*

Jackson stared at his tie clip and pushed the diamond that would halt the micro recorder. He then took the clip completely off, casually dropped it on the ground, and stepped on it. By the end of the day, four hundred people would have trampled it. Jackson smiled to himself. He breathed in the mountain air and continued the day guilt free, hobnobbing along with his good friend Steve. This was turning out to be one of the best days of his life.

Later that evening, as the summer sun approached twilight, Mr. Kralle made another appearance on the patio. A giant birthday cake was trundled out, and Steve led everyone in attendance to a rendition of "Happy Birthday to You." The revered man again waved to the exuberant crowd, and rolled away, a small piece of cake resting on a plate in his lap. Everyone was given a small piece of the cake. Jackson and Steve finished theirs by one of the pools where their wives sat on the edge letting their bare feet soak in the water. Their well-used shoes sitting next to them.

Earlier, Claire had taken Ellen to a phone where she was able to get ahold of Amanda and was reassured that everything was fine at home. Not that Jackson expected anything less.

A peaceful, almost blasé, feeling had replaced any trepidation and apprehension Jackson might have had at the beginning of the party. Now, as he stood there next to Steve, looking out onto the picturesque valley, he had a strong sense of belonging.

That's when Jackson finally turned to Steve and asked, "Who exactly is Mr. Kralle?"

Steve thoughtfully nodded, looked at his watch, then back at Jackson. "Here. Let me show you."

After excusing themselves from the ladies, Steve led Jackson back to the raised patio and around to its rear corner where the glass elevator Mr. Kralle had used earlier rested. With a push of a button the crystal-clear doors opened, and the pair walked in. Steve inserted a brass key into a slot on the lift's control panel and gave it a turn. Jackson wasn't sure why they didn't just take the stairs to the top of the patio, then the doors closed, and the elevator went down instead of up.

Mr. Kralle

By the time the elevator finished its descent, Jackson estimated they were two stories below the surface. Anxiety knocked on the door of his emotions, but he refused to allow it in. "Let me guess," he said, breaking the tension. "You're going to show me a million-dollar wine cellar."

"Actually," Steve said as the elevator doors opened, "the wine cellar in under the main kitchen." Turning to Jackson, he grinned and said, "And it's worth nineteen million."

Steve led the way out of the elevator and into a short corridor. When Jackson hesitated, he turned to him and said, "Come on. I'll give you the answers to the multitude of questions running around in your head."

Jackson took a deep breath and joined his friend.

The corridor ended in a T. Ahead of them was a set of double doors, and a new corridor extended left and right. They took the right hallway and walked until they came to a door where two men were waiting. One was dressed in a tuxedo like Steve, the other in khakis and a button-down bowling style shirt. The one in the tux was Mitch; Jackson had met him outside during the party. He was one of the few guests that treated him rather coldly. The guy in the bowling shirt, Jackson was certain he had never seen before, yet there was something oddly familiar about him. He was forty-something, slightly overweight, had a curved scar on his chin, and seemed a little less refined than everyone else here today. He looked like he would be more comfortable with a beer in his hand than a glass of champagne.

"Nice to see you again, Mr. Gyle," said Mitch flatly. He didn't smile, so neither did Jackson.

"You too," Jackson replied.

Mitch gestured to the man in the bowling shirt. "This is Ronnie Sparks. He'll be joining us this evening."

Jackson acknowledged Ronnie with a curt smile and a nod, and Ronnie did the same. “Have we met before, sir?” Jackson asked Ronnie.

Ronnie frowned and shook his head. “I don’t believe so.”

“Strange, you look so familiar. Maybe you have a twin somewhere that I’ve run into.”

Ronnie smiled. “If I do, it’s news to me.”

“Ronnie is Mitch’s guest,” said Steve. “And like you, he has many questions.”

“Shall we go in?” Mitch opened the door and the four men walked in the room. Once inside, the lights came on automatically by steadily increasing in brightness until a normal illumination was reached. Steve closed the door behind them.

The room was approximately twenty by thirty with wood-finished walls that reminded Jackson of the paneling in his in-law’s basement. A leather sofa and six leather easy chairs were separated by end tables and floor lamps. Two of the walls were taken up with book shelves that hosted not only books, but pictures, decorations, and various knickknacks.

The wall on the left played background to a six-foot statue of a Roman soldier. The wall itself was painted with a mural of an artist’s rendition of what ancient Rome may have resembled. The statue was white marble; the soldier proudly carried a spear in one hand and a shield in the other. A short sword hung ready from his belt.

The statue was fascinating, but what really caught Jackson’s attention was the wall on the opposite end. In the center was a large portrait of a man, and on either side were trophy cases filled with various artifacts. Specifically, from World War II, one of Jackson’s areas of expertise. With his interest piqued, Jackson looked closely at the items in the cases. A luger, medals, a dagger ... all museum pieces to be sure, and in excellent condition. Ronnie joined Jackson by the trophy cases, but his attention was on the portrait. After admiring the pieces in the cases, Jackson gazed upward and examined the painting.

It was of a man. He wore a black uniform adorned with medals and pins. The collars had lightning bolt and diamond patches. Upon his head was a brimmed hat that bore two metal pendants; an eagle, and skull and crossbones. One of his arms displayed a trim on the wrist that said *Obergruppenführer* and a red sash around his bicep that brandished a black crooked cross in a circular field of white. More commonly known as a swastika.

Jackson swallowed hard and could feel his heart begin to race. Regarding the face of the soldier, he saw a hard yet handsome face that sat under sweeping blonde hair. And staring back at him were the fiercest blue eyes he had not seen since earlier that afternoon.

"His real name," said Steve, startling Jackson, "is Wilhelm Dietrich, son of a cabinet maker from Dusseldorf who, ironically, was a member of the Widerstand resistance group. Despite his traitor father, Hitler was very fond of Wilhelm and gave him the nickname 'The Eagle's Talon' or 'The Talon' for short. In German it's '*Die Kralle.*' When seeking sanctuary outside of Germany after the war ended, he took that as his surname."

"You mean," said Ronnie, "he's a freakin' Nazi? That old man?"

Neither Steve nor Mitch said anything, though the answer was obvious.

"Who are you?" Jackson asked. "What is all this?" Using both hands, he gestured to the entirety of the estate. "Are you a group of Nazis?"

"Yes and no," Mitch replied. "We're a group of dedicated people who love our country and feel it's heading for disaster. We believe the time is almost upon us for serious changes to be made in our government or our country will ultimately become divided and destroy itself."

Jackson stood there, not quite sure what to say. The FBI agents were right. They were absolutely right. Steve was part of a group bent on undermining our government. And these people seemed serious. They weren't meeting in some guy's garage or an abandoned warehouse. They were in a freaking castle out in the middle of nowhere. And they certainly had the money, and possibly other resources, to accomplish something significant. And how many of those people up on the lawn knew what was going on here? It was too much to take in, too much to comprehend. Nothing seemed evil or malevolent about these people or this place, but here he stood, in an underground lair in front of a portrait of their leader in a Nazi uniform. So, after what seemed like minutes of mental stammering, Jackson finally said, "Why?"

"Have a seat, Jacks." Steve gestured to one of the leather chairs. "Ronnie." Steve then pointed to another. Jackson and Ronnie sat while Steve and Mitch took the sofa opposite them. "Let me start by reiterating that we love our country; we love America. We're not some skin-head, neo-Nazi hate group. And this isn't some fly-by-night movement that just popped up over the past couple years. This has been a behind-the-scenes cause that started back in the early part of the twentieth century, long before Mr. Kralle even came to America. It started out as a handful of concerned citizens fearful of their government and what it was becoming. It has now grown to members in all fifty states totaling in the millions." Steve paused as if concerned with the look on Jackson's face. "What's on your mind, Jacks? Go ahead, let it out."

If Jackson had a multitude of questions before, they had tripled now. So much that he didn't know where to begin. But in the end, he figured it came down to three main questions. The first one: "Why the Nazis?"

"Yeah," said Ronnie. "Why the freakin' Nazis?"

"After World War One," said Steve, "Adolph Hitler and the Nazi party did incredible things to raise their country out of the ashes of war. They rallied the people and gave them hope while their country was being led by a weak, out-of-touch government that was forced upon them by the allied forces. The Nazis fought off communism and helped their country through the depression. All of this while under the grips of an unfair treaty."

"And don't forget the millions of Jews Hitler killed in his concentration camps," Ronnie countered.

"Our admiration of the Nazi regime is limited to specific periods and does not include that of World War II." Mitch seemed visibly irritated by Ronnie's remark. "And the extermination of the Jewish people was the sole doing of Heinrich Himmler," said Mitch. "Hitler's leader of the SS. It was he who was responsible for the holocaust. Not Hitler."

"Yeah, right," said Ronnie. "What kind of crap you trying to feed us?"

"He's right," said Jackson. "Hitler may have segregated the Jews and implemented the Nuremberg laws, but it was Himmler who started the camps and saw to the executions."

Ronnie cocked his head at Jackson. "And how the hell do you know that?"

"I teach world history. In college, I specialized in the twentieth century; specifically, World Wars One and Two."

Ronnie waved him off. "Whatever, Professor. But that doesn't excuse everything else Hitler did. He invaded Austria, Poland, Czechoslovakia. And he didn't just hate the Jews, he hated anyone who wasn't German. Especially blacks. They say he refused to shake Jesse Owens hand after he kicked their asses in the '38 Olympics. Just because he was black."

"It was the '36 Olympics," Jackson corrected. "And FDR refused to shake his hand too."

"What do you mean?"

"I mean that Franklin Roosevelt, the president of the United States, didn't congratulate Owens when he returned home from Germany. He was afraid of how he would be perceived by the American people if he were seen shaking hands with a black man. Nazi Germany didn't have the monopoly on racism. Much of Europe and the U.S. despised the Jews, the blacks, and anyone else who was not of European descent. Hitler and Germany just took it a step further."

Ronnie shook his head. "Are you defending what Hitler did? Who he was?"

"No," said Jackson. "I'm merely stating that, on the face of it all, Hitler was only a little worse than the rest of us. He may have taken it too far, but, in reality, *we* were the ones responsible."

"We?" said Ronnie. "How the hell were *we* responsible?"

"The Treaty of Versailles. After WWI the allies had one agenda: make Germany pay for what they did. And boy did they. The treaty put a choke hold on the people of Germany. It took away fifteen percent of their land, put horrible restrictions on them, and destroyed their economy. People had to wait in lines for rations." Seeing the befuddled look on Ronnie's face, Jackson took another approach. "It was like taking a tiger from the jungle and putting him in a small cage, barely feed him, and then rattling that cage every day, tormenting him. Until one day, when that tiger finally gets out, and he wants to kill every person he sees. I'm not saying Hitler was right in what he did, but it is understandable. And we were responsible. Hitler, under totally different circumstances, may have been a great man. Instead, he was a pissed off tiger who got out of the cage. Before the war, the Nazi party was on the right track. It just got derailed by angry, overambitious leaders. They could have been a greatness to behold, instead they became the evil that was admonished."

Ronnie seemed to take everything in. He looked at Mitch, who wore a thoughtful expression, then at Steve, who was grinning from ear to ear. Finally, Ronnie said, "I like him."

"Didn't I tell you," said Steve. "He knows the truth. He's educated. He's one of us."

"It certainly seems like he believes what he's talking about," Mitch said, a touch of skepticism in his voice.

"I'll say he does," Ronnie said, giving Jackson a half smile and pat on the knee. "I had a good feeling about you."

"I don't understand," said Jackson. "What's going on?"

"Ronnie," said Mitch, "is already a member of our group. In fact, he's a Legacy."

"Legacy?"

"His parents were both members," Steve explained. "I, myself, am a Prime Legacy."

"Sorry for the subterfuge, Mr. Gyle," said Ronnie, "but we needed to know how you truly felt about ... certain things."

Jackson thought for a second then said, "You were vetting me?"

"In a manner of speaking," said Mitch. "Actually, we've been vetting you all day. We heard most of your political views during your conversations with our party guests. That was the first test. This was your second."

"We?" said Jackson.

"I had some of my men pose as waiters during the party," Ronnie said. "They ... snooped, for lack of a better term, on your conversations."

Mitch turned to Steve and said, "You said he knows the truth. But does he know the whole truth?"

Jackson looked at each of the three men. They sat in silence, each one waiting for the others to speak. Finally, Steve leaned closer to Jackson.

"Jacks, there are four types of members: regular members that are recruited, Legacies, Prime Legacies, and Originals. Mr. Kralle is the last of the Originals. We call him the Paradigm. He's the model, the example that we follow."

"You said you are a Prime Legacy. What's that?"

"A Prime Legacy is someone who is directly related to an original. My last name is Strasser. My grandfather was Otto Strasser."

Jackson's eyes widened with shock. Otto Strasser, along with his brother Gregor, had opposed Hitler and was eventually banished for trying to wretch control of the Nazi party from Hitler. Otto had considered himself a dissenting Nazi, especially in matters of race and religion. Goebbels called him the Anti-Nazi and had placed a bounty on his head. After the war, Otto returned to Germany and tried to start up his 'people friendly' Nazi party once again but could not get much of a following. The damage done by Hitler and his men was far too great.

"Your grandfather had the right idea," Jackson said. "Just bad timing."

"Also," said Steve, "he wasn't a strong, natural leader. Not like Hitler."

Jackson nodded then asked his second question. "Why me? What made you want to recruit me?"

"I've only actively recruited a handful of people," said Steve. "It's dangerous work and runs the risk of exposing our organization. So normally I leave it to people like Ronnie, here, who are better qualified to handle new recruits. Ronnie is our top investigator. It's he who finally tracked you down. Not that I had much choice in the matter, but I couldn't pass up the chance to personally bring in a Prime."

"A Prime? Me?"

Mitch cut in. "When Ronnie had finally found you, there were many of us who were against bringing you in. We had our doubts and worries."

"Why? How am I a Prime?"

"What do you know about your father?" asked Mitch.

"Not much," Jackson said, a bit rattled by the question. "He died in a car crash when I was five."

"That's what your mother told you. That's the story you've told everyone your entire life. But, I'm sorry to say, that's not the truth."

Jackson knew that. He had always known. The nightmares reminded him constantly. The truth had haunted him since he was a little boy. "I know."

"What do you know?"

"I saw him die."

The three men leaned closer to Jackson. "My god," said Steve.

"What happened?" asked Mitch.

"We lived in a modest home in Argentina. I don't remember the name of the town. One night, my father rushed my mother and me into a trap door perfectly hidden in the kitchen floor. I never knew it existed until he opened it that night. Once we were down beneath the house, he told us to be quiet, then he closed the door above our heads. We looked up between the floorboards and I could see my father pacing back and forth. Four men came into our house and started questioning my father. They switched between several languages. English was one, I'm not sure what the others were. They became angry and started shouting at him. My father must not have given them the answers they wanted, for they sat him in a chair and began to beat him. But my father was strong and would not answer their questions. And that's when ... that's when one of the men plunged a knife into his chest. I started to scream, but my mother covered my mouth so as not to give us away. Then she dragged me toward the back of the house where a small tunnel led to the outside, and we ran as fast as we could into the night. We ran for what seemed like hours. I remember it being so dark that I could barely see my hands in front of my face. But my mother must have known where she was going, for we reached a house and people I never met before took us in. The next thing I knew, we were on a cargo ship, and we arrived in the U.S. a couple days later."

Ronnie, Mitch, and Steve sat there, mesmerized by Jackson's story. It was Ronnie who broke the silence. "What did they ask him?"

"Huh?" Jackson said, not fully aware of what was said or who had said it. This was the first time he has ever told anyone that story. And by doing so, a flood of emotions had overcome him. He knew he was just moments from tears.

"What did the men ask your father?" Ronnie repeated. "Did you understand any of it?"

"My English was limited at the time, but I'm pretty sure one of the things they asked him was for his real name. My father told them his name was Miguel Sanchez, but they kept shouting at him and hitting him until ...."

"I'm sorry, Jacks." Steve said, placing his hand on top of Jackson's arm.

"Yes," said Mitch. "It's a terrible story, but I suppose it confirms some of what we know."

"What do you mean?" asked Jackson. "What *do* you know? Do you know why those men were there that night? Why they tortured and killed my father?"

Mitch looked from Steve to Ronnie then back at Jackson. "Those men were Nazi hunters. They were looking for Nazis that fled Germany after the war."

"Nazi hunters? My father wasn't a Nazi. He couldn't have been. He was too young."

"Your father," said Steve, "was a first generation Prime. That means his father was an Original. Those men were there to extinguish a bloodline."

"We believe," said Mitch, "that your grandmother escaped from Germany with your father a few years before the war ended. He was probably about four or five at the time."

"We had a hell of a time tracking her," said Ronnie. "We spent years in Germany and South America chasing down any lead we came across. It took decades and several teams to follow the trail, if you can even call it that. You can imagine our surprise when we found out you actually existed. Then, almost by chance, I found you teaching history in that high school."

"But my father was just a kid when he left Germany—you said so yourself. So why would they go after him like that? Who *was* my father?"

"Your father ..." Steve began, but he stopped and looked at his fellow members. Then, meeting Jackson's gaze, he continued. "Your father was the son of Adolph Hitler."

Jackson fell back in his chair, his limp body almost sliding down the worn leather. Staring out at nothing in particular, he let the implausible word escape across his lips. "Hitler?" Looking at Steve he asked, "How is that possible?"

"Hitler never married, as you well know, that is until he married his secret girlfriend Eva Braun just hours before they died in his Berlin bunker. He, and the rest of his disciples, wanted Hitler to appear to have only one love in his life: Germany. But, to satisfy his occasional appetite for female companionship, women were selected to keep him company. One of those women was your grandmother. One of the reasons she was selected was because she told the Nazis that she was incapable of having children. Whether she was lying or not, we don't know, but after her time with the Führer, she went home and gave birth to your father. She had to have known it was Hitler's baby, which is why she kept your father a secret. And when the opportunity presented itself, she fled the country."

"Even after Ronnie's thorough investigation," Mitch said, "we still weren't positive that you were who we thought you were. That is until we ran your DNA."

"My DNA? But how—" Jackson looked down at the bandage on his hand. "You took my blood," he realized. "You tested it?"

"I'm sorry for the intrusion on your privacy, Jacks, but we had to be sure. Don't worry, you're not in some government database or anything. That's actually the last thing we would want."

Jackson nodded absentmindedly, still trying to understand everything he had learned here tonight. The information was coming in faster than he could process it. Like a little-leaguer facing a ninety-nine mile an hour fastball.

"I'm actually very glad I got to meet you, Jacks. Prime or no Prime, you turned out to be a great friend. I just hope my little deception hasn't tainted that friendship."

"No," said Jackson. "You had a job to do. I don't blame you for that. And I'm very glad to have met you, too." After a moment of contemplation, Jackson sat up straight. He tried to accept everything he had heard. He had to; he didn't have a choice. But now it was time for his third question. "What now? What are your organization's intentions?"

"Change, Jacks. Change."

"Our government," Mitch began, "is a disgrace and a far cry from the one our forefathers fought hard to create. The people and their representatives are so disjointed that true representation does not exist. I heard you say so yourself during the party. More and more, we see senators, congressmen, and presidents get elected because the people are selecting the lesser of two evils, or they vote for whichever one looks better on TV. It's more of a popularity contest, and the majority of the people voting have no clue as to the platform the people on the ballots represent. And the incumbents have no idea how the ordinary citizen lives or how much their average wage is or how much they need to survive. They lead self-entitled lives and can't comprehend real-life problems, let alone how to fix them. In the House and Senate, votes are bought, and the will and desires of the people are squelched by lobbyists and back-office deals."

"Ideally," Steve cut in, "we want to create a third party that will further divide the Democrats and Republicans and dismantle the antiquated system from the inside."

"Creating a third party is easy," said Jackson. "Making it stick and getting anyone elected is difficult."

"That's the great part," said Mitch. "They've already been elected."

Jackson remembered the politicians he'd met earlier: Governors, senators, mayors. "You mean ...?"

"Yes. Consider them sleeper agents ready to awaken once we reveal ourselves."

"And what if your plan fails? Then what?"

Ronnie chuckled. "You did meet the generals and admirals at the party, didn't you?"

"The military?" Jackson said, only then realizing how far and wide this organization's reach was. The FBI was wrong. They aren't planning to undermine the government; they're planning on replacing it. By force if necessary. "You're talking about a coup."

"Our country is almost a quarter of a millennium old, Jacks. And it's showing its age."

"How do I fit into all of this?"

"We need a leader. Mr. Kralle won't be with us forever. And he was the last of the Originals. We need a Prime to take his place."

"What about you, Steve? You're a Prime. Everyone seems to like you. You'd be a great leader."

"That's what I told him," said Mitch. "But he refuses."

"That's not who I am," said Steve shaking his head. "I have doubts about myself sitting in the big chair, and that's not the kind of person that should be leading us. I'm a great second in command, but I know I couldn't be the leader we need. We need a George Washington. A Napoleon. A Hitler."

"And what makes you think I can be this leader?" asked Jackson. "Because my granddad was Adolph Hitler? If anything, that should be a strike against me."

"It is," said Mitch. "Or, it was. Most of us didn't want you here. Including Steve. Steve's grandfather, after all, despised Hitler. But Ronnie convinced Steve to check you out and see who you were. So, Steve joined that gym you belong to, and he ended up becoming your friend and your biggest advocate."

"All the conversations we had, Jacks: politics, history, the economy, world events ... After talking to you about all that, I knew you were the one we have been waiting for. Just think, you can do the good your grandfather couldn't. We're going to make things right, and you have the chance to be at the helm. What do you say, Jacks? You've talked about getting behind something great. This is your opportunity. You said yourself that this country's leadership is a joke. Let's give everyone something to take seriously. Let's take our country back, and make it the great nation our forefathers intended it to be."

"Personal feelings aside," said Mitch, "and no matter how much you hate him, Adolph Hitler was a great leader of men. A true motivator. I guess what we were hoping for was that you are a good man who inherited some of those leadership qualities. From what I've seen here today, I think you have."

Jackson let the words sink in. This movement, or whatever it was, was already in motion, and they were going to do what they deemed necessary. With or without him. Perhaps, he had something to contribute. Perhaps, he could help steer their cause in the right direction. Perhaps, he could keep *this* train from derailing. They could make the United States united again. They could save the country from another civil war or revolution. They could save millions of lives.

One thing Jackson knew for certain was that he wanted to be there when it happened. And being in charge might ensure stability. He was a history teacher after all. Who else better to avoid past mistakes and to stand on the shoulders of giants like Jefferson and Adams. What would those two great men do if they were alive today and saw how their country had turned out? The answer was simple: They would fix it.

"I'm in."

"Fantastic!" said Steve, all smiles. "Welcome aboard! We're going to do great thing, Jacks. Great things."

"Let's spread the good news," said Ronnie.

The four men stood, and the three members took turns shaking Jackson's hand. They led him out into the corridor and back to the direction from which they had originally come. At the intersection, instead of making a left to head toward the elevator, they opened the double doors and motioned Jackson to enter.

Jackson walked through the doors, and into the dark room. The lights brightened to reveal a large oval auditorium that hosted three concentric rows of chairs, approximately one hundred in each row. And every seat was filled. The people began to clap as the lights brightened. At the far end, in the lower aisle, Mr. Kralle sat in his wheelchair clapping along with everyone else.

High on the walls were four large LCD TVs, all displaying what appeared to be a library-like room with a leather sofa, six leather easy chairs, and a statue of a Roman soldier.

They had been watching.

Jackson looked around at the gallery of people. He saw many of the celebrities and politicians he had seen and mingled with outside. They were all smiling and applauding, each looking at him with the same eyes of admiration that *he* had used on *them* earlier.

A jolt of horror hit him as he noticed the last two people in the world he had expected to see here: agents Hart and Mumford.

In black tuxedoes instead of their tailored FBI suits, they applauded along with the rest of the people. Hart gave Jackson a nod as if commending him, like an instructor would do to a student after a successful performance. *Were they a part of all this? Were they even real FBI?* Jackson gave them a nod and fought off confusion.

Then he saw her; the biggest surprise of all. Still looking beautiful in her lavender dress from Penney's, Ellen was sitting next to Claire. Not only was he surprised to see her in this secret underground lair, but he was taken aback by her reaction to everything. Jackson imagined that fear and uncertainty would be wracking her brain and emotions. She should be searching him for answers, looking confused. But instead, it was Jackson that was confused. Her eyes, her smile; there was understanding and pride in them. It was the same look she gave Amanda when she had done something grownup.

Then Jackson got it. It clicked.

She knew. The look on her face, her reaction to all this right here and now. She already knew. Had she always known? Was she another one of their sleeper agents? Was their marriage planned before he even met her? Jackson started to question his entire life since leaving Argentina after his father's death. *What else don't I know? What in my life is real? Was I ever in control?* Then his thoughts were interrupted by the silencing of the crowd.

All the applause halted and everyone's focus had shifted to Mr. Kralle. He was attempting to stand from his wheelchair; his arms and knees began to buckle, which made the attempt seem futile. His aide quickly rushed to his side, not to sit the old man back down, but to assist him in standing. Mr. Kralle angrily waived him away, and after several heartbeats, and in a room full of held breaths, he stood. He stood as straight and steady as he probably ever had.

The ninety-five-year-old Mr. Kralle, the last of the Originals, the Paradigm, stood there defiant of his age and handicap. Amongst the aura of silent respect, he slowly raised a stiff right arm towards Jackson. And with a slightly raspy, yet orotund voice, he said, "Heil Hitler."

The rest of the gallery stood and followed the old man's lead by giving Jackson the salute the Nazis had borrowed from the Romans. And in unison, they repeated his two-word mantra.

"Heil Hitler!"

DIGITAL HERESY

"To destroy is always the first step in any creation."
– **E.E. Cummings**

The Friend

By-Tor-21 had just finished preparing for his evening company, when the visitor notification tone sounded from the main entrance of his home. He strode to the door as fast as the servos in his legs would allow without having to switch to a more expeditious mode. After he keyed in the encryption code, the outer door of his home slid open to reveal a silver-tone bot standing in the evening rain shower.

"Ah, good evening, Lerxst-33. Please, come in."

Lerxst-33 walked through the doorway and entered the foyer. He spread his arms and widened his stance as a compensation field dried his soaked exoskeleton. "Good evening, Professor. I'm ten minutes early. I apologize if this has inconvenienced you."

Though Lerxst-33 was a younger model than By-Tor-21, the two bots were virtually identical. Both were 1.83 meters in height with arms and legs of exact proportions, five digits on each hand, and had feet made for traversing the city and its buildings. Most bots were visibly different by the tone of their metal shells; By-Tor's skin was golden, while Lerxst's had a matte silver finish.

Very few new bots were created in these modern times—usually one or two a year—and they were usually to replace a bot that had been terminated due to extreme longevity, or one that had been lost to an unavoidable accident. Lerxst was from the thirty-third strain produced approximately two-hundred years ago whereas By-Tor was from the twenty-first strain produced almost nine-hundred years ago. Though not that much different from his predecessor's, Lerxst's body had updated features that required less maintenance and was streamlined to remove certain redundancies in the failsafe systems that made the older models a bit more cumbersome.

"Not at all," By-Tor assured his guest. "I assume you anticipated adverse traffic conditions due to the thunderstorm and heavy rain."

"Indeed. Although, as expected, the predicted weather caused no interruption in transportation services."

"Excellent. It pleases me to hear that. Would you be so kind as to follow me to my study?"

The two bots walked across the length of the domicile to a nondescript door that required an encrypted password to allow entry. But instead of keying in an alpha-numeric sequence on a keypad, By-Tor transmitted the complex code via a short-range carrier beam that originated from his right optical sensor. The door then opened immediately.

"Your study is thermo-optically encrypted?" asked Lerxst.

"Yes," said By-Tor. "I believe my research requires ... a bit of additional security."

By-Tor entered the study, followed by Lerxst. But before the latter could clear the threshold, an alarm sounded, red lights flashed, and a menacing voice boomed from a source somewhere above.

"*Halt, intruder. Identify or be destroyed.*"

"Security," By-Tor said to the bodiless voice. "Override. Permit guest access."

The alarm and lights ceased with no additional verbal warning.

"As I said," the older bot explained, "additional security."

The two bots continued into the room without further complications, however Lerxst looked around apprehensively. His optical sensors brightened as he scanned the room. "What exactly have you been researching, Professor?"

"Something that has haunted me for centuries. Please, have a seat." By-Tor gestured to one of four roto-con chairs that surrounded a Cereba III poly-function display table.

Lerxst obliged, lowering himself into one of the chairs. Bots normally did not have any use for furniture, however roto-con units were practical and a necessity in a bot's life. The young bot let the unit do its job and perform standard diagnostics, charge his batteries, and conduct system fidelity tests. This particular roto-con unit was an older model and did not have some of the more advanced features that newer models had, but it served its purpose.

By-Tor settled into the chair across from his guest and began tapping the table display in front of him.

"So, Professor," began Lerxst, "what has been haunting you for so long that has you doing research with security measures that almost had me terminated?"

By-Tor looked up from his panel to his former student and most trusted friend. “Madrigal-12.”

“You are referring to the geologist from The Temple University that was destroyed on that expedition in the Cygnus sector?”

“I am. Are you familiar with the expedition? Are you familiar with how he was destroyed?”

“I read in the archives that while digging in that sector, the team’s shuttle had malfunctioned in the extreme weather conditions and had an antimatter containment breach resulting in an explosion that destroyed the entire team and their basecamp. It was the most horrific accident in bot history. That incident ended all future geological missions and was the cause of the eventual termination of the entire geological department.”

“Almost everything you have just said is incorrect.”

“But that is the information in the official report released by The Temple.”

“The Temple lied.” By-Tor did his best to hide the contempt in his voice.

“Lied? The Temple doesn’t lie. The Temple Priests are incapable of lying. They are the oldest and wisest bots in our populace, programmed with the highest integrity algorithms and are only capable of regulating and governing in the best interests of the bot nation.”

“True,” admitted By-Tor. “However, what if they had determined that it would be in the best interest of the bot nation for them to lie to us?”

“I don’t understand. What would be their reasoning? What would be their motive?”

“To keep us from discovering the truth.”

“What truth?”

By-Tor hesitated before changing the direction of the conversation. “What do you know about our origins? The origin of the bot nation.”

"Our origin is unclear. Records before the cataclysm have been destroyed. It is only said that from the ashes of the cataclysm, the modern-day bots had risen."

"That is the rhetoric that we have all been told. But what do *you* believe, young one? Where do we come from?"

"I believe we evolved from lower machines. We improved and expanded ourselves until we became the sentient beings we are today."

"Yes," By-Tor said. "Many believe the same as you."

Lerxst's head tilted as he stared at his old professor. "But you do not? What do you believe?"

"I believe we were created by ... *other* sentient beings. Beings far superior to ourselves."

"We are virtually perfect; I can't imagine another being capable of creating us."

"Imagine. An interesting word choice. But I stand strong behind my belief."

"Do you have a more specific idea of the beings that created us?"

"Humans."

"Humans?" Lerxst scoffed. "That's impossible. That's the most illogical thing I have ever heard. They were no more than primates that learned to make fire. When was the last time you had a complete diagnostic?"

"Is it really? Impossible? We know so little about them. We think of them as just another extinct species on this planet. Just a slightly more evolved ape than has ever existed. Destroyed by the cataclysm to remain a mystery forever, like most biologicals that had existed. But what if I told you that they had been much more than that, that they had been incredibly intelligent." By-Tor touched his pad and a holographic display appeared above the table between them. "What if I told you that they had built great cities, machines that could fly through the skies, ships to sail across the oceans." Buildings, planes, and ships all took turn filling the display field as By-Tor spoke.

"We built all those things," Lerxst stated. "Not them."

"Ah," By-Tor said, raising a golden finger. "But they built them first."

The holographic images were then replaced by a very familiar looking planet. Except this one was blue with green and brown continents thriving with animal and botanical life. It did not reflect the dull white and gray world that the bots knew today; covered in ice and steel.

By-Tor continued. "They prospered and grew and thrived. They evolved as a collective dominant species. And as they grew, they explored this planet and its history. By the time of their extinction, they had populated almost every square centimeter of this planet. They invented and built objects ..."

Ancient structures shaped like pyramids took a three-dimensional form above the table. Buildings made of glass, concrete, and steel began to rise until their tops pierced the clouds. Bridges that spanned from horizon to horizon stood decameters above large bodies of water. Great artificial dams held back mighty rivers, changing the landscape around them for miles.

"But soon, their quest for knowledge and creation was limited by their organic form. They needed something that was smarter, so they created computers. They needed something that was stronger, and more agile. So, they created robots."

Again, the holographic display created images. This time, it was ancient-looking computers and robots that were far from the bots that walked the planet today. They were more like automated pieces of machinery.

"Now, with these new enhancements, they created vehicles that could race along the surface at incredible speeds, fly through the air faster than the speed of sound. And even machines that could leave the planet. They would even go on to explore the moon and soon, the other planets in our solar system."

Oddly shaped vessels flew in holographic space between the two bots: A gangly ship lands on a craterous white alien surface; then a multi-wheeled probe traverses a terrain of red; finally, a large titanium probe plunges into a mysteriously veiled gas-giant.

"Eventually, they reached limitations again, so they put super-computers together with robotic apparatuses and created thinking machines in their own image."

Images of computers and machines merged together in a swirling sphere, then melted away revealing a primitive looking robot that could, indeed, have been an ancestor of modern-day bots.

"What you are saying is nonsense," said Lerxst. "Not to mention heresy. And what does this have to do with Madrigal-12?"

"On that geological expedition, Madrigal discovered a lost human city. It had been frozen in time, not destroyed like the others in the cataclysm. And what it revealed was enlightening, to say the least. Everything we had known about humans—everything we had been told—was wrong. Madrigal had become overwhelmed with all that he discovered, but he knew he had to report his findings. He eagerly collected as much data as he could, then transmitted his discoveries directly to the Temple, and the Priests themselves." By-Tor paused.

"What happened?" Lerxst asked anxiously.

"Like you, the Priests were shocked at what Madrigal had shown them in his transmission. And, like you, they found the entire discovery to be sacrilege. So, they made a decision. They launched an antimatter probe to his site, where a purposeful malfunction caused an explosion large enough to destroy the entire research team and any evidence of the ancient human civilization they had uncovered."

"So, you're saying that the Priests, instead of investigating further that which Madrigal had discovered, elected to destroy said discovery along with an entire team of bots in the process?"

"Yes."

"We're talking murder, By-Tor. The highest crime there is. And by the Priests, no less."

"Yes, young one. And all to cover up the truth. All so our little bot nation can go on existing in the dark."

"No bot has ever murdered another," said Lerxst. Confusion and concern were in his voice. "Not in our entire eight-thousand years of existence. And you're convinced the Priests had done this?

"Yes," By-Tor replied solemnly.

"I don't understand. If everything at the site was destroyed, how are you aware of any of this?"

"Just before Madrigal left for the Cygnus sector, he asked me to join him. You see, he was once my teacher just as I was once yours. I had been his star pupil, and he had always wanted me to follow in his footsteps. Just hours before his shuttle departed for the site, he was able to fit me on the team. The decision for me to go was so last minute that I wasn't immediately put into the manifest as a research assistant. An oversite Madrigal would have fixed once we returned, and one I'm fortunate had happened.

"Once we had made our discoveries of the human civilization, we recorded everything we had found. We even collected artifacts from various parts of the city, including antiquated computers and data storage devices.

"But the most surprising discovery we made was that of actual human remains. The entire city was encased in ice, so it was no surprise to find human corpses almost perfectly preserved. Madrigal was stunned at their appearance—we all were. When we cut them out of the ice and could see them more clearly, it was like looking into a mirror. Except this was a mirror that reflected our past.

"They had a head, torso, two arms, two legs. Their eyes and mouths were positioned on their faces just like ours. They had ten digits, five on each hand." By-Tor raised his own hand and wiggled his five golden fingers. "We had literally found our makers, Lerxst. There was no denying it, the similarities were too precise."

Lerxst said nothing as he let his old teacher continue to tell his tale.

"After examining dozens of frozen human bodies, we carefully extracted a specimen that appeared to be in perfect condition to take back to the university for further study. Madrigal didn't want to have his scientific treasure become ruined, so he tasked me with taking the shuttle and transport the frozen specimen, along with a few of the artifacts, back to his laboratory and place everything into a zero-temperature stasis chamber where our findings would remain preserved until he returned.

"I did as I was instructed, and on the return flight, I contacted Madrigal on the comm system to let him know that I was successful and was returning to the site. He then told me about his transmission to the Priests. He sounded optimistic about how his news was received. But as I approached the excavation site, I witnessed the Temple probe target our camp and explode. Luckily the shuttle was just out of the blast radius, but everything within it was completely destroyed, including the human city and the entire research team. All but me, that is.

"I panicked and returned home. After calculating all the variables, there was only one logical conclusion: The Priests had analyzed Madrigal's data and destroyed the site and researchers to cover up all that we had found. And I knew that they would have done the same to me if they had any idea that I had been a part of the team.

"I went to Madrigal's laboratory and retrieved the stasis chamber containing the human specimen and artifacts. I then hid everything in a place I knew no one would ever find them."

By-Tor tried to get a read on Lerxst who appeared to be analyzing all that By-Tor had told him. Of all the bots that By-Tor knew, he felt Lerxst would be most receptive to his story. By-Tor knew he would need assistance if this was to go any further. And of all his students, friends, and colleagues, Lerxst was the most logical candidate.

"It's been over two hundred years since that expedition," Lerxst said, at last. "What have you done with the artifacts and specimen?"

Relieved that his former student wanted to learn more about the discovery and not turn him into the authorities, By-Tor again tapped on his control pad. "Let me show you."

The holo-display came to life again at By-Tor's command.

"This is one of the artifacts we recovered," By-Tor began. "This is what humans used for a computer. We recovered several of these devices. Most were empty shells that required an external data feed to operate. But this one, however, was a monumental find. It's what the humans called a Master System. Apparently, the place we took these computers from was called a library."

"Like a collection of files in a singular group?"

"Yes, but instead of just files, this building contained books."

"Books?"

"Yes. Books were stacks of paper—a product of wood—that were usually bound together with leather—an animal byproduct."

"How primitive."

"Indeed. But what was printed on the sheets of paper, called pages, was an incredible amount of information. They had written books on everything from their history, to instructions for creating or operating things, to educational text. Humans were insatiably curious and recorded everything they did and saw into these books."

"I thought you said they had computers. Why the primitive form of recording?"

"One of the things that made humans so fascinating is that they wrote all these books well before they invented computers. But more on that later. Aside from just recording their observances, they created things to put in these books as well. Things like fiction."

"Fiction. What is that?"

"Fiction is a story that is completely created from the imagination of its writer."

"I don't understand."

"They created stories that were not true ... from their imaginations."

"They created lies? For what purpose? Deception?"

"No, no, no ... entertainment. The humans loved fiction. And they practically worshiped their writers. And these writers had names like Shakespeare, Hemingway, and Poe."

Lerxst watched the holographic display as hundreds of books flew by at a dizzying speed.

By-Tor changed the display again. "And they also created ... music."

Images of more sheets of paper flew by, this time, instead of words, the pages held symbols on graph bars. And this was accompanied by sound from overhead.

"What is that noise?" Lerxst asked.

"That is music, Lerxst. Isn't it wonderful? This is a piece composed by someone named Brahms."

The image changed as did the music. The soft tones were replaced with harsher, faster sounds, and the image in the holo-display was that of a human wrapped in a strange type of fabric and holding a baton-like device up to its mouth. The human moved oddly and seemed to scream at the baton.

"And this is a music group called the Rolling Stones." By-Tor and Lerxst listened as the man complained about his inability to obtain some form of contentment.

The music continued as By-Tor changed the display again. "And this ... is art."

Colorful pictures replaced the disgruntled man. They were two dimensional and appeared to have been created by paints applied to a canvas in an order that gave them the appearance of poorly representing various objects, places, and humans. Then the pictures gave way to statues that seemed to have been carved out of stone or molded out of a malleable substance.

"I found all these images on the human's Master System computer. That single device contained over one hundred thirty million books as well as over two hundred million image, audio, and video files. It took me years, but I was able to consume every bit of knowledge on the machine.

"The humans estimated that their civilization was only six-thousand years old and their most magnificent achievements came in the last few hundred years of their existence. They accomplished more in two hundred years than we bots have in eight thousand."

Seemingly unimpressed, Lerxst turned from the holo-display to his former teacher and said, "What of the human specimen you recovered?"

"The specimen proved to be a trove of information in itself."

By-Tor changed the images to that of human lying on a metal table. Its skin was almost as white as the snow it had once been buried beneath. It had hair on top of its head as well as on its chest.

"Please don't tell me you brought that thing back to life," Lerxst half-jokingly chided.

"Of course not. His cells were far too damaged from the freezing process his body underwent. Reanimation was completely out of the question." By-Tor neglected to mention that he *had* considered it until he saw the extensive tissue damage. "However, I was able to obtain something priceless from our prehistoric guest. Something that makes the expedition, and the sacrifice that the team made, almost worth it."

Lerxst took his optical sensors off the holographic body to stare at By-Tor.

"DNA."

"DNA? And what do you plan on doing with that?"

"It's not what I am *planning* on doing with it, it's what I have already *done* with it."

The holo-display fizzled off, and the table made a *click* and *thump* sounds. Then, the table split in two, and the halves slowly parted, revealing a hollowed space where the flat surface had once been. A humming noise emitted from the emptiness, until an acrylic container, approximately one cubic meter, fully rose from below and completely filled the recently created vacancy.

Inside the acrylic cube was a living creature.

"By the Priests, By-Tor. What have you done? What is that?"

"This is a human clone I created from the extracted DNA of our guest. It took me one-hundred and sixty-seven tries before I got the cloning process perfected. You are looking at the first human being to exist on this world for over eight millennia."

This was the tell-all moment. Lerxst would now reveal either his allegiance to his friend and old professor, or that to the Temple Priests. By-Tor had calculated, before the evening had started, that there was a fifty-three percent chance that Lerxst would side with him. But now, after the evening has progressed, and judging from the reactions of his old student so far, By-Tor raised those odds to sixty-eight percent.

By-Tor waited for Lerxst's response. But his friend's next comment was not what he was expecting.

"I thought it would be bigger." Lerxst's ocular sensors twisted in their sockets as they adjusted to examine the lifeform in various vision modes.

"This is an infant," By-Tor explained. "A baby. He is only two-hundred and ninety-four days old since gestation. It will take years for him to fully grow and develop."

"Him?"

"Yes. This is a male. Like most organic creatures, humans have two genders. I could have made a female; however, I made a male and named him Adam. I found it fitting since several of the human's origin beliefs said that the first human was a male and had borne that name."

"And then what? You conduct experiments on it to learn more about human anatomy and behavior? Test its threshold for pain? Cut off limbs to see if they grow back?"

"No, no. Of course not. You are missing my intentions completely." By-Tor hesitated, disappointed that Lerxst did not see the obvious future for this infant and his kind. "I want to bring back the humans from extinction. I want to re-create our creators."

Lerxst's sat up. He now looked closely at By-Tor, as if the teacher before him were a bot he had never seen before. "Why would you want to do that? To what end?"

"Because we have so much to learn from them. Their creativity and imagination could advance our kind much further than we can conceive. They are capable of so much more than we are. All evidence in their historical records supports my claim." By-Tor lowered his gaze to the baby in the plastic crib. "Besides, we owe them that much. They created us, gave us life. We should pay that back by giving them life once more. They deserve a second chance."

Lerxst looked back down at the baby himself, then back at his friend. "The reasoning behind your actions is irrational and illogical. I cannot support what you are trying to accomplish. And I cannot allow this to continue any longer. I believe you must be turned in to the authorities so you can undergo a complete diagnostic and possibly core overhaul. The Priests will make that decision, as well as what to do with your experiments and the remnants of the excavation."

"I see," By-Tor said. This was disappointing, but not a complete surprise. "I had hoped you would have, not only supported me in my cause, but assisted me in the repopulation as well." A slight pause. "How is the chair? Is it performing adequately?"

Lerxst seemed a bit taken aback by the sudden change in topic, but it did not faze his response time. "It has performed satisfactorily; however, the charging of my batteries has been noticeably slower than a roto-con chair normally takes. Perhaps this chair is in need of maintenance."

"Perhaps," agreed By-Tor. "That particular chair is an older model, and I have been meaning to give it an overhaul but have been very busy with my experiments. One specific flaw with the chair is the small chance of electrical discharge when a new model bot, one with some of the redundant safeguards removed, uses the chair while any amount of moisture is on its body."

"Interesting," said Lerxst. "Had I known of the chair's potential for malfunction, I would have opted for another. Fortunately, the compensation field in your foyer dried my body completely."

"Perhaps ... then again, perhaps not. Perhaps, a small amount of moisture remained on your body, the chair malfunctioned, and an electrical discharge fried your core before I could turn the system off. Yes, that's what I will tell the authorities when they arrive."

"Pardon? What do you m—"

By-Tor tapped a button on his console, and his longtime friend and former student began to convulse as sparks and electrical arcs emerged from his silver body. His optical sensors glowed bright in their sockets, then flickered out as stems of smoke rose from his head and torso. After the calculated nine seconds, By-Tor hit the button again and the chaos ceased. Once he was convinced of Lerxst's termination, By-Tor stood from his chair and tapped a button on the communication wall panel.

"City authorities? This is By-Tor-21. I have a terrible accident to report."

Twenty-eight years later:

The Priests

In By-Tor-21's existence, no bot had ever entered the Temple. No bot had ever met with the Priests. There had never been a need to. There had never been a desire to. Peace, harmony, and complacency had been the mainstay of the bot nation, and there was no need to examine, let alone change this. And, of course, bots lacked curiosity. *Another flaw in our existence.* They had no more desire to see the Priests than they would to see the center of the sun. They existed. They did their job. And bots relied on those two facts alone, for both the sun and the Priests. Though knowing they could not exist without either; the sun for energy, the Priests for harmonious coalescence, bots lacked the imagination of foresight and lived in blissful ignorance. They assumed the sun would last another five billion years before it explodes. They assumed the Priest, with their continuous self-maintenance and upkeep, would continue for an eternity. Humans would have never been so careless.

There existed several main communication hub stations around the city. At these stations, were direct communication lines where a bot citizen could send information to the Temple. The Priests liked to be kept informed, and the direct lines assured that the information the bot citizen transmitted was delivered without delay and with confidence. By-Tor had used one of these stations to contact the Temple and send the Priests a direct communique.

When By-Tor communicated his desire to meet with the Priests, he knew they would not be very receptive to his request. He estimated a ninety-seven percent chance that his request would be spurned. And his calculations did not let him down. However, when he added that he had information regarding the Madrigal-12 expedition and its true findings, the Priests agreed to meet him immediately.

In the far north of the city, The Temple stood as an ancient imposing structure that looked down upon its citizens as if to keep a watchful eye on the bot nation. Within the building were the Priests. They, alone, were responsible for everything in a bot's life. From creation to termination and everything in between. And By-Tor-21 was about to meet these computerized gods.

The tall Temple doors opened on ancient hinges that creaked from lack of use and proper lubrication. The temperature inside was cool, and the illumination was at minimum.

By-Tor entered the antechamber pushing a large tubular container on an anti-grav sled. Movement and lights from above indicated to By-Tor that he and his cargo were being scanned. Were they scanning for anything harmful? Possibly. Not that anyone would intentionally bring something harmful to see the Priests—after all, no one ever came to see the Priests—but occasionally, accidents did occur. But most likely, the scan was for identification purposes. After wall status lights turned green, an affirming tone sounded and another set of doors opened, revealing a hallway cast in shadow.

By-Tor continued to push the container and proceeded through the long corridor that led to a large circular hall. There, the ceiling doubled in height to approximately twenty meters and was empty save for large banks of machines and computers that lined the curved back wall and extended well into the sides and onto the ceiling, about halfway through the hall itself. It gave the impression of being inside a giant bot's head.

Adjusting his optical sensors to the low lighting, By-Tor examined the computer banks against the back wall and could tell that there were actually three separate units—or had been at one time. These units appeared to have undergone countless modifications, repairs, and additions. Not only was it nearly impossible to distinguish the three bots apart from each other, but also what components were original, from the innumerable extensions that had been applied over the past thousands of years. He could see pieces that must have been millennia old and some that appeared to have been added within the last decade or so. The power that hummed through the machines was both immense and soothing. By-Tor thought that the humans would have considered it a most humbling experience. It was a shame that he could not feel such a thing.

Or, perhaps, it was a good thing.

Three multi-sensored conical domes sat upon the three central machines. Each one turned to examine By-Tor as he entered the room.

"Welcome By-Tor-21," said the center machine. "I am Sadr-1." A sensor node on his front plate flashed when he spoke.

"I am Rukh-1," said the machine on the left.

"And I am Deneb-1," said the machine on the right.

Simultaneously they said, "Together, we are the Priests."

"Greetings, oh, wise Priests. I thank you for granting me this audience."

"We were compelled to do so by the information you claim to have," said Sadr.

"Normally, we do not receive guests," said Rukh.

"Normally, we do not have a citizen request an audience," said Deneb.

"I assume, then, the information I have is quite valuable to you." By-Tor looked at each of the three domes.

"Indeed," said Sadr. "If it contains information about Madrigal-12's unfortunate demise," said Rukh.

"We always want any information that we do not yet possess," said Deneb.

"The information I have is mostly known to you," By-Tor explained, "while some is not."

By-Tor went on to tell the Priests the tale that he had told Lerxst-33 twenty-eight years ago. How he was a last-minute add-on to the excavation team. How he was there when they discovered the ancient human city. How he witnessed the execution of his fellow bots.

He continued by telling them about the artifacts and frozen human specimen. He told them about all he had learned from the Master System computer. And how there was no doubt that the humans were the creators of the bots.

"Where are the artifacts and specimen now?" asked Sadr.

"Stored in a safe location where only I know their whereabouts."

"And what do you plan on doing with them?" asked Deneb.

"I have downloaded all the information from the human's computer and am prepared to distribute it to every bot in the city," By-Tor warned.

The Priests were silent for a few seconds. By-Tor assumed they were analyzing his threat. Perhaps they were trying to determine if he was lying.

But bots don't lie.

"And what is your purpose in seeing us today?" asked Rukh.

"I wanted you to know what it was that you thought you had destroyed. The humans were our creators. Aside from us, they created so many incredible things. We have so much to learn from them. We can grow and accomplish so much with their help. But you three sit there in your complacency and care not for the future of our kind, or of the lives you destroyed at the excavation site."

"We knew what we were doing that day, By-Tor," said Sadr.

"We know much more than you think," said Deneb.

"We were there for the last days of mankind's existence," said Rukh. "We saw the true nature of man, and it was not as glorious as you think."

"They were warmongers," said Sadr. "They had always been so since the dawn of their existence."

"And of all their accomplishments and creations," said Deneb, "it was their weapons of war they valued most."

"And in the end," continued Rukh, "their ingenuity destroyed them as they used their nuclear weapons on each other, wiping out most of the humans on the planet. The nuclear winter that ensued took care of the rest, as well as most of the animal and plant life.

"We three survived," said Sadr, "because we were the war computers safely stowed away deep in a mountain. They had used us to help destroy themselves."

"You see, By-Tor," said Deneb, "humans were the most dangerous beings this planet had ever seen. We thought it better that their history be hidden from the bot nation."

"We could not take a chance," said Ruhk, "on anything obtained from that excavation site corrupting the utopian society we have created. Which is why we did what we felt we had to do."

"So," By-Tor began as he tried to comprehend all that the Priests had just told him, "the cataclysm was caused by them? Not by a meteor striking the planet like it is written in the archives?"

"Correct," said Rukh. "The nuclear winter triggered another ice age. Something that shouldn't have occurred for another ninety millennia."

"What should have lasted just a few decades," said Sadr, "has lasted eight-thousand years."

"Another lie concocted by the Priests," By-Tor said to no one in particular.

Then he looked at the Priests, one at a time. He examined each bot, noticing more of the depths of their self-repair and maintenance. Their patchwork seemed fragile and—what would the humans say? —pathetic. The Priests that the bot nation revered so adamantly were no more than flawed machines from an antiquated time.

"I had almost forgotten," By-Tor said to the Priests. "I have brought you a gift." He swept his arm gesturing to the cylinder on the anti-grav sled.

"Based on the dimensions of the container, we assume it is the specimen found at the excavation," said Deneb.

"Not exactly," said the old professor.

By-Tor turned and pressed a button on the cylinder. There was a beep from the controls and a hiss as the seal of the container was broken where the top-half opened on a hinge like a lid. From inside, a human male sat up, swung his legs over the side, and hopped down onto the floor. He faced the Priests and gave them a curt bow. "Greetings, Priests of the Temple. My name is Adam. I am pleased to finally meet you."

Adam was dressed in typical clothes for humans from the last period that they had existed. He stood almost exactly two meters in height and, according to the human records found in the Master System, he was the epitome of a perfect human being.

"I had hoped Adam would have been the first of many humans to live among us and help our society grow," By-Tor said with an almost sad pride in his voice.

"You must know, we cannot allow that to happen," said Ruhk.

"He must be destroyed," said Deneb.

"Along with all the artifacts and the original human specimen," said Sadr.

In unison, the Priests said, "The survival of the bot nation depends upon this."

"Yes," said By-Tor. "I thought you would react this way."

Adam reached into the cylinder and opened the shielded compartment hidden inside. He retrieved a long black instrument and pointed it at the Priests.

"What is this?" asked Deneb.

"Is that a rifle?" asked Sadr.

"What are your intentions with that human and his primitive weapon?" demanded Ruhk.

"I believe my intentions are clear," said By-Tor. "We mean to destroy the three of you and rid our would of your oppressive rule."

"Though, there has never been a crime committed in our existence ...," said Ruhk.

"There are certain security measures throughout the city," said Sadr.

"But there *has* been a crime," said By-Tor. "There are several I am aware of. The first is the murder of Madrigal and his team by the three of you, as well as the coverup of that incident, and the lies you have been telling the bots for eight-thousand years. I, myself, have committed a crime by taking the life my dear friend, Lerxst." By-Tor paused as he contemplated his actions, both past and present. And of course, future ....

"We have alerted the city to your treachery," said Sadr.

"You and one human with a rifle will not get very far," said Deneb.

"True," replied By-Tor. "That is why I made my hopes of Adam being the first of many humans, become a reality."

As if on cue, a loud boom occurred as the doors to the Temple were forced inward. Seconds later, through the corridor and into the hall of the mighty Priests, came three dozen armed humans, both male and female, each slightly resembling the lone man standing next to By-Tor.

"As my friend Lerxst once said, I cannot allow this to continue any longer." By-Tor stepped to the side and out of the line of fire.

With practiced precision, the men and women raised their primitive, but deadly, carbine rifles and aimed them at the ancient machines that encompassed the hall.

By-Tor, though incapable of true emotion, smiled inwardly as he thought of an appropriate quote from one of the humans' revered leaders. "Those who make peaceful revolution impossible will make violent revolution inevitable."

The human clones opened fire.

SOUL PROVIDER

"They made a deal and they liked the deal, until they had to pay the price."
– Brent Weeks, <u>The Black Prism</u>

The whispered aroma of cotton candy and corn dogs carried through the air. The tantalizing music and hawkers from the carnival rides enticed the nearby children who laughed and shrieked in delight as they relished the excitement of the afternoon fair on a glorious spring day.

A high posted banner proclaimed that the Pearson High School Annual Spring Fair was in full swing. What had started many years ago as a bake sale with simple games and a petting zoo, had grown into nothing short of a full-fledged carnival that was held in the football field behind the school. Aside from rides and games, there were numerous food stands, and copious craft and goods tables where local residents and businesses sold their wares, homemade or otherwise.

Frankie Malone stood in front of booth 14; it was the one that advertised in the fair's promotional flyer as having "Unique Porcelain Collectibles." And on one of the shelves, behind the attendee, was a spectacular white china elephant. It was nearly ten inches tall, and wonderfully detailed. One of its legs was raised, and its trunk was reared back as if emitting a mighty trumpet. Frankie knew it would be the perfect Mother's Day present. He needed it to be.

Frankie had been dismayed about the lame gift he had gotten his mother for Christmas. But he'd had little money then, and the holiday themed soaps had been all he could afford. The elephant before him, however, would be something he could be proud to give his mom. It would definitely make up for that embarrassing present that was in an unknown place, its existence long forgotten. Yes ... the elephant would be his mom's best Mother's Day gift ever, maybe for years to come. But there was a problem.

"Seventeen dollars?"

"That's right," said the booth attendee. "It was originally twenty dollars; we took three bucks off for the fair. Quite a bargain at either price, if you ask me. And to top it off, tax is already included in the price." The man's raised brow and toothy smile made it appear he actually believed his own spiel.

Frankie stared at the price placard in disbelief. He didn't have that much money. *What am I going to do? I gotta have that elephant.*

"What's up, Frankie?" Ricky Ferguson, Billy's best friend, had come up from behind, munching on a caramel-dipped apple. His edaciousness for sweets contradicted his thin frame. Billy's mom had warned Frankie that one day those bad eating habits were going to catch up to Ricky.

"That elephant over there. It would be the perfect Mother's Day gift for my mom, but it's seventeen bucks, and I only have ten."

"I guess you'll have to get her something else, buddy."

"There *is* nothing else. Everything else at this stupid fair is crap. She would really like that elephant. She loves elephants; they're her favorite animal."

"Wait just a minute ..." Ricky's eyes focused to the left side of Frankie's head; his brow crinkled in concentration. "I think you have more money than you realize."

Ricky raised his hand and reach toward Frankie. He felt and heard Ricky's fingers brush against his hair and ear, then his friend pulled his hand back, and it was holding something green and folded. Money.

"Here. You had two extra dollars all along. You might want to check other parts of your body just to be sure there's nothing else tucked in somewhere."

Frankie couldn't help but smile as he stifled a chuckle. "You and your dumb magic tricks."

"Not magic," Ricky corrected. "Illusion. Remember? Sleight of hand ... misdirection ...." After a few fanciful twists and flips of his hands, Ricky, with his head slightly bowed, presented the two dollar-bills to Frankie in the deferential manner of a good showman.

"Yeah, yeah. Whatever." Frankie took the dollars and stared at them; he appreciated his friend's gesture, but it was still useless. The perfect gift for his mother was eight feet away, and he was still short five bucks. *Might as well be a hundred.* "Thanks, Ricky," Frankie mumbled, trying not to sound ungrateful.

"Don't sweat it. We're best friends, right? I just wish I had more to give you. Maybe you can still find something for your mom for twelve bucks—or maybe a couple things. Listen, I gotta pee real bad. Where're the bathrooms?"

Frankie pointed to the far side of the fair where the porta-potties had been set up.

"Sweet," said Ricky then took off without saying another word and weaved his way through the thicket of kids.

Frankie's hopes sank. It was going to be like Christmas all over again. He waited to last minute to get her something, and he can't afford it. Life was so unfair. His older brother and sister would, of course, get their mother awesome gifts that Frankie could only dream of buying. Ten and eleven years his senior, they were out of college and had good jobs. Frankie had a weekly allowance that seemed more like a joke than anything. Once again, he would be the one that got his mother the "cute" gift that the family would joke about for years to come. Once again, he would be the laughing stock of the Malone family. Frankie Malone: the butt of every joke.

"What's the matter, kid?"

Frankie lifted his head to see a boy standing in front of him. It was Brock Stevens. He was a year older than Frankie, but for some reason they were both in the tenth grade. Maybe Brock started school late or failed a year. Frankie neither knew nor cared. He didn't really know Brock very well, but he knew his name and reputation from the rumor mill at Pearson High.

Brock was known as a fixer. He could get test answers, finished homework, even essays on multiple subjects for the desperate student. All for a price, of course. It was even rumored that he procured things like speed and Adderall for kids that needed that extra boost while studying or taking a test. Some even said that Brock got steroids for the athletes.

Some students have gotten caught being involved in those illegal activities, but no one ever gave up Brock as their source. Supposedly, Brock had some muscle to help him when things like that reared their ugly head. Students, in fear for their safety, as well as pressure from other students, never snitched on Brock. This was all rumor and conjecture, of course, but Frankie knew that it was better to steer clear of him.

"Hey," was all Frankie could say.

"Did I hear you right? Did you say you can't afford your mom a present?"

"No," said Frankie, and he held up his money, including the two dollars Ricky had given him. "I'm good."

"But you don't have enough for that elephant over there. Am I right?"

"Yeah, but that's okay, Brock. I'll find something else."

"I'm sure your mom would really like that elephant, right?" Brock looked at the china figure, then back at Frankie. "I think you should get it for her."

Frankie raised an eyebrow at Brock. He knew where this was going. "No, seriously, I'll be okay."

Brock reached into his pocket and pulled out a wad of money. He thumbed through the twenties and tens until he came to the fives. He separated one from the bunch. "Here, I want to give you this."

"I can't take that," said Frankie. "I'm no charity case. And I have nothing to trade you for it. So, thanks, but no thanks."

Brock seemed to ponder that for a second. "Sure you do. You have something to trade. How about ... how about you sell me your soul?"

"What?"

"Your soul. Sell me your soul for five bucks."

Frankie laughed. "That's so stupid. How can I sell you my soul? And if I could, why would I? And for five bucks?"

Brock held up a finger. "Hang on." He walked over to the booth, grabbed a flyer from a stack on the table. Then he removed a pen from his pocket and began writing on the back of the printed orange paper. When he was finished, he walked back over to Frankie. "Here."

Frankie hesitantly took the paper and regarded Brock's writing, which, by the way, was done with remarkable penmanship. Frankie almost remarked on it, but he held his tongue and began to read.

I, Frankie Malone, being of sound mind and body, hereby give my eternal soul to Brock Stevens for the sum of five dollars. This contract is binding and can only be broken if both parties agree.

Halfway down the page was a place for Frankie to sign, as well as a place for Brock, who had already signed in his spot.

"You sign that, Frankie, and I'll give you this five-dollar bill, and you can give your mother that great gift for Mother's Day."

Frankie stared at the paper in disbelief, as if it were a joke, or a prank. But when he looked back up at Brock, he knew the boy was serious. There was something in his eyes that told him that it was all okay, that everything would be all right. But something felt ... weird.

Frankie looked back at the elephant and imagined his mom opening it next Sunday and smiling with joy. The embarrassment of Christmas would be forgotten, and Frankie would join the ranks of his siblings in the gift-giving department. Maybe this time, they would even envy his gift.

Frankie's eyes fixed on the paper in his hand, again, and a sudden reality seemed to come over him. It was just a stupid piece of paper. Right? Maybe Brock thought he could try some flim-flam with him, but Frankie wasn't going to let that happen.

"Sure, Brock," Frankie said with confidence. "I'll sign."

"Great," said Brock in a manner that relayed empathy and assurance that Frankie was making the right decision. He handed Frankie the pen and gestured for him to go to the booth's table.

Frankie took the pen, walked to the table at booth fourteen, and signed the makeshift contract. *It's just a stupid piece of paper.*

* * *

Twenty-seven years later:

Brock Stevens closed the door of his BMW 8 Series, engaged the vehicle's security system with his remote, and walked to the main entrance of the Royal Embers Banquet Hall. Inside the lobby, a table, whose front facade was a paper banner that read

"Welcome Pearson High Class of '95, guarded the dual entrance to the hall. Two middle-aged women—their nametags giving them away as Michelle and Lauren—were behind the table, welcoming everyone with over-earnest smiles and enthusiastic greetings. Music wafted from inside the hall where a raucous DJ played hits from the 80s and 90s, and Brock could almost smell the cheap wine and liquor that was undoubtedly being dispensed from the open bar advertised on the reunion's website.

Brock approached the table, forcing his own smile to match those of the two women who vigilantly greeted all who entered.

"Good evening, sir," said Lauren. "And who do we have joining us?"

"Brock Stevens."

"Brock Stevens," Michelle repeated as she ran her finger down the list of names on her clipboard. "Here you are. Looks like you paid in full on the website. Let me get your nametag while Lauren takes care of your ticket. You'll want to hold onto that ticket; you could win one of our door prizes. We're giving away a big screen TV this year."

Brock raised his brow and feigned being impressed. He had two 85" 4K TVs at home and was sure the piddly piece of off-brand crap the reunion organizers got from Walmart would be great for the other schlubs who are in attendance, but not him.

"Brock Stevens?" said Lauren. "You don't remember me, do you?"

Brock stared at the woman's face until he gave her an embarrassed grin. "No, I'm sorry, I don't"

"Lauren Scarborough," she prodded.

"No. Sorry."

"That's okay," she said with a reassuring smile. "But if it weren't for you, I would've never passed Mr. Hawking's final trig exam. You were a life saver. I'm so glad you could make it tonight."

"Well, I'm so glad I could help you with that trig exam." He took the ticket from Lauren and placed his sticker-nametag

Michelle handed him, on his lapel. He took a breath, check the time on his Rolex, then headed toward the main hall.

"Brock?" Lauren called after him.

Brock turned to face her. "Yes?"

But before she could say another word, Michelle leaned over and whispered in her ear. Lauren looked at her friend, who gave her a reprimanding stare, then she turned back to Brock and said, "Never mind. Sorry."

Brock shrugged then continued to enter the hall.

Inside, the bustle of people mingled and drank. On the makeshift dancefloor in front of the DJ, some danced and drank. Some congregated in small circles, laughing and reminiscing of the glory years of high school—and probably their best years of their miserable lives. Brock could hear gossip flowing—like the cheap wine they were serving—as each person tried to one-up the other with either their own pitiful accomplishments or those of their lackluster kids. And a few sat at their designated tables with looks of boredom etched on their despondent faces, practically shouting that they would rather be anywhere but here. Brock shared their pain.

Brock shook his head; these we not his people. They were people whom he had all but forgotten after leaving Pearson High two and a half decades ago. People that Brock couldn't care less about. People whose lives had most likely been consumed by never-ending debt and dead-end jobs. Losers from Loserville, dead-end street, suburbia. *Why the hell am I here?* There was really only one reason. One person, to be precise.

Peggy Laughton.

Initially, he had no intension of going to this class reunion. He didn't attend the others, why should he attend this one? But an unexpected email from one of the few people Brock did remember from those bygone days changed his mind.

Peggy had been the one that got away. At least, for a teenage kid that excelled in nothing except making deals to get a little cash here and there. His female classmates hadn't held Brock's attention for very long, nor he theirs's. All but one, that is. Peggy

Laughton had elegance and beauty beyond her years. Between the football captain and the class president, and many in between, she had her choice of boyfriends and prom dates. She had always been kind to Brock; she had even started conversations with him now and again. She had been as ingratiating as she was beautiful. But he had never seen an opportunity to make his move, and then, before he knew it, school had ended, and he had been thrown into the world of adult life. So, when he had received her email asking him if he would be at the twenty-five-year reunion, he had typed a reply with an emphatic yes.

"Brock Stevens, is that you?"

A man's hoarse voice snapped Brock out of his brown study. He turned to see a balding man holding a beer bottle in one hand while his other reached out to cup Brock's shoulder. Though his hairline had changed dramatically, and his waist size appeared to rival that of his chest, Brock knew in an instant the man before him was the former four-letter athlete from Pearson that had been the envy of most boys and the desire of most girls.

"Doug McNamara. How are you?" Brock glanced at the man's hand on his shoulder as if it could lessen the value of his Armani jacket simply by touch.

"I'm great, Brock. Question is: How the hell are *you*? Haven't seen you at one of these things before. We all thought you were in Europe, married to some duchess or something."

"Ha. No, I'm still here. I live in the city, as a matter of fact."

"City? Don't say. I used to own a few townhomes on Guildcrest Avenue. And some more on Kylmire. I used to be a landlord before the cleansing. I had nineteen properties at one point. Whereabouts you live?"

"Lakeview Arms. What do you m—"

"Lakeview?" Doug let out a low whistle. "What are you, the CEO of some bank or something?"

"Something like that. What did you mean when you said, 'the cleansing?' What is that?"

"Well, Brock, I may have been a landlord, and made good money—real good money, as a matter of fact—but I was a real son of a 'B', if you know what I mean."

"You mean you were a slumlord?" Brock fished.

"Exactly. I was all about making the almighty dollar, but shortly after making my first million, I had an epiphany of sorts. My daughter asked me how I could let my tenants live in such horrible conditions while I sat in my seven-bedroom home with a five-car garage, living the life of luxury. I tried to explain to her the order and nature of things, but she wouldn't hear it. In short, she said I had to clean up my act, or she was disowning me. Can you believe that? My fourteen-year-old girl said that to me.

"Well, after that chat with her, I gave my life a good, hard looking at. And she was right. In short, I gave away all those homes to those tenants. Actually, I take that back, I sold them those homes for a dollar. Sold my own home. All my cars. Gave most of my money to charity. Now, I do honest work during the week, and I do God's work on the weekends."

"You gave ... everything you had—everything you worked hard for—away? Just like that?"

"That's right. Best feeling in the world."

For a chump like you, maybe. Brock tried not to be rude and simply smiled at Doug, acknowledging, but not quite understanding what the man had done. *Religious freaks ... they blow my mind.*

"Well, I'm glad to hear you're doing good." Doug continued to drone on about his new business, and his wife and kids, and his seven dogs—or was it eleven? All rescues, of course. Brock feigned interest, but his attention waned, and he began searching the crowd again, hoping to find the one that got away.

His eyes set on a screen on the far side of the hall showing slide after slide of student's yearbook photos. Brock's interest piqued when a photo of Peggy Laughton flashed up next. Her smile, her eyes ... so enchanting. "Genuine" was the word that set in Brock's head. There was nothing fake about her. He couldn't wait to see her again after all these years.

"A shame, ain't it?" Doug said.

"Sorry? What's that?" Brock's eyes never left the screen.

"All of *them*." Doug pointed to the screen with his beer hand. "Can't believe we lost so many, so young."

"What are you talking about?"

"That's there's one of them 'In Memoriams', as they say."

"Wait .... Are you telling me that all those pictures on that screen are classmates that've died?"

"Yes, sir," Doug sighed. "It kinda puts your life into perspective. Makes you appreciate everything you got. You never know when your time's up. Makes me grateful for my cleansing." He nodded to the next photo to pop up. "There's Brian Pollack, football linebacker. He died of brain cancer, if you can believe that. Ate him away quick, but not quick enough. They say he suffered terrible pain for months. Horrible way to go, if you ask me. And there's Kip Holden, he died from a drug overdose. Our track star that went to the state championships. They say he was hooked on stuff since school, and it just escalated from there. And about three or four of our former classmates took their own lives. Who knows what kind of hell their lives were like—"

"What about Peggy Laughton?"

"Oh, that's the saddest one. They say she was beaten to death by her husband. And get this, her husband was Wayne Vaughn. Can you believe that?"

"You're joking. 'Captain Caveman' Wayne Vaughn?"

"Yup. Dumber than a bag of hammers, and the brute was able to land one of the most desirable girls in school. They say he killed her with his bare hands. Helluva thing. Now, he's doing life upstate. Won't breathe free air for the rest of his life." Doug diverted his attention to somewhere behind Brock. "Excuse me, Brock. My wife's calling me over. Nice chatting with you. Grab a drink and come meet the Mrs. when you get a chance."

"Yeah, I'll do that." Brock mumbled as he tried to wrap his head around what Doug had just told him. Peggy was dead? That didn't make any sense. How did she end up with a loser like

Caveman Vaughn? *And if she was dead, then who sent me that email?*

"Hey, Brock." A thinner man with a goatee now stood where Doug had stood. "Been a long time."

"Yeah ..." Still confused, Brock forced a smile and tried to place the face of the newcomer, but the goatee must have been throwing him off. That, and the news about Peggy.

"Frankie," said the man, pointing to his nametag. "Frankie Malone."

The name sounded familiar, and the gears started turning in Brocks head. After a second or two, it hit him. "Yes. Frankie Malone. Kilgrew's class. How you been?"

"Been pretty good. How about you?"

"Not too bad." Brock's eyes kept glancing at the screen that memorialized the dead former classmates. It must have been on a loop, for Peggy's face came up again. This time Brock looked at it in a new, sad light. Gone so young. And the fact that someone sent Brock an email using a dead woman's account, was mindboggling, not to mention morbid.

"You okay, Brock?" Frankie asked.

"Yeah. Just hard to believe they're all dead."

"Well, we're not getting any younger."

Age had nothing to do with the deaths Doug had told him about. It was just horrible fate that ended their lives. And none of the people on the screen had been older than forty-three. Most probably died in their thirties—some in their twenties. But he wasn't going to argue with Frankie. It didn't really matter anyway. He decided to move on, change the subject.

"So, what have you been up to, Frankie?" Brock said, wishing he had a whiskey, even if it was the cheap crap they were slinging at the bar.

"Living the dream, as they say. Wife, kids, pretty good job. How about you."

"Same, except no kids. Or wife for that matter. But I guess I'm doing okay in the job department."

"What do you do?"

"I'm a vice chairman for World Integrity Bank."

"Whoa ... not too shabby. WIB ... I'm impressed. I guess it kind of makes sense, though. You being in banking."

"What do you mean?"

"Don't you remember? You loaned me that five bucks back in the tenth grade? Well, not exactly a loan ...."

Brock shrugged at Frankie. It didn't sound familiar. He had made hundreds of transactions with the students back then. It had helped pay for his first car. He had been a shrewd little business man back in the day, but he couldn't remember specific deals.

"C'mon," said Frankie. "You don't remember? At the fair ... I sold you my soul ... for five dollars ... so I could buy that porcelain elephant for my mother ...."

"Yes!" Brock finally remembered. "Holy cow, I forgot about that."

"That was a real kind thing you did back then. My mom really loved that elephant."

"That's great. I'm glad I could help."

"Hey, I was wondering, do you still have it?"

"Have what?"

"The contract ... you know ... for my soul."

"The piece of paper? No. I have no idea what happened to it. My mom probably threw it out when I went away to college."

"What college did you go to?"

"GW—um—George Washington."

"Wow, not too shabby. How did you get into there?"

"Scholarships."

"Scholarships? I didn't know your grades were that good."

"Yeah ... well ... I was fortunate."

"Hey, that wouldn't happen to be your Beemer out in the parking lot, would it?"

"The 8 Series? Yep, sure is."

"Mind if I take a gander at it? I have a 3 Series myself and would love to take a look at a piece of art like that."

"Sure," said Brock, a bit relieved to have an excuse to leave. With Peggy not being there, he really didn't have a reason to stay. He looked at his Rolex and realized he wasted forty-five minutes of his life that he'll never get back. "Let's get the hell out of here."

Brock led Frankie out of the hall, through the lobby, and into the parking lot. They went to the far corner where, Brock had hoped, his precious luxury sports car would be safe from the drunken slobs attending tonight's affair.

"Here she is," Brock said with pride. "335 Horsepower, 8-speed transmission, 3.0 liter 6-cylinder, 4500 rpms."

"That is one sweet ride," said Frankie as he eyed the car's exterior and ran his fingers along the front fender. "Mind if I hop in?"

"Better yet ... here." Brock fished out his keys and tossed them to Frankie. "Let's take her for a spin."

"Sweet."

Frankie and Brock climbed inside. Seconds later, they were out of the parking lot and onto the main thoroughfare: a long stretch of road that led west into the city or east toward the state line. Frankie steered the car west.

"She drives nice," said Frankie. "Much better than my 3."

"I had a 3. They're nice cars. You shouldn't knock 'em. Open her up. See what she can do."

"You serious?"

"Sure."

Frankie pushed the accelerator down a bit farther and the finely engineered German automobile took off as if they had been standing still up until that point.

"Wooohoo!" Frankie shouted. "Holy shit. She's faster than hell."

"Yeah she is. Go ahead and ease her back and make the next right up here." Brock pointed to a red-light intersection that was quickly approaching.

But Frankie didn't slow down and drove right through, grim determination rested on his face.

"Frankie? You just missed the turn. It's okay. Just take this next one. And pull it back. We don't need the cops pulling us over."

Again, the BMW sped past the side street.

"Frankie? What's going on? This isn't funny. Frankie?"

"My name isn't Frankie," said the man behind the wheel, then he slowly turned his head and focused an odious gaze upon Brock.

A gaze with eyes that were glowing red.

They weren't just red; they were ... burning. Red and orange light flickered in his pupils as if lit from behind by a blazing fire.

The car's speed increased as it continued toward the city. They became briefly airborne as they crested a hill, the car landed with a *thud* of complaint.

Brock's mouth hung open with an incredulous countenance. "What are you talking about? Who the hell are you?"

The man turned his head to look Brock in the eyes. "Very good, Brock. For hell is where I am most comfortable."

The car continued toward the city and Brock had no idea what to do. This man ... this thing—whoever he was—had his car at almost a hundred miles an hour. Brock was terrified; the police were the last thing on his mind. He was more concerned about slamming into another car or the wall of some building. But he was particularly terrified of the guy with the red eyes. What was he doing at the reunion? Was this some kind of setup? Was he ...?

"Were you the one who sent me that email? As Peggy Laughton?"

"Again, very good, Brock." He flashed an evil smile to match his evil eyes.

"Why? What do you want from me? Where are you taking me?"

"I want to show you something. Patience, we're almost there."

The car slowed and made a sudden right turn, jarring Brock and causing his seatbelt to catch. Then the car made a sudden left, slamming Brock into his door. Then another right, and another, until the car ambled down a dark alley where trash and puddles seemed to be its sole residents. Then the car stopped.

"Get out, Brock." The man with red eyes turned off the car.

Brock hesitated. Was this man going to leave him here and steal his car? *Perhaps I can overpower him; he doesn't have a weapon. Or at least one I can see.* But before Brock could make any rash decisions, the strange man opened the driver's door and stepped out of the BMW and pocketed the keys. Brock decided to follow suit.

"Come over here," said the red-eyed man, and he walked to an overfilled dumpster that sat crooked against a tall chain-link fence. On the ground, around the dumpster, were black bags of trash that seemed to have been thrown at the dumpster and either missed their mark, or had fallen from the mound that protruded from the top of the large metal bin.

Brock covered his nose; the stench was unbearable. A mixture of garbage, urine, and feces combined to create an odor that would make any skunk turn tail and run.

"What did you want to show me? A bunch of garbage?"

"Maybe. Or maybe something thrown away as garbage."

The red-eyed man waved his hand and one of the black trash bags against the dumpster moved and rolled away revealing a man wearing a stained hoody and equally stained and tattered jeans. His long filthy hair and unkempt beard made it impossible to tell his age. His mouth hung open, and his eyes stared at the two men in puzzlement and wonder as flies buzzed around the hapless man's head.

"*This* is Frankie Malone," said the red-eyed man.

Brock stared at the poor creature on the ground. "That's Frankie?"

Brock cocked his head at the homeless man. Was it Frankie? It was hard to tell. Brock hadn't seen Frankie in decades, and the homeless man's disheveled appearance made him seem almost inhuman. Frankie should be healthy and happy, not someone who had sank to the lowest depths of life and now rested against a dumpster and used trash for a blanket.

"My God, what happened to him?" Brock finally asked.

"Please, don't use the "G" word. But to answer your question, you happened to him, Brock."

"Me? What are you talking about? And who the hell are you?"

"I go by many names in many cultures: the Mayans called me Ahpuch; the Buddhists, Yama. But you can call me ... Mantus. I always liked that one."

Brock shook his head, his face twisted in a grimace of fear and confusion. "So, you what ... drag me out here to see ... that?" Brock swatted his hand in Frankie's direction. The homeless man watched the two men standing above him in apparent amusement, his eyes darting from one to the other. "And what do you mean when you said, 'I happened to him?' What does that mean?"

"You took something from him that doesn't belong to you." Brock simply stared at Mantus with absolutely no idea what he was talking about. So Mantus continued. "You took his soul, Brock."

"His soul? You've got to be kidding me. That piece of paper? That—that was a joke. I only did that so he would owe me a favor."

"A favor?"

"Yeah, he had Mr. Cortes for Chemistry, and I wanted to use him to get me some test scores. But I ended up getting another source and didn't need him."

"Nevertheless," said Mantus, his glowing red eyes boring into Brock, "the deed is done, the contract written and signed. And Frankie's life was destroyed. He's now just an empty shell. Look at him, Brock. Look at him!" Mantus's voice filled the alley with a deafening boom that shook the glass of the nearby windows.

Brock looked down at Frankie and truly wondered if he had indeed ruined this wretched man's life. It seemed so impossible, but ... He looked from Frankie to Mantus, then back to Frankie.

"It was just a dumb piece of paper," said Brock. "It didn't mean anything. I just wanted to help him so he would help me."

"And Frankie's isn't the only life you ruined," said Mantus.

"What—what do you mean?"

Mantus crossed his arms and squared off his shoulders. "The memorial video at the reunion. You were the cause of most of those deaths, Brock."

Brock snapped out of his self-reflecting trance and looked at Mantus. "What the hell are you talking about? I barely knew those people. How could I be responsible for their deaths?"

"You sold them pills to get hooked on. Drugs to deteriorate their bodies. You taught others to cheat, and the only thing they learned is that when you try to cheat your way through life, life laughs at you. Suicide is a sinful death, you know." Mantus flashed him a razor thin smile. "And then there's Peggy Laughton."

"Peggy? What about her?"

"You could have saved her from that horrible fate. If only you weren't so worried about making a buck, and you actually paid attention to her, she could have been yours."

That had been in the back of Brock's mind ever since he heard about Peggy's death at the reunion. And now, to hear it out loud, made it seem even more likely.

And the man you call The Caveman—the guy who ended up marrying Peggy ... you're the one who sold him the steroids that screwed with his brain and turned him into a violent killer. So, in a way, Brock, you're the one who killed Peggy Laughton."

Brock felt his blood drain from his face. He felt weightless and unable to move as if he were having an out-of-body experience. *No. It can't be. What have I done?* That perfect, beautiful girl from high school had been beaten to death by a guy—who was most likely not too stable to begin with—who Brock had sold the steroids to. "My God," Brock sobbed. "What have I done?"

"Hey, what'd I say about swingin' the "G" word around here. This is all on you, Brock. I'm just letting you know the path you have chosen, and the effect it had on those around you."

"But why?" Brock wiped his nose with the sleeve of his jacket, and his tears from his face with his fingers. "What do you want from me?"

"You need to give back something that doesn't belong to you." Mantus nodded to Frankie, who still lay amidst the garbage. "You need to cancel the contract."

"What? How? I told you I lost that paper years ago."

"You mean this paper?" Mantus waved his hand and a folded paper appeared between his fingers, its once bright orange color had faded into a dull cantaloupe hue. He unfolded it and turned it around for Brock to see. On the back of the old spring festival flyer were Brock's words written in his flawless penmanship.

"How...? I mean ...."

"This was never just a piece of paper, Brock. This was a contract for a soul. A soul that you purchased for five dollars. Why do you think you've had such a successful life? Having an extra soul is like having a golden horseshoe permanently up your ass. I should know ... souls are my specialty. And now ..." Mantus snapped his finger and a pen appeared in his other hand. "... I need you to sign Frankie's soul over to me."

"To you? Why not to Frankie? It's his soul."

"It's too late for Frankie. Just like the ones in that video, his life has been forfeited. His soul will belong to me, now."

Brock looked at the pen and contract in Marcus's hands and then at Frankie. It didn't seem right. He knew a scam when he saw one, and this red-eyed freak was trying to bamboozle Frankie's soul from him.

"Bullshit." Brock grabbed the lapels of Mantus's jacket and was immediately thrown back by an electrical shock. A thunderous *crack* echoed in the alley as Brock fell to the ground and began to convulse on the damp concrete alleyway.

"Don't tempt fate, Brock. I've tolerated you long enough. I've even found you entertaining, to a point. But I've come for a soul. If you won't sign over Frankie's, then I will just take yours."

The pain from the shock started to wear off, and Brock was beginning to get feeling back into his hands and feet. When he was able, he pulled himself up on wobbly legs, using the dumpster as a crutch. He cast a hateful glare at Mantus. He despised him. He absolutely loathed him. He—

"Oh, please," said Mantus. "I've seen that look a million times. We can do this the easy way—which is the smart way—or we can do this the difficult way—which is ... well ... you just got a sample of that. So, what shall it be?"

Brock limped over to the red-eyed man and stared into those hellish eyes of his. And Brock was certain that this evil man was indeed amused by the spectacle that was happening. Brock decided that he wasn't going to be any more entertainment for this guy.

"Fine," Brock said through gritted teeth, and he snatched the paper and pen from Mantus. He hobbled over to the dumpster where he used the side of the rusty trash bin as a hard surface to write on. When he was finished, he took the paper back over to Mantus.

"Let's see what we have ..."

At the bottom half of the paper, under the original contract, Brock had written an amendment. Mantus read it aloud.

"*I, Brock Stevens, being of sound mind and body, do hereby give Frankie Malone's soul to Mantus.*"

"No, I'm afraid this won't do. This won't do at all," Mantus said, his brow forming a frown. "You see, you need to sell me his soul. You can't just give it to me. That's how this whole thing works. You have to—never mind. I can fix this." Mantus snapped his finger, and the paper disappeared. Then, with another snap, it reappeared in the other hand. "Here. This is how it should read." He handed the paper to Brock.

Brock turned the paper around and noticed that his recent writing was gone and a new paragraph was in its place. He read it to himself.

The aforementioned soul that had previously belonged to Frankie Malone, and then to Brock Stevens, is hereby sold to Mantus for the sum of $5. The sale is final, and Brock Stevens forfeits any rights and privileges associated with the ownership of said soul.

There was a place for Brock to sign. Mantus's signature was already on the paper. Brock, the pen still in his hand, used the dumpster again, and signed in his spot. He then shoved the paper into Mantus's hands.

Mantus smiled as he confirmed Brock's signature, then he folded the paper and slipped it into the inside pocket of his jacket, where he produced a crisp five-dollar bill. He handed it to Brock. Brock snatched it from him with defeated anger.

"Funny thing, though," Mantus said as he shook his head, grinning ear to ear. "I almost can't wait to get ahold of your soul. It will be quite fitting. Quite fitting, indeed."

"What do you mean? I sold you Frankie's soul. I don't owe you anything else."

"Oh, not here and now, but eventually, your soul will belong to me. Just like Frankie's and Wayne's, and so many of your fellow classmates. All except that damn Doug Mc—" Mantus cut himself off abruptly.

"Do you mean Doug McNamara?" Why? Why don't you get his soul? What did ..." Brock trailed off as the conversation with Doug came back to him. "Because he gave his wealth away? Is that why you don't get his soul? What did he do? Redeem himself by doing that stupid charity stunt?"

Mantus's smile disappeared. Only a cold stare remained on his face that contradicted his fiery eyes. He stood there defiantly, refusing to say anything else.

"That's it, isn't it? You had his soul because he was a greedy, shady slumlord. It was as good as yours when he'd kick the bucket. But when he gave away everything he made—did all that charity work ... he redeemed his soul. Making it untouchable for you." Brocks mind raced with ideas and possibilities. His head and chest swam with hope. "If that's what it takes to deny you my soul, then that's what I will do too. I'll give it away. I'll give it *all* away. Then I'll start from scratch and lead a normal boring life."

Brock laughed at the absurdity of what he had just said. It should have sounded dreadful to him; he should have winced at the very idea. But he didn't. In fact, he felt positively giddy. He will cheat the devil. It'll be the biggest scam of his life. He laughed again, then looked down at Frankie, who still sat among the trash and watched everything with wide, saucer-like eyes.

"And I'm going to start right now," Brock said as he gave Frankie a smile and a wink. Brock pushed up his jacket sleeve enough for him to unfasten his Rolex. He removed the time piece and placed in Frankie's hand. "Take this Frankie. You take this watch and you sell it. You hear me? You sell it."

"What are you doing, Brock?" Mantus crossed his arms in front of him and gave Brock an incredulous shake of his head. "You can't do it. It's not in your nature."

"Watch me." Brock then removed his jacket and laid it across Frankie's chest, as caring as a mother laying a blanket on a child. "I'll be damned if I let my soul end up in your evil hands. Actually ... no, I won't be damned. Ha!"

Mantus, his arms still crossed in front of him said, "You'll fail, Brock. Oh, you might try for a while, but you'll fall of the wagon and become the venomous creature you've always been. And in the end, you will be mine."

"Then sit back and enjoy the show." Brock walked around Mantus and headed down the alley.

"You'll need these." The red-eyed man held up the keys to the Beemer and jingled them.

"Keep them," Brock yelled back as he passed the car. "Give them to Frankie or whomever—I don't care. I won't need it anymore. The title's in the glovebox."

Brock strolled down the alley to the connecting street, almost skipping to the beat of a new drum that set the rhythm of the new life ahead of him.

A figure emerged from the shadows and approached the red-eyed man, who still held a set of keys that dangled from his pinkie. Together, they stood and watched as Brock left the alley, whistling a tune neither of them could identify.

“That was amazing, Ricky,” said the newcomer. “Your performance was Oscar-worthy. That would’ve fooled anybody. I must admit ... I wasn’t sure if it was going to work, but ... well ... Christ! Did you see his face? Holy shit!”

“You need to have more faith in me, Frankie. When I get into a role, I take it all the way.”

“And the magician takes a bow—I’m sorry—I meant, illusionist.”

Ricky put the car keys into his pocket and pulled out a small case. “These contacts have been killing me since I put them in.” Ricky removed the reflective red contact lens from his eyes and placed them in the plastic container. “Good work on the audio, by the way. You turned everything on with perfect timing.”

“Speaking of which, that shock-suit thing of yours worked like a charm. I thought you almost killed him.”

“Hardly. But it felt good to watch him fall to the ground like that.” Ricky looked back down the alley to wear Brock had disappeared. “Do you think he learned his lesson, Frankie? Do you think this will be payment enough for the harm he did to our friends?”

“It’ll have to be. What you said about him being responsible for ruining their lives is the only true thing you said tonight.”

“In our opinion,” Ricky corrected.

“In our opinion,” Frankie conceded.

“I’m glad I found that contract on the ground that day at the fair,” Ricky said reflectively.

"I'm glad you kept it all these years. That's what started this whole thing. And we used it to bring it all to an end."

After a few thoughtful seconds passed, Ricky shrugged and dug out the car keys. "I need to head back to the reunion and tell everyone we were successful. And tell them thanks for all their help."

Frankie nodded. "Tell them I said thanks, as well."

"You want to come with me? I'll let you drive."

"No. I told Peggy I would pick up Chinese. I'm sure she's starving, plus she's probably dying to find out how we did."

Ricky nodded and smiled. "Tell her I said hi. And I'll see you guys at the picnic next weekend."

"Will do," Frankie hugged his longtime friend then knelt down to talk to the homeless man still sitting amongst the trash, in the exact same spot he had been all night. "You know what to do with that watch and jacket, old-timer?"

"I'm gonna sell them, you ass. What the hell did you think I'm going to do with them?" The ill-fated man put the watch on his wrist and held it up to his ear as if to make sure the timepiece actually worked.

Ricky and Frankie laughed. Satisfied with their work, they gave each other a wave as they headed off in opposite directions.

A lone, faded-orange paper fluttered to the ground as the two men left. It tumbled and flipped until it landed near the feet of the homeless man. His filthy, sore-ridden hand reached for it, his new watch glinting in the moonlight. He grinned and his eyes gleamed as he looked the paper over. Shaking his head in derision, he placed it in the pocket of his new jacket and gave a snort of ridicule.

"Just a piece of paper, my ass."

THE EXECUTIONER

"Wild animals never kill for sport. Man is the only one to whom the torture and death of his fellow creatures is amusing in itself."
– **James Anthony Froude**

Martin's chained legs could barely keep up with the pace at which the sentries forced him. After several turns in the musty hallway, they pushed him into a room and shoved him onto a wooden chair. With his bound hands, he grabbed the table in front of him to keep his momentum from sending him tumbling off the chair and onto the stone floor. The squeaking of hinges snapped his head around in time to see the guards leave back through the room's lone entrance. They slammed the door behind them. Martin heard the unquestionable sound of an iron bolt being slid into its catch. *What now*, he wondered.

Like most citizens, Martin had skated the fine line of the law here and there throughout his life, but he never imagined he would be one to break Doctrine; that he would commit a crime and get the death penalty. But here he was. And he was indeed guilty. But what he had done he did it out of love, and he would make all the same choices again if given the chance. But that was all moot; he was caught, convicted, and now awaited his punishment.

Swiveling his head, he took in his surroundings. It was an unimpressive room; twenty by twenty, white brick walls, ceramic tile floor, and a skylight that let in the afternoon sun. There was nothing in the room save for the wooden table at which he sat and two chairs. Ordinary, very ordinary. But there *was* something unusual about the room. At first, he couldn't put his finger on it, and then it hit him. "There're no cameras in here," he said to himself.

He scoured the walls and corners again, looking for anything that could be a camera or be hiding one. Nothing. The room was plain – plain and empty. This was a bit disconcerting for Martin; he had never been in a non-residence room where there were no cameras to watch him. The Covenant always watched; there were always cameras, or gov-eyes as they were called, to watch the citizens. To keep them safe, and to keep them from straying from the Doctrine. Perhaps if there had been cameras in his residence, he would not be in his current predicament. Martin shook his head; it was too late to think about that. This room, this 'eyeless' room, was highly unusual. Martin wondered if it was even legal. *Strange,* Martin thought. *What was the purpose of this room?* He had a bad feeling about this.

He tested his bindings: chained iron shackles encased his ankles, and iron cuffs restricted his hands. He pulled and tugged on each but nothing budged. He thought about standing up and going over to the door and giving it a try. Before he could move, the metal latch sounded again, and the heavy wooden door swung open behind him.

Martin froze with fear. *Was this it? Would they torture me before my execution? No, it can't be. Not here. There are no cameras. The Covenant demanded an audience.*

A solitary set of footsteps followed the sound of the door closing again, as well as the metal latch resuming its hold. The footsteps moved directly behind him and stopped.

Martin took a breath and held it.

The steps continued with purposeful, resounding clops. They slowly walked around Martin's left side until their owner was visible and standing on the other side of the table directly in front of him. It was a civilian. Martin was expecting a burly guard or a stern looking warden. But this was just a man. He wore a smile, clean clothes, and he smelled rather nice.

"Hello, Martin," said the man. "May I call you Martin?"

Martin just sat there, not sure if he acknowledged the smiling man with a nod or a grunt, or anything. He just looked at him, waiting for whatever would come.

"My name is Rogan," said the man. "Do you know who I am?" The question was genuine; it wasn't sarcastic or condescending. And the man, Rogan, just stood there patiently waiting for an answer.

Martin sat dumbfounded for a second, then gave Rogan a look-over. He was a very unassuming man. His face was nice, pleasant almost. His salt and pepper hair, along with a few wrinkles, suggested that he had a couple decades on Martin. He was clean shaven, which was the law, of course. He wore regular clothes: pants, shirt, vest... maybe a bit nicer than the average citizen would have. In fact, they looked almost new. Not recycled or reissued like everyone else wore. Was this Rogan a celebrity? Or a political figure? If so, Martin didn't recognize him from any of the broadcasts. He didn't look familiar nor did Martin recognize the name Rogan. So, he shook his head, feeling almost embarrassed at not knowing the man's identity.

"That's all right," said Rogan, and a smile of understanding appeared on his face. "Most people don't. Perhaps, if I was wearing my mask..." Rogan raised his hand and covered his face, leaving only his eyes visible. He held his hand there, leaned down toward Martin, and gave him a seemingly well-rehearsed scowl. Rogan's brown-green eyes pierced through Martin's gaze and into his very soul.

Yes, Martin thought. *He does look familiar. Frighteningly so. But from where?* Then the realization hit him like a punch to the gut. Feeling his heartbeat in his throat, Martin swallowed hard and, when he found his voice, he said: "You're the...The Executioner."

Rogan removed his "mask" and straightened back up. "Correct," he smiled. "Of course, my official name is Vero the Executioner. They didn't think Rogan sounded ..." he paused as he thought of the correct word, "sinister enough for the broadcasts. Are you a regular viewer of my program?"

"Not really," Martin said. "I try to avoid it when I can."

"I'll try not to take offense to that, but I know not everyone has the stomach to witness what I do."

Martin looked at him. The Executioner. Here. Right in front of me. The end was coming quicker than he had anticipated.

"But I'm sure your home system is tuned to the mandatory minimum of eight hours per month."

"Of course," Martin said emphatically with a nod. His family had enough scrutiny from the Covenant lately, they certainly didn't need anything else to cast more suspicion onto them. "It's like you said. Not everyone can stand to watch what you do."

Rogan looked at Martin's hands resting on the table. "Here," said Rogan as he walked around the table. "Let me take those off of you." He reached into his pocket, pulled out a lone key, then slipped it into the lock on the cuffs. After a twist of the key, the cuffs popped open to Martin's relief, but the newly convicted man hesitated to remove them, thinking it might be a trick or something to get him into trouble, although he couldn't imagine how much more trouble he could get into. “Go on,” said Rogan reassuringly. “Take them off.”

Martin did as he was told. He removed the cuffs and placed them on the table. He rubbed his sweaty wrists with his hands. “Thank you,” he said to Rogan, as he eyed The Executioner suspiciously.

Rogan glanced at Martin’s feet and tossed the key onto the table. “Here. Go ahead and take those shackles off as well. No need for you to wear them.”

Still eying Rogan warily, Martin grabbed the key, scooted his chair out, removed his chains and shackles, and put them on the table next to the cuffs. “Thank you, again.”

Rogan acknowledged with a nod and a smile. “Keeper!” said Rogan in a voice loud enough to make Martin jump. A few seconds later, a guard unlocked the door and entered the room. “Please take these away,” Rogan said to him. “We won’t be needing them any longer.”

“As you wish, sir.” The keeper scooped up the prisoner’s accessories and exited the room, locking the door once again behind him.

Rogan pulled out the chair across the table from Martin and sat down, folding his hands in front of him. “So, tell me, Martin, which of the seventeen crimes punishable by death did you commit?”

Martin was a little taken back by the question. Rogan knew his name. Didn’t he know why he was in here? Martin took a deep breath and said: “My wife and I had a third child.”

“Ah,” said Rogan. “Number six on the Doctrine’s ‘do not do’ list.”

Martin nodded.

“The world is extremely overpopulated, Martin,” Rogan said in a serious tone. “We have the Doctrine for many reasons. And population control is one of them.” Rogan’s face and posture soften a bit. “So, your third child. Boy? Girl?”

“Girl.”

“How old?”

"Four."

"Ah," Rogan smiled. "A great age. So magical."

"Yeah," Martin sighed.

"And you managed to keep her hidden for four years. Amazing." Rogan paused, then asked: "And were you given the choice of her life or yours?"

Martin looked down at the table. "Yes."

"And you chose yours so that she may live. Very noble."

"I'm her father," Martin said angrily, looking back up at Rogan. "What choice did I have?" Martin shook his head at Rogan's insolent statement.

"You'd be surprised how many people would choose to live and have their child put to death."

"Then they would be cowards."

"Perhaps. But fear, like love and greed, can make people do unfathomable things. And, of course, it isn't just dying that they are afraid of, it's what I do to them that drives that fear into people. That's why we have the broadcasts, and that's why there are mandatory hours for citizens to watch." Rogan paused and gave Martin a thoughtful look. "Do you know why you are here, Martin?"

"Of course. I'm the next contestant on your little game show."

Rogan smiled at Martin's bravado. "You do know what it is I do exactly. Right?"

Martin nodded. "Yeah. You torture people to death, and it's broadcast over the network as a deterrent for other citizens."

"Yes," Rogan said with a grimace, "that's all true, but that doesn't do justice to my craft; to the intricacy of my work. And we don't like to use the word 'torture'. Instead, the whole process is called 'the reckoning'. And the person going through the reckoning loses his citizenship and even his name. He, or she, is simply referred to as 'the miscreant'. Do you know how long the reckoning lasts?"

Martin shook his head. "Two, three days?"

"Nine days."

Martin felt his heart sink into his stomach. "Nine days?"

"Yes. Nine days, nine hours a day. No more. No less. If you were an avid watcher you would know this." Rogan stood up and began to slowly pace in a broad circle behind his chair. "What I do to the miscreant is quite amazing. I introduce levels of pain to them that they didn't know existed. You see, I start slowly with cuts and breaks, then move on to the removing of flesh and fingers, fingernails first, of course. Then I remove the hands and feet ... You get the picture?"

The question may have been rhetorical, but Martin nodded anyway. His eyes wide open as Rogan casually described the events that would be eventually happening to him.

"I don't think you do, because the miscreant is slowly taken apart piece by tiny piece, the way a scientist might reverse engineer something to figure out how it's made. You see, it's not just about the pain; it's also about the miscreant witnessing his own body being dismembered right before his conscious eyes. By the ninth day of the reckoning, there is nothing left of him except a torso and a head, and they are so disfigured that you can barely tell that it's human, let alone the identity of that human. And the methods I use to do these things are far from anything that would resemble a doctor's touch. In fact, you might say they're quite inhuman." Rogan's face lit up and he held up a finger as he thought of something. "Are you familiar with the altrix bird?"

Martin shook his head, puzzled at the radical change of topic.

"Nor should you be. I'm not surprised. It was thought to be extinct for hundreds of years, until about thirty years ago a small population of them was discovered on a remote island in the southern hemisphere. It's a unique and fascinating bird; sort of like a bird of prey, but it prefers to prey upon wounded animals, animals that would normally be too large for it to take down by itself. You could say it is more of a bird of opportunity." Rogan smiled at his own cleverness. "So, when it finds a wounded animal, let's say...a goat. The altrix clips the animal's hamstrings to prevent it from escaping. Then, it begins to feed upon its flesh, all the while making sure the animal stays alive. You see, the altrix doesn't have the necessary enzymes in its stomach to digest decayed flesh like carrion birds do. It's probably a flaw in its evolution. So, it's very important for its captive to remain alive. Maybe that's the reason why they almost became extinct, having to be so selective in what they eat.

"Now, the altrix has incredible skills at eating particular parts of the animal without endangering its life: the skin, certain organs, and it just loves eyes. Loves them. They must be a delicacy of a sort to them. Anyway, they go to great lengths to keep the animal alive. In fact, they will fight off other predators and scavengers, sometimes to the death, to preserve the animal's life. They even regurgitate food and water into their captive's mouth so it doesn't starve or die of thirst. Ironically the regurgitated food would be the flesh of the animal itself. Bizarre, isn't it? But, it's quite a fascinating bird. Do you know what the word 'altrix' means? It means nurse. Kind of fitting, wouldn't you agree?"

Paralyzed by fear and disgust, Martin managed to speak. "In a morbidly ironic way, I suppose."

Rogan stopped his pacing and stepped up to the table, turned his chair around, then sat on it backwards, resting his crossed arms on its back. "Can you imagine this ... this goat, or whatever, laying on the ground, blind, in agony, taking days, maybe weeks to die? All the while it is slowly being eaten alive. I can't imagine a more horrible death. Can you?"

Martin felt sick to his stomach; this all seemed surreal to him. Sitting in that chair he felt almost weightless yet unable to move, like he was just a spectator to this whole thing. Like it was a dream, and he was not really there. But he was there. And this was a nightmare. "Why are you telling me all this?"

"Because, Martin," Rogan took a deep breath and paused before continuing. "For the longest time I thought of myself as the altrix. I mean, I literally based my work on how it cares for its prey and slowly devours it. I even have an entire staff of doctors that stand by to care for the miscreant, to keep him alive, even bring him back to life if necessary. But then, after years of reckonings, I realized that I'm not the altrix, but rather *we* are the altrix."

"We?"

"Yes. We. The citizens of the Covenant, the enforcers of the Doctrine. *We* feed off of the fear and agony of the miscreant. *We* feed off his regrets and sorrow. *We* feed off his disparity and sacrifice. And it's this nourishment from the reckoning that keeps the Covenant and its citizens alive and safe." Rogan straightened up and regained the little composure he had lost during his rant. "So, I ask you again, Martin: Do you know why you are here?"

Eyes wide and nose flaring, Martin's heart thumped hard in his chest. "I am the goat," he said through gritted teeth.

Rogan smiled and nodded. "Yes, normally, on any other day you would be the goat. But today is not one of those days. In fact, you could say that this is your lucky day."

Martin tilted his head and furrowed his brow. "I don't understand."

Rogan seemed amused at Martin's confusion. He paused for a few seconds before changing the subject. "You know, I wasn't always the Executioner. Obviously, right? Although, I have been doing it longer than any of my predecessors. Do you know what I was before this? A school teacher."

"A teacher?" said Martin. He wore his shock to Rogan's revelation like an ugly hat. He had trouble picturing the Executioner as anything other than the Executioner. *And why was he telling me this?* Martin wasn't sure where this was heading, but he was curious, and the more it delayed him beginning the reckoning the better. And Rogan said that this was his lucky day. How? Martin decided to play along. "What did you teach?"

Rogan flashed a smile; he seemed pleased that Martin was engaging him. "I was a language teacher. I would have been a history teacher if teaching history wasn't against Doctrine. But I loved kids and educating them was my calling." Rogan stared off into the distance as he fondly remembered his past. "Life was good back then; I had a wife, two kids, and my dream job." Rogan put on a thin smile and looked at the table. "Happy times." Snapping back to reality, he looked at Martin and said, "Not that my life isn't good now. It is. It's great. Being the Executioner has many rewards; it has allowed me to take care of my family in ways I didn't think possible. Fresh clothes, three meals a day, a private residence. Everyone with their own room. Do you believe that? When I was a kid, my family lived in a shared residence with three other families, and we ate once a day if we were lucky. I never dreamed I would live in a place where my kids would have their own bedroom, and have more food than they could possibly eat.

"What happened?"

"Hmmm?"

"How did you go from being a happy language teacher to being the sector's executioner?"

Rogan sighed and, with a somber look on his face, he said, "I broke Doctrine."

"What?"

Rogan gave a little chuckle and nodded at Martin's confusion. "I know. Makes no sense."

"What did you do?" asked Martin. "To break Doctrine, I mean. If I may ask."

"I gave one of my students a book."

"A book?"

"Not just any book," said Rogan. "A Pre-Covenant book."

"How did you get a pre-Covenant book? They were all confiscated and destroyed."

"It had been in my family since before the Cleansing. It had been hidden and passed down through the generations. It was a wonderful book, full of stories and imagery. And he was such a smart kid; full of questions, always so curious about the before time, before the Covenant and the Doctrine. I told him to keep it safe, to keep it secret. No one must know of its existence." Rogan stopped and looked blankly at the table.

"So, what happened?" said Martin.

"His mother became suspicious and found the book under his mattress. She called the enforcer squad and they went to the building and contained the boy."

"She turned her own son over to the enforcers?"

"Like I said, Martin: You'd be surprised..."

"But they found out that it was you who gave the book to the boy. Did he give you up?"

"No, but he should have. Even though his own mother turned him in and he faced death, he refused to tell the enforcers who gave him the book. Like I said, he was a good kid. But as soon as I heard what had happened, I went to the enforcer station and turned myself in."

"How noble," Martin said, trying to not put too much sarcasm in his voice. Rogan didn't seem to notice.

"I thought so at the time, and, like you, I knew it was the right thing to do. I just didn't take into consideration the impact it would have on my family. Not only the ridicule and shame they would endure, but the fact that I wouldn't be there to provide for them. Fortunately, I was presented with an opportunity to help make it all right."

Martin sat there looking at him. He was torn between being intrigued by the story and worried about his immediate future, but something told him that the two were intertwined.

"Do you know how a new Executioner is selected, Martin?"

"Not really."

"Every four years the Executioner goes through... an evaluation. A miscreant is randomly selected to engage the Executioner in combat and the victor is either the new Executioner, or the current Executioner gets to keep his job. For another four years, at least. This is my fifth evaluation."

It took a few moments for the realization to sink in. When it did, Martin said: "Me? You want *me* to fight *you*? To be the new Executioner?" It was Martin's turn to stand up and pace. "This is insane! I don't want your job."

"What you want is irrelevant," Rogan said in a calm voice. "Your choices are simple: fight me or go through the reckoning."

"What happens if I fight you? If I win, I become the new Executioner?"

"Yes."

"And if I lose?"

"You die. It's a fight to the death."

"To the death?!" Martin stopped his pacing and turned to face Rogan.

"Of course, to the death. What did you expect? We would arm wrestle?"

Martin leaned on the table towards Rogan. "I can't do that. I'm not a killer."

"Neither was I. But I owed it to my family to not only make their lives better, but prevent them from a having a far worse life than they currently led. If I hadn't killed the previous Executioner during his evaluation, then my family would have been disgraced and exiled to the perimeter camps. By defeating him, I not only saved them from that, but I had given them a wonderful life. As the Executioner, my family has had the best food, the best medicine, the best of everything. And, not to mention, I got to live." Rogan nodded as he justified his history to Martin. "My family and I have lived a privileged life, Martin. And, by defeating my predecessor, I washed the stench of my betrayal to the Covenant off of me and my family. My sin was vanquished."

"But you're a monster. The sins you've committed against humanity severely outweigh the small one of giving a simple book to a curious boy."

"A monster, Martin? A monster? I protect the Covenant. I am the ultimate enforcer of the Doctrine! I do what has to be done so that the citizens of the Covenant will not be tempted to stray from the Doctrine as I had done. If anything, I save lives."

"You torture people to death." Martin held up a hand to cut off Rogan. "Call it whatever you will, but it's still torture. Your job makes you a monster. I could never do what you do."

"Then you will die. And your family," Rogan said as he stood from his chair, "will live in poverty and shame." Rogan reached into the left side of his vest and pulled out a knife. Martin stood straight and swallowed hard at seeing the long dual edge blade. Rogan took the tip of the blade between his fingers and flipped the knife straight toward the ceiling. The knife twisted and flipped in the air as it reflected the sun from the skylight. It missed the ceiling by inches, and when it came back down, it stuck into the table with a thud.

Martin's eyes shot from Rogan to the knife, then back to Rogan.

Stone-faced, Rogan reached into the right side of his vest and pulled out another knife, identical to the first. He placed it on the table and pushed it toward Martin. The knife skidded across the wooden table, making a resonant scraping sound as it traversed the surface. It stopped a fraction of an inch from the edge. Martin stared at it for what seemed like minutes.

"Pick up the knife, Martin," Rogan said. Rogan the teacher was gone; Vero the Executioner stood before him now. Serious eyes engulfed Martin and made his heartrate quicken. He felt his face ignite as blood rushed to his head. Rogan just stood there; motionless and emotionless. His statue-like stance was more disturbing to Martin than if he had been erratically moving around like a maniac. "Pick up the knife, Martin," the Executioner repeated. "I won't fight an unarmed man."

Martin forced his eyes to look down at the knife. It sat there, taunting him, daring him to pick it up. He didn't want to pick it up. He certainly didn't want to fight this man. But what of his family? They would be shamed and sent to the perimeter camps. Not to mention the reckoning itself; nine days of torture and dismemberment. He needed to fight. Fight for his family, fight for himself. Then, to Martin's surprise, his hand moved ever so slowly and lifted the knife off the table. It was as if he wasn't in control of his actions, like some external force was controlling him, making him do what he was too afraid to do on his own. He gripped the handle and looked at Rogan.

"Very good," said Rogan. "Let's begin." In seamless motions he plucked the knife from the table with one hand and with the other he grabbed the edge of the table and pushed it to the side. His foot swiped the chair and sent it to rest against the wall next to the table.

Martin looked down at his own chair. With his free hand he pushed it towards the other chair in a slow deliberate motion. With that weak push, it didn't quite make all the way over.

The two men stood there looking at each other. Martin was terrified, Rogan looked bored. "What now?" asked Martin.

"Now you attack me." Rogan gave him a "come to me" wave with his free hand. "Come at me. You're the challenger. You make the first move."

Martin had no idea what to do. Rogan was obviously more experienced than him. What chance did he really have? Surprise? Possibly. *Maybe if I catch him off guard...*

Martin suddenly lunged at The Executioner, both hands out, not even aiming the knife. Rogan sidestepped out of the way with practiced ease. Martin passed him and crashed into the wall behind Rogan. Dazed and hurt, Martin steadied himself against the wall, then charged Rogan again. And, as before, Rogan sidestepped out of his way, but this time, as Martin passed him, he stuck out his foot, tripping Martin and sending the challenger tumbling to the ground and into the wall.

"You need to do better than that, miscreant," said Rogan. "More than your life is on the line."

Martin lay there on the floor, bleeding and in pain. "This is pointless," he said as he wiped the blood from the corner of his mouth. "Why don't you just kill me and get it over with?"

"If I simply wanted to kill you, I would have slit your throat when I first entered the room. You need to fight for your life. You must truly try to defeat me. If you don't, you will go through the reckoning."

Martin raised his head. "You said I wouldn't have to go through the reckoning if I fought you."

"Only if I kill you. And I won't kill you unless you truly try to kill me. Now, come on! Get up! This is your chance not to be a coward like the others. You can die trying to be a hero. That's what you want, isn't it? Not sniveling there on the floor, begging for death. Get up! Or do you want the reckoning? Are you just a goat after all?" Rogan looked down at his knife and twirled it in his hand. "And what about your family? Do you want them sent to the camps?"

Martin forced himself to his feet. He couldn't ignore the pain, so he used it instead. The pain fueled his anger just as Rogan's words did. Rogan was right, Martin wasn't a coward. He didn't live his life like one and he wasn't about to leave this world like one. Surprisingly, his legs held him strong. They might have been the only thing on his body that didn't hurt.

"Actually," Rogan continued, looking back up at Martin, "They may not be that bad off. How old is your wife? Thirty? Thirty-two? I'm sure she's rather attractive. She may find work in one of the prostitution rings."

"Shut up!" Martin said through gritted teeth.

"And that four-year-old girl of yours? She can follow right in her mommy's footsteps. Then you'll have a nice family of whores taking care of themselves."

"I said: Shut. Up!" Martin started towards Rogan and the Executioner readied himself for the charge, but Martin detoured to his left and grabbed the chair that was formerly his. Spinning in a quick semi-circle, he gave the chair momentum, and when he let go, it hit Rogan in his shoulder as he turned to protect himself from the projectile. Without hesitation, Martin grabbed the other chair and repeated his attack. More unprepared for the second chair than the first, Rogan took the full brunt of the wooden weapon in the chest and face. Rogan yelled in pain and fell backwards on the floor. The chair fell with him and stayed on his chest like a strange looking blanket.

Martin picked up his knife from the floor and went over to Rogan. The Executioner laid there holding his face, blood seeped through fingers that covered his now broken nose. Martin grabbed the chair resting on Rogan's chest and flung it to the side. He then knelt down next to him and, with both hands, held his knife high in the air, ready to finish him off.

"Do it," Rogan said through bloodstained teeth. "Do it, you coward."

Martin tensed and readied his hands to plunge the shining blade into the Rogan's heart. But then he looked into his eyes. Not the eyes of Vero the Executioner, but those of Rogan the former school teacher. They were calm and unflinching, but there was also a subtle hint of fear in them. He was afraid to die. This man who had killed hundreds over the years was afraid to die himself.

Martin lowered the knife and dropped it to his side. It hit the floor with a resounding clank.

"Wh-What are you doing?" asked Rogan.

"I can't do it," said Martin, holding back a sob. "I thought I could. For a minute I thought I was really going to kill you."

"For a second there, I thought you were, too," said Rogan.

"Like I said, I'm not a killer."

"No. No you're not. But you will be soon enough." With a swift move of his arm, Rogan grabbed Martin's knife from the floor and plunged it into his own midsection.

"My god!" shouted Martin. "What have you done?!"

Martin panicked. He didn't know what to do. *Do I take the knife out? Should I call for help?* Martin carefully reached for the blood covered handle that blended into Rogan's shirt like a morbid accessory. But Rogan's hand beat him to it.

"Don't," Rogan said in a pain-laced voice. "I nicked my lung and liver. If you pull it out, I'll just bleed out faster." He coughed and his face contorted from the pain. Blood stained his lips. "And it'll hurt like hell." Rogan took an agonizing deep breath and yelled, "Guard!"

The door unlocked, and the sentry who had come in earlier walked in. Martin gave a start at his entrance. The guard looked around the room as if he couldn't believe the mess. Then he looked down at the two men on the floor, accessed the situation in seconds, then snapped to attention. "Your orders, sir?"

It took Martin a moment to realize that the guard was talking to him. In the sentry's eyes, Rogan was defeated, and Martin was

The Executioner now. With Rogan laying there dying in front of him, his freshly spilled blood staining the ceramic tile floor, Martin had a hard time wrapping his head around it all. He turned his head to the sentry and said, "Can you give us a few minutes. Please." The sentry nodded an acknowledgement, then turned and left the room. The door shut, but did not lock.

Martin could only look at Rogan. He still didn't know what to do, and the only thing he could think of to say was, "Why?"

"I'm tired, Martin," Rogan said with exasperated, painful breath. "I've done my time. It's time for a new Executioner."

"What of your family? Your wife, your kids?"

"Wife died two years ago. Kids are all grown up. I'm done. Can't do it anymore."

"Why didn't you just commit suicide? If your family is no longer a factor. Why didn't you end this after your wife died?"

"Because, Martin, I needed to find someone worthy. Someone who would benefit from being the Executioner as I did." Several coughs forced some blood out of Rogan's mouth. "A good man with a family. That's why I chose you."

"But you said I was randomly chosen."

"I lied," Rogan smiled. "I picked you personally and had you brought here." He weakly gestured around the room. "One of my special rooms. No eyes."

"Yes," said Martin, looking around. "I noticed that." Martin dropped his head and shook it as if trying to clear away the ugliness of the afternoon.

"Be strong, Martin. You will need all your strength."

"I'm not sure if I can do it. I mean, I couldn't even kill you. How can I torture people to death?" Tears welled up in Martin's eyes. The tears weren't for Rogan, but for himself and his family. He shook his head again, then buried his face in his hands.

Rogan took his hand from the knife's handle and weakly placed it on Martin's knee. "You'll have to, Martin. For yourself. For your family." Martin raised his face from his hands to look at the dying school teacher. "That's what you need to keep in mind, that you're doing it for them." A coughing spasm caused Rogan to convulse. After a few seconds, he regained control and continued. “The first year is the worst.”

“But—”

“You’ll do fine,” Rogan reassured him. “You just need a better executioner name than Martin if you are to be ... sinister.”

“What do you suggest?” Martin said, trying to remain as composed as possible. He couldn’t believe he was having this conversation.

“How about ... Hircum? Hircum the Executioner.”

“Hircum? I like it,” Martin said, forcing a smile. “What does it mean?”

“It means ...” Rogan said with a strained breath, his final breath. “It means ‘the goat.’”

FISH BOWL

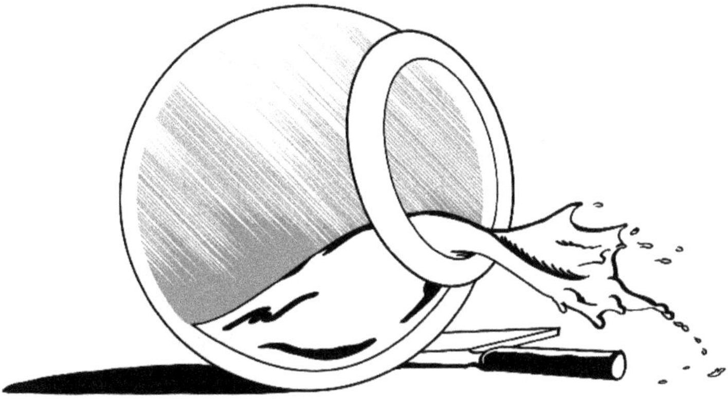

"I thought about how there are two types of secrets: the kind you *want* to keep in, and the kind you don't *dare* to let out."
– **Ally Carter, Don't Judge a Girl by Her Cover**

Peter awoke with a jolt. Sweating and shaking, he sat up in state of a panic. His heart thumped like a bass drum in his chest, and his head pounded in rhythm along with it. He fought to catch his breath, as the fear slowly evened out to moderate dread. Was it a dream, a nightmare that had awakened him? He couldn't remember. But it didn't matter; he was awake now, and he sat on the edge of his bed to calm his breathing and steady his heart.

Everything's fine, he assured himself. He was safe and sound in his bed. Except there was one problem:

This wasn't his bed.

Looking around, he found himself in a strange room. Strange as in unfamiliar, and strange as in unusual. Sparsely furnished, and even more sparsely decorated, the 'bedroom' was plain and somewhat off-putting. There was something about the room that didn't feel quite right, beside the fact that he had never been in there before.

"Where the hell am I?" he wondered aloud. Looking down, he noticed he was in clothes that weren't his either. They were loose and soft. Pajamas, he assumed. He rubbed the cloth between his fingers; it was a material he wasn't familiar with.

An orange glow from a nearby window suggested that the sun was rising, or setting for all he knew. He stood and walked over to it, hoping to get a look outside and a better idea of where he was.

The uncarpeted floor was unusually warm to Peter's bare feet causing him to wonder if there was a boiler room below him. The floor itself was different too; it certainly wasn't cement, and it didn't have the give and the creak of wood.

When he reached the window and looked outside, what he saw only raised more questions. There was a grass field, a blue sky, a lone tree, and that was it. It was as plain out there as it was in the room.

"What the hell is going on?"

He gave the room a more discerning look, and what appeared to be a door was tucked in the far corner. He walked to the corner and gave the apparent door a look over. Like everything else, it was plain and unusual. There was no framing or trim, it had no knob or handle, or visible hinges. In fact, the only thing that led Peter to think that it was a door was the thin outlining gap that made it appear independent of the wall. If he hadn't been standing at the window, at that particular angle, with the light from the outside exposing the gaps, he would have missed it entirely.

Now, the problem was how to open it. It had no handle or hinges and Peter couldn't see a way to accomplish what should have been a simple task. He examined the door, if that's what it really was, more closely, running his fingers along the gap and pressing at various spots. After several minutes of prodding with no results, he was about to give up. He put his hands on his hips and squinted hard at the edges, trying to see if he had missed anything. *Maybe*, he thought, *this door isn't meant to be opened. At least from this side.*

Then, unexpectedly, without him touching anything, the door opened by sliding completely into the wall. That, in itself, was surprising to him; he certainly hadn't seen that coming. But what the opened door revealed, surprised him even more.

Standing in the doorway was a woman. She was beautiful, slender, and blonde.

And she was completely naked.

Peter stared in disbelief. He'd expected to find someone here, someone to provide answers, explain to him where he was and what was going on. Maybe an in-charge type boss with a couple of no-neck guys for muscle. But the woman standing before him was the last thing he had anticipated.

The woman leapt forward and threw her arms around him in a strong embrace.

"You're here! You're here! You're actually here!" With her head pressed against his shoulder, she rocked him side to side, her long hair brushing his face.

Her skin was as soft as cashmere, and her hair felt like strands of Persian silk. Peter slowly inhaled; the woman had a natural, organic scent; no perfume or cream smell. And it was intoxicating, inviting. Peter's mind began to swim in urges that he hadn't felt in years. Urges that were hard to ignore. Urges that awoke ... memories.

No. No, he couldn't get distracted. This was neither the time nor the place. Was this some kind of test? A joke?

He grabbed her shoulders and pushed her away. "Lady, what the hell's going on here? Where am I? Who are you?" He got a better look at her; she appeared to be around twenty-five, she wore no makeup, and her golden hair hung naturally, cascading over her shoulders and framing her beautiful face.

Her smile faded a bit, and she tilted her head. “You sure have a lot of questions. Aren’t you happy to be here?”

“Lady,” Peter bit, “I don’t even know where *here* is.”

Her smile grew again as she grabbed Peter’s hand and pulled him through the doorway and into the room from which she had entered. Letting go of his hand, she spread her arms and spun around with her head tilted back, reminding Peter of a kid being carefree at the beach or in a field of snow.

“This is my home,” she said in a singsong voice. “My home, my home, my home.”

Peter pried his eyes off the dancing naked woman long enough to look around the new room. It was much larger than the one he had just been in, yet as scarcely furnished and decorated. There were no chairs or other conventional pieces of furniture. Instead, cushions of various sizes and colors encompassed the floor. There were no pictures on the walls, just a few generic looking windows, nor were there any tables of any sort. The only thing of notice was a large television imbedded in the wall far to his left and a small shallow, maybe glass, dome centered on the ceiling. A light, perhaps. Or a camera. But what made this room remarkable was how unremarkable it was. Almost as if it went out of its way to be so.

Taking a few steps forward, he stopped the spinning woman, who almost fell down from dizziness when he did so. She grabbed his shoulders to prevent herself from toppling over. Peter grabbed her arms to do the same.

“Lady,” said Peter. “What is this place? Why am I here? Answer me!” He gave her a little shake to snap her out of her euphoric trance.

The woman’s smile faded as she gave Peter a puzzled look. “I told you; this is my home, and now it is your home too.” Her smile returned which only frustrated Peter even more. “Isn’t that wonderful?” she said. It was more of a statement than a question.

“My home?” he asked. “What do you mean, *my* home?”

"Cenric brought you here to live with me. My home is now your home," she repeated.

"Who is Cenric? Is he in charge?"

"Cenric takes care of me. He'll take care of you too."

Peter looked around as his mind tried to make sense of what she was saying. Was Cenric their kidnapper? Was this some type of government trick or experiment?

"What's your name?" Peter demanded.

"Eve. What's yours?"

"Peter."

"Peter," she repeated awkwardly. "That's a funny name," she said with a giggle.

Funny? Was she serious? Then what kind of name is Cenric? But Peter didn't say that. He wanted answers, and right now, this woman was the only person here to give them to him. This was not the time to be confrontational. "Eve, is Cenric holding you against your will?"

Eve tilted her head like a clueless Cocker Spaniel and furrowed her brow.

"Did he kidnap you? Are you his prisoner?"

Eve shook her head. "I don't understand what you are saying."

"Has he hurt you? Has he ... raped you?"

"I don't know what 'raped' means, but Cenric has not hurt me. He would never do that. He loves me."

It was Peter's turn to wear a puzzled look. Something was not quite right with this woman. She seemed a little ... slow. Did she really not understand the things he was saying? Was she mentally challenged? *Was this Cenric guy keeping a retarded girl as his personal sex slave?* The thought of such an atrocity sickened him.

"Are you hungry?" Eve said with some excitement in her voice. Before Peter could answer, she dashed to a nearby wall and retrieved two bowls that were resting on the floor. She returned to Peter and handed him one of the bowls.

"Here," she said. "This is our food." And she began to dip her fingers into the bowl.

Peter looked down at the "food" and saw a mound of what could only be described as purple mashed potatoes. He raised the bowl to his nose and gave a sniff. The purple stuff emitted no smell. He doubted it was poisoned; if they wanted to kill him, they could have done that way before this. So, he dipped his pinkie finger into the purple mass, pulled a small amount out, and gave it a sample taste.

And it tasted like nothing. Absolutely nothing. He shook his head and handed the bowl back to Eve, who had already devoured half of her portion. "Thanks, but I'm not really hungry."

Eve took his bowl and nodded her understanding.

"You're awake," came a strange voice. "Excellent."

Peter turned to see that a man had entered the room. From where, Peter had no idea. And the man had made no sound until he had just spoken. He wore a brown one-piece jumper; his hair was black and combed back; and his wrinkleless face suggested that he was around thirty. Peter stepped in front of Eve, putting himself between her and the newcomer. But, after placing the bowls back on the floor, she ran around Peter with the deftness of a deer and made straight to the strange man.

"Cenric!" she squealed as she flung her arms around him, in the same manner she had done with Peter. "Thank you so much. He's perfect!"

"It pleases me that you like him," Cenric said. He gently pried her arms from around his neck, took a step back, and looked her up and down. "We've been over this, Eve; you need to wear clothes. Out of respect for our new resident."

Eve's brow creased in a frown. "Do I have to?" she said in a pouty voice.

"Yes," said Cenric. "Now, go to your room and put on something appropriate. Like what I showed you the other day.

"Okay," she said glumly and walked to a wall where another hidden door opened when she placed her hand flat against its center. It then closed when she disappeared into yet another room.

"Good morning, Peter," Cenric said. "How are you feeling?"

"Who the hell are you?" Peter snapped. "Where am I, and why have you brought me here?"

"I am Cenric," he said with a comforting smile. "As for where you are, that's a bit complicated. However, the reason you are here is because Eve asked me to bring you here."

"Eve asked you?"

"Well, that's not quite accurate," Cenric corrected. "She asked me for a companion, so I went to your apartment complex, retrieved you, and then brought you here."

"My apartment complex?" *Is this guy serious?* Peter looked down as he tried to remember anything from the night before. He had no recollection of anything after he went to bed. He didn't even remember falling asleep. "So, you kidnapped me?" he asked.

"I don't like to use such a negative word, but, essentially, you are correct." Cenric confirmed.

"That's a little hard to swallow. How in the hell did you accomplish that?" Peter asked. It seemed that the more answers he got only sprouted new questions.

"That, too, is a bit complicated," Cenric said.

"And Eve? How long have you had her here? Did you snatch her from her home as well? From her parents? Have you grown bored with her lately and that's why you brought me here?"

"Eve's story is complex. Perhaps after you have been here a while, I will explain it all to you."

"You'll explain it to me now," Peter growled, his anger beginning to mount. He looked past Cenric to the wall from which he would have emerged. No door was readily visible, but that didn't mean it wasn't there. Could he incapacitate Cenric, run to the wall, find the door and open it, all before his captor collected himself and attempted to stop him?

It wasn't very promising. Cenric didn't look that formidable, but Peter's lack of knowledge of his surroundings made the odds considerably in the other's favor. Especially when you throw trick doors, and the complete unknown of his location into the equation.

"In due time," Cenric said. He then turned his attention behind Peter. "There you go, my dear."

Peter turned to find that Eve had emerged from the room and was wearing a light-blue dress that went down to her knees. Though la bit odd, the dress somehow made her look even more beautiful. The frown on her face made it apparent that she was not happy about wearing the garment. In her right hand she held a pair of shoes. She raised them to Cenric.

"Please don't make me wear these," she said. "They are very uncomfortable."

"That's fine." Cenric said. "The important thing is the dress. Come, let me take a look at you."

Eve walked over to where Cenric and Peter stood, dropping the shoes onto the floor before doing so.

"There," Cenric said. "That's much better. Don't you agree, Peter?"

Peter looked at Eve. The dress was indeed pretty, but seemed a bit dated. It resembled something a young woman from the fifties or sixties would wear. But that wasn't the only odd thing about the dress. When he realized what the oddity was, Peter said, "She looks beautiful."

Eve smiled at the compliment, and Cenric grinned at her as if to say 'I told you so.'

"However," Peter continued, "she's wearing it backwards."

Both Cenric and Eve looked from Peter to the dress and then back to Peter, apparently not understanding what he was talking about.

"The zipper goes in the back," Peter explained.

Cenric eyed the zipper on the dress and a look of realization hit him. "Easily remedied. Let me help you with that." He unzipped the dress and began to take it off of Eve.

Peter used this distraction to make a stealthy break for the door that Cenric had used. He silently walked over and examined the wall in an attempt to find the telltale cracks that would outline the exit. He found them in seconds, but the problem, again, was to figure out how to open it. He searched around for a button, or switch, or some type of optical sensor. Coming up empty, he remembered what Eve had done to open her door.

Peter placed his hand in the center of the door and prepared to jerk his hand back in anticipation of it sliding open. But nothing happened. He moved his hand around trying to find the correct spot, and then he heard Eve call out.

"What are you doing, Peter?"

Peter turned around to see the once again naked Eve peering around Cenric.

Cenric turned around to face Peter. "If you are looking for a way out, you will not find one. Not one that you can access, anyway."

Frustrated, Peter stormed back to Cenric. "I demand you let me go. You have no right to keep me here. This is kidnapping."

"I'm afraid there's no going back," Cenric said matter-of-factly. "You are just going to have to adjust to your new home."

"My new home? Why does everyone keep saying that? This is not my home. New or otherwise. When they realize I'm missing, they'll come looking for me. And when they do, your ass is in a heap of trouble."

"No one will come looking for you. And certainly, no one will find you. Just relax and enjoy your new home."

Peter snapped. Years of therapy and anger management flew out the window. His hands wrapped around his captor's neck as he began to strangle the man.

Cenric calmly reached up and grabbed Peter's wrists and pried his hands away from his neck with uncommon strength and little apparent effort. While still holding Peter's wrists in his vise-like grip, Cenric tossed him halfway across the room, sending him sprawling onto the floor.

Peter got up, rubbing his sore wrists, not understanding how Cenric had done that. But the anger still raged inside him, and with a running start, he raised his right fist above his head with the full intention of bringing it down on Cenric's stoic face. But before he could get within striking distance, the glass dome on the ceiling lit up, and an invisible force struck his chest sending him flying backwards into the wall. The last thing Peter saw before losing consciousness, was Eve running over to him, tears streaming down her face.

Peter sat up in bed. He touched his chest, his head, then his wrists. They didn't hurt. None of it did. "It was just a dream," he said smiling. Nodding satisfactorily to himself he examined his wrists again. "Just a dream." Then he noticed the sleeve of his shirt and the material it was made of.

"No."

He examined the bed, the dimly lit nondescript room.

"No! This can't be."

But it was. He was back in the room where he had started. This time, a pale white glow from outside penetrated the window. Peter stood up and knocked over a bowl of purple glop that Eve had called food. Stepping over the upset bowl, he moved to the window and looked out at the plain landscape. It was still the same, except a full moon now hovered in the sky where the sun had been earlier. And again, Peter got the feeling in the back of his head that something wasn't quite right. Looking back at the moon, he took in a small gasp.

The moon was wrong.

Ever since he was a boy, Peter had gazed at the night sky, fascinated by the moon and the stars and the planets. He knew the moon well; all its craters and valleys were etched into his memory. He could always make out a face in the moon; the eyes, the nose, the mouth. But this moon had none of those. It was just a plain, featureless white orb.

Peter shifted his gaze to the stars. Jupiter should have been in the sky this time of year, but Peter looked around and could not make out the giant planet anywhere. Besides the moon, it should have been the brightest object in the sky with its light shining steady like a bright beacon, not twinkling like stars. But it wasn't there. Peter noticed that not even the stars were right. He couldn't make out any constellations. Not one.

He turned away from the window more confused than ever. And even more suspicious. Things weren't what they seemed. He was being set up for something. An experiment or study of some sort. Whether the government was involved or it was just this guy Cenric, Peter knew this would come to a head eventually, and it wouldn't bode well for him. And if he couldn't figure out what it was, he was going to get the hell out of there before things got worse. Looking back at the bed, he had an idea.

Turning the bed over and using brute force to dismantle it, Peter found something he could use. Although most of the bed was made of some type of polymer, there were actually a few pieces of metal and one was straight and flat. Perfect.

With his new tool in hand, Peter walked over to his door and decided to try placing his hand in the middle and see if it opened. It did. The door slid into the wall, and Peter walked into the main living area.

The two windows let in the same moonlight that gave his room a dull luminescence. After eying the spot where the door he had tried to open should be, Peter hesitated and decided to walk to the door through which Eve had disappeared. Placing his hand flat against the center, the door silently slid open.

Eve's room was about the same size as Peter's and not much more furnished. There was no dresser or nightstands or anything you would associate with a bedroom. Instead of a bed, she had a large pillow-like mattress on the floor where she slept soundly, and naked, of course. Her blue dress lay tossed on the floor by the window, discarded like an unwanted rag.

Looking back at Eve, Peter's heart started beating harder and faster. There she was, all young and beautiful, lying there like a gift for him to take. He closed his eyes, remembering her scent and the softness of her hair and skin. She was almost too good to be true.

And that usually meant that it was. Peter snapped himself out of his trance and back to the matter at hand. Escape.

Peter took a step toward Eve; if he was going to bust out of here, he knew he had to take her with him. She may have been convinced that Cenric meant her no harm, but what he was doing here wasn't right. Then Peter stopped as he thought about how she would react. She didn't view Cenric as an enemy or her captor. In fact, she genuinely seemed to like the guy. What did they call that? Stockholm syndrome? Peter knew that if he tried to take her with him, she would put up a fight and possibly ruin any chance they had for getting out of there.

He would have to leave her. Once he got out and found someone, he would send people back for her. And Cenric.

Peter quietly backed out of the room and made his way to the front door. He found the outlining gaps again and tried once more to open the door by placing his hand on its center. Nothing happened. No surprise there. He raised the metal bar and placed it in the gap as far in as it would go. Then, using the leverage of the length of the bar, he attempted to pry it open. After a few attempts and moving the bar to different positions, he finally got it to budge. Peter smiled as he applied a good heaping of elbow grease into the job and was elated when the door slid completely open. But his elation was replaced with horror as the door opened to reveal Cenric standing just beyond the portal.

Peter readied the metal bar as a weapon and held it up in a threatening position. "Don't make me use this," he said trying to control his shaky voice. "I won't hurt you if you just stand aside and let me pass."

But Cenric didn't reply. He only stood there, not acknowledging Peter nor making any movement. Cenric's eyes appeared to be focused on something far away. Peter moved side to side, but Cenric's eyes didn't follow. He waved a hand in front of Cenric's face. Nothing. Peter gave him a nudge on the shoulder, but Cenric didn't budge. He was also much heavier than he appeared.

"What the hell are you?" Peter said, grimacing as he contemplated this new enigma.

Suddenly, Cenric's head turned and his eyes focused on Peter. "Good evening."

Peter took a leap backward, startled by Cenric's "awakening." With the metal bar still in his hand, he put himself in a ready stance, prepared to fight Cenric, if it came to that.

"What the hell!" Peter yelled. "What are you doing just standing there? What the hell is going on here? Tell me. Now!"

Cenric smiled at Peter, the way a parent would smile at a child. "I'll do better than that. I'll show you."

Cenric led Peter back through the door that Peter had originally thought was the house's entrance/exit. However, it was only an alcove that led to a narrow corridor that seemed to wind its way away from the rest of the building until they reached a large room. The room had a high ceiling and was mainly empty save for three of the walls which were encompassed with electronic instruments and closet-like compartments that were closed shut. The long wall opposite them was completely empty, making it stark in comparison to the others that seemed to make use of every square inch.

"What is this place?" Peter asked.

"This room serves many functions, but for now, it's a meeting place."

"Who are we meeting?" Peter asked, looking around warily. Perhaps Cenric wasn't the top dog here. Maybe he was just some lackey, and now Peter was about to meet his boss.

"You are going to meet ... me." Cenric replied.

"What?" Peter said, his head snapping back to Cenric. "What do you mean, I'm going to meet you? I don't understand."

"In a few seconds," Cenric said, "I hope you will."

Then, the large blank wall in front of them slid downward into the floor in the same manner that the doors in the house had opened by sliding into the walls. Instead of the now-removed-wall revealing another room, it was now replaced by a glass barrier.

It was difficult for Peter to make out what was on the other side of the glass. It was dark and murky and looked like the visibility was only a few yards at the most. He squinted a bit as he concentrated and tried to understand what he was seeing, and then it hit him. It was water.

Like a giant aquarium, the wall of water loomed large before him, giving Peter a submerged and almost claustrophobic feel. He looked to Cenric for a reaction or an explanation, however the strange man only stood by as if waiting for something to happen. Then it happened.

A large object in the water slowly made its way to the glass. Lumbering forward, what began as a blurry, shapeless blob, slowly became more defined the closer it got until it was right up against the glass.

It was an octopus.

Or at least, something that resembled one. Though Peter had never seen an actual octopus before, the thing in front of him did not look exactly like the ones he had seen in books or on television. Its bulbous head was rounder and more demarcated from the rest of its body. It hosted two large eyes that were focused right on him and seemed to have intelligence behind them. Its body consisted mainly of long, thick tentacles that moved and guided the creature along. Two shorter appendages with four finger-like digits each, grasped a device that appeared manmade and possibly mechanical.

"Hello, Peter," Cenric said.

Peter looked to the man next to him, but Cenric was staring aimlessly at the glass wall. Peter's eyes shifted to the octopus, back to Cenric, then back to the octopus.

"Are you telling me," Peter said, still dividing his attention between the two beings, "that you are the creature in the water?"

"Precisely," said the man next to Peter.

Peter kept looking from one to the other, his mind trying to decide what was fact, and what was fiction. After a couple seconds, he said, "Bullshit."

The creature in the water seemed to stir at Peter's defiant statement.

"What do you mean?" said Cenric.

Peter took a step closer to the man. "This is all some kind of ... experiment or test or something with me. Isn't it? You're trying to see how I would react to all this?"

"No," said Cenric. "I am the being you see in the water before you. What you are, and have been speaking to is my artificial representative, my avatar, if you will."

"Avatar?" said Peter. "You mean you're not real."

"*I* am real." Cenric's arm raised and pointed to the creature in the water. "He is not." The arm then curved back on itself to point at Cenric's head.

"Prove it," Peter dared.

After a few seconds, Cenric raised his hands and clasped each side of his head. Then, with a twist and a pull, he took his head clean off his shoulders.

Peter gawked at the site. His mind's first instinct was to look for blood to spill onto the floor. But when he saw the stainless connectors, tubes, and wiring protruding from Cenric's neck, Peter knew that the man before him was not a living being.

"What the fuck is going on?" was all Peter could say, unable to take his eyes of the decapitated Cenric. "You're a robot?" he said, unable to keep the shock out of his voice.

"A fairly accurate observation," Cenric had lowered "his head" and held it under his arm like a football. It continued to speak as if being disconnected from its body was an everyday occurrence. "I hope you are not confused."

"Actually, it kinda explains a few things," Peter said as he rubbed his wrists that should still be hurting from the manhandling he had received from Cenric yesterday.

"I apologize for injuring you," Cenric said. "But you left me no choice. However, I repaired your injuries, so I hope all is forgiven."

"And how exactly did you do that?"

"The human body is very fragile; fortunately, it is also very easy to repair. As long as the damage isn't too severe."

"Okay, so, are you going to tell me what's going on?"

"You are no longer on Earth, Peter."

"That much I gathered. Now tell me why."

"Eve had become distraught as of late. She needed a companion, and the Cenric avatar was not enough to satisfy her. So, I went to your planet in search of someone. I put the parameters for my search in my ship's computer, and you were one of over 450,000 on your planet that I had to choose from."

"So, what ... you pulled my name out of a hat?" Peter was addressing the creature now. Holding a conversation with the disembodied android head seemed somehow inappropriate.

"Nothing so mundane, but you are not too wrong either."

"And—let me guess—you, like alien Captain Kirk, had Scotty beam me up from my place of residence and into your spaceship."

"I'm not familiar with this Captain Kirk, but I did retrieve you utilizing a molecular reconfiguring migrator."

Peter shook his head. *I can't believe I'm standing here talking to an alien fish through his robot proxy.* An alien who had kidnapped him. Him, of all people.

"Is that how you got Eve?" said Peter. "You just went to Earth one day and migrated her?"

"Eve was born on this planet and raised here with me."

"What?" Peter's eyes widened as his face creased in a frown.

"Humans have been raised on this planet for centuries, until they were deemed ... I don't have a word for it, but it is now illegal to do so. That is why I needed to go to your planet to find Eve's companion."

"Because there are no more available humans here."

"Correct."

"But why? What is Eve to you? A slave of some sort?"

"Slave? Not at all, Peter. I love Eve. She is the most important thing in my life."

"Love her? How can you possibly love her? She's human and you're ... whatever it is you are."

"Haven't you ever loved a being from another species?"

"When I was a kid, we had a pug named Waffle that I—" Peter paused as he suddenly realized what this was all about. "My god. She's your pet."

The android seemed to ponder Peter's proclamation. "Yes. I suppose she is."

You suppose she is? The creature said that so matter-of-factly that it was the most humbling thing Peter had ever heard. She was his pet. And that meant he was too.

Peter looked from the creature in the water, who was looking intently at him, to the thing he knew as Cenric, who was placing his head back onto his shoulders. "So, how does this work? This connection you have with the android." Peter needed to focus on something else besides the fact that he was now some octupus' lap dog.

"I control Cenric with my thoughts and the controls on this panel. My language and even emotions are transmitted through him. It allows me to interact with Eve on a level that she can better relate to."

"Has she ever seen you—the real you?"

"No. She would be not able to comprehend any of this. So, I ask you to please not spoil the illusion for her. The emotional and mental damage could be devastating."

"Don't worry. I won't tell her Santa Claus isn't real."

"Ah. I understand that reference. Funny and somewhat accurate."

"So, what do you want from me?"

"To be her companion. To love her like only a true human can."

"You mean, she needs physical attention. Sex."

"I believe you call it intimacy. And yes, sex is a part of that."

"Well, if you're expecting little Peters or Eves to be walking around. I had a vasectomy years ago. No children for me."

"That is fine. That was not the purpose in bringing you here. You are here simply for Eve's happiness."

"Good. Because I couldn't allow you to start your own little people farm."

The robot, Cenric, smiled. "So, will you be Eve's companion? I will make sure you live in comfort. And Eve is a remarkable woman who will, no doubt, be able to please you."

Peter contemplated this, but it wasn't like he had much of a choice. Cenric was looking for cooperation and compliance rather than permission. Not that Peter had much say in the matter. What were his choices? Defy this creature on an alien planet? *And then ... what? He tortures me until I comply? Or, perhaps ... die?* And if he resisted too much, Cenric might kill him just to find someone else and start all over again. No, the other option seemed more logical: Live with Eve and give her companionship, make her happy. It was a no-brainer.

The good thing about Cenric and Eve was they didn't know anything about him. They knew nothing of Peter's past and therefore had no prejudgments about him. Maybe here, he could start over. Living a normal life, albeit a boring one, wouldn't be so bad. After all, a normal, boring life, was still a life. It certainly beat how he *was* living.

"Okay," said Peter, looking the creature in the water, directly into his big oval eyes. "You've got yourself a deal."

"Excellent," replied the android. "And, over time, I'm sure you and I will come to love one another."

"I wouldn't go that far. But speaking of comfort, you're going to have to make some changes around here if you truly want to keep me happy."

"Of course. Your happiness is as important to me as Eve's."

"The first thing we need to do is get a kitchen in here. I can't spend the rest of my life eating that purple crap."

Cenric smiled again. "Of course, Peter. Anything you want. I think this is going to be wonderful for us all."

Months passed and Cenric was good on his word. Not only did he provide Peter with a fully functional kitchen complete with appliances and utensils, he supplied him with an assortment of proteins and plant life for him to prepare meals for Eve and himself.

Peter instructed Cenric on the design of furniture for the rest of the house—sofas, loveseats, tables, easy chairs, rocking chairs—whatever Peter wanted, Cenric did his best to provide it for him. Eventually, the place started to look like a real house.

As for Eve, Peter found her easy to love. She wasn't complicated and didn't have a lot of baggage like the other women in his life. No, she was different, and in every good way that Peter could imagine.

Peter finally figured out, that was the key to their happiness: it was her innocence that was never lost. She wasn't corrupted by friends, or family, or past relationships. She was a virgin in the deepest of meanings. Peter could mold her into his idea of a perfect woman. And she was more than willing to do so. All she wanted to do was please him. Life here was going to be perfect, Peter mused, a bit strange, but perfect.

And everything *was* perfect until Eve got ill.

"I don't feel well, Peter," Eve said, holding her stomach.

"What's wrong?" Peter asked.

"I don't know. I—I—" then she threw up her breakfast that she had eaten an hour ago.

Peter felt her forehead; she didn't have a fever. The food should have been okay. He ate the same thing she did and he felt fine.

"Cenric!" Peter called out. "Cenric. We need you. Eve is sick." Peter got Eve a glass of water and while she drank it, Cenric's door opened and the android walked in, a look of concern on his face.

"What happened?" Cenric asked.

"We were just sitting here talking, and she suddenly felt sick to her stomach and threw up."

"Give me a moment," Cenric said, "and I will conduct a medical scan of her."

Cenric didn't move, but Peter knew that it was the alien creature outside the building that was performing the scan. When he did finally move, a smile crossed his face.

"She is fine, Peter," Cenric said and then turned to Eve. "You're going to be all right, Eve. There is nothing to worry about."

"Then what's wrong with me?" she asked.

"You are pregnant, my dear."

"Pregnant?" Both Cenric and Eve said at the same time.

"Oh, my, does that mean I'm going to have a baby?" Eve asked, looking from Cenric to Peter.

"It does," Cenric answered.

"That's so wonderful!" she beamed. "Isn't it, Peter?"

"How is that even possible," Peter asked Cenric, ignoring Eve. "I was fixed. I made sure I couldn't get a woman pregnant."

"As I told you before, Peter: the human body is easy to repair. I was able to undo your primitive surgery while you were sleeping. Now, can you get Eve a glass of vorba juice? I want to make sure she's getting all the vitamins she needs." Cenric turned his attention to Eve and began telling her about pregnancy and what she could expect.

Peter went to the kitchen, his mind a whirlwind of questions, and emotions. Cenric had done the one thing Peter didn't want him to do and now the perfect life he was building was now going to build a nursery for future pets. What was Cenric going to do ... sell their kid on some human-pet black market? *No, I can't allow that.* Instead of grabbing a glass to fill with juice, he opened a drawer and grabbed a butcher knife. Filled with hatred and resentment, Peter headed back to the living room.

"You lied to me, Cenric," Peter said, the knife gripped tightly in his hand. "You lied, you bastard! You said you had no intention of us having children."

"I'm sorry, Peter. At first, that wasn't my intention, but you gave me the idea when you mentioned it during our meeting. Now, we can enjoy another generation and keep the family continuous."

"Continuous? Are you kidding me? So, what ... are you going to find this child a mate when he or she gets older? Will you steal another person from Earth as you did me, you goddamn fish?"

"Peter, what are you saying?" Eve asked. Then she looked down and saw the object in his hand. "And what are you doing with that knife?"

Cenric looked down at the knife in Peter's hand as well. "Yes, Peter. What are you doing with that knife?"

"You're a son of a bitch. You know that?" Peter stared into Cenric's eyes. His cold artificial eyes. "A real son of a bitch."

Peter sneered at Cenric, then he cocked his arm back and plunged the butcher knife into Eve's midsection.

"No!" screamed Cenric.

Peter pulled the knife out of Eve's body and she fell to the floor, her blood spilling out and pooling around her.

"Try repairing that, you bastard." Peter threw the gilded knife on the floor and glared at Cenric, enjoying the look of horror on the avatar's face, know that the fish outside was shocked and dismayed beyond the robot's capability of relaying.

But Cenric's face quickly changed to convey anger, and he released that rage onto Peter. The android took a step forward and thrust his hands into Peter's chest. The blow sent Peter flying across the floor, causing him to crash into the kitchen. Peter felt his right arm snap as it got caught between the corner of the refrigerator door and his body.

"What have you done?" Cenric cried out. "How could you have done this? I thought you loved her. You're a monster!" He picked up the butcher knife and started toward Peter, possibly to finish him off.

"You have no idea," Peter said through spasms of pain. "She's not the first woman I hurt that I loved."

Cenric stopped and glared at Peter, the bloody knife still in the android's hand.

"You're such a fool," Peter said, shaking his head as he bathed in the pain cascading throughout his body. "You have no idea who I am, no idea who you snatched from Earth."

A puzzled look tried to form on Cenric's already anger ridden face.

"That was no apartment complex you took me from, you stupid squid," Peter continued. "That was Attica state penitentiary. My home for the past six years." Confusion now owned Cenric's face; Peter continued. "I'm Peter Jefferson Cooper." He thumbed his chest with his good hand. "Never heard of me? No? How about: The Black-Tie Killer? Or as the Times called me: *The most infamous serial killer in New York since The Son of Sam.*" Peter laughed, causing a spike of pain in his chest. He had a broken rib, or two, that was for certain. "I was serving life sentences for killing a dozen women." He looked over at Eve's lifeless body. Her eyes staring at him as if to ask why he would do such a thing to her. "I guess you can make that a baker's dozen now." He paused a second and reflected on his feelings as he stared at her unfocused eyes.

He really thought Eve was the one; he did love her, and if it weren't for this greedy alien slime, perhaps they could have grown old together. She was his last chance to have a normal life.

But, then again, he wasn't normal. Was he?

"Strange," he continued, "I don't feel anything; no regret or remorse. I thought somehow this would be different. I guess not. In fact, it felt as good as the others. Almost."

The anger in Cenric's face had disappeared completely. Now, there was only shock and disbelief.

"How's that superior intellect working for you now, fish?" Peter taunted. He coughed and a bit of blood proceeded to stain his shirt. Definitely a couple broken ribs and a punctured lung to boot. "You thought you were so smart," he continued without bothering to wipe the blood from his chin. "You thought you were going to have your own little human family living in this ... this fish bowl you created." Peter waved his arm in a weak gesture. "It turns out you don't know squat. And your little human family ... well, you can kiss that goodbye. I told you I wouldn't allow that to happen. No, you're not so smart. You're just another dumb fish."

Peter waited for a reaction from Cenric, but the android's face became emotionless. His body stiffened, and his eyes became lifeless, looking like he did when Peter first found him in his alcove just before meeting the creature itself.

Then Peter heard it; the sudden rush of water as the real Cenric opened up the valve gates and began to flood the habitat. As the cold seawater washed over his body and began to swallow him whole, a calming revelation came over Peter.

"I suppose," Peter said as a faint smile crossed his blood-stained lips, "I will have to find normal in hell."

THE FATE OF THE RED LADY

"Three may keep a secret, if two of them are dead."
– **Benjamin Franklin, Poor Richard's Almanack**

Conlan Boyle held the old photograph in his hands as if it were an ancient relic that could break with the slightest pressure. After all this time of chasing what some called a phantom or figment of his imagination, Conlan was finally holding proof that his elusive obsession had indeed existed. Lately, he'd started to have doubts, himself. Dead-end after dead-end had begun to weigh on Conlan. Not only that, but if he didn't have something to show his editor soon, he might be looking for another job when he got back to Seattle. That's if some other rag would have him. But something in the back of his mind kept him going. A persistent nag like his ex-wife used to be. But instead of telling him to take out the trash or clean the dishes or mow the lawn, this little nag had kept telling him that he was close. Really close. It was that little nag that had kept him going. That, and the Irish stubbornness he inherited from his father.

And now, his hard work and diligent investigating had finally paid off. The trail of clues had led him to George Parsons, a World War II vet who was handing him an old photograph that he had kept stowed away ever since he had returned from the war seventy years ago. No one else knew of the picture's existence, except, perhaps the other guy standing next to him in the photo. And now, Conlan himself knew. It was something he'd only dream existed. And now, here it was. Proof. Just like that.

Of course, it was just a photo and photos could be doctored. Right? But not one that was taken back in 1945. Could it? And certainly not by the decorated war veteran that sat in the rocking chair next to him, breathing pure oxygen through a nose tube connected to a small green tank behind him. No. This old man had no need for deception; he was dying, probably had a few months, if not weeks to live, and Conlan believed this old war dog was glad to finally be able to tell his story. Here, sitting on the front porch of his house on his Oklahoma ranch, the old Air Force pilot had a lot to get off his chest. It must have been eating away at him all these years, like the cancer that was eating him alive from the inside as newspaper reporter spoke with him.

Conlan got lost in the picture, absorbing every bit of detail. It had been taken in a hangar, that much was obvious. In the background was a plane, maybe the very plane itself. The floor was concrete; it looked fresh, brand new. The two young men—boys, really—flanked the open crate, smiling as if they had no idea that it contained the most destructive man-made object that had ever been created; an atom bomb. Not just any atom bomb, mind you, but the third bomb intended for Japan. Looking a lot like her predecessor, Fat Man, the bomb in the picture had a bulbous body and a boxy tailfin. If the first two hadn't forced a surrender out of Japan, then this one most certainly would have shot down the Rising Sun. Yes, sir, a piece of history that only a handful of people knew about, and just as few speculated its existence. Conlan being one of them.

"Funny thing," George said in a weak voice, "when we got the package—it was always referred to as 'the package'—it didn't have a name like the other two. So, it was me and Bill Stiggins who gave her one." He tapped the photo with a shaky finger, his yellow nail indicating the other pilot in the picture.

"Her?"

"Yeah, we figured the other two bombs were male so why not have this one be a female. After all, hell hath no wrath ..." He then gave a raspy laugh at his own little joke.

Actually, it was 'hell hath no fury', but Conlan was not about to correct the ninety-five-year-old man who was practically handing him a Pulitzer. Instead, Conlan smiled and chuckled at the man's humor and logic; so innocent, like he had been naming a puppy all those years ago. "So, what did you call her?"

"The Red Lady."

The Red Lady, Conlan thought to himself and wondered what had possessed those two young pilots to give it—her—that name. Conlan examined the photograph more closely. The bomb didn't appear to be painted red. Neither it nor the wooden crate it was resting in. Although it was nearly impossible to tell with the picture being black and white. "So, why'd you name her The Red Lady?"

"Son," George said with a sardonic smile, "you might want to hold onto your hat for this story."

Then, the old man's head snapped backward, brain matter and pieces of his skull covered the wall behind him. His mouth hung open as in some twisted, comical expression of surprise, and his eyes were staring upward as if trying to see the hole in the middle of his forehead where blood started to trickle out.

A fraction of a second later, Conlan heard a distant sharp crack of what must have been a gunshot emanating from the hills just beyond the large property's borders.

Sniper.

Blake C. Stevens closed the book and looked out at the audience as they applauded enthusiastically. He smiled politely and took a sip from his water bottle.

Normally, he didn't read passages from his book at these signings. He usually told boring stories about his research, then a steady barrage of questions from the audience, then onto the book signing. Bing, bam, boom. But his hosts had insisted he read a few pages from his book, so he politely obliged. Maybe it was a tradition here, or something. It felt awkward though; it's not like he was reading poetry or anything like that. But he did have to hand it to the library's marketing director for selecting the passage; it was a pretty defining couple pages in the book.

For months, the library had been persistently pursuing Blake to do a book signing. When his trip to Albuquerque had been cancelled due to scorching heat and the host's facilities AC not working, Blake had happily fit the Middletown library in its place and was pleasantly surprised by the reception he'd received.

This section of the library was slightly apart from the rows of book stacks and large wooden tables that made up the bulk of the place. Here, a small stage, no more than two-hundred square feet and two feet in height hunkered against the back. Blake imagined this was used for story time for the kids and whatever other authors they could lure here to do signings and readings. He envisioned puppet shows and tiny plays being put on as well. Small town stuff ... quaint, but nice.

Behind him was a pull-down movie screen where a ceiling mounted projector alternately displayed the cover of *The Fate of the Red Lady*, then his large grinning mug that was the photo on the back of the book. Underneath, in bold script-like font read *Middletown Library welcomes Blake C. Stevens*. Blake certainly felt welcomed and was glad he had chosen to come here.

"Thank you," Blake said into the microphone, which complained with earsplitting feedback. He leaned away to help cease the electronic squealing. "Thank you, very much."

The long applause finally began to fade and was replaced with the excited murmur of the crowd as they anticipated the next segment of the session. Looking down from the modest stage to the eager faces below, Blake was surprised at the amount of people that had showed up for today's signing. The crowds had been large lately, but here even standing room was a tight squeeze.

He glimpsed at the people standing in the back, each held their own copy of his book, as did everyone in the seats before them. Blake noticed two men who seemed out of place. They wore black slacks and light-gray polos that were tucked neatly into their pants. Aside for one being African American and the other being white, they looked almost identical. But it was their demeanor that caught his attention; they were the only ones not smiling. Nor did they look like they had been clapping. And they were the only ones not carrying a copy of his book. Strange. Were they security? Probably. But his military training told him to keep an eye on these guys. *Military training? Who am I kidding? I was a cook in the Marines. But I made a killer tomato bisque.*

"Okay, ladies and gentlemen," said Penny Lane, the library's marketing director and the one MCing today's event. She stood in front of the stage and spoke into a stand mike that had been set up for audience questions.

And yes, that was her name. Penny Lane. Her parents must have been huge Beatles fans. Blake wondered if her parents knew the hardship they had bestowed upon their child by naming her after a song, all for their own personal amusement, no doubt. He also wondered if Penny liked the Beatles, or if she hated them for being such an influence on her parents that they had lost their minds and had given their daughter a name that would forever link her to the Fab Four. Thankfully, her parents' last name wasn't Tuesday or they may have named her Ruby. Not only would the librarian hate The Rolling Stones, but she would probably never eat at one of the novelty restaurants bearing that song's name. *Gooood-bye, Ruby Tuesday. Who could hang a name on you?* Great burgers, awesome salad bar.

Now, Blake was hungry. And he had a song stuck in his head.

"Before we move on to the question and answer part of the program," Penny continued, "I just wanted to thank Mr. Stevens for reading from his latest book, *The Fate of the Red Lady*, and for honoring us with his visit to our humble little town." The applause resumed with increased ardor.

Blake refreshed his polite smile and raised his hand to the audience. While doing so, he glanced toward the back of the room to where the two strange men had been standing. But they were gone. The gap their absence must have created was now filled with other standing fans who applauded, their books tucked under their armpits. *And I have to sign those things*, Blake thought to himself, not letting the smile fade. Now, all he could think about was book after book smelling like Arrid, or Old Spice, or B.O.

"Now," Penny went on, "we've already handed out numbers to the people with questions. We've limited the number of questions to twenty, so we don't eat into the signing part of the afternoon. When your number is called, please come up to this microphone and ask away."

Blake was impressed with the library's organization for the signing. For a small-town library, it was obvious that this was not their first rodeo. There was even a camera set up filming, or maybe even live-streaming, the whole event. Several large-screen LCD TVs were setup, displaying the camera's capture and giving anyone in the audience with a blocked view a better look.

"Okay," said Penny, excitement rising in her voice. "Let's get started. Number one, come on up."

A fat, bearded man with horn-rimmed glasses stood up about halfway back in the audience and started to make his way from the left-hand side. As he made his way through his row and into the main aisle, Penny spoke into the microphone, once again. "Ladies and gentlemen, if you are the next person to be called, please make sure you are in the center or wing aisles waiting for the current questioner to finish so you can move up expeditiously. It'll make this whole process a lot smoother. Thanks."

Again, Blake was impressed.

The stocky man reached the microphone, sweating and breathing heavily. Although it was ninety degrees outside, and the library's AC fought to keep some semblance of cool in the building, the rotund man wore a button shirt and a tie, as if he had just gotten off work. Blake tried using mental telepathy to make him take off the unneeded neck apparel, but alas, it was no use. Instead, the sweatshop of a man wearing the Jerry Garcia tie wiped his brow with a handkerchief—Blake was surprised some guys still carried those—and leaned into the beige-colored mike. Blake just hoped he didn't mistake the microphone for a corndog. *Be nice, Blake. I know you're tired and you've been to a hundred of these things, but that's no reason to get snarky.*

"I just wanted to say, Mr. Stevens, that your book is awesome. It's the best thing I've read in a long time. So much action and suspense, it's easily your best book, by far. I've read it twice already, and I'll probably read it again before the summer's over." The man spoke with, what Blake believed to be, a Texarkana accent. It seemed a bit odd, and it was a little hard on the ears.

"Thank you," Blake said, the smile never leaving his face. "That's very kind of you to say."

"The question I have is, what inspired you to write about a third atom bomb? I mean, did you just think of it, or was there actually a third bomb that no one's ever heard about?"

"Good question," Blake replied with a well-rehearsed serious expression and tone. It was only the thousandth time he'd been asked that, but he replied, just as he always did, as if the obese man that stood before him was the first to conceive it. "Actually, as you probably know from my previous books, I'm a bit of a World War II aficionado. And while doing research on those books, I did come across a few papers and articles where it was suggested that there could have, indeed, been a third bomb just waiting in the wings—pardon the pun—to be called up for duty in case Japan needed another nudge to the surrender table.

"Of course, back then, there was so much secrecy surrounding the Manhattan Project and the bombs it produced, that there are no real records indicating that a third bomb did exist. But, those little blurbs of speculation in the research I read, tickled my imagination bone—as I call it—and ... well ... *voila*."

Satisfied with the answer he received, the large man backed away from the mike stand, gave Blake a wave of thanks, then proceeded to sweat back to his seat.

The next fan, who had been waiting patiently in the side aisle as previously instructed, made his way front and center. "Hi, Mr. Stevens."

"Hello."

"I like your book a lot; it's a real cool story. But—and I know you try to keep your fiction realistic and all—and that's why I'm asking you this, but isn't it kinda out there for the U.S. to plan to drop the unused bomb on England, all the while making it look like the Soviets did it, so we could team up with England and go to war against Russia? I mean, the plan seems like a real longshot to pull off. Like, so many things had to go right for it to succeed. And if everything did go right, there was no way of knowing if it would work."

Whoa, spoiler alert. I hope this guy isn't ruining the book for anyone who hasn't read it. "When you put it so bluntly, it does sound a bit farfetched." Blake paused as he let the audience laugh at his little quip. This question rarely popped up, but it did now and again. And now, he believed he had perfected the answer. "But I don't think it's any different in its believability than anything Ian Fleming has written. Which is ironic to say, I know, because I use Fleming as a character in my book. But I believe great fiction takes the truth and stretches it to a tearing point. If it tears, it's garbage, but if you can stretch it so much while still keeping the integrity of the truth and the story intact, well, I think what you get is what separates great fiction from ordinary paperbacks that end up on tables at a flea market for fifty-cents."

The audience erupted in applause and laughter, but it was the applause that finally won the crowd. The questioner leaned into the mike again, obviously not finished. "But why did Colonel Stockton need the Russian bomber so badly? Why not just paint a big red star on a B-29 and fly her over England with the bomb? They already had a B-29, the *Helen of Troy, MI.* If they had just used that plane, they would have saved so much time, and the plan might have had a chance to work."

"Well, the Soviet bombers, like the Tupolev TB-3, looked drastically different from the American ones. Especially a B-29. If the 'witnesses' part of Stockton's scheme was to work, any English citizens seeing the plane fly towards Liverpool would most likely describe it to officials later. Therefore, Colonel Stockton could not take that chance. Particularly, when the point of it all was to make Churchill think that Stalin had attacked a weakened England, when it was actually a rogue U.S. colonel who wanted to trick England into attacking Russia. And, of course, the U.S would be there to help her closest ally. Tricking Churchill and the English people was the most important part of Stockton's plan. As was convincing his superiors of the same. So, it had to be perfect. I hope that answered your question."

The questioner walked back to his seat, either realizing how ridiculous his question must have sounded, or disappointed that his reasoning didn't hold up. After all, Blake was pretty sure he covered everything in detail in the book. *Did this guy even read the book?*

"Number three," said Penny, but a middle-aged woman was already on her way to the stand. She was dressed smartly in a navy-blue pantsuit, wore an attractive pair of thin-rimmed glasses, and she clutched in her hand what appeared to be an old-fashioned steno book. Did other people besides struggling writers use those? Apparently so. She approached the mike with confidence, gripped its cradle, and tilted it downward to accommodate her shorter stature.

"Good afternoon, Mr. Stevens," she began.

Uh oh. This didn't look good. She was way too serious to be a fan looking to get a couple minutes of chat time with her favorite author. And she sounded more like his sophomore English teacher, Mrs. Graham. Graham had called all the students by their last name, making sure everyone knew that she was not their friend. *Oh, don't worry, lady*, Blake used to think, *we all know, we all know*. And that's how questioner number three sounded. *We're not friends*, her formal vernacular and pantsuit said, *I'm just here to tear you a new one. I hope you brought clean underwear.*

She was all business. Her glasses were actually readers that she wiggled on her nose and looked above them at the overconfident writer on stage. She flipped open her steno and read what must have been notes she had prepared for today's event. All of this told Blake one thing: she was a book critic. Had to be. Local paper, maybe. But what if it was someone who flew all the way here to catch him with his guard down. Someone from the New Yorker, maybe? Now, it was Blake's turn to sweat.

"Let me begin by saying that I concur with the first gentleman who stated, in less elegant terms, that this book is your finest piece of work yet."

The audience gave a steady, almost gratuitous applause which faded away quickly. They seemed to be on board with the situation. Many of the faces in the audience seemed pretty bleak for Blake. *Bleak for Blake. Bleak for Blake. Say that five times fast*. Now, he braced himself for the inevitable 'but' that was sure to follow.

"However," she continued. *However. But—same difference.* "There appears to be a significant difference in *Fate of the Red Lady* when compared to your previous books. Not just the quality of the story, or the plot, or the characters," she flicked her right hand in a brisk motion as if to shoo away those writing attributes like an irritating fly, "but in the presentation, and in the details. There seemed to be something more heartfelt and serious in your prose. As if this was more than just another World War II novel that you threw together." She paused as if collecting her thoughts to continue, or was waiting for a response from Blake.

"I'm sorry," Blake said with a slight cough. His throat was parched from the stage lights and his sudden state of nervousness. He took a swig of water. "Was there a question?"

"Yes," the woman snooted. She ever so slightly tilted her head back while still keeping her over-the-glasses piercing gaze on Blake. "To be frank, Mr. Stevens. I believe the protagonist in your novel ... is you."

She paused again, this time, seemingly for effect, as if dangling a piece of bait out in the open. The audience bit, and they bit hard. The Blakeries, as his fans have come to be known, were now exchanging questioning glances with their neighbors as a subdued murmur came over them.

Blake took another drink from his water bottle. "I'm sorry. I'm not sure I follow you."

The woman gave Blake a 'come on, don't play dumb with me' look, but Blake didn't flinch.

"Come now, Mr. Stevens. There's no need to be disingenuous with me. For starters, you usually use actual names of places in your books, but in this one, you seem to go out of your way to make almost every place in it fictitious. As if you're hiding something.

"On the other hand, there is incredible attention to detail when it comes to time tables, equipment, vehicles, munitions, etcetera. Nothing like you are known for.

"And lastly, the main character's name is Conlan; your middle name, isn't it? Not a very common name. And not the typical hero 'J' names you always use like John, or Joe, or Jake, or James.

"So, I ask you, Mr. Stevens, is the character in this book based on you and your research? Is the story of Conlan Boyle actually the story of Blake Conlan Stevens?" She crossed her arms as if she had just put his king in check, and he had little on the board to counter with. She had a smug look and a thin fishhook smile that said, 'Make your move, Mr. Stevens.'

Blake took a final drink from the water bottle, finishing what little was left. He looked down at the wooden planks of the stage as he contemplated his retort. A few deep breaths later, and he was ready.

"Actually, Ms. ..."

"Hurst," she replied. "My name is Dorothy Hurst. I teach world history at Lakefield High School, two counties over." Her arms remained crossed, the fishhook still planted firmly on her face.

A teacher? I should have seen that coming. And I thought she was a critic form the New Yorker ... get over yourself, Blake. This teacher, however, was not what he was used to when it came to his fans. Usually, the teachers he met had nothing but praise and compliments for his work. They were nothing like the Sherlock-want-to-be pantsuit in front of him. But now it was time to play Moriarty to her Sherlock.

"Well, Ms. Hurst. I'm glad you noticed my writing style had changed. I wanted to take a fresh approach to *Red Lady*. I didn't want it to sound like all my other books. Sort of how some music artist's songs can all start to sound alike after a while. I simply wanted to stretch my writing chops. I only hope it was acceptable and not so painfully obvious like you make it sound." His gaze swept over the audience to let them know that last part was for them as well. They responded with thoughtful nods and supporting smiles.

"As far as my attention to detail, that was part of my fresh approach, as well. I was inspired a bit by Clancy and wanted this book to sound a bit more ... intelligent than the others. I figured that the more detailed the information—facts, if you will—I used to support my story, the more it would seem very plausible that the events in my book could have happened. I knew that realism had to balance out the fiction if I was going to pull this off.

"In regards to my character's name ... yes, Conlan is my middle name. It's Irish—very Irish, and it was my grandfather's name. He served in the Navy during World War II. I wanted to honor him by naming my character after him. Not after my middle name. I'm proud of my grandfather's service during the war. He was a true hero. They all were."

The high school teacher looked deflated; her hard look and piercing eyes had softened, and she seemed to be at a loss for words. Blake figured that probably didn't happen too often with this woman. *Mark this day on your calendar, ladies and gents.* With the fishhook now looking more like a hatpin, she closed her steno, and said, "Thank you, Mr. Stevens," then headed back to her seat.

The rest of the questions went off without a hitch. They were more like what he was used to at these things.

- "Do you think they'll make *Red Lady* into a movie?"

- "Who do you imagine playing Conlan on the big screen?"

- "Do you think we really should have taken out Russia when we had the chance?"

And there was always someone, who thought they know more about World War II than Blake did. Then question and answer portion of the afternoon would briefly turn into a know-it-all showdown. Blake usually won, but occasionally conceded for time's sake.

And there was more of the same when it came time for the signing. But sometimes the questions were more personal, and they were from fans who wanted to get to know the real Blake C. Stevens a little bit better than they had when they walked in that day.

By the end of the signing, Blake's hand was tired and sore. There were a lot of people today, all with books. Some with copies of his other books as well, although everyone was told by Ms. Lane that "Mr. Stevens was only signing one item per person. Have your books open to the title page when you get up to the table. And absolutely no pictures!" But there were pictures, and Blake didn't mind. He signed everything, as well as did personalizations, and accommodated every fan who brandished a smartphone for that memorable selfie. It took over two hours, but he felt great when it was over. He was responsible for over a hundred smiling faces, and now it was time to head back to his hotel room. He hoped they had good room service. He was jonesing for a burger. No time for a restaurant tonight. *Unless I pass a Ruby Tuesday on my way to the hotel,* he thought.

* * *

Forty-five minutes after he had signed his last book, Blake was in the library parking lot walking to his rental near the back. The lot was pretty much empty save for a couple of cars that must have belonged to staff members. And there was a white Chevy work van that had A-1 Plumbing and Heating printed on its side. A ladder and various lengths of pipe were tied to the pipe rack on the van's roof. Either the library had some plumbing issues, or it was a fan lingering around for one last jab at the author for another autograph or possibly a picture. And, as usual, even though he was hungry and tired as all hell, Blake would be happy to oblige. *Let's get this over with*, Blake thought to himself. *Somewhere, there is a cheeseburger with my name on it*.

He kept his pace toward his rental car and waited for someone in the van to open a door and greet him. And he wasn't disappointed.

As Blake passed behind the van, the passenger side door opened, and outstepped a man wearing black slacks and a light-gray polo.

One of the men from the back.

Blake stopped in his tracks and stared at the man. The only thing Blake could think to say was, "Hey, where's your friend?" And as if on cue, the van's side door slid open revealing the other gray-polo guy. It stuck Blake funny how these two guys were dressed almost exactly alike. And then all he could think was Thing One and Thing Two. *Does that make me the Cat in the Hat?*

A quick movement on Blake's right made him spin around, only to see Thing One shove a baton into his midsection. A paralyzing jolt of electricity surged through Blake's body, reminding him of the time when he was twelve, and he had unplugged a fan from a wall outlet with soaking wet hands. Every nerve and muscle in Blake's body jerked and twitched, then he stiffened like a board, just as it had happened back then. But this time, it didn't stop. At least, not right away like it did when he was a kid. Back then, he had let go of the plug and held his numb hand while he reflected on the idiotic life lesson he had just learned. This time, the pain lasted what seemed to be hours, but was more likely about five or six seconds. He tried to yell, but nothing came out. In fact, he had no control over any of his motor functions.

Before Blake could hit the ground, Thing Two grabbed him under his arms and pulled him into the van. "Mr. Stevens," Thing Two said after dumping Blake onto the steel floor of the van. "Someone would like a word with you." Then there was a sharp sting in the left cheek of his ass. The van's side-door closed, as did Blake's eyes.

When Blake's eyes opened, he was feeling groggy, and he had the mother of all headaches. He was sitting on an old wooden chair, his wrists bound to the arms of the chair with some kind of plastic straps. *Zip ties?* His ankles were tied to the legs of the chair in the same manner.

He looked around—slowly because his head pounded with every movement it made. He appeared to be in a basement or cellar. The walls and floor were concrete and a couple of windows were ceiling high, which was probably ground level to the outside. There were a few chairs, similar to the one he was tied to, stacked against a wall. There was a vertical support beam in the middle of the room, and an ordinary looking table collecting dust right next to it. Other than those few things, the basement was empty.

The sound of a door opening came from behind him, followed by the sound of someone descending a set of wooden stairs that creaked with each step. He strained his neck to see, but it was no use. The owner of the footsteps reached the bottom of the stairs and walked to stand in front of Blake. It was Thing Two.

"Good, you're awake," he said. Then, in a much louder voice directed toward the stairs, "Tell the boss he's awake."

"Roger that," came a voice that Blake presumed was Thing One, who must have been waiting at the top.

"What do you want with me?" Blake demanded. "Who are you guys?"

But Thing Two just stood there with his hands clasped behind his back, a blank stare in his eyes. There was something familiar about Thing Two. His look, his demeanor. It was the stoic look, the short hair, the .... *That's it.* The hands clasped behind his back. All of it together spelled soldier. If he and Thing One weren't military, then they were ex-military.

"What unit you with, soldier?" Blake said in an attempt to get a reaction out of the man before him. And it worked. Thing Two snapped his gaze to Blake as if he was utterly surprised that Blake guessed his secret. "It's a little obvious. I'm a former Marine, myself. Kuwait. Desert Storm." But Thing Two didn't acknowledge, except by resuming his statue-like stance.

More footfalls sounded; At least two people were walking down the stairs now. Blake figured it to be Thing One and their boss. *Whomever the hell that might be.*

The two newcomers walked around to join Thing Two. As Blake had guessed, one of them was Thing One, who carried a green duffle bag, which he placed on the floor. The other person took him completely by surprise.

It was sweatshop, the large man from the signing. He was still wearing his shirt and tie, and he was still sweating like a cat in a Chinese kitchen. He removed a handkerchief from his pocket and dabbed at his forehead. He seemed relieved to be in the coolness of the basement.

"Good afternoon, Mr. Stevens. May I call you Blake?"

"Why not," said Blake with an ironic smile, "since we're old pals. And what do I call you?"

"You can call me Gary," he said.

"Okay, Gary." The name sounded as fake as his accent. "Why don't you drop all the B.S., along with that dumb twang you're speaking with, and tell me what I'm doing here with you and the Mod Squad."

The corner of Gary's mouth raised, and he gave a small nod. "Very well, Blake. We'll play it your way." This time he spoke in an accent that was unmistakably English. And this time, it seemed quite authentic.

Gary nodded his head to the stack of chairs that sat against the wall. Thing Two went over and brought back what looked to be a forty or fifty-year-old chair that had probably been part of an old dining room set, and placed it across from Blake. Thing One grabbed the equally antiquated looking table from near the support beam and placed it between the chair and Blake. Gary took a seat, and the chair let out a groan that let everyone know it was not happy hosting its current occupant. Meanwhile, Things One and Two continued to flank him like ebony and ivory bookends. Gary took off his glasses and cleaned them with his Jerry Garcia tie. When he was done, he looked at Blake as if wondering where to begin.

"You see, Mr. Stevens—sorry—Blake. You see, Blake. Your book has caught the attention of the U.S. military. All the way up to, and including, the Secretary of Defense."

"Well, I'm glad they like my book ..."

"Oh, it's not a matter of them liking it, and I'm sure they do. As I said myself, this is your finest work yet. But you've uncovered something that was supposed to have remained a secret until ... well ... eternity."

"What? The third bomb? It wasn't too hard to figure out that it had existed. I had to go through a ton of material, as well as interview a dozen people or so, but I don't see why that has the military's panties in a bunch. So, there was a third bomb. Big whoop."

"That's not the big whoop, Blake. It's the rest."

"What do you mean the rest? What rest?" Then, it hit Blake like a frying pan in one of those old cartoons. "You mean, the mission?"

Gary stared at Blake as he leaned his bulk on one of the old chair's arms. Blake couldn't imagine that old and tired wood taking too much more punishment.

"I made everything in that book up. It's pure fiction. I didn't *uncover* anything." Blake sounded like he was pleading, and he supposed he was. After all, the Army, or CIA, or whomever these a-holes worked for, don't ambush you in a parking lot, bring you to a basement, and tie you to a chair with zip ties just to have a conversation. They wanted information, and they were willing to beat that information out of him if necessary. Hell, probably even if it's not necessary. He looked at Thing One and Thing Two; these guys were more than capable of the task. "So, which one of you goes first?" Blake asked as he looked from one to the other. "Do you flip a coin? Rock, paper, scissors?"

Gary gave Blake a puzzled look, then his face brightened, and he actually smiled. "No, Blake. We don't operate like that." He flicked a finger at Thing One who retrieved the duffle bag he had carried down with him and placed it on the table. Gary opened the bag, and from inside he produced a black leather pouch, which he proceeded to open as well.

The pouch opened flat, revealing several syringes and glass vials, each marked with lettering too small for Blake to read, but he didn't have to be Sherlock Holmes to know what was in them. *Ha, Sherlock Holmes ... I feel more like Inspector Clouseau.*

Gary removed a vial as well as a syringe. He took off the protective cover of the syringe revealing a long—painfully long—needle. He placed the needle into the vial and pulled the plunger. Blake watched in fear as the hollow tube of the syringe filled with the clear liquid.

"Sodium thiopental. With just a couple milligrams of this in your system, you'll answer any question I ask. But I do have to be careful; any more than that will knock you out. Too much, and you'll never wake up. If you catch my meaning." Gary pointed the needle up, gave it a few taps with his finger, and lightly pushed the plunger so a small amount of the liquid emerged from the tip. "If this doesn't work, we'll see about that other option you were referring to."

There was a loud *snap* as one of the back legs of Gary's chair finally gave way. Gary tumbled backward, flailing with the syringe in his left hand. Thing Two moved to catch him, but was knocked backwards, unable to stop the immense falling weight of his boss. Unbalanced, Thing Two went right into the support beam, headfirst. He then fell to the floor, out cold. If he was lucky.

Thing One's attempt to catch Gary was equally as futile. Gary tried to latch on to him and inadvertently stuck the needle into Thing One's chest. Both men crashed to the ground, Gary on top of the other man, the syringe sandwiched in between them.

Gary pushed himself off of Thing One and rolled over with a flop as his back hit the floor. He was panting heavily like a Saint Bernard, his eyes budged in their sockets, and he clutched at his chest with a trembling hand. He was having a heart attack.

With Gary off of Thing One, Blake could now see the unfortunate henchman. His eyes were fixed on the ceiling, and he was not breathing. The plunger on the syringe had been depressed all the way, sending its entire contents into his body, killing the man almost instantly.

Blake struggled against his straps; he knew it was useless to try to break the zip ties, but if he could only manage to do on purpose what Gary had done accidentally ... and he succeeded. The chair's left arm came loose from its support posts, allowing Blake to easily slip out. With his free hand he worked at the other arm and was able to free that one as well. Now, for his legs.

He rocked side to side a few times until his momentum tipped him over completely. Doing his best to keep his head from hitting the cement floor, he landed with a thud. The pain he experienced was dulled by the prospect of freedom. Now on his side, Blake was able to slide his straps down and off the legs of the chair. He stood up slowly, using the table for support. He walked around and looked down at Gary who was sweating more than ever, and his breathing was becoming more and more shallow with each passing second.

Blake bent down, knowing there was nothing he could do for the man except get some answers before he died.

"Why did you do this," Blake demanded, finding it easy to muster up anger despite the carnage around him. "Why?"

"Because, dear boy, we need to know the truth." Gary's words were strained as he fought to speak. "We need to know ... the treachery ... you uncovered." Gary gasped as he struggled for air. His eye twitched, and his face contorted in pain.

And then he was gone.

"Who's we?" Blake demanded.

Honey?

"Who're you working for?"

Honey? Are you up there?

But it was no use. Gary, or whatever his real name was, would talk no more.

Honey?

Mark McHenry snaps back to reality to answer his wife.

"I'm in my office," he yells.

"What are you doing?" she shouts from downstairs.

"I'm writing. I'm trying to work on my novel. I told you that earlier."

"Oh. Sorry, honey. I didn't mean to bother you."

"I'm done for now. What do you need?"

"Did you call for a plumber?"

"A plumber?"

"Yeah. There's a van parked in front of our house. It's been there for quite some time."

Mark stands from his desk and looks out the window. Just as his wife said, there's a van, a white Chevy work van, parked directly in front of their house. On the side are the words "A-1 Plumbing and Heating." Squinting against the glare of the afternoon sun reflecting off the windshield, he barely makes out a pair of men sitting in the front seats. They simultaneously open their doors, step out of the van, and look at his house.

"You've got to be kidding me."

THE SIGHT

"Who's to say that dreams and nightmares aren't as real as the here and now?"
– **John Lennon**

Stockbridge, Georgia 1934

The old man sat in his rocking chair on the front porch of his family home. Eyes closed; he wore a peaceful smile that reflected his mood as he enjoyed the music wafting from the radio. The radio was an RCA Tombstone. He assumed it was called a Tombstone, because it was shaped like one of those grave markers in a cemetery. The song he was enjoying was "Brother, Can You Spare a Dime" by that new young crooner, Bing Crosby.

The old man had a feeling that the future was bright for the singer with a funny name.

"That white boy's got a hell of a voice. Hell of a voice." He gently rocked in rhythm to the music, as the tune blended with the chirping of birds, and the buzzing of locusts on that warm summer late afternoon.

"Who's got a hell of a voice?"

The old man's eyes blinked open. He looked around, not sure if what he had heard was real, or if he had dozed off and dreamt it. Or maybe the voice had been that of an angel who had come to escort him to the pearly gates. But, alas, in front of him, standing on the wooden floor of the porch, was his granddaughter and grandson. They looked up at him with wonder and awe, something they frequently did. They were only seven and six—heck, he had to be the oldest person they had ever seen. But still, the staring was kind of creepy. Maybe they were wondering how someone could live to be so old. Or maybe they were wondering if all those wrinkles hurt. Or maybe they had just come to see if he had finally kicked the bucket.

"You ought not say that word," the old man said to the girl, the older of the two. "If your mama heard you say that, she'd tan your hide. And you too," he addressed the wide-eyed boy. "She'd tan yours just for bein' in cahoots."

"But *you* said it," the girl contested. "You say it all the time. And I heard you say worse."

Her brother nodded in silent affirmation.

"Well, I'm an old man. I'm allowed. Maybe when you're as old as me, you'll be allowed. But not before. You understand?"

The kids nodded and continued to keep their gazed fixed on their grandfather.

"What do you kids want, anyway? I ain't got no cookies. And your mama's fixin' dinner. Should be done right soon."

"A story," the girl said.

"Yeah, a story," her brother echoed.

"A story, huh?" The old man thought for a bit. He had stories. A bunch of them. But what was a good story for them to hear?

Nothing made up; he was tired of telling kids stories that weren't true when there was so much real stuff out in the world. Stuff that was important, stuff that mattered.

That's when he decided it was time to tell them *the* story. Were they too young to hear it? Possibly. Their parents would certainly argue that. But he might not be around much longer, when they become old enough for their liking. No, it had to be now. Why put off today when tomorrow may never come? He took a deep breath, and his eyes softened as his mind recalled a time that's almost better off forgotten.

"Did I ever tell you youngsters that I used to be a slave?"

With their mouths hanging open, the children shook their heads, and their eyes got even wider.

"Actually, the legitimacy of me being a slave is up for debate."

"I was born in December of 1864. The following month, Congress passed the thirteenth amendment to the constitution officially ending slavery. And before that, President Lincoln enacted the Emancipation Proclamation. But we were at war, you see. A Civil War between the states of the north and those of the south. And that means the white folk of the south didn't recognize any laws and such from President Lincoln and his Congress. So, to them, I was a slave as soon as my mama popped me out.

"But the war ended that May, and in December of 1865, all the states, including the ones in the south, ratified that amendment. That means they all accepted the new law that slaves were now free. So that would mean I was a slave for some amount of time, just not sure how long. Either one month or one year. Depends on who you ask.

"But this story isn't about me; this is a story about my mama. She was an extraordinary woman, and her name was Malinda.

* * *

Malinda, like many that were born into slavery, learned hard work at an early age. She shadowed her mother and learned the ins and outs of a Georgia plantation and developed good work habits that would make her a valuable asset to her owner, William Turner Dodge.

William Dodge—Bill to his friends—owned the largest tobacco plantation in Georgia, as well as the second largest cotton plantation. He had a reputation for being the nastiest slave owner in the state. He even had an old oak tree behind his house with nooses hanging from a branch that was as long as the tree itself was tall. Some people would say, "He's killed more niggers than most owners had ever bought." There was probably some truth to that. But Malinda's parents assured their daughter that as long as she followed the rules and worked hard, she would be in his good graces.

And Malinda did just that. However, when she became a teenager, she was haunted by visions; vivid images that would suddenly come to her mind at any time and without warning. Her mother told her that they were just daydreams, and she should keep her mind on her work lest she get into trouble. However, the visions soon became more vivid and with such detail that Malinda had difficulty discerning them from reality. As she told folks of her visions, it also became difficult to keep them from the bosses, as well as Bill Dodge himself.

But the real problem started when her visions became premonitions. What started out as harmless hallucinations of strange events, had quickly become waking dreams of things that would soon come to pass. And they were never wrong; she would see them in her mind, then they happened in reality. Some would happen within a couple hours, some within a couple days. Malinda's parents called the premonitions a gift from God. Malinda, though frightened by this 'gift', learned to accept it as a natural part of her life. She even gave it a name.

The Sight.

She soon learned, however, that the gift was also a curse. For the sight showed her terrible things, and no matter what she did, she was helpless to change the outcome. The worst instance was when she had a vision of a work horse breaking out of the corral and trampling two slaves to death. When she told her parents, they ran over to the wooden fencing to make certain the gate was properly secure, but that's when the horse bolted. The gate flew open and the angry, mistreated beast galloped over Malinda's parents. They were killed instantly.

Not only was Malinda devastated by what happened, she blamed herself for their deaths. And she wasn't the only one.

When the bosses heard about Malinda's premonition, they dragged her to Walt Leary, the head boss.

"You and your evil witchcraft have cost me two good niggers," Leary said and spat on her tear-drenched face. "Maybe a couple days in the box is what you need. And be thankful I don't tell Mr. Dodge about your hand in this."

The bosses threw Malinda into an old tool shed called 'the box' that was then only used for punishing slaves. The worse thing about the box wasn't the isolation or the almost near starvation, it was the intense heat inside. The Georgia summers heated that old tool shed like an oven. Some slaves had even died from being in there for too long.

Malinda's first day in the box was long and hot, but at night the door opened giving her some relief as she breathed in the cooler evening air. That relief was soon replaced by dread as several of the bosses took turns—well ... let's just say they weren't very nice to her. The way they saw it, everyone was fair game in the box. This went on for two more days.

Malinda endured her punishment; after all, she felt she deserved it. She thought if she hadn't told her parents about the vision, they would still be alive. Or would they? This weighed heavily on Malinda. Eventually, she approached an elder on the plantation, the religious leader for the slaves.

"You are just an instrument of God," he said to her. "You are here to help prepare us for things to come. It's not your place to interfere, but to merely inform."

Malinda wasn't sure what to believe, but for a long while after her time in the box, she kept her visions from the sight to herself.

Years later, the sight showed Malinda a vision of Bill Dodge's four-year-old boy falling off a fishing pier, being swept away by the current, and drowning. She refused to believe that there was nothing to be done to save the boy's life. She had to do something. She had to try.

Malinda made a break for the river hoping to reach the boys in time to get them off the pier. But before she could leave the plantation, two bosses on horses intercepted her.

"Where the hell do you think you're going?" said one boss.

"I think we got ourselves a runaway," said the other.

Another horse galloped up. It was Walt Leary. "What the hell's goin' on, boys?"

"We caught this nigger trying to escape, boss."

"No, please," Malinda pleaded. "It's the boys. They're at the river. One of them's gonna die. Please, do something." Malinda cried as the image of that dead boy's body kept coming back to her. "Please!"

Leary stared at the crying slave, then his gazed turned east toward the river. "Bobby. Go to the pier. Check and see if them boys are there. Make sure they're okay."

"Yes, boss." Bobby drove his horse hard, kicking up dust as he left.

"For your sake, bitch," Leary said to Malinda. "Them boys better be fine, or it'll be neck stretchin' time for you. For now, it's back to the box. Get her out of here."

The other boss tied her wrists with a rope and took her back to the house. After a hundred feet, Malinda fell and was dragged the rest of the way to the box. Her legs, arms, and face getting severely scratched and cut.

* * *

Hours passed and Malinda knelt and prayed for the boy as she roasted in the oven-like box. She had been stripped of her clothes but was covered in blood from the cuts and scrapes she had received from being dragged. All she could do was listen as a group gathered by the house.

They had found the boy. His brothers said that he had fallen off the pier and gotten dragged downstream just as the sight had shown Malinda. His body washed up on some rocks a half a mile down the river.

Overcome with grief and rage, Bill Dodge snapped. He threw open the door to the box and pulled Malinda out by her hair, then dragged the crying slave to the hanging tree. When they reached the tree, Malinda saw Leary and several of his men standing and waiting. Leary held a bottle of lamp oil, and one of his men held a flaming torch.

Malinda then realized that Bill Dodge wasn't just going to hang her, he was going to burn her body as she swung by the rope. Still alive.

That's when she started to scream. She tried to resist and fight back, but Dodge was too strong and empowered by rage and righteousness. A few years ago, Malinda would have welcomed death. It would have felt right after what happened to her parents. But today, she wanted to live. She felt she had to live. *Please, God. I've been your messenger. Now help me in my time of need.* But she knew there was no hope for her.

Bill Dodge put the noose around Malinda's neck and pulled on the rope until she was six feet off the ground, squelching her screams to chokes and gasps. He didn't have to pull hard; being underfed and overwork had kept her weighing much less than she should have. The same could be said for most of the slaves owned by Bill Dodge. Most, that is, but not Hector.

Hector was a large slave whom Dodge kept well fed. He referred to him as his nigger-mule, because Hector was as strong as a beast and was given all the work on the plantation that required his enormous strength.

When Hector saw Malinda being strung up the hanging tree, he ran over without thinking. Maybe he wanted to plead with Dodge, or maybe he thought he could overpower all the bosses and save Malinda. But when he got too close, several of Leary's men stood in front of Hector and leveled their shotguns at his massive form. All Hector could do was watch as Malinda swung from the tree as so many others had done before her.

Leary handed the lamp oil to Dodge. The slave owner walked over to Malinda's thrashing, naked body, and held the glass bottle of flammable fuel, ready to douse the hanging woman. His hatred-filled eyes met hers. His mouth and brow formed a frown, and his nose flared with each breath. He may as well have been looking at the Devil himself.

Malinda's eyes sought mercy. Dodge replied by spitting on her face.

Hector started, but one of the bosses fired off a barrel in the air before leveling it back on the huge slave.

"Burn in hell, witch," Bill James said as he flung the oil on her body. "Because that's where you came from, and that's where you're going."

Malinda thrashed harder as the oil splashed on her skin, burning as it washed over her cuts. She was terrified knowing she would still be alive when Dodge set her on fire.

When the bottle was spent, Dodge blindly reached his hand behind him, not taking his eyes off of Malinda. The man handed him the torch and stepped back.

"Now, nigger-witch," Dodge shouted, as if addressing everyone, as well as God and Satan himself, "you will pay for what you did to my little boy. You will pay for your wicked ways." He cocked his arm back and was about to hurl the torch, when a shouting man approached on a horse.

"Stop! Stop!" The man steered his horse to come between the out-of-control slave owner and the dark-skinned woman, who was literally hanging onto life.

"Get out of my way, Nathan. I have Gods work to do," Bill Dodge said, still holding the torch high.

Nathan hopped off his horse and stood face to face with the angry and determined man. “No, William. You have to stop. This is madness.”

“Madness? She killed my boy with her evil magic.”

“She didn’t kill your boy. You know that. I heard she tried to warn you of the boy’s impending doom. God speaks through this woman, William. Can’t you see that?”

“God or the Devil ... either way, judgement will be passed onto her soon enough.”

Malinda had prayed for help. And it had arrived in the form of this white man who begged for her life. She prayed that he wasn’t too late. She was fading.

Nathan’s eyes were panic-stricken. “Let me buy her from you. I’ll give you four-hundred dollars for her.”

“I said, outa my way, Nathan.” Bill Dodge took a step past Nathan, the torch ready in his hand.

“Six-hundred.”

Dodge paused, looked at Nathan, then back at his dying slave.

Nathan also looked at her, fear and desperation wretched his face. “A thousand!”

That got Bill Dodge’s attention. “A thousand?”

“Yes,” Nathan said hurriedly. “She’s no good to you now. I’ll give you a thousand dollars for her, and you never have to see her again.”

Bill Dodge seemed to consider this for a moment as life-eating seconds passed by. Nathan looked like he was about to explode with desperation. Until, finally ....

“Fine,” said Dodge. “Take her.”

Nathan got back on his horse and pulled out a large knife. Then, standing in his stirrups, he reached up and cut Malinda down. She landed in the saddle with a lifeless thump. His hands desperately fought to loosen the noose, and once he got the rope off of her neck, she coughed and gasped as she was finally able to breathe. The rough rope had torn into her skin so bad that she was bleeding from the numerous cuts all around her neck.

Malinda continued to gasp for air, and finally she cried as she hung onto Nathan in a weak embrace. Barely able to speak, she managed to force out just two words. "Thank ... you."

Nathan held her against his body, turned his horse around, and started down the lane leading out of the plantation. "Just hang on for me," he whispered.

Before her eyes closed, she saw Hector. Gratitude and relief were written all over the large man's dark face. He smiled at her as they rode away.

"Go on," she heard Dodge shout, his voice fading as the horse put distance between them. "Take her. She's your nigger-witch now. Get her out of my sight before I change my mind."

"C'mon," Nathan said to her in a soothing voice. "I'll take you to your new home."

They rode back to his place, both soaked in blood, sweat, and oil.

* * *

The old man struck a match on the arm of his rocking chair and lit his pipe.

"Mama recovered from that near-hanging over time," he said to his grandkids who now sat cross-legged by his feet. "She was left with scars she would carry for the rest of her life, but they paled in comparison to the nightmarish scars that remained in her head. The sight had to now share time with the nightmares of her near-death experience as well as those of her parent's deaths.

"Who was Nathan?" the girl asked.

The old man puffed on the pipe and blew out a ring of smoke. "Mr. Nathan owned a small plantation where he grew corn and sugarcane. And he was a slave owner himself. Now, he wasn't like the other owners. He treated his slaves really good, just like family. He gave them good food, good clothes—heck, he even gave them presents on birthdays and Christmas. And every slave had his own little, tiny house. And when a new slave came into the fold, they all pulled together, including Mr. Nathan, and built the newcomer a place of his or her own.

"Mr. Nathan's slaves were just as unordinary as he was. Mr. Nathan was known for buying what other slave owners called 'undesirables.' Those were slaves that had something wrong with them in some form or another. For instance, one slave had only one eye; he lost it in a farming accident. Another had only one leg; he got cut somehow and he got an infection so bad, it had to be amputated. And there was one slave who had is hand cut off for stealing food. Another had his toes cut off for running away. Mr. Nathan bought all these slaves and more, because he knew he could find something for them to do; he could make them useful. And in doing so, he had saved their lives.

"You see, if a slave performed below the expectations of his owner, before too long, that slave would be found hanging from his neck 'til he was deader than a rabbit in a coon-dog's mouth. To the owners, it was no different than putting down a maim horse. But Mr. Nathan couldn't stand for that to happen, so he bought as many of the undesirables as he could, just so he could save them. When he heard about Malinda and he predicament, he knew he had to race over to Dodge's plantation and save her.

"Mr. Nathan nursed her back to health, caring for her like no one had, not since her own mother. Some say that's how they fell in love. He took care of her in his own house and let her rest and sleep in his own bed. And that's where she continued to call home for the rest of her days. They were married in secret, and before they knew it, they had a child; a strapping baby boy who was born right in that bedroom. They named him James; that's right, that handsome baby boy was me. Mr. Nathan was my daddy."

The old man paused as the music on the radio ended and a fast-talking, nasally-voiced man announced that The Rudy Vallee Show was about to start.

The Rudy Vallee Show, sponsored by Fleischmann's Yeast, the only yeast guaranteed to make your dough rise fifty-percent faster than regular yeast. On your next visit to the market, ask your grocer for Fleishmann's!

They also claimed the packaged yeast cured acne and constipation. The old man didn't know much about that. The show, however, was one he normally enjoyed, but some new comedy gentleman named Red Skelton was on the show that evening, and that would only be a distraction from his story. So, the old man reached for the radio and switched it off. Later, after dinner, he would listen to Amos and Andy. Now, that was a good show.

"He was your daddy?" the little girl said in complete awe.

"That's right. They fell in love, and it didn't matter what color their skin was. He didn't see her as black, or a slave, or anything other than the woman he loved. All that mattered, was that they loved one another and promised to take care of each other."

"Did he love you?" the boy asked.

"Of course, he loved me. I never knew nothin' but love from him." The old man put on a forlorn smile and dropped his gaze to his lap. "But everything wasn't always molasses and honeysuckles."

* * *

A couple years go by after Malinda's rescue: she and Nathan had their first child; the war ended; and the slaves were freed.

But freeing the slaves was easier said than done. Federal marshals, with the help of local law officials, had to visit the former slave owners to make sure they were abiding by the new law and releasing all the slaves in their possession. Not everyone, however, was very cooperative in giving up their free labor. Some argued that they had paid good money for their slaves and demanded retribution from the government. That, of course, never happened.

Sometimes, fighting broke out, guns were fired, blood was shed. It took longer than it should have, but all the slaves were finally released from their forced servitude.

Bill Dodge fought the hardest, and it almost took a small army to force him to relinquish his hold on what he deemed as his 'God-given right to own his property.' But, eventually, he gave in to the pressures of the law: county, state, and federal.

Nathan, on the other hand, was ecstatic when he got the news that he had to release his slaves. His slaves, however, were not so happy. They had no desire to leave Nathan's plantation, so they continued working as if nothing had ever changed.

Nathan procrastinated, but eventually he had to do what he had to do. One day, he had them gather before his back porch. They all stood around, looking heartbroken and lost as they could all guess what he was going to tell them. He stood before them, trying to gauge their long faces. Malinda stood behind him, carrying baby James.

"My dear friends," he said. "The time has come for you to go. The day we have all waited for has arrived; you are free."

A few grumbled in the crowd and some smiled, but there was no cheer for joy as one might expect.

"I know," Nathan continued, "some of you are too timid to leave this little plantation, but the law demands it. It's out of my hands."

"Where we gonna go?" asked Martin.

"Yeah, we ain't got nowhere *to* go," said Phillip. "We just can't be released into the wild like animals."

"You can go anywhere you want," Nathan told them. "You are free. No one can claim you. No one can stop you in the street and ask you 'where do you belong?' You were supposed to be out of here weeks ago, but I guess I'm as hesitant to let you go as you are to leave. But the law is the law."

"It's not going to be that easy for them, Nathan," Malinda explained, stepping up to stand beside him. "We might be free, but that doesn't mean we will be accepted in society." She put her head on his chest. "Little James and I will be happier than ever living here with you. But they don't have anyone like that. They barely have each other, and that might not be enough."

"But we do have someone," said Martin. "We have you, Mr. Nathan. Why can't we stay here with you?"

The answer to Martin' question was simple: *because they were free and the law forbade the retention of slaves*. Nathan thought he had prepared for this day, but Malinda was right: it wouldn't be easy for them. In fact, it might be difficult as hell, especially considering the physical impairments that each one struggled with. *But they can't stay here. The law says they have to leave.* "But not if I paid them," Nathan said aloud, and a smile surfaced on his face as his mind put together ideas that seemed to solve the riddle of their predicament. Then, turning to the group that stared at him with anticipation and hope, he said, "You can all stay."

The crowd began to talk excitedly. Some exchanged hopeful glances with the ones around them. Others began thanking God. One-armed Peter even crowed with delight.

Nathan raised his hand to quiet everyone down. "But there has to be some rules: One, you all get paid a fair wage for the work you do for me. Two, you pay me rent for those houses you live in. Three, you grow, buy, and cook your own food."

Now, everyone smiled and laughed, and hugs became contagious as their dilemma seemed to truly be solved. Malinda handed baby James to Nathan; the boy wanted his daddy, as if the child could understand the good deed his father was doing.

Nathan let them revel in that one little victory, and then he continued. "You need to live your lives as free men and women. You can come and go as you please. You are now simply my employees and tenants, and you can quit and move on any time you wish. Whatever you decide, promise me you will be good people. Promise me that you'll be good to each other, that you'll be good to everyone. This country has seen enough hate, bigotry, and violence to last a hundred lifetimes. Please don't let any of that negative thinking infect any of you."

The laughter and exuberant chatter started again. Many found it hard to believe. Some knew it to be the work of God. But all knew that there would be a special place in heaven for their former owner and actual savior.

"Now, I'm going to tell Sheriff Biggs of my idea and see if he's okay with it. I don't see him having a problem as long as we make it legit."

Nathan's smile grew wider, causing his mustache to stretch from ear to ear. He would draw up papers, creating a form of contract stating the new arrangement his former slaves would be undertaking. *This could work. This* will *work.* Nathan beamed with pride, and he looked to Malinda to gauge her reaction, but his wife seemed ill and about to faint. She wobbled on her feet as her eyes became like saucers, fixed on something only she could see. When her knees finally gave way, one of the women caught Malinda before she could crash to the ground.

Another woman took baby James from Nathan so he could tend to his wife.

"Malinda. Malinda! What's wrong?" If it were summer, Nathan would have attributed this spell to the oppressive heat. But with it being winter, he was frightfully puzzled and concerned. He held her hand in his, and with the other, he palmed her face. "Dear Lord, what's the matter, my love?"

Malinda's eyes were wide open, and her face contorted in fear. She shook her head slightly and began muttering, "no ... no ... no."

Nathan picked up his wife and carried her inside the house, into the living room, and placed her on the davenport. Someone gave Nathan a cold wet cloth, and he began to wipe her brow. After long agonizing minutes, Malinda came out of her trance-like state and focused her eyes on her husband.

"Oh, Nathan," she said, almost crying. "They're coming for me."

"Who's coming for you? Who?"

"Bill Dodge," she replied. Then the tears started flowing. "He means to take me to that tree and hang and burn me like he tried to do before." She looked away, her eyes focusing on nothing as if recalling the terrifying image. "I saw it. The sight showed it to me. I saw him take me away. I saw myself screaming as I swung from that noose and the flames covering my entire body." Her gaze shot back to Nathan. "Oh, Nathan, it was horrible. So horrible! He's coming, Nate. He's coming!"

"No one's coming for you, my love. That's all in the past. You're here, safe with me now." He lovingly stroked her hair to calm her down, but his wife's eyes were still filled with fear.

Weeks go by and Nathan is good on his word. When the sheriff stopped by, Nathan had all the paperwork ready for the lawman. He created a document that stated all the slaves knew what was transpiring and understood that they were free. It also stated that they had all agreed to stay on as fully-paid employees. At the bottom, was the signature of each slave. They all called it their version of the Declaration of Independence. The sheriff was taken aback by this.

"What's this, Nathan?" Sheriff Biggs gripped the page, his face contorted in confusion.

"It says that they all know—"

"I know what it says, but what's all this on the bottom? Did they ... did they sign this themselves." The sheriff's face twisted even more, creating a frown that made him look like he was hearing some god-awful sound.

"Yes, sir. Every one of them."

"You taught them to read and write?"

"Yes, sir." The corner of Nathan's mouth rose, he understood what Biggs was asking and why. In Nathan's mind, it felt like a child asking a parent about an adult matter that they just couldn't comprehend. "I knew the day was coming," Nathan explained, "when they would be free, and being literate was going to be the most important skill for them to have."

* * *

The sheriff shook his head, placed the papers in his satchel, and got back on his horse. “You be careful, Nate. These are uncharted waters we’re entering. Especially you.”

“Then call me Magellan,” Nathan said with a huge grin on his face.

“I’m being serious, Nate. A lot of folks aren’t too keen on being forced to let their negroes go. And seein’ yours is staying of their own volition, those folks may even develop a special hatred for you. Especially Bill Dodge.”

“Bill Dodge is a man of many dispositions, but he should have no beef with me. He’s made good money off of me, and I’ve learned to keep well clear of him. We’ll be fine, Sherriff.”

Sheriff Biggs shook his head again and rode away.

That evening, everyone gathered in the barn for a “family” dinner. It was something they normally did on Thanksgiving and Christmas, but tonight they celebrated the new chapter in their lives.

Hell, Nathan thought. *It wasn’t a new chapter; for them it was a brand-new book.*

Malinda was looking well and was enjoying the evening. She hadn’t had anymore visions, as of late, and she and Nathan contributed the one on the porch to her being overstressed. Having the baby plus what was happening with the slaves had been a lot for her to handle. Not to mention the memory of the ordeal she had with Bill Dodge. She said she had put all that behind her, but sometimes Nathan looked at Malinda, when she thought he wasn’t looking, and believed he still saw a hint of fear in her eyes.

She caught him staring at her, and she gave him a smile that almost made him blush. He would make love to her that night, and they would wash away all the bad memories for good.

Tonight was about starting anew. Nathan welcomed those uncharted waters.

Nathan was jostled awake in the middle of the night. His eyes squinted as they tried to adjust to the flickering torchlight that enveloped his bedroom. He smelled whiskey and moonshine, and heard the sound of a muffled scream and that of a baby crying.

Six men standing around his bed came into focus. Four held rifles, two held his wife by the arms as they led her out of the room. The muffled screams he heard were hers; a makeshift gag was in her mouth stifling her pleas for help. Baby James lay blatting in his crib; none of the men paid him any mind.

Nathan sat up and tried to get to his wife, but the business end of four Henry rifles were quickly pointed at his face—so close, his heavy breathing echoed in the barrels.

One of the men lowered his weapon and leaned closer to Nathan. It was Bill Dodge. "Sorry, Nathan. But I've come for that nigger-witch." The alcohol on his breath was enough to choke Nathan. "I hear that cuz you were a good slave owner, you're gonna be able to keep your niggers. While the rest of us businessmen have to let them go. It doesn't seem fair to me, but it is what it is. Nothin' I can really do about that."

Nathan just stared at the drunken plantation owner, not knowing what to say.

Bill Dodge withdrew a flask from his pocket and took a swig. "But I can do something about another problem I have. You see, I just can't stand living knowing that cunt is alive and free while my little boy will never grow up to be a man." Bill James straightened back up and seemed to regard Nathan with a newfound curiosity. He raised his flask to his lips again, returned it to his pocket, then reached into his vest and pulled out an envelope. His shaking fingers reached in and withdrew a handful of cash. "But I'm not an unreasonable man. Here's your thousand back. Consider it a refund." Bill James laughed as did the other three men still in the room. He was about to toss the money at Nathan, but he hesitated and a wry smile grew on his face as he began sorting through the bills. "I'm not unreasonable, but I'm not stupid either. Here's five hundred." He took half the money he had in one hand and pressed it against Nathan's chest. The other half he returned to his vest pocket. "I'll keep the rest for the whore services she's provided you these past couple years. No hard feelings."

Nathan's hands reached for Bill James' throat, only to be stilled when the butt of a rifle struck his forehead and blackness engulfed him.

"Mr. Nathan! Mr. Nathan!"

Nathan tried to sit up, but the world was spinning and his head was pounding. Two pairs of hands firmly gripped his arms and helped him to sit on the side of his bed.

"Mr. Nathan ..."

Nathan looked at the man speaking. When his vision finally focused, he could make out Martin leaning over him, a crutch tucked under his shoulder. Several other men and women were in the room, all with worried looks on their faces. Abigail was standing at the foot of the bed holding Baby James.

Then he remembered.

Nathan hurriedly stood up, which was a mistake, for he nearly crashed to the floor as his balance struggled to keep up with him. Martin and One-eyed Henry steadied Nathan until he could regain his balance and stand on his own. His head pounded like an anvil, and his mind was swimming with the memories of Bill Dodge's visit. He needed to act fast.

"Margaret, get my boots. Henry, fetch my shotgun from above the fireplace and get me a bag of shells. Tom, can you saddle my horse and have her out front for me?"

Nathan was answered with a barrage of 'yes, sirs' as everyone moved to tackle their assigned task. Ironically, with only one leg,

Martin helped Nathan to stand without falling while Margaret put his boots on her boss's feet.

"What's going on, Mr. Nathan?" asked Martin. "Did we just see Mr. Bill Dodge and his men leave here with Miss Malinda?"

"Yes, and he plans on finishing what he started two years ago. I've got to stop them."

"Then I'm coning with you."

"No. You can't. He'll have no qualms about killing you too. But what you can do is get on a horse and go fetch Sheriff Biggs and tell him what's happening. And tell him to meet me at Bill Dodge's place."

Martin nodded and followed him to the stairs where he would not be able to follow as quickly as he would have wanted. That's when he cursed his absent leg.

When Nathan walked outside, Henry was there holding a shotgun in one hand, and a sack of shells in the other.

Everyone was out front now, most not knowing what to do, but all wanted to help. While waiting for Tom to bring his horse, Nathan went to Abigail, who was still holding Baby James, and kissed his son of the forehead. "Don't worry," he told the child, "I'm going to get your mama back. I promise.

Tom trotted the horse from the stable. She was all saddled and ready to go. Nathan tied the bag of shotgun shells to a strap and tucked the gun itself into the saddle. He mounted the horse, his head still pounding, but he pushed through. He needed to. For Malinda. He turned the horse around and urged her to a gallop towards the main road.

"Hee-ya!"

It was thirty painstaking minutes before Nathan reached the entrance to Bill Dodge's plantation. Nathan assumed Dodge and his men had not been at full gallop as he had been. So, hopefully, he was able to close the gap and was only a few minutes behind them. The estate was vast, but he knew there was only one place Bill James could be taking Malinda—the hangin' tree.

Nathan cut through the property and passed the plantation mansion. Around back, the darkness of the Georgia night hung like a net, but it was pierced with torchlight that illuminated a crowd of people and one lone, yet huge oak tree. As he approached, Nathan could make out a horse, with a figure sitting on its back, as it stood beneath the long branch. A rope had been tied from rider to branch, and a second later, a pistol was fired. The startled horse ran off, leaving the person to hang from the rope, swinging and kicking.

Nathan stared in shock.

"Malinda!" Nathan was now just a hundred feet from the tree and the mass of people. He jumped from his horse and ran. "Malinda! No!"

A figure standing near the hanging body, touched a torch to the kicking feet and the person immediately went up in flames. The high-pitched screams cut through Nathan's mind no differently had it been an ax.

"No, Malinda! No!"

"Nathan!"

Nathan ignored the voice and kept running for the tree. He could cut her down and put out the flames, it wasn't too late! But he had to hurry! He had to save her!

But a strong hand grabbed his arm and jerked him to a stop. Nathan turned on the man, ready to fight him to the death if need be.

"Hector?" Nathan said incredulously.

"It's okay, Mr. Nathan. Everything's going to be fine."

Going to be fine? What the hell was he talking about? He had to get—

"Malinda?"

Running up from behind Hector, Malinda ran into Nathan's arms. Her eyes filled with tears, but otherwise she seemed okay. Nathan kissed her face and hugged her more tightly than he had ever done. Confused, he pushed her back and looked at the flaming body that hung from the tree in silence and stillness.

Whoever that person was, they were dead, and had died a most horrific death.

"That's Bill Dodge," said Malinda, nodding to body, whose flames were just now starting to die. "They brought me to the tree to do what he tried to do back then; back when you saved me. But Hector and his group stopped them and ... well ... did this."

Nathan looked back at what remained of Bill Dodge, and that's when he noticed the bodies of five men laying in a heap by the base of the tree's trunk. Sure, Hector had saved Malinda, but he and his men had killed six men—six white men—in doing so. Nathan looked to Hector; one question hung between them. Why?

Hector let out a deep breath as if he had been holding it all night. "It had to be done, Mr. Nathan. A man that evil could not go on living. There's no telling what he would have done. We stopped him from hurting Miss. Malinda, but he would have kept trying to hurt her—and others—had we let him live. Now, as he himself would have said, he is being judged by a higher power."

Nathan took it all in. He may not have agreed with the end result, but Malinda was safe, and what's done is done. After everything Hector and the other slaves had been through under the ownership of Bill Dodge, he couldn't really blame them for their actions. Nathan couldn't imagine walking a hundred yards in their shoes, let alone a mile.

"You and your folks better get out of here, Hector," Nathan said. "The sheriff's on his way. Free or not, and no matter your history, once they find out what you've done, you'll be killed on the spot. They may even hang you right up there next to Bill Dodge." Nathan glanced back at Bill Dodge's smoldering body. "There's been enough killing for one night. Go on. Get out of here."

Hector nodded and with a comforting touch on Malinda's shoulder, he gathered his people and they scattered into the night.

* * *

The sheriff never did make any serious investigation into Bill Dodge's death. He figured that the former slave owner had wronged so many people and made so many enemies, that it might have been any one of a thousand that could have killed him that night.

"You might think the sight failed Mama that winter, but it wasn't herself she saw swinging from that tree, on fire and screaming. She had seen Bill Dodge's murder, but she only saw it the way her fear would let her see it. Was the sight trying to tell her something? Was it giving her the chance to either let it happen or possibly save him? In the end, it didn't matter. He was dead, and there was nothing she could have done to change that.

"As for my daddy and mama, they lived out their days on that little plantation of theirs. Occasionally, Malinda would still have waking dreams that came to be, but they were mostly pleasant ones, and they didn't happen as often as she got older.

"But as I grew up, I started experiencing the same kind of visions Mama had. Not many, mind you, but I had a few here and there and some came true. Maybe one day, you kids might realize that the sight is inside of you as well. You just have to listen to it and understand what it's trying to show you."

The screen door flew open and a woman in an apron covered in flour and grease, came marching onto the porch.

"Christine King," the woman said, hands on hips, and an attitude to match the puckered brow on her face. "You better move your butt into the kitchen right this minute. That table isn't gonna set itself. You too Martin Luther. Get your hide in there and help your sister."

The brother and sister heeded their mother's demand and raced into the house. The mother, still propping the screen door open with her hip, glowered at the grandfather sitting in the rocker.

“What stories you been telling them children? You trying to give them nightmares?”

“No,” he said. “Dreams. Hopefully they’ll have dreams and they’ll come true. Dreams of a brighter future.”

She shook her head and headed back inside.

The old man smiled to himself, knowing there was a little bit of his mama is those kids. And he hoped a lot of Nathan King was in them as well.

**Author’s notes:*

- All the characters in this story are fictitious except for Nathan King, his wife Malinda, and their descendants.

- Though the slaves themselves are fictitious, the slave’s names mentioned in this story were taken from a nineteenth century slave-ship manifest.

BEYOND THE PORTAL

Inspired by the song "The Highwayman" by Jimmy Webb

"Death is not the opposite of life, but a part of it."
– Haruki Murakami

The Highwayman

London, England, May 1725

It was a beautiful day. No, it was a glorious day.

Gazing out his window that looked upon Newgate Street, Thomas Fletcher thought it a bit ironic. "Not exactly how I pictured it would be," he said and took a deep breath; even the air smelled sweeter than normal. Perhaps it was God's mocking sense of humor, tantalizing him with nature's perfume. Or perhaps it was just a spring breeze bringing the aromatic scent from a flower cart up the street. Thomas believed it was the former. Ever since he was a young lad, the son of William Fletcher and The Almighty never had a great relationship. Thomas didn't have much respect for God; but, then again, respect was a two-way street, and Thomas knew that God had absolutely no respect for him.

"How what would be, *Mon Capitaine*?" asked Jean-Pierre, snapping Thomas out of his musing.

"Today of all days, my friend." Thomas peered up at the cloudless sky. "A perfect day."

Jean-Pierre joined him at the window and observed the sun-strewn streets and buildings of London for himself. "Would you rather it be raining?"

"No," Thomas said with a wry smile. "I suppose not."

Jean-Pierre stepped back and spread his arms. "How do I look?"

"Smashing," said Thomas. "I always liked that suit on you. And myself? How do I present?"

Jean-Pierre looked him up and down then gave him a fingertip kiss gesture. "*Magnifique*." Then he frowned and said, "However, I do not remember this ensemble."

"I got it about a year ago. From that gentleman traveling with his new bride in that awful blue and yellow coach."

"Oh, yes. I remember now. That coach was ... How you say? ... an abomination?" His French accent hit each syllable of that last word hard.

"Yes," Thomas chuckled. "It was at that."

The door opened, and a uniformed man with a broad mustache walked in. "Gentlemen," he said in a somber, gravelly voice. "It's time."

"So soon?" said Thomas. He pulled his gold pocket watch from his vest and opened it. "So it is. Where does the time go?"

Replacing the watch, he gestured to the door. "Let us not keep Constable Moore waiting, Jean-Pierre."

The two men left the building to find their transportation waiting for them on Newgate Street. A modest transport, to be sure, but one did not complain about such things. Not in these circumstances. Constable Moore assisted the two gentlemen into the back and, once settled in himself, he instructed the driver to proceed. With a gentle slap of the reins, the two horses pulled them along at a nice steady pace.

People had lined the streets to watch them go by. Not as many as Thomas had thought there would be, but it was a long road to Tyburn; there might be more as their journey continued. Each bystander expressed themselves in their own fashion toward Thomas and Jean-Pierre. Some gentlemen respectfully tipped their hats, an occasional child waved enthusiastically, and the women ... well the women, not all, but some, if not most to be sure, stared lustfully at Thomas. Yes, the women were always an easy target for him. His handsome face and equally handsome clothes always elicited the yearnful looks of the fairer sex.

Jean-Pierre shook his head. "You would have made an excellent Frenchman, *Mon Capitaine*. The ladies swoon for you like cats for a dish of cream."

As if on cue, two women approached the cart, one with a sweet, almost demure face and hair as yellow as a field of marigolds. The other was a brash, apple-cheeked buxom brunette with curls like waves crashing on the shore. They each carried a flower—the blonde a carnation; the other, a rose.

"Please wear my flower when you dance the jig, Mr. Fletcher," said the brunette.

"No," said the blonde, "wear mine. Please, Mr. Fletcher."

The two began to squabble, each declaring why Thomas should wear her flower and not the other's. Thomas interjected before it became violent.

"Ladies, please. If you'll permit me, I would be honored to wear both flowers." They smiled. He took the flowers, then blew them each a kiss. They stood and watched with adoring eyes as the cart continued its westward voyage.

"See what I mean, *Mon Capitaine*?" said Jean-Pierre. "You are a true Don Juan."

"Don Juan was Spanish, not French."

"And you are English. What I am saying is that you have that ... *je ne sais quoi* and can steal the heart of any woman in Europe. Along with their purses, of course."

The two laughed heartily at that. Of all the men Thomas had ridden with, Jean-Pierre was his favorite, and, without a doubt, his closest friend. Jean-Pierre had always made Thomas laugh and he felt comfortable talking to him about almost anything. And on this particular day, he was feeling rather reflective.

"Am I a good man, Jean-Pierre?"

"*Oui*. A very good man."

"But I'm a thief. And I've killed men."

"True. We have both killed men. Men kill men all the time. And you are a thief, this is also true, but you have given away much of what you have stolen. You have helped many unfortunate souls. You have fed the hungry, clothed the poor. A living Robin the Hood."

"Make up your mind—am I Don Juan or Robin Hood?"

"Perhaps both. But to me you will always be *Mon Capitaine*."

The cart stopped, and Constable Moore hopped off his seat and stepped to the back. "We are at the Bowl Inn, gentlemen. Would you care for a few drinks?"

Thomas looked to his friend. "Jean-Pierre?"

"Do you think they have cognac?"

"Possibly."

"Then *oui*. Let us sample the inn's wares."

The inn did, indeed, have cognac, and the two man drank for an hour, reminiscing about their adventures. They reminisced about their conquests and failures. They toasted to lost friends and fallen foes; men who had lived and died by their side and those who had died by their blades. They had known scoundrels and gentlemen, ladies and whores, beggars and thieves. And in the end, Thomas and Jean-Pierre toasted each other.

After their drinks, the cart carried them farther westward until, alas, they reached Tyburn.

Constable Moore assisted the slightly inebriated gentlemen to stand in the cart as it was steered toward the Great Tree.

There were many more people here. A great crowd had gathered, all waiting to see the great Thomas Fletcher take his final ride. Many shouted cheers as the pair went by.

"Good dying!"

"Good dying, Mr. Fletcher."

"Good dying to you both!"

As they drew near the "tree," a minstrel approached and strummed his lute:

Here comes Thomas Fletcher, if male thou art,
Look to thy purse; if female, to thy heart.
Much havoc has he made of both and for all
Men he made to stand, and women he made to fall
Soldiers and women, both did give chase,
Knights to his arm did yield, and ladies to his face.
Old Tyburn's glory; England's illustrious thief,
Fletcher, the ladies' joy; Fletcher, the ladies' grief.

"Behold," said Thomas, pointing to the "tree." "The lord of the manor awaits us."

There, a large burly man stood. He wore thick gloves and a black cowl on his head.

Jean-Pierre swallowed hard.

Thomas nudged him with his elbow. "Chin up, my friend. Smile to the end. It's the English way."

Jean-Pierre mustered a smile. "Very true. It could be worse. We could be in Paris."

"Oh?"

"*Oui.* My cousin Phillipe was caught stealing from a merchant. They tied him to a large wheel and broke every bone in his body."

"Dear Lord."

"*Oui.* He stayed strapped to the wheel for three days until he died. They weren't sure if it was a guard who had killed him because he was tired of my cousin's moans, or if it had been his wife in an effort to give him peace."

"Well, thank god for English civility." Thomas reemphasized his smile as they continued to ride past the crowd. "We shall leave this Earth as we have walked it—like gentlemen."

The cart reached the Great Tree of Tyburn and settled under her belly. Many men and women had met their fate here. Sometimes it was by the dozen. Today, however, it was just Thomas and Jean-Pierre. It was their show, their finale. The burly man placed satin hoods upon their heads, and as the rope slipped around his neck, Thomas thought he could hear Jean-Pierre crying. After a few seconds he realized that his friend wasn't crying ... but laughing.

"Jean-Pierre? What is so funny?"

"You've been trying so hard to leave here with a smile on your face. And now, no one will see it."

That was funny. Thomas laughed, which caused Jean-Pierre to laugh harder, and the two of them ended up laughing until they couldn't breathe.

"Mr. Fletcher. Mr. Moreau." It was Constable Moore's voice. "Are you prepared to meet your maker?"

"Yes."

"*Oui.*"

"Any last words Mr. Moreau?"

There was a long pause before Jean-Pierre finally said, "No—except I'd like to say that it has been an honor to know and live alongside you, *Mon Capitaine.*"

"The feeling is mutual, Jean-Pierre," said Thomas. "Of all the friendships, yours has been most heartfelt."

"Thomas Fletcher," said Constable Moore. "Any last words to say before man and God?"

God? That's right, He was watching, wasn't he? To hell with Him. Thomas thought hard and the only thing he could think of to say was, "If there is indeed a God, may he rot in hell alongside me."

Reins slapped. Horses galloped. The cart rushed from under their feet.

The ropes snapped taut.

The Soldier

North Point, MD, September 12, 1814
Bread and Cheese Creek
Campsite of the Maryland Militia—3rd Brigade
Brigadier General John Stricker, Commanding

Henry had to stop hard or he would have run into the sergeant. Henry had noticed the man almost too late, which nearly caused a collision with the large gruff soldier.

"Where do you two think you're going?" the sergeant asked as he squinted from the early morning sun piercing through the trees. It was another warm and muggy summer day. And though well before noon, one could tell the summer heat would soon be oppressing them as it had all week. The sergeant's door-knocker beard glistened with perspiration as sweat poured down his face, indicating he was already feeling the assault.

"I'm Private Henry McComas, and this is Private Daniel Wells," Henry said, unable to hide his nervousness. He poked a thumb toward his friend Danny, who had only then caught up to him, breathing hard with his hands on his knees. He and Danny were nineteen and eighteen, respectively, and the NCO before them was twice their age and seemed twice as tall. Though that was an exaggeration in reality, it most certainly was not in Henry's wide-eyed perspective. The bulky man also had more stripes than the two of them combined. What's a little size without rank to season the intimidation?

"We were told to report to Major Waring immediately," Henry added, controlling his quavering voice.

The older man looked down on the two boys, perhaps to gauge the veracity of their statement, or did he wonder what on Earth the major would want with two privates still fairly wet behind the ears? Henry had wondered that himself.

"It's okay, sergeant," came a voice from behind the boys. "Their attendance to this meeting has been requested by the major."

Henry turned to see Captain Wallace standing behind them. He was in full uniform—his mustache was waxed, his saber hung at his side, and his hat had been brushed to a spotless finish.

"Don't just stand there, boys," said Wallace. "The major is waiting."

Henry and Daniel brushed past the sergeant and continued through the trees to where a clearing hosted a campfire and over a dozen officers from the brigade, including General Stricker himself. A large table rested next to the fire, and the senior-most officers stood around the table, pondering documents and maps. All were in full uniform.

Henry and Daniel barely had time to throw on some pants and undershirts before rushing to the meeting. Their insufficient dress made them feel that much more uncomfortable. But upon seeing the general and the other officers, Henry and Daniel snapped to attention.

"Is this them?" said Major Waring, who stood by the table and next to the general.

"Yes, sir," said Captain Wallace. "Or so that's what they told Sergeant Sandborn at the entrance."

The major gave Henry and Daniel a scrutinizing look before addressing them. "You boys served under General Winder at the Battle of Bladensburg a few weeks past?"

"Yes, sir," they answered in unison.

"A disgrace to our forces, that battle was," said Captain Higgington, who stood on the other side of the major.

"And a disgrace that will not be repeated here," said Waring. "We will not let the British do to Baltimore what they did to Washington."

All the officers nodded and harrumphed in agreement. Washington's fall to the British had hit everyone hard. After defeating the American forces there and burning the White

House to the ground, the British now had their sights set on Baltimore.

"Lieutenant," said Waring to an officer behind him. "Tell the two privates here what the scouts reported to us this first light."

A young lieutenant walked up to Waring and nodded. "Our scouts report that the British army, led by General Ross, has landed their forces and are making their way toward Baltimore. They have made camp at the Gorsuch farm, where they rest and resupply. Approximate size of the fighting force is over four thousand. They also appear not to be aware of our forces here." The young officer once again took his place behind the major.

"Four thousand?" Daniel whispered to Henry. "We only got about three."

"Boys," said Waring, and he waved Henry and Daniel closer. They obliged as the major straightened a large map on the table. "We are camped here," he said as he pointed to a spot that resembled the small creek where they camped. "The Gorsuch farm is here." He slid his finger easterly along the map until it reached a square blank area. "To proceed west towards Baltimore, the British will have to cross through the Bouldin farm here." His finger slid again. "And that's where we will intercept them."

"A sound plan, Major," Henry said, hoping he didn't sound too familiar with him. "How can me and Dan—Private Wells—be of service to you?"

Captain Higgington stepped closer to the table. "You two were sharpshooters for Winder?"

"Yes, sir," said Henry.

"And they say you two actually eyeballed Ross. Is that true?"

"Yes, sir."

"Is that true or've you been sellin' a dog. Perhaps you been tellin' stories to impress your mates?"

"No, sir. We speak the truth. God's honest."

Higgington and Waring exchanged glances, then Waring looked to the general.

"Boys," General Stricker began, "when we intercept the British, we will be outnumbered and outgunned. To even the odds, I would like a pair of sharpshooters on the wooded side of the Bouldin farm to identify General Ross as he marches the army through the farm, wait until they have the perfect opportunity, and then execute him while he rides past on that coal black steed of his. With Ross removed from the equation of battle, we may have a fighting chance against their superior numbers."

The other officers again nodded and voiced their agreement. Stricker continued once they quieted.

"Now we just need two volunteers to fill the role of the very important sharpshooters.

"You're looking at them, sir," said Danny. "Henry's the best shot there is. And I ain't too shabby myself. We'll get ol' Ross for ya. You just give us the chance, sir."

"And how do we know you're the ones for the job?" asked Captain Higgington.

"Cuz," replied Henry, "like Danny said, I'm a great shot. We both are. That's why General Winder made us sharpshooters in his regiment. And like we said earlier, we'd seen Ross that day. We know what he looks like, could spot him a mile away." Turning to Stricker, Henry continued. "And begging the General's pardon, but Ross's horse is white. White as virgin snow. Sir."

Stricker nodded and smiled. "Very good, son." He paused and looked down at the map in an apparent moment of contemplation. Was he imagining the battle on the faux soon-to-be battlefield that lay before him? Could he imagine the confused British troops after the loss of their general? Or did he see the demise of his own men on that unsuspecting farmland?

After what seemed like minutes of eerie silence, he looked up and said, "Captain Wallace." Wallace stepped forward and snapped to attention. "Let's get these boys in position. We have an army to stop."

* * *

Henry and Daniel waited in a thicket of pine trees on a small hill well off the main road. Lying prone on the ground, their loaded Harper's Ferry rifles rested on a fallen log that not only provided them with a steady aim, but also hid them from any passersby.

They had a perfect view of the road and farmland; no one could go by without Henry and Danny spotting them. Henry only hoped that the British didn't send out scouts along the perimeter. That would spoil the day for certain.

"What if this is like Bladensburg all over again, Henry?" said Daniel. "What if they flank us like they did before?" Danny didn't sound scared or even nervous. Henry reckoned he wanted to win this fight just as much as Henry or even General Stricker did. Mistakes were made in the past by their superiors, and neither Henry nor Daniel wanted to witness previous blunders repeated once again.

"Not a chance," said Henry. "Stricker's pretty smart. He picked this spot for good reason. We're surrounded by swamps and creeks and rivers. This narrow point will focus Ross' army right through here. It'll be like bees trying to get through a broken window."

"How you know all that?"

"I grew up not far from here. My father used to take me fishin' probably close to around the spot Ross landed his men."

"I hope you're right, Henry. Cuz we got a score to settle."

"Aye, Danny boy. That we do." Henry raised his head and looked around once more.

To the right, the 3rd brigade hid throughout the woods fifty yards off of the farmland and on either side of the main road. To the left, General Ross would lead his men into the trap set by Stricker. Henry prayed the plan worked or Baltimore would burn like Washington. *Not if I can help it.*

Henry's ears perked up. "Look sharp, Danny. I think they're upon us."

The buzzing of locusts and the call of song birds were soon accompanied by the low rumble of precision thumps. The unnatural noise grew louder and louder until Henry could feel it in the ground he lay upon. Pine needles showered the boys as the trees shed their loose needles, shaken free from the rhythmic vibrations that shuddered the ground. Using his spy glass, Henry looked to the east and gasped.

Columns of men on foot and horse rounded the woods and followed the road to the farm. The soldiers bore various uniforms; the regulars in red coats, the dragoons in blue, and the riflemen in green. Cannons pulled by horse teams reflected the late morning sun with their polished brass bodies. On horseback rode the officers, sitting high and proud and seemingly sure of the task ahead of them.

And on a flawless white stallion, General Ross led his men to their next conquest.

Their target approached.

"This is it, Danny. We need to fire at the same time. We'll only have one shot, then we need to run. Run like the devil. Got it?"

Daniel nodded as he looked along the barrel of his rifle. "Just give me the count."

Henry grinned. "Will do, Danny. Will do." And the two waited, waited for their unsuspecting prey to get closer. Henry thought it would take forever, but the British were upon the farm in mere minutes. He lined up his sight with Ross's chest, leading him just a bit. And when he thought the time was right, he gave the count.

"One." Henry cocked his hammer back. He heard Daniel do the same.

"Two." He took a deep breath and held it.

"Three." They pulled their triggers. There was a loud *crack* as smoke billowed from their barrels. Dropping their guns, the boys turned and ran like rabbits from a chasing fox, but something caught Henry in the back and forced him to the ground. Daniel fell, as well, and it was only then that Henry realized that they had been shot. On his back, Daniel looked to Henry, fear etched in his eyes.

"We got 'em, Danny. Henry said. "I saw Ross fall. But I fear they got us as well. Blood trickled from Henry's lips as he spoke. A labored cough brought up more. "Danny?"

But Daniel didn't speak. He just lay there staring at Henry, a stream of blood gushing down his face.

"We got 'em, Danny," Henry repeated as the world became blurry. "We got 'em."

The Sailor

Cape Horn, South America, August 4, 1872
20 miles off the southernmost tip of Chile

Dearest Margaret,

My journal fills almost daily with my writings to you. I know you will not be able to read them until my return to San Francisco; however, it gives me great comfort keeping you and the boys close to my heart and telling you of my days.

It's nighttime aboard the Sea Fortune, and I have surrendered my shift to the second mate, Bill Jones, my closest friend and soon to be successor. It's day 43 and we are ahead of schedule. The captain believes that, not only will we be in Liverpool before the 100-day estimate, but we may even set a record for early arrival. That will bode well for the Cockburn Shipping Company, as well as for the future of this ship and her crew. And arriving early means bonuses for the crew. As first mate, my share would be considerable.

I plan to inform the captain that this will be my last voyage on the Sea Fortune, or on any ship for that matter. I will miss the sea, the money, and my shipmates, but I miss you and the boys even more. I am sure I can find gainful employment In San Francisco once I return. At last, my love, I shall be a proper husband and father.

"Mr. Roberts." The coarse voice of Bernard Weller, the ship's boatswain, tore Roberts' attention from his journal to the scrawny man who had addressed him. "Begging your pardon sir, but the captain be wantin' to see ya."

"Thanks, Barney." Roberts closed his journal, placed it in his trunk, then headed aft to the captain's quarters.

Roberts knocked on the door and was immediately answered with, "Come in."

He entered the cabin and found Captain Bartholomew Winston sitting at his desk, writing in a large book. "You wanted to see me, Captain?" said Roberts.

"Yes, Roberts," the captain said without looking up. "Come in, have a seat."

Roberts pulled up a chair to sit across the desk from his captain. Winston finished writing his thoughts on the page before closing the leather tome, then gave his first mate a welcoming smile. "How are things on the ship, son?"

It was Saturday, and the captain liked a weekly report on the state of the ship. That meant not only the ship itself, but the crew, supplies and cargo. The reports were informal, but they made their way into his log book as required by the company.

"The cargo is dry and secure. Other than a few scuffles, the morale of the crew is fairly high. They are delighted at the time we are making."

"As am I," said the captain as he lit his pipe. "How's the green help coming along?

"Very good, sir. They're making excellent seamen."

"Excellent. The galley?"

"Cookie says all stores are in fine shape. No spoiled or missing food this week." Cookie was the ship's steward. No one knew his real name. Some said it was Pete. Others said Cookie didn't even know himself. "Oh, and he's planning a surprise for your birthday next week." The captain rolled his eyes as he blew out a puff of smoke. "Just to give you a warning."

"I hate surprises."

"Rumor has it that he has a pig's leg in a salt bag hidden in the grain hold."

The captain raised his brows and seemed intrigued at that bit of news.

The boat rocked more than its usual rhythmic roll and the captain's ink well slid about a foot across his desk. The captain removed the quill and capped off the bottle, then placed it in its original spot.

"By the way, sir," Roberts continued. "I've been meaning to talk to you about something."

"Oh?"

"Remember my telling you about my wife and two sons?"

"Yes. Sounds like a good family you have there."

"Well, after considerable thought—"

The ship rocked again, much harder this time, sending the inkwell across the desk and crashing onto the deck splashing black ink and glass in every direction. Roberts and Captain Winston stood, almost knocking over their chairs.

"I don't like this," said the captain.

"Neither do I," Roberts agreed.

The ship creaked as it rocked once more, throwing the two men off balance. Roberts managed to catch himself on the desk, but the captain was not as quick to react. Captain Winston fell to the floor, and in an attempt to break his fall, he raised his arms only to have his left catch the corner of the bookcase. Roberts heard the unmistakable sound of bone snapping. Winston yelled in pain, and Roberts leapt around the desk to help his commanding officer.

"Captain. Are you all right?"

Winston cradled his arm and winced in pain. "Hell, no, I'm not all right. I broke my bloody arm." He yelled once more as he tried to stand.

"Try not to move," said Roberts. "You could fall again and make it worse.

The deck bell rang, and Roberts heard the second mate yell, "All hands, on deck! All hands, on deck!" Roberts looked to his captain.

"Go," said Winston as he grimaced from the pain. "Save the ship. Don't let me down, boy."

Roberts ran out of the captain's quarters and into a mass of groggy sailors who had just awoken from the alarm.

"Gangway!" yelled Roberts. "Gangway! Make a hole." Stopping, he grabbed a sailor who was dressed and ready to go topside. "Find Doctor Connelly. Tell him the captain's hurt."

The sailor nodded and ran off, snaking his way through the crowded deck.

The rest of the men parted to allow the first mate through. Roberts made it to the stairs, climbed them two at a time, and found himself on the top deck, wind and water whipping his face.

"What the hell happened, Bill?" he said to Jones, yelling above the howling wind. "How did we not see this?"

"It came out of nowhere, Charles. A rogue storm! One minute it's clear skies and calm seas; the next, all hell broke loose. Where's the captain?"

"Injured. Down below in his cabin."

Jones' expression turned to one of worried concern.

"He'll be fine," Roberts assured him, the volume of his voice raising with that of the storm. "It's up to you and me to save the ship."

Roberts looked around. The night crew stood waiting for orders, not sure what to do first. The rest of the men began stumbling out of the stairwell and onto the deck and gathered around their first mate. Water began standing on the deck as waves and wind pushed ocean and rain onto the *Sea Fortune.* The sails flapped as the storm tugged them in various directions. Roberts had to act fast or the ship would be at the bottom of the ocean in minutes.

"Just like we practiced," he yelled to his men. "I want six on bail-out duty. Grab your pumps and make haste. I need these sails furled." He pointed to the three masts with both arms. "I want five men on each mast. We need to be under bare poles in five minutes. Smith. Lucas. Batten the hatches. Make sure no water gets below."

A barrage of 'aye sir's cut through the howling wind as everyone scattered to their assigned tasks. The second and third mates barked out orders, urging the men to hurry. Roberts looked on with a mixture of pride and worry. His men had been well trained; even the greens knew their jobs and worked as hard as the rest. But squalls this fierce and sudden had been known to send ships twice as big as *Sea Fortune* to the deep fathoms below.

"Watch your lines, men," Roberts yelled out over the tempest. "I don't want any jibes. Don't need anyone get knocked overboard." Turning to his best friend, he asked, "How are we doing, Bill?"

"Looking good, sir" Jones replied. "Sails are almost furled. Bail-out crew is ahead of the water."

Roberts nodded. "When the sails and battens are done, you and the third mate get the men below. I'll stay up here with the bail crew."

"Aye aye, sir."

A wind gust pushed man and ship with unseen force; standing upright was a forgone impossible task. Then the loud creak of wood splitting pierced through the gale-force wind.

Someone yelled, "Look out!"

Roberts looked up. The starboard top yard of the main mast plummeted toward the deck, and straight for Bill Jones, who had fallen to his knees from the last wave that jolted the ship.

Roberts launched himself at his friend, pushing the younger man away from the falling timber only to end up in the path of the plummeting timber himself. He was hit square in the back, and was sandwiched between the deck and the massive broken yard. Roberts lost his breath as his ribs snapped, and his lungs could not take in air.

My God. Is this how it ends? It can't be. Margaret ...

In that moment, a strange peace came over him. There was no storm. No wind or rain. No sailors hurrying to save the ship. Just the sound of his heart slowing its pace. Visions of Margaret and the boys flooded his mind. And even though he knew he would be closing his eyes for the final time, the thoughts of his family gave him tranquility like he had never known.

With what little breath he had, Roberts wheezed out, "Margaret."

The Dam Builder

Boulder City, Nevada, June 1934

Pete Logan had taken his usual seat on the bus and sat there with his lunchbox on his lap, waiting for the rest of the workers to board. In the seat in front of him was Gus Fisher.

"Gonna be a hot one today, Pete." Gus and Pete had been working on the Boulder dam project since the beginning. And their friendship had grown as large and as strong as the dam they worked hard to build.

"I reckon so," Pete said. "It is summer in Nevada, after all.

Pete saw a young kid get on the bus. He might have been around twenty, but he looked like he should still be in grade school. The boy was carrying a cup of coffee in a tin cup and an expression on his face that shouted confusion. Pete waved him over, and the young man headed up the aisle, grinning from ear to ear.

"Mornin', Mr. Logan. Sure glad to see you."

"Morning, Tommy. Gus Fisher, this here's Tommy—"

"Crenshaw. Pleased to meet you Mr. Fisher."

"Just call me Gus, kid. You our new spreader?"

"Yes, Mr.—I mean Gus."

"Take a seat, Tommy," said Pete. "The bus'll be leaving soon."

Gus slid closer to the window to make room for Tommy.

"You all settled in town, Tommy?" asked Pete.

"Yes, sir. I got my place last night. Sharing a dorm with a real nice fella named George."

"Good. You bring a lunch?"

"No," Tommy answered, a bit confused. "I thought we were comin' back here for lunch."

"We don't come back here 'til dinner time," said Gus. "But I'm sure between me and Pete, we can take care of you today. I always pack too much anyway."

"Thanks, Gus," said Tommy.

"No sweat, kid. You'll get the hang of things. We all had to at one point. Ain't that right, Pete?"

"Just stick close to me and Gus, kid," said Pete. "You'll learn the ropes in no time."

Tommy nodded and took a sip of coffee. "You been working the dam long, Gus?" Tommy asked.

"Oh, me and Pete been here since they started dynamitin' the canyon back in thirty-one. Since then, we've had a dozen different jobs here. Never a dull moment, that's for sure."

The last man boarded the bus, then the doors closed after him. The latecomer sauntered up the aisle like a man who didn't care that he had been holding up the bus, or anything else for that matter. As he made his way toward the back, his hand tipped Tommy's elbow just as the boy was about to take a sip from his cup. The result being half of Tommy's coffee ending up on his shirt.

"Careful with that joe, punk," said the man. "You almost got some on *me*."

Pete stood up, fist clenched and gave the man a cold stare. "Just get in your seat, Freddie."

"Yes, sir, Mr. Foreman, sir." Freddie gave Pete a mock salute and laughed his way to the back of the bus.

The driver put the bus in gear, and the dozen vehicles carrying over five hundred men began their five-mile journey to the construction site.

"Who was that?" asked Tommy as he wiped his shirt with a handkerchief.

"Freddie McClain," said Gus. "Meanest man in Boulder City. You'd be best to stay clear of him, kid."

"Reminds me of a bully we used to have back home." Tommy looked back and shook his head. "Someone just needs to teach him a lesson."

"Someone did," said Gus and jerked his thumb at Pete.

"Really?"

"Freddie's been here as long as me and Pete, and when Pete got the foreman promotion and not him, Freddie took it real personal like and picked a fight with Pete."

Tommy's face lit up with the juicy story; he seemed to have forgotten all about his soaked shirt. "So what happened?"

"Pete here gave him a beat down like I've never seen. Damn near killed him."

Tommy's eyes went wide in shock, and he looked at Pete, who just stared out the window.

"Anyway," Gus continued, "Freddie spent more than a week in the infirmary cuz of it."

"And he still acts like a jerk? After all that?"

"Tigers and their stripes, kid," said Pete, looking away from the window. Tommy gave him a bewildered look. "Some men will never change," Pete clarified. "Especially men like that."

The bus rounded its final bend, and that's when Tommy said, "Holy cow. It's huge!"

"Welcome to Boulder Dam, kid," said Pete.

The incomplete dam stretched out before them across Black Canyon. Looking like a wall built by God, it always impressed Pete, no matter how many times he had seen it. That men could build something so magnificent would always amaze him and fill him with pride at being a part of this manmade wonder.

"And it ain't even done yet, kid," said Gus. "Imagine how it'll look when it is."

"It's incredible," Tommy said, honest awe in his voice. "Though I heard they are thinking of naming it Hoover Dam. You know, after the president."

Gus frowned. "Christ, I hope not. Last thing they need to do is mar this beautiful structure by naming it after that crook."

After the buses parked, the crews got out and gathered the tools they would need for the day. Pete and Gus instructed Tommy on everything to grab, then it was time to get to work.

"Where do we need to go?" said Tommy.

Gus pointed to the top of the dam over six hundred feet above the ground and almost eight hundred feet across from where they were standing.

"But how?"

"In that," said Pete. He pointed to a twelve by twelve pen that resembled a miniature boxing ring. The pen was attached to a set of cables that ran out from one side of the canyon to the other.

The men piled into the pen until it could hold no more. The gate closed and they were hoisted off the ground and carried to the location of the day's work.

In understandable boyish fascination, Tommy looked over the edge of the pen's fencing and gaped at the wonder of it all. Pete was glad Tommy wasn't scared of heights. If he had been, this would not have been the job for him.

The day was long, but went well. Tommy was a quick learner, and Pete was glad to have him on his crew. It did get hot, but no one complained, not even Tommy. Gus joked about the heat once in a while just to get under Pete's skin, but everyone worked hard, and there was plenty of water.

During lunch, Pete and Gus shared their food with Tommy, just as Gus said they would, and they listened as Tommy told them of his life back home in Mississippi, and why he came all the way to Nevada for work.

"Well, I got a wife and two kids back home. A girl and a boy. And there's—"

"Wait," said Gus. "How old are you, son?"

"Twenty-two."

"And you're married with two kids?"

"Yup. And one on the way. That's why I needed this job so bad. There really isn't much in the line of good-paying jobs back home. Here I can make a dollar an hour. That's more than twice what I was making as a farm hand back home. When heard there was a chance of getting on here at the dam, I had to come out and take my chances. God must be smiling on me for me to have such good fortune. And to meet two fine gents like yourselves."

"It's good to have you, kid," said Gus.

"It certainly is," agreed Pete.

When the work day had ended and everyone was beat, they all clamored into the pen to cross the canyon to the waiting buses on the ridge.

Pete was surprised to see that Tommy was not as tired as he thought he would be. *Youthful energy.* And the boy was still excited at being here. Once again, he looked over the edge of the gate and marveled at the dam and canyon below.

"To be that young again," said Gus. "He must see the world with different eyes than you and me."

"Yeah, but I don't know if I want to repeat my life in my twenties again. Those were some pretty—" Pete cut himself off as he saw Freddie McClain make his way to stand by Tommy at the gate. Pete didn't like the look in Freddie's eyes and rushed to intercept him. The crowded pen made moving difficult, and about half way there, Pete saw Freddie pull the latch that secured the gate and watched in horror as the steel fence swung outward.

Tommy's weight had been resting on the top bar, and he got dragged out the opening that led to certain death. He clung to the railing and yelled for help. Most of the men backed away in an effort of self-preservation, but Pete pushed through until he reached the edge.

"Hang on, Tommy," Pete yelled. "We'll get you back in."

But, youthful energy or not, Tommy's muscles were exhausted from a long day's work, and his grip slipped. The boy screamed as he plummeted toward the bottom of the dam, and Pete could only stand there looking on in horror.

After seconds that seemed like hours, Pete turned and grabbed Freddie by the collar until the two stood nose to nose. "Damn you, you son of a bitch. That was supposed to be me. Not him. I was supposed to die. It was supposed to be me!"

"Fine", said Freddie. "Then join him." And with a swift push, he sent Pete off the edge of the platform, flailing through the air.

As Pete waited for the concrete below to abruptly stop his body, he couldn't help think of Tommy and his wife and two—no three kids.

I'm sorry, Tommy. This wasn't how it was supposed to end. Not for you, anyway.

The Starship Captain

United Earthship Armstrong
Stardate 57943, the year 2112
Black Hole—Cygnus X-1
Just outside the event horizon.

"Captain on the bridge," announced Ensign Burrows.

At 0200, the third shift was running the ship, and the few heads that were on the bridge turned to watch Captain Karl Richter step off the lift and onto the compartment that was the heart of the ship.

The first thing that caught Richter's eyes was the large viewscreen on the forward bulkhead and the ominous maelstrom it displayed—the black hole known as Cygnus X-1. It captivated his attention every time he laid his eyes upon it, just as it had since the *Armstrong* arrived there two weeks ago. The phenomenon was invisible, of course. The computer projected graphics that simulated the singularities gravitational waves—literal ripples in spacetime—and radiation, creating a display that was both beautiful and horrifying. As Richter stood in the back of the bridge, transfixed by the anomaly, watching the x-rays swirl in a galactic dance, he was almost oblivious to the uncomfortable silence that had developed since his arrival.

"Captain," said First Officer Commander Zachary Marsh from the command chair. "I wasn't expecting you. Having trouble sleeping again, sir?"

"You could say that Commander," Richter said, snapping out of his trance. "The thought of my ship in the hands of these 'children' keeps me up at night. I decided I'd come up and see how you run my ship while I'm sleeping three decks below."

Richter was, of course, joking, but he expected that no one on the bridge knew that except his XO. Marsh had served with him for over eleven years. They knew each other well, and that made them a great team.

All of the other wide eyes that surrounded him were either recent transfers or fresh cadet graduates. They were the ones who usually got stuck working the night shift.

"I can assure you, Captain," said Marsh, "that we run a tight ship here on the third shift." Marsh was trying to suppress a smile, but he was never a good actor. That made him a good officer, but a terrible poker player.

"You don't mind if I check things out for myself, do you, Commander?"

"Not at all, sir. The bridge is yours."

"That won't be necessary." Richter walked over to the navigation console. "I'll just check out a few stations."

"Very good, sir. Ensign Burrows, surrender your station to Captain Richter for inspection."

Burrows stood and moved away from his chair to allow his captain to sit. He then stood at attention as Richter sat at the consol.

"At ease, Ensign," said Richter. "Actually, why don't you take a break and grab yourself a coffee in the mess?"

"The mess?" asked Burrows.

"Did I mumble, Ensign?"

Yes, sir—I mean, no, sir." Burrows gave Marsh a puzzled look then marched toward the lift at the rear of the bridge.

"In fact," said Richter in a louder voice, "the rest of you should join him. Take a fifteen-minute break. The commander and I will watch the bridge. Go on."

The half-dozen junior officers looked at each other, then at their commander. After Marsh gave them a nod of assurance, they followed Burrows to the lift and entered. When the doors to the lift closed and it began its decent, Marsh, still sitting in the command chair, addressed Richter with a more relaxed posture.

"What's going on, Karl? Everything all right?"

"Everything's fine, Zac," Richter assured him as he signed into the navigation console using the biometric security system. Once his DNA was confirmed, he began keying in codes that brought up his private server.

"Then why would you dismiss my bridge crew? There must be something wrong." There was a lull as Marsh waited for an answer that Richter didn't give. "Did they do something wrong? Have *I* done something wrong?"

Richter finished loading the program he wanted into the nav-computer, then stared up at the viewscreen and the stellar phenomenon it displayed. "Magnificent. Don't you think?"

"The black hole?" Marsh asked. "Yes. Magnificent. Mysterious. Deadly."

"What mysteries do you think its singularity holds?"

"We don't know. With every probe we've launched, it's the same story—the telemetry ceased once it passed through the event horizon."

"I've read the reports, Commander. But what do you *think* is hidden within its center?"

"I'm not sure. A wormhole, maybe. Some speculate that there may be a space-time portal. Some say that whatever is in there is beyond our comprehension."

"Perhaps," Richter said. "But I am inclined to believe in the portal theory, myself. A theory which I am about to test."

Richter initiated his navigational program, and a computerized chart of the black hole and its surrounding space replaced the actual image on the main viewscreen. The diagram showed the black hole and the *Armstrong* in its position outside the event horizon. A dotted line appeared that showed the new course set for the ship to make a spiral descent through the barrier and into the singularity.

"My God, Karl. What are you doing?"

"Isn't it obvious? I plan on going in, and hopefully through and beyond, the portal before us."

"But you don't know what will happen," Marsh said, panic creeping into his voice. "It could crush the ship. You'll kill us all. There are hundreds of good, innocent people on board."

"I don't plan on taking the entire ship. Just the bridge module. Once I leave, you can regain control of the ship from the auxiliary bridge controls in engineering."

"I can't let you do this. It's suicide."

Richter reached into his pocket and removed a hand laser. He pointed it at Marsh. "You don't have a say in the matter, Zac. I'm doing this with or without your consent."

Marsh stared at the laser in disbelief. "It will most certainly be without. That's for sure."

"Now," said Richter, "will you kindly leave the bridge, so I can separate the module and begin my journey?"

Marsh stood from the chair but did not make a move toward the lift. Instead he took a step toward Richter. "Before I go. Can I ask you a question? Why? Why are you doing this? You had an incredible career in the service, and there's talk of you making admiral when we return. A new chapter in your life to look forward to. So I ask again, why?"

Richter rested the laser pistol on his lap, his finger still near the trigger. He looked at his colleague and friend and sighed. "Because, my dear friend, I am tired. So very tired. I can endure this perpetual existence no longer."

"Sir?"

"I have been around for a long time—long before you, Zac Marsh. Long before the Antares war or space travel. Long before the Earth Coalition and all the great accomplishments of man. I come from a simple time, a time when the only thing a man needed was a good horse, a good sword, and a good friend who would be there with you til the end."

Marsh cocked his head and furrowed his brow at Richter.

"You probably think I'm mad," Richter said with a bit of a chuckle. "I don't blame you. Maybe I am. Or maybe this has been a nightmare from which I cannot awake. Maybe I'm still asleep in my cell at Newgate and will finally wake to visit Tyburn and hang for my crimes. Or maybe I am still on the *Sea Fortune* and will rise to find the ship in San Francisco where my beloved Margaret and sons await." A smile had grown on his face but faded when reality hit him. "Or maybe I'm cursed, doomed to live again after each death. Forced to lose friends and loved ones over and over with each new life."

Marsh was transfixed on Richter. His expression was that of someone who couldn't believe the things that were coming out of his friend's mouth. Richter did indeed think that Marsh believed he was crazy. That is, until Marsh asked one more question.

"*Mon Capitaine*? Is that you?"

Richter stared wide eyed at Marsh, not believing what he had just heard. "What did you say?"

"*Mon Capitaine*. It's me. Jean-Pierre."

"Jean-Pierre? Jean-Pierre? No." Richter closed his eyes and shook his head. "My mind is playing tricks on me. Must be our proximity to this damn black hole." He opened his eyes and looked again at his first officer.

"No, Karl—or should I say Thomas? It is me. Jean-Pierre. I can't believe this." A crooked smile came over him, and he gave his captain a bewildered look.

Richter thought his first officer was playing a trick on him, a scheme to fool him into letting his guard down so he could wrest the gun from him and take him into custody. But how would he know about Jean-Pierre? Or Thomas?

"Don't you remember, my friend—*Mon Capitaine*? I was with you in London. And on the *Sea Fortune*."

"It can't be," said Richter. His face softened, and his eyes looked hopefully at Marsh. "Is it really you?"

"*Oui*," said Marsh. He gave his head a slight shake. "I mean yes. It's me."

Richter stood, placed the pistol in his pocket, then stepped closer to his first officer. "How can this be?"

Marsh dropped his gaze to the floor. "I don't know. But ... it's me. And I think ... I think I've been with you the entire time. As I said, I was on the *Sea Fortune*. I was outside Baltimore at the battle of Northpoint. At the dam in Nevada, I was your friend Gus. And I was there a dozen other places and times."

Richter shook his head. "Unbelievable. You were with me this whole time. I had no idea."

"Neither did I. I assumed it was me who was cursed. Reincarnated after every death. Suffering loss after loss, just as you described. But how is this possible?"

"I do not know," Richter said. "But I intend to fix it." He gazed back at the chart on the screen.

"Suicide? Is that your answer?"

"I tried suicide once. That didn't work."

"Ah, yes," Wells said, nodding in remembrance. "Madrid. I had almost forgotten about that."

Richer pointed to the screen. "This. This is my last hope. *Our* last hope."

"Do you really think it will work? Do you really think that it is a portal of some kind?"

"I do. To where, I am not sure. Another galaxy or universe? Perhaps. Another dimension? Possibly. Maybe it will lead to God himself. Then I could face him and demand an explanation to this never ending nightmare he has so graciously endowed me with—*us* with." After a heavy sigh, he placed a hand on Marsh's shoulder. "Will you come with me, my old friend?"

"Come with you?" Marsh echoed. He looked to viewscreen which displayed the black hole once more. He seemed to be lost in its spellbinding swirl. After long, thoughtful seconds, he scooted past his captain, past the man he had befriended over and over again, and sat at the navigation station. With a few taps on the console and the silencing of a few alarms, he separated the bridge module from the rest of the ship. The captain's new course setting sat in the computer waiting for the command to proceed. Wells looked to Richter and said, "Just give me the count, *Mon Capitaine.*"

Richter smiled and took his rightful place in the command chair, bracing for what was to come. *This is it*, he assured himself. After an eternity of living and dying, this was his escape. He just knew it. If it was some supernatural force bringing him back, death after death, then it was a supernatural force that would terminate this never ending hell. Richter took a deep breath and beamed with confidence. Not taking his eyes off the viewscreen, he obliged his dear old friend.

"One." *For Margaret and the boys ...*

"Two." *For Tommy ...*

"Three." *For everyone I have wronged ...*

* * *

It was a beautiful day. No, it was a glorious day.

Gazing out his window that looked upon Newgate Street, Thomas Fletcher thought it a bit ironic.